THE LONG ROAD HOME

Danielle Steel

PARAGON

CHIVERS PRESS
BATH

First published 1998
by
Bantam Press
This Large Print edition published by
Chivers Press
by arrangement with
Transworld Publishers Ltd
1998

ISBN 0 7540 2132 7

British Library Cataloguing in Publication Data available

Printed and bound in Great Britain by
REDWOOD BOOKS, Trowbridge, Wiltshire

For the children who have died, those we know about, and those we should have. And those who have lived through it, and come from that terrible place of knowing their lives and souls constantly in danger ... the children of a war that should make us all cry more than any other.

May we grow wise enough, and brave enough to protect them. Let no child die again for lack of our love, our courage, or our mercy.

And for Tom, who made me brave enough to say it.

With all my heart
and love,

d.s.

CHAPTER ONE

A clock ticked loudly in the hall as Gabriella Harrison stood silently in the utter darkness of the closet. It was filled with winter coats, and they scratched her face, as she pressed her thin six-year-old frame as far back as she could, deep among them. She stumbled over a pair of her mother's winter boots, as she moved farther back into the closet. She knew that here, no one would find her. She had hidden here before, it had always been a good hiding place for her, a place they never thought to look, especially now, in the heat of a New York summer.

It was stifling where she stood, her eyes wide in the darkness, waiting, barely daring to breathe, as she heard muffled footsteps approaching from the distance. The sharp clicking of her mother's heels clattered past like an express train roaring through town, she could almost feel the air whoosh past her face with relief in the crowded closet. She let herself breathe again, just once, and then held her breath, as though even the sound of it would draw her mother's attention. Even at six, she knew that her mother had supernatural powers. She could find her anywhere, almost as though she could detect her scent, the pull of mother to child inevitable, unavoidable, her mother's deep, inky-brown eyes all-seeing, all-knowing. Gabriella knew that no matter where she hid, eventually her mother would find her. But she hid anyway, had to try at least, to escape her.

Gabriella was small for her age, undersize,

1

underweight, and she had an elfin quality about her, with huge blue eyes, and soft blond curls. People who scarcely knew her said that she looked like a little angel. She looked startled much of the time, like an angel who had fallen to earth, and had not known what to expect here. None of what she had encountered in her six brief years was what they could have promised her in heaven.

Her mother's heels rattled past again, pounding harder on the floor this time. Gabriella knew instinctively that the search had heightened. The closet in her own room would have been torn apart by then, also the equipment closet under the stairs, behind the kitchen, the shed outside the house, in the garden. They lived in a narrow town house on the East Side, with a small, well-kept garden. Her mother hated gardening, but a Japanese man came twice a week to cut things, mow the tiny patch of lawn, and keep it tidy. More than anything, her mother hated disorder, she hated noise, she hated dirt, she hated lies, she hated dogs, and more than all of it, Gabriella had reason to suspect, she hated children. Children told lies, her mother said, made noise, and according to her mother, were continually dirty. Gabriella was always being told to stay clean, to stay in her room, and not disturb anything. She wasn't allowed to listen to the radio, or use colored pencils, because when she did, she always got the colors on everything. She had ruined her best dress once. That had been while her dad had been away, in a place called Korea. He had been gone for two years, and come back the year before. He still had a uniform in the back of a closet somewhere, Gabriella had seen it there once, when she was hiding. It had bright shiny

2

buttons on it, and it was scratchy. She had never seen her father wear it. He was tall and lean, and handsome, with eyes the same color as her own, blond hair, like hers, but his was just a little darker. And when he came home from the war, she thought he looked like Prince Charming in 'Cinderella.' Her mother looked like the queen in some of the storybooks Gabriella read. She was beautiful and elegant, but she was always angry. Little things bothered her a lot, like the way Gabriella ate, especially if she dropped crumbs on anything, or knocked over a glass. She had spilled juice on her mother's dress once. She had done a lot of things over the years that she wasn't supposed to.

She remembered all of them, knew what they were, and she tried hard not to do them again, but she couldn't help it. She didn't want to upset anyone, didn't want her mother to be mad at her. She didn't mean to get dirty or drop things on the floor, or forget her hat in school. They were accidents, she always explained, her huge eyes imploring her mother for mercy. But somehow, no matter how hard she tried, the wrong things always happened.

The thin high heels walked past the closet again, more slowly this time, and Gabriella knew what that meant. The search was ending. She had narrowed it down to the last of the hiding places, and it was only a matter of time before her mother found her. The child with the huge eyes thought of turning herself in, sometimes her mother told her that she wouldn't have been punished if she had been brave enough to do that. But most of the time, she wasn't. She had tried it once or twice, but

3

it was always too late, by then, her mother said, if only she had confessed earlier, it would have been different. It would all have been different if Gabriella behaved properly, if she answered when she was spoken to, or didn't when she wasn't, if she kept her room clean, if she didn't push her food around on her plate, and let the peas fall over the edge until they left grease spots on the table. If only Gabriella could learn to behave, speak only when spoken to, and not scuff her shoes in the garden. The list of Gabriella's failings and transgressions was endless. She knew only too well how terrible she was, how bad she had been all her life, how much they would love her if she could only do what they told her to, and how much they couldn't because of the constant grief she caused them. She was a bad child, she knew, a sad disappointment to both of her parents, and that pained her greatly. Knowing that was the crushing burden she had carried throughout her short existence. She would have done anything to change that, to win love and approval from them, but so far she had done nothing but fail them. Her mother made that clear to her constantly. And the price Gabriella paid for it was the constant reminder of her failings.

The footsteps stopped outside the closet door this time, and for a brief moment, there was an interminable silence before the door was suddenly yanked open. Light filtered back into the bowels of the closet where Gabriella hid, and she closed her eyes as though to shield herself from it. It was the merest crack of light reaching toward her through the coats, but to Gabriella it felt like the bright sunlight of exposure. She could smell her mother's perfume heavy in the air, and sense her closeness. The rustle of the petticoats her mother wore were like a warning sound to Gabriella, and then slowly the coats were pushed apart, creating a deep canyon leading straight into the back of the closet. And for a long, silent moment Gabriella met the eyes of her mother. There was no sound, no word, no exchange between them. Gabriella knew better than to explain, to apologize, or even to cry. Her already too-big eyes seemed to outgrow her face as she watched the inevitable rage grow in her mother's eyes, and with a single superhuman gesture, her mother's arm lunged toward her, grabbed her by one arm, yanked her off the ground, and pulled her forward with such speed that the air seemed to leave Gabriella's lungs with a small whooshing sound as she landed unsteadily on her feet next to her mother. And within an instant the first blow fell, dropping her to the ground with such force it left the small child breathless. There was no whimper of pain, no sound at all, as her mother slapped her hard across the top of her head, and then pulled her to her feet again with one hand, and hit her as hard as she could across the face with the other. To Gabriella, the sound of the blow was deafening.

'You're hiding again,' the tall, spare woman shrieked at her. She was almost beautiful, and might have been, had there been something different in her eyes, something other than rage running rampant across her face. Her long, dark hair was woven into a loose bun. She was elegant and graceful and had a lovely figure. The dress she wore was well cut, an expensive navy silk. And on her hands she wore two heavy sapphire rings. They

5

left their mark on Gabriella's face now, as they had done before. There was a small cut on her head, and bright red marks where she had been slapped, a welt from one of the rings already visible on her cheek. Eloise Harrison slapped the child across her right ear, and then shook her, holding her by both arms, shouting into the tiny, devastated face. 'You're always hiding! Always giving us problems! What are you afraid of now, you little brat? What have you done? You did something, didn't you? Of course you did ... why else would you hide in the closet?'

'I didn't do anything ... I promise ...' The words were barely more than a whisper as Gabriella gasped for air. The beating seemed to take all the wind out of her, all the life out of her soul, as she looked up imploringly with tear-filled eyes at her mother. 'I'm sorry, Mommy ... I'm sorry ...'

'No, you're not ... you never are ... you're never sorry, are you? You drive me crazy all the time, doing stupid things like hiding ... What do you expect from us ... miserable child ... My God, I can't believe what your father and I have to put up with ...' She flung the child away from her then, as Gabriella slid across the well-waxed floor, a few feet away from her, never far enough, as a blue suede high-heeled shoe kicked her with blinding venom in the small thin thigh that trembled. The biggest bruises were always on her legs and arms, her body, where they were unseen by others. The damage to her face always subsided in a few hours. It was as though her mother knew instinctively where to place the blows. She'd had plenty of practice at it. She'd been doing this for years.

Nearly all of Gabriella's life now.

There was no remorse, no words of comfort to Gabriella lying at her feet. No effort to apologize or soothe her. She knew that if she got up too soon, it could start her mother's fury all over, so she waited there for a long time, head bowed, cheeks drenched in silent tears, still wincing from the blows delivered by her mother. Gabriella knew that looking up at her with her tear-stained face would only make her mother angrier, so she kept her eyes focused on the floor, as though she might disappear if she lay there forever.

'Get up . . . what are you waiting for?' The biting words, followed by another yank on the arm, and one last blow on the side of her head. 'My God, Gabriella . . . I hate you . . . pathetic child . . . look how disgusting you are . . . you're all dirty . . . look at your face!' Suddenly, from nowhere, two smudges had appeared mixed with tears on the angelic face.

Anyone even minimally human would have been in agony seeing her, but not her mother. Eloise Harrison was a creature from another world, and anything but a mother. Abandoned by her parents as a small child, sent to live with an aunt in Minnesota, she had lived in a cold, lonely world with a maiden aunt who had rarely spoken to her, and most of the time had her carrying firewood or shoveling snow in the freezing winters. It was the Depression then, her parents had lost most of their money, and had gone to Europe to live on the little they had left. There was no room for Eloise in their world, or their hearts. They had lost their son, Eloise's brother, to diphtheria, and neither of them had ever had great affection for their daughter.

Eloise had stayed with her aunt in Minnesota until she was eighteen, and then returned to New York, to stay with cousins. She had met John Harrison at twenty, and married him two years later. She had known him as a child, he'd been a friend of her brother's. And his parents had been more fortunate than hers had been. Their fortune had remained intact during the Depression. Well born, well bred, well educated, though without great ambition or strength of character, John had gotten a job in a bank, and met Eloise again shortly thereafter. He was instantly dazzled by her beauty.

Eloise had been pretty then, and young, something of a beauty, and there was a coolness about her that drove him into a frenzy. He begged, he pleaded, he courted, he wanted desperately to marry her, and the more he pursued her, the more aloof she was. It took him almost two years to convince her to become his wife. He had wanted children almost immediately, had bought her a lovely house, and he was so proud of her he almost crowed every time he introduced her. But it took him nearly another two years to convince her to have a baby. She always said she needed more time. And although she never said it openly, having children wasn't really what she wanted. Her own childhood had been so unpleasant, she wasn't particularly attracted to the idea of having children. But it meant so much to John, that eventually she relented. And regretted it almost immediately after. She had a difficult pregnancy, was violently ill almost to the very end, and the delivery was a horror she knew she would never repeat and always remember. In Eloise's mind, despite the adorable pink bundle they placed in her arms the next day, it

8

simply wasn't worth it. And it annoyed her right from the first to see how much attention John lavished on the baby. It was the kind of passion he had once had for her, and suddenly all he seemed to think about was Gabriella ... was she warm enough ... was she cold ... had she eaten ... had someone just changed her diaper ... had Eloise seen how sweet she looked when she smiled ... He thought it was remarkable how much she looked like his mother. Just listening to him, Eloise wanted to scream every time she saw her daughter.

She went back to her own activities rapidly, shopping, going to tea parties in the afternoon, and having lunch with friends. And more than ever, she wanted to go out every evening. She had absolutely no interest in the baby. She admitted to several of the women she played bridge with on Wednesday afternoons, that she found the child incredibly boring and quite repulsive. And the way she said it always amused them. She was so outspoken they thought it was funny. If anything, she was less maternal than she had ever been. But John was convinced she would come to it slowly. Some people just weren't good with babies, he told himself, each time he saw her with Gabriella. She was still very young, she was twenty-four, and very beautiful. He was sure that when the baby started doing more interesting things, she would rapidly conquer her mother. But that day never came, not for Eloise, or for Gabriella. In fact, when Gabriella started crawling everywhere, pulling at things, standing up next to the cocktail table and throwing ashtrays on the floor, she nearly drove her mother crazy.

'My God ... look at the mess that child makes ...

she's constantly knocking things down and breaking things, and some part of her is always dirty . . .'

'She's just a baby, El . . .' he said gently, scooping Gabriella up into his arms and hugging her, and then blowing raspberries on her belly.

'Stop that, that's disgusting!' Eloise said sternly, looking at him in revulsion. Unlike John, Eloise hardly ever touched her. A nurse they had early on had figured it all out easily and shared her thoughts with the baby's father. She said that Eloise was jealous of the baby. It sounded ridiculous to John, but in time even he began to wonder. Every time he talked to the child, or picked her up, Eloise got angry. And by the time Gabriella was two years old, Eloise slapped her hands every time she reached out to touch something in their living room or their bedroom. She thought Gabriella should be confined to the nursery, and said so.

'We can't lock her up in there,' John objected when he found her in her room, whenever he came home from the office.

'She destroys everything,' Eloise would answer, as usual looking angry. But she was even more so when John commented on what pretty hair Gabriella had, what lovely curls. It was the next day that Gabriella got her first haircut. Eloise took her to Best and Co. with the nurse, and when they returned, the curls had vanished. And when John expressed surprise, Eloise explained that having her hair cut was healthy for her.

The rivalry began in earnest when Gabriella spoke in sentences and would run down the hall squealing to see her father. Sensing danger near at hand, she generally steered a wide berth around

10

her mother. Eloise could barely contain herself while she watched John play with her, and when he finally began criticizing Eloise for how little time she spent with the child, a chasm began to grow between Eloise and her husband. She was sick of hearing him whine at her about the baby. She thought it was unmanly, and frankly disgusting.

Gabriella's first beating occurred when she was three, on a morning when she accidentally knocked a plate off the breakfast table and broke it. Eloise had been sitting uneasily beside her, drinking her morning coffee. And without hesitating, the instant the plate fell, she reached over and slapped her.

'Don't ever do that again ... do you understand?' Gabriella had simply stared at her, her eyes filled with tears, her face a mask of shock and sorrow. 'Did you hear me?' she shouted at the child again. Her curls had reappeared by then, and the huge blue eyes stared back in confusion at her mother. 'Answer me!'

'I sorry, Mommy ...' John had just entered the room and saw what was happening with disbelief, but he was so shocked, he did nothing to stop it. He was afraid to interfere, and make things worse. He had never seen Eloise so angry. Three years of anger, jealousy, and frustration were erupting from within, like a long-overdue volcano.

'If you ever do that again, Gabriella, I'll spank you!' Eloise said ominously, shaking the child by both arms until her teeth shook. 'You're a very, very naughty girl, and no one likes naughty children.' Gabriella glanced from her mother's face suffused with rage, to her father standing in the doorway, but he said nothing. He was afraid to. And as soon as Eloise was aware of him, she

11

scooped the child up in her arms, and took her back to her room, and left her there, without her breakfast. She gave her a sharp slap on her bottom before she left. Gabriella was lying on her bed, whimpering, when her mother left her to go back to breakfast.

'You didn't have to do that,' John said quietly when Eloise came back to the breakfast table for another cup of coffee. He could see that her hands were shaking, and she still looked angry.

'If I don't, you'll wind up with a juvenile delinquent on your hands one day. Discipline is good for children.' His own parents had been kind to him, and he was still startled by Eloise's reaction. But he was also well aware that their daughter made her extremely nervous. Eloise had never been quite the same since Gabriella was born, and nowadays she was always angry at him about something. His hopes for a large, happy family had long since vanished.

'I don't know what she did to upset you, but it couldn't have been that awful,' he said calmly.

'She threw a plate on the floor intentionally, and broke it. I'm not going to put up with tantrums!' Eloise said sharply.

'Maybe it was an accident,' he said, trying to mollify her, and succeeding only in making the situation worse. There was nothing he could ever say to defend their daughter. Eloise simply did not want to hear it.

'Disciplining Gabriella is up to me,' Eloise said through clenched teeth. 'I don't tell you how to run your office,' she said, and then left the table.

Within six months, 'disciplining' Gabriella became a full-time job for her mother. There was

12

always some fresh crime she had committed that required a slap, a spanking, or a beating. Playing in the garden and getting grass stains on her knees, playing with the neighbors' cat and getting her arm scratched, or her dress dirty, falling on the street and scraping her knees and getting blood all over her dress and socks was a particularly heinous offense that cost her her most serious beating to date, just before her fourth birthday. John knew of the beatings, and saw it happen many times, but he thought there was nothing he could do to stop Eloise, and even comforting the child afterward made it worse, and it became simpler to accept Eloise's explanations of why she had to beat, slap, or spank her. In the end, he decided it was best to say nothing, and he tried not to think about what was happening to their daughter. He tried to tell himself that maybe Eloise was right. He didn't know. Maybe discipline was good for children, if she said so.

His parents had died in an auto accident and there was no one he could talk to, no one he would have dared tell what Eloise did to Gabriella.

Gabriella was certainly a model child, she barely spoke, cleared the table carefully, folded her clothes neatly in her room, did everything she was told, and never answered back to her mother. Maybe Eloise was right. The results were certainly impressive. And when she sat at dinner with them, her eyes were huge in her face, and she remained completely silent. It was only unfortunate that her father came to mistake terror for good manners.

But in Eloise's less generous eyes, Gabriella always fell far short of perfection. There was always something more to scold her about, punish her for,

13

or a new reason to give her a 'spanking.' Eventually the spankings became longer and more frequent, the slaps seemed to punctuate every exchange between them, the shakings, the sharp blows, the resounding slaps to every part of her body. There were times when John feared that Eloise might seriously hurt Gabriella, but he kept his comments to himself about the way his wife was bringing up their daughter. To him, it appeared that discretion was the better part of valor, and he did his best to convince himself that what she was doing wasn't wrong, and he was careful never to see the bruises. According to Eloise, the child fell constantly, and was so awkward they couldn't let her ride a bike or learn to roller-skate. The deprivations her mother inflicted on her were clearly for her own protection, the bruises a sign that she was as clumsy as Eloise declared her.

And by her sixth birthday, Gabriella's beatings had become a habit, for all of them. John avoided them, Gabriella expected them, and Eloise clearly enjoyed them. If anyone had said as much to her, she would have been outraged. They were for the child's own good, she claimed. They were 'necessary.' They kept her from becoming more of a spoiled brat than she was, Eloise would have explained. And Gabriella herself knew how truly bad she was. If she weren't, her mother wouldn't have had to hit her . . . if she weren't, her father would have stopped her mother from beating her . . . if she weren't, they might have loved her. But she knew better than anyone how unworthy she was, how truly terrible were her crimes. She knew all of it, because her mother told her.

And as she lay on the floor that summer

14

afternoon, and her mother dragged her off the floor by one arm, and slapped her one more time before sending her to her room, she saw her father watching them from the doorway. She knew he had seen the beating and done nothing about it, just as always. His eyes looked mournful as Gabriella crept past him, and he said nothing. He didn't reach out to comfort her, he didn't try to touch her, he simply looked away, refusing to see the look in her eyes, unable to bear it any longer.

'Go to your room and stay there!' Gabriella's mother's words rang in her ears as she walked softly down the hall, feeling her cheek with tiny trembling fingers. She knew she was a big girl now, she knew that the things she did that made her mother so angry were really awful, and as she crept into her room and closed the door, a sob escaped her, and she ran to the bed and clutched her dolly. It was the only toy she was allowed to have, her grandmother had given it to her before she died, her father's mother. It had big blue eyes and eyelashes and pretty blond hair, and Gabriella genuinely loved her. The doll's name was Meredith and she was Gabriella's only ally. Gabriella clutched her now, rocking back and forth, sitting on her bed, wondering why her mother hit her so hard ... why she herself was so awful ... and all she could remember now was the look in her father's eyes as she walked past him. He seemed so disappointed, as though he had hoped that she'd be better than she was, instead of the little monster her mother accused her of being. And Gabriella believed her. She did everything wrong, and she knew it. She tried so hard, but there was no pleasing them ... no way to stop the inevitable ...

no way to escape it. And as she sat there, holding her doll, she knew deep in her soul that it would never stop. She would never be good enough, she would never win them over. She had known all her life that they didn't love her, and was long since convinced that she didn't deserve love. She didn't deserve anything more than the pain her mother inflicted on her. She knew that, but she wondered still why it had to hurt so much . . . why her mother was always so angry at her . . . what she had done to make them hate her . . . And as she lay crying silently on her bed, the one thing she knew was that there were no answers, and no one could save her from this. Not even her father. All she had in the world was Meredith, her only friend, her dolly. She had no grandparents, no aunts or uncles, no friends or cousins. She was never allowed to play with other children. Probably because she was so naughty. They probably wouldn't like her anyway. No one would. Who could possibly like her if her parents didn't, if she was so bad? . . . She knew she couldn't tell anyone what they did to her, because it only proved how bad she was, and when they asked her in school what had happened to her, she always told them she fell down the stairs, or over the dog, even though they didn't have one. But she knew this was a secret she had to keep, because if she didn't, people would know how truly terrible she was, and she didn't want anyone to know that.

It wasn't her parents' fault, she knew that as well. It was her fault for being so bad, for making so many mistakes, for making her mother so angry. It was all her fault. And as she lay on her bed and thought about it, she could hear her parents' voices. As they often did, they were shouting, and she knew that was her fault too. Sometimes after her mother punished her, she could hear her father shouting at her, as he did now. She couldn't make out the words, but it was probably about her ... probably her fault ... she was even worse than they said. She made them fight. She made them angry at each other. She made everyone so unhappy, almost as unhappy as she was.

She cried herself to sleep, at dusk, without dinner, and as she drifted off to sleep, feeling her cheek ache and her thigh throb where her mother had kicked her, she tried to think of other places, other things ... a garden ... or a park ... with happy people in it ... and children laughing as they played ... everyone was playing, and they wanted her to play with them ... a tall, beautiful woman came toward her and held her arms out to her and told her that she loved her ... It was the most wonderful feeling in the world, and as she thought of it, everything else in her life faded away, and she drifted off to sleep, holding her dolly.

*　　　*　　　*

'Aren't you afraid you're going to kill her one of these days?' John said pointedly to his wife, and she looked at him in contemptuous amusement. He'd had more than a few drinks as he stood looking at her, gently reeling. The drinking had started at about the same time as the beatings. It was easier than trying to stop the beatings, or explaining Eloise's behavior. The drinking took the edge off and made an intolerable situation nearly bearable for him, if not for Gabriella.

'Maybe she won't end up a drunk like you, if I

17

beat a little sense into her now. It might save her a lot of heartache later.' Eloise sat calmly on the couch looking at him with disdain, as he made himself another martini.

'The sickest thing is, I think you believe that.'

'Are you suggesting I'm too hard on her?' Eloise said, visibly furious at being challenged.

'Too hard? *Too hard?* Have you ever taken a good look at her bruises? How do you think she gets them?'

'Don't be ridiculous, if you're trying to blame me for that. She falls on her face every time she puts her shoes on.' She lit a cigarette, and leaned back to watch him drink his martini.

'Eloise, this is me you're talking to. Who are you kidding here? I know how you feel about her . . . so does she . . . poor kid, she doesn't deserve this.'

'Neither do I. Do you have any idea what I have to put up with? She's a little monster underneath those curls, with those big innocent blue eyes you're so in love with.'

He looked at her as though a veil had been lifted from his eyes, swept away by the force of the alcohol in his system. 'You're jealous of her, aren't you, El? That's what this is all about, isn't it? Just plain jealousy. You're jealous of your own daughter.'

'You're drunk.' She dismissed him with a wave of the cigarette, unwilling to listen to what he was saying.

'I'm right, and you know it. You're sick. I'm just sorry for her that we ever had her. She doesn't deserve a life like the one we give her . . . you give her . . .' He took no responsibility for his wife's cruelty and took great pride in the fact that he had

18

never laid a hand on Gabriella. But he had never done anything to protect her either.

'If you're trying to make me feel guilty about her, don't bother. I don't. I know what I'm doing.'

'Do you? You beat her senseless practically every day. Is that what you had intended for her?' He looked horrified as he drained his glass, and felt the effect of his fourth martini. Sometimes it took more than that to drown the things that he remembered her doing.

'She's not an easy child, John. She needs to be taught a lesson.'

'Well, you've done that, El. I'm sure she'll always remember the lessons we taught her.' His eyes began to glaze as he said it.

'I hope so. Children don't need a lot of fussing over. It's not good for them. She knows I'm right too. She never argues with me when I punish her. She knows she deserves it.'

'She's too afraid to argue with you, and you know it. She's probably afraid you'll kill her if she says anything, or tries to resist you.'

'You make me sound like an ax-murderer, for God's sake.' She crossed one shapely leg over the other, but for several years now he was no longer moved by her. Seeing what she was doing to their child had made him begin to hate her, but not enough to try and stop her, nor leave her. He didn't have the guts to do that, and was slowly beginning to hate himself for it.

'We should send her to school somewhere in a few years, just to get her out of here, away from both of us. She deserves that.'

'She deserves a proper education from us before that.'

19

'Is that what you call this? "Education"? Did you see the bruise on her cheek when she went to her room tonight?'

'It will be gone by morning,' Eloise said calmly.

He knew it was probably true, but hated to admit it. Eloise always seemed to know just how much force to use so that the bruises never showed on the exposed areas of Gabriella's body. The marks on her upper arms and legs were usually a different story. She was an expert at it.

'You're one sick bitch,' was all he said to his wife as he left the room and walked unsteadily to their bedroom. She was, but there seemed to be nothing he could do about it. He stopped in the open doorway of his daughter's room on the way, and stared into the darkness. There was no sign of life there, no sound, and the bed appeared to be empty, but when he walked softly into the room and looked more closely, he saw a small lump at the bottom of the bed and knew it was Gabriella. She always slept that way, hidden way down in the bed, so that her mother wouldn't think she was there if she came to find her. Tears filled his eyes as he looked at the small, barely visible lump of battered terror that was his daughter. He didn't even dare pull her back up to the empty pillow. It would only expose her to Eloise's anger again, if she came in to see her. He left her there, lonely and alone and seemingly forgotten, and turned and walked on to his own room, wondering at the injustices of life, the inhumanity that had befallen his child, and yet he knew as he walked away from her, he knew that there was nothing he could do to save her. In his own way, he was as powerless against his wife as

20

Gabriella. And he hated himself for it.

CHAPTER TWO

The guests began arriving shortly after eight
o'clock at the town house on East Sixty-ninth
Street. A handful of well-known socialites were
there, a Russian prince with an English girl, and all
of the women Eloise normally played bridge with.
The head of the bank where John Harrison worked
had come with his wife, and waiters in dinner
jackets were serving champagne on silver trays as
the guests arrived, as Gabriella sat hidden at the
top of the stairs, watching them. She liked watching
the guests when her parents gave parties.

Her mother looked beautiful in a black satin
gown, and her father looked handsome and elegant
in a well-cut tuxedo. The women's dresses
shimmered as they came into the hall, and their
jewels sparkled in the candlelight as they took their
glasses of champagne, and seemed to drift away
toward the voices and the music. Eloise and John
loved giving parties. They did it less often now, but
they still entertained lavishly from time to time,
and Gabriella loved watching the guests as they
arrived, and lying in her room afterward listening
to the music.

It was September, the opening of the New York
social season. And Gabriella had just turned seven.
There was no special occasion for the party that
night, just a gathering of their friends, some of
whom Gabriella recognized as she watched them.
There were a few she had always liked, and who

21

were nice to her on the rare instances when they saw her, which wasn't often. She was rarely introduced to their friends, seldom seen, never made much fuss of. She was simply there, hidden away upstairs, mostly forgotten. Eloise didn't think children should be seen in social situations, and Gabriella's existence in their lives was anything but important to her. Now and then one of her friends asked about the child, mostly at her bridge club, and she dismissed their inquiries with a graceful hand, like an annoying insect that had crossed her path and could be brushed away just as quickly. There were no photographs of Gabriella in the house, although there were many of Eloise and John, in silver frames. There were never any photographs taken of Gabriella. Recording her childhood was of no particular interest to them.

Gabriella smiled as she saw a pretty blond woman walk into the hall downstairs. Marianne Marks was wearing a white chiffon dress that seemed to float as she moved, talking to her husband. She was one of her parents' closest friends, and her husband worked with Gabriella's father. There was a diamond necklace glittering on her neck, and her hands moved gracefully as she took a glass of champagne from one of the waiters. And then, as though sensing something, she glanced upstairs, and stopped when she saw Gabriella. The woman's face seemed to be suffused with light, and from the glow of the candles in the chandelier, she almost seemed to be wearing a halo, and then Gabriella realized that the sparkle she saw there was from a tiny diamond tiara. She looked like a fairy queen to Gabriella.

'Gabriella! What are you doing up there?' Her

voice was gentle and warm, as she smiled broadly, and waved to the child hiding on the top step in her pink flannel nightgown.

'Shhh . . .' Gabriella put a finger to her lips with a worried frown. If they knew she was sitting there, she would get in terrible trouble.

'Oh . . .' Marianne Marks understood instantly, or thought she did, as she ran upstairs quickly, on light feet, to see her. She was wearing high-heeled white satin sandals, and made no sound, as her husband waited for her downstairs, smiling at his wife and the pretty child who was whispering now, as Marianne embraced her. 'What are you doing up here? Watching the guests arrive?'

'You look so pretty!' Gabriella said with an awestruck air as she nodded in answer to the question. Marianne Marks was everything that her mother wasn't. She was beautiful and fair, she had big blue eyes like Gabriella's and a smile that seemed to light everything around her. She seemed almost magical to Gabriella, as she watched her, and sometimes she couldn't help wondering why she couldn't have had a mother like this one. Marianne was about her mother's age, and always seemed sad when she said that she had no children. Perhaps there had been a mistake somewhere, perhaps Gabriella had been destined for a woman like this, and had come to her own parents by mistake instead . . . maybe because she was so bad, and needed to be punished. She couldn't imagine Marianne punishing anyone. She was always so kind and so gentle, and she seemed so happy, particularly now as she bent down to kiss Gabriella, and as she did, Gabriella could smell the warm, delicious smell of her perfume. Gabriella hated the

23

scent of her mother's perfume. 'Can't you come downstairs for a little while?' Marianne asked, wanting to whisk the little girl into her arms and take her downstairs with her. There was a quality to the child that always seemed to reach out to her and seize her heart. Everything about the little girl made her want to love and protect her. She didn't know why she felt that way, but Gabriella was one of those rare, fragile souls that reached out and touched you, and Marianne felt the pull of her now as she took her hand in her own and held it. It was small and cold and the fingers felt unbearably frail, the grip firm and almost pleading.

'No, no ... I can't come down ... Mommy would be really angry. I'm supposed to be in bed,' she whispered. She knew the penalty for leaving her bed and disobeying those orders, yet she could never resist the temptation to watch the people arriving for her parents' parties. And now and then there was a bonus like this one. 'Is that a real crown?' Marianne looked like the fairy godmother in 'Cinderella' to her, and Robert Marks, waiting for his wife patiently at the foot of the stairs, looked very handsome.

'It's called a tiara,' Marianne giggled. Gabriella had to call her either Aunt Marianne, or Mrs. Marks. There were severe penalties for calling her parents' friends, or any adult, by their first names, and she knew that. 'Isn't it silly? It belonged to my grandma.'

'Was she a queen?' Gabriella asked solemnly with the huge, knowing eyes that always touched Marianne Marks' heart in ways she didn't quite understand, but felt acutely.

'No, she was just a funny old lady in Boston. But

24

she met the Queen of England once, that's when she wore this. I thought it would be fun to wear it tonight,' and as she explained, she unpinned it carefully from her elegantly coiffed blond hair, and set it gracefully on Gabriella's head of blond curls with a single gesture. 'Now you look like a little princess.'

'I do?' Gabriella looked awestruck at the prospect. How could anyone as bad as she look like a princess?

'Come ... I'll show you,' the pretty blond woman whispered, and took her hand and led her across the upstairs hall to a large antique mirror. And as Gabriella stared at her own reflection with wide eyes, she was startled by what she saw there. She saw the beautiful woman standing next to her, looking down at her with a warm smile, and the elegant little diamond crown shimmering atop her own head, as Marianne held it.

'Oh ... it's so beautiful ... and so are you ...' It was one of the most magical moments in her short life, a moment engraving itself forever on her heart as they stood there. Why was this woman always so kind to her? How could she be? How could she and her own mother be so different? It was a mystery that, to Gabriella, defied explanation, except that she knew, and had for years, that she had never done anything to deserve a mother like this one.

'You're a very special little girl,' Marianne said softly as she bent to kiss her again, and then took the tiara gently from her head and pinned it easily onto her own head again, with a last glance in the mirror. 'Your parents are very lucky people.' But Gabriella's eyes only grew desperately sad as she said it. If Marianne only knew how bad Gabriella was, she would never say things like that. She knew her mother could have told the woman a very different story, and would have. 'I think I probably should go back downstairs now. Poor Robert is waiting for me.'

Gabriella nodded wisely, still overwhelmed by what she had done, the kiss, the tiara, the gentle touch, the kind words. She knew she would remember it for a lifetime. It was a gift to her beyond anything the woman could have known or suspected.

'I wish I lived with you.' Gabriella blurted out the words as she held the woman's hand, and they walked slowly to the top of the stairs. Marianne thought it was an odd thing for Gabriella to say and she couldn't imagine what would make her say it.

'So do I,' she said gently, hating to let go of the child's hand, feeling her tug at her heart, and seeing something so sorrowful in the child's eyes that it physically pained her. 'But your mommy and daddy would be very sad, if you weren't here with them to keep them happy.'

'No, they wouldn't,' Gabriella said clearly, and Marianne stopped for a long moment, looking down at her, wondering if the child had gotten into trouble that day, or been scolded by her parents. To her, in her naïveté, it seemed as though it would be impossible to scold a child like this one.

'I'll come back and wave to you in a little while. Shall I come upstairs and visit you in your room?' Promising her something at least seemed the only way to leave her, to soothe her own conscience at leaving those eyes, that pleading look that tore at her heart now. But Gabriella shook her head wisely.

'You can't come upstairs to see me,' she said solemnly. The price to pay for it would have been almost beyond bearing, if she was discovered by her mother. Eloise hated it when her friends talked to Gabriella. It would be worse still if she found out someone had come upstairs to see her. Gabriella knew her mother would blame her for annoying their guests, and her fury would know no measure. 'They won't let you.'

'I'll see if I can slip away later . . .' Marianne promised, as she started down the stairs and then blew her a last kiss over an elegant shoulder. The gown seemed to float around her again as she moved, and she stopped halfway down the stairs, and looked back up to the child watching her. 'I'll be back, Gabriella . . . I promise . . .' And then, feeling something odd and uneasy in her heart, which she didn't quite understand, she ran the rest of the way down the stairs to her husband. He was drinking his second glass of champagne by then, and speaking to a very handsome Polish count, whose eyes lit up instantly when he caught sight of Marianne. He kissed Marianne's hand as Gabriella watched them. It was like watching a dance as she gazed at them, talking, laughing, and then moving slowly away toward the other guests. Gabriella wanted to run down the stairs and cling to her, to find safety with her, and protection. And feeling the child's eyes still glued to her, Marianne glanced upstairs one last time, and waved, as she disappeared on her husband's arm, as the count said something funny to her and she laughed a silvery sound. Gabriella closed her eyes at the sound of it, and leaned her head against the banister for a little while, just remembering, and

27

dreaming. She could still see the little tiara on her own head, and remember the look in the woman's eyes, and the delicious smell of her perfume.

It was another hour before the last of the guests arrived, and Gabriella sat there silently, watching them. None of the others spotted her, or ever glanced upstairs. They arrived, smiling, and talking, and laughing, left their wraps, took their champagne, and moved inside to see the other guests and her parents. There were more than a hundred people there, and she knew that her mother would never come upstairs to check on her. She just assumed that she was in bed, as she was supposed to be. It never occurred to them that she'd be watching the guests and being wicked, as usual, disobeying their orders. 'Stay in bed and don't move, don't even breathe,' had been her mother's last words to her. But the lure of the magic downstairs had been too great for her. She wished she could go downstairs and get something to eat. She was starving by the time the last guests had arrived, and she knew there was a lot of food in the kitchen, pastries and cakes, and chocolates and cookies. She had seen a huge ham being prepared that afternoon, a roast beef, and a turkey. There was caviar, as there always was, although she didn't like it. She had tasted it once, and it was terribly fishy, but her mother didn't want her to eat it anyway. She was forbidden to touch it, or any of the things they served at their parties. But she would have loved to have one of the little cakes. There were éclairs, and strawberry tarts, and little cream puffs that were her favorites. But everyone had been so busy that night, no one had thought to offer her dinner. And she knew better than to ask

28

her mother for something to eat when she was getting ready for a party. Eloise had been in her dressing room for hours, taking a long bath, doing her hair, and putting on her makeup. She didn't have time to think of the child, and Gabriella knew that it was better if she didn't. She knew what would have happened if she'd asked for anything. Her mother always got very nervous before their parties.

Gabriella could hear the music playing louder now. There was dancing at the far end of their huge living room, and the dining room and library and living room were full of people. She could hear them talking and laughing, and she waited for a long time, hoping to see Marianne again, but she never returned, and Gabriella knew she had no right to expect it. She had probably forgotten. Gabriella was still sitting there, hoping for a last glimpse of her, when her mother suddenly swept through the hallway downstairs, looking for something, and instantly sensed Gabriella's presence. Without hesitating for a moment, she glanced up at the chandelier, and then beyond it, to the top of the stairs, where Gabriella was sitting in her old pink nightgown. Her breath caught instantly, and she leaped to her bare feet and moved backward, falling over the first step, and landing with a hard thump on her thin bottom. And the look on her mother's face told her instantly what was coming.

Without a sound or a word, Eloise came up the stairs, as though on winged feet, a messenger from the devil. She was wearing a tight black satin gown, which revealed her spectacular figure and shone like her black hair, pulled back in a tight bun. She

29

was wearing long diamond dangling earrings, and an elaborate diamond necklace. But just as Marianne's gown and jewels seemed to soften her, to surround her in an aura of light and gentleness, what her mother wore seemed to accentuate her harshness, and made her look truly scary.

'What are you doing here?' She spat out the words in whispered venom. 'I told you not to leave your room.'

'I'm sorry, I just ...' There was no excuse for what she had done. Even less for having lured Marianne Marks up to see her ... or worse yet, trying on her tiara ... If her mother had known that ... but fortunately, she didn't.

'Don't lie to me, Gabriella,' her mother said, grabbing her arm so tightly it instantly stopped the circulation, and almost as quickly made it tingle. 'Don't say a word!' she said through clenched teeth as she dragged her down the hall, unseen by the people enjoying her hospitality downstairs. Had any of them seen what was happening, they would have been shocked into silence. And as though she knew that, she continued in a poisonous whisper to Gabriella, 'Don't make a sound, you little monster ... or I'll rip your arm off.' And Gabriella knew with absolute certainty that she would have. She didn't doubt it for a moment. At seven, she had learned many valuable lessons about her mother, and she knew that whatever tortures she promised, she generally delivered. That was one thing about Eloise you could always count on.

Gabriella's feet were literally lifted off the ground, as her mother half carried her to her room, with the rest of her body dangling as she tried to run along beside her mother, so as not to annoy

30

her further. The door was still open, and she threw Gabriella inside, who fell with a sharp thud to the ground, twisting her ankle, but she knew better than to make a sound as she lay on the floor in the darkness.

'Now you stay in there! Do you understand? I don't want to see you out of this room again, is that clear? If you disobey me this time, Gabriella, I promise you, you'll regret it. No one wants to see you out there . . . no one likes you . . . no one cares about you sitting at the top of the stairs like some poor pathetic little orphan. You're just a child, you belong in your room, where no one has to see you. Do you hear me?' There was silence from where Gabriella lay, crying silently in the darkness from the pain in her ankle and her arm, but she was too wise and too proud to complain about them to her mother. 'Answer me!' The voice sawed into the darkness and Gabriella was afraid her mother would approach her and deliver her message even more succinctly.

'I'm sorry, Mommy!' she whispered.

'Stop whining. Go to bed where you belong!' Eloise said, and slammed the door. She was still scowling over the incident as she hurried back to the stairs, and then as she descended them hurriedly, her face seemed to transform, and the memory of Gabriella and what she had done to her seemed to vanish entirely as she reached the hallway. Three of her guests were standing there, putting on their coats, and she kissed each of them warmly as they left, and then returned to the drawing room to chat and dance with the others. It was as though Gabriella had never existed. And to her, she didn't. Gabriella meant nothing to her.

Marianne Marks said to give Gabriella her love as she made her exit. 'I promised to go up and visit her before I left, but she must be asleep by now,' she said with regret as the child's mother frowned and looked startled.

'I should hope so!' she said sternly. 'Did you see her tonight?' she asked Marianne, almost vaguely, seeming surprised but not particularly concerned about it.

'I did,' the pretty woman confessed sheepishly, forgetting what Gabriella had said about not being allowed to see the guests, and not giving it much importance. Who could get angry at an angel like Gabriella? But there were far too many things Marianne did not know about the child's mother. 'She's so adorable. She was sitting at the top of the stairs when we arrived, in the sweetest little pink nightgown. I ran upstairs to give her a kiss, and we chatted for a few minutes.'

'I'm sorry,' Eloise said, looking mildly annoyed. 'She shouldn't have done that.' She said it apologetically, as though Gabriella had done something appalling to offend them, and in Eloise's eyes she had. She had made her presence known, which was an unpardonable sin to her mother, but Marianne Marks couldn't have known that.

'It was my fault. I'm afraid I couldn't resist her, with those huge eyes. She wanted to see my tiara.'

'I hope you didn't let her touch it.' Something in Eloise's eyes told Marianne not to say more, and as they left the Harrison house that night, Marianne said something about it to Robert.

'She's awfully hard on that child, don't you think, Bob? She acted as though she would have stolen my tiara, if I'd let her.'

32

'She may just be very old-fashioned about children, she was probably afraid Gabriella had annoyed you.'

'How could she annoy me?' Marianne said innocently as they drove home behind their chauffeur. 'She's the sweetest little thing I've ever seen ... so serious, and so pretty. She has the saddest eyes...' And then, wistfully, 'I wish we had a little girl like her.'

'I know,' he said, patting her hand, and glancing away from the disappointment in his wife's eyes. He knew what it meant to her that in nine years of marriage they had never been able to have children. But it was something they both had to accept now.

'She's hard on John too,' Marianne volunteered after a few moments of silence, thinking of the children they would never have, and the pretty little girl she had talked to that evening.

'Who?' Robert's mind was on other things by then. He'd had a busy day at the office, and was already thinking ahead to the next one. He had dismissed the Harrisons from his mind, and his wife's comments about their daughter.

'Eloise.' Marianne brought him back to the evening at hand, and he nodded. 'John danced with that English girl Prince Orlovsky brought several times, and I thought Eloise looked as though she were about to kill him.'

Robert Marks smiled at his wife's assessment of the situation. 'And I suppose you would have been fine if I'd danced with her?' He raised an eyebrow, and his wife laughed at him. 'The woman scarcely had any clothes on.' She'd been wearing a flesh-colored satin gown that clung to her like skin, and

33

left absolutely nothing to the imagination. She'd been quite spectacular and John Harrison had clearly found her very entertaining. Who hadn't?

'I suppose I can't blame Eloise,' Marianne admitted sheepishly. And then, seemingly without guile, as she turned her big blue eyes innocently to her husband, 'Did you think she was pretty?'

But he knew better than to answer, as he laughed heartily, just as they reached their house on East Seventy-ninth Street. 'I'm not going to fall for that one, Miss Marianne! I thought she was dreadful-looking, a complete harpy, and with a figure as bad as hers, she should never have attempted to wear that dress. I can't imagine what Orlovsky was thinking when he brought her!' They both laughed at his extricating himself from his wife's question, and they both knew that she had been a striking beauty and more than a trifle racy. But Robert Marks had never had any interest whatsoever in any woman other than his pretty wife, and it didn't matter a fig to him that she couldn't have children. He adored her. And his only interest now was in getting her upstairs to their bedroom. He didn't give a damn about Orlovsky's new mistress.

But the same was not quite so true for John Harrison, who was engaged in a similar, though far more heated, conversation with Eloise in their bedroom.

'For God's sake, why didn't you just take her dress off?' Eloise said tartly. He had danced repeatedly with the much-discussed English girl in the skintight beige satin dress, and his amorous dances with her had not gone unnoticed, either by Eloise or Prince Orlovsky.

34

'For chrissake, Eloise, I was just being polite. She'd had a lot to drink and didn't know what she was doing.'

'How convenient for you,' Eloise said coldly. 'I suppose when her strap slipped off her shoulder, and her breast was exposed, it was entirely an accident that you were practically kissing her at the time.' She was pacing around the room, smoking, and they'd both been drinking heavily all evening.

'I wasn't kissing her and you know it. We were dancing.'

'You were nearly making love to her, right there on the dance floor. You humiliated me in front of our friends.' And as far as she was concerned, he needed to be punished for it.

'Maybe if you were more interested in sleeping with me, Eloise, I wouldn't need to dance that way with a total stranger.' Not that he cared anymore. How could he after what he'd seen her do to Gabriella? He was standing over Eloise, and their voices were raised, but for once Gabriella couldn't hear them. She was sound asleep in her bedroom. The last guest had left at two o'clock, and it was nearly three o'clock in the morning as her parents argued. They had been at it ever since the party had ended, and their words were getting more and more heated, as were their tempers.

'You're disgusting,' Eloise said, standing as close to him as she dared. They both looked enraged, and the truth was that he would have loved to have taken the girl from Vladimir Orlovsky, and might still do it. His fidelity to, and his feelings for, Eloise had disappeared years before. As far as he was concerned, cruel as she was to their child, and cold as she was with him, she deserved it and he owed

35

her nothing. 'You're a bastard, and she's a whore!' Eloise said, wanting to humiliate him and to hurt him, but she couldn't. He didn't care what she thought anymore, or what she said. He hated everything about her, and she knew it.

'And you're a bitch, Eloise. It's no secret anymore. Everyone knows it. There isn't a man worth a damn in this town who'd want you.' She didn't answer him with words this time, but reached back and slapped him as hard as she could, almost as hard as she might have hit their daughter.

'Don't waste your energy. I'm not Gabriella,' he said, giving her a furious shove as she fell backward against a chair and knocked it over. She was still picking herself up off the floor as he strode out of the room, and slammed the door behind him. He never looked back, he didn't care, and for a crazed moment he almost hoped that he had hurt her. She deserved it, she had inflicted so much pain on him, and their little girl, she deserved to get some of it back. He didn't know where he was going that night, and he didn't care. He knew that the English girl would be in bed with Orlovsky by then, so he couldn't go to her, although he knew where she lived. But there were plenty of others, girls he called from time to time, professionals he used, or married women who were happy to spend an afternoon with him, or single ones who deluded themselves he might leave Eloise one day, and didn't care how much he drank when he was with them. There were lots of women willing to go to bed with him, and he took advantage of them as often as he had time to. He never hesitated to seize an opportunity to cheat on her. Why should he?

He flew down the stairs and hailed a cab, and as

36

he got into it, and it drove away, Eloise limped to the window, wearing one shoe, and watched him. There was no sorrow in her eyes, no regret for what she'd said, or what had happened. There was only anger and hatred on her face, and she had bruised her hip in the fall and was furious with him for it. So furious that her anger needed to vent itself, and there was only one place where she could do that. With a look of outrage she took off the other shoe and hurled it across the room, and walked on soundless feet out into the hallway. Everything she felt for him, or didn't, was in her eyes as she hurried down the hall to the familiar door, and all she knew as she walked into the darkened room was that she wanted to hurt him.

With a single gesture, she flipped the light on so she could see what she was doing, and ripped the covers off the small bed. It didn't deter her that there appeared to be no one there. She knew she was always there, hiding, just as evil and wicked and repulsive as her father. She was as disgusting as he was, and Eloise hated her with every ounce of her being as the small pink form was revealed, crouched in a little ball at the bottom of the bed, clutching her doll ... the stupid doll his mother had given her and she clung to all the time ... Eloise was in a blind rage as she grabbed it, and battered it against the wall, and broke off its head, as Gabriella came awake in a blinding flash and saw what she was doing.

'No, Mommy, no! Not Meredith! ... No ... Mommy, please ...' Gabriella was sobbing as her mother destroyed the doll she had loved for years, and then Eloise turned to her daughter in the same white rage and began to hit her.

'It's just a stupid doll ... and you're a wicked little brat ... you dragged Marianne up to see you tonight, didn't you? And what did you tell her ... did you cry to her ... did you tell her about this? Did you tell her you deserve this ... that you're a rotten little bitch ... that you're a little whore, and Daddy and I hate you because you give us so much trouble? ... Did you tell her we have to punish you because you're so bad to us ... did you? Did *you*? *DID YOU*?' But Gabriella could no longer answer her, her sobs had been drowned by screams as her mother hit her again and again and again, at first with the body of the doll she had called Meredith, and then with her fists, battering her chest and her body and her ribs, pounding at her, ripping at her, grabbing handfuls of her hair and nearly tearing it off her head, and then slapping her until she couldn't catch her breath any longer. The blows were continuous and endless and brutal beyond belief. All her hatred for the child, and for John, the humiliation she had felt that night when he'd gone after the English girl, were visited on the child, who had no idea what she had done to deserve it, except that she knew that in some part of her she was so evil that surely she deserved her mother's hatred.

Gabriella was nearly unconscious when her mother left her that night. There was blood in her bed, and a knife sliced through her each time she tried to breathe. Neither of them knew it, but two of her ribs were cracked. She couldn't breathe, she couldn't move, and she had to pee desperately, and she knew that if she did it in her bed, her mother really would kill her. The remains of her doll had disappeared. Her mother had taken it and thrown it in the trash when she left the room, exhausted, and somewhat sated. Her fury against John had dimmed. She had fed the monster within her. It had eaten Gabriella instead, devoured her, chewed her up and spat out what remained of her. There was blood matted in the child's hair as she lay in bed, and the bruises she would wear the next day would be the worst she'd ever had. It was the first time her mother had actually broken bones, and Gabriella was terrified and never doubted it would not be the last.

She lay in her bed, unable to cry after her mother left, it hurt too much. She shook violently instead. She was desperately cold as her entire body trembled. Her lips were swollen, her head ached, and every inch of her body hurt, but the worst was the searing pain from within whenever she tried to breathe and found she couldn't. She thought maybe she would die that night, and hoped she would. There was nothing she had left to live for. Her dolly was dead. And she knew that one day she would meet the same fate at her mother's hands. It was only a matter of time before her mother killed her.

Eloise slept in her black satin evening gown that night, too tired to undress. And Gabriella lay in her own blood, waiting for the angel of death to claim her. She tried to think of Marianne and the moments she had shared with her that night, but she couldn't think of that now, couldn't think of anything. She was in too much pain, and hated her mother too much. The hatred she felt took over everything. It almost made the pain bearable. And as she lay in her bed, at that very moment, her father lay in the arms of a pretty Italian prostitute

39

he knew well on the Lower East Side. Gabriella had no idea where he was, nor did Eloise, and it no longer mattered to either of them. Eloise told herself she didn't care where he was, she wished him in hell, and with her he was. And Gabriella knew that wherever he was, he would never save her. She was alone in the world, without saviors, without friends, without even her doll now. She had nothing. And no one. And as she lay there, unable to move that night, in too much pain, she finally peed in her bed, and knew with utter certainty that in the morning, when her mother discovered it, she would kill her. She lay thinking about it, welcoming it, wondering how the end would come, how much more it would hurt, or maybe it wouldn't hurt at all . . . and as she thought of it, welcoming death into her life, she slipped mercifully into an inky blackness.

CHAPTER THREE

The front door of the town house on Sixty-ninth Street closed quietly, shortly after eight o'clock, the morning after the party. John Harrison walked silently up the stairs, and paused briefly outside Gabriella's room, knowing she would probably be awake by then. But when he looked into her room, he couldn't see her stirring. Her eyes were closed and she lay on top of the sheets, which was rare for her, but he thought it was a good sign. Instead of hiding at the bottom of the bed as usual, she was lying in the open. More than likely it meant that her mother hadn't bothered her the night before.

Eloise had probably been too tired after he left, she had had too much to drink anyway to waste her time with Gabriella. At least for once the child hadn't been punished for the sins of the father. Or so he thought anyway, as he walked down the hall to his own room.

Eloise was still sleeping in her dress, her diamond necklace was still on, her earrings were loose in the bed, and she was still so sound asleep that she didn't move when he slipped into bed beside her. He knew her well enough to know that when she woke, she would say little about his hasty departure. She seldom did. She would be cool with him, distant for a day or two, but once the battle ended, it was never again mentioned. She just held it silently against him.

And just as he thought she would, she woke at ten, stirred lazily, and when she came fully awake, she glanced at him, not surprised to see him beside her. He was still half asleep by then, catching up on the sleep he'd missed the night before, in the apartment on the Lower East Side. There were a number of addresses just like it that he went to. Eloise had no idea where he went when he left her. She suspected, but would never have asked him.

She said nothing to him as she got up, left her jewelry on her dressing table, and walked slowly into her bathroom. She remembered everything that had happened the night before, particularly the part after he left, but there was nothing unusual about it, nothing worth commenting on now. She had nothing to say to her husband.

Gabriella was still in her room when Eloise went downstairs to make breakfast. The housekeeper had stayed to help the caterers clean up the night

41

before, and she was off now because it was Sunday. She was a quiet, unobtrusive woman, who had worked for them for years. She didn't like Eloise, but was civil to her, and Eloise liked her because she minded her own business. Although she silently disapproved of it, she never interfered with Eloise's disciplining of Gabriella.

Eloise put a pot of coffee on, sat down at the breakfast table, and picked up the paper. She was reading it, sipping coffee in a Limoges cup, when John finally came down and joined her, and asked about their daughter.

'Where's Gabriella? Still in bed?'

'It was a late night for her,' Eloise said in a chilly voice, without looking up from the paper.

'Should I go and wake her?' Eloise said nothing and only shrugged in answer. He poured a cup of coffee for himself, took the Business section of the *Sunday Times*, which Eloise never touched, and read for a half hour before commenting again on Gabriella's absence. 'Do you suppose she's sick?' He sounded worried, it didn't occur to him what had happened the night before, although it should have. He didn't realize that Eloise always took it out on her when he left at some ungodly hour after an argument. He should have suspected instantly, but as usual, he didn't really want to know. It was nearly eleven when he went upstairs to find her.

He found her changing her bed, moving with the awkward stealth of someone in great pain, but still he seemed not to see what had happened.

'Are you okay, sweetheart?' Her eyes bulged with unshed tears as she nodded. She'd been thinking about Meredith, her doll, and she felt as though someone had died the night before. And

42

someone had. Not only the doll, but she had. It had been the worst beating ever administered by her mother. And it had dissolved whatever small hope she had had left that she might survive her life here. She had no further expectation of that now. She knew it was only a matter of time before her mother totally destroyed her. She had no illusions anymore, no dreams, nothing at all, just the unbelievable pain in her side, and the memory of her doll being pounded against the wall, just as she knew her mother would have liked to do to her, but had not yet dared to.

'Can I help?' He offered to put the blanket back on the bed with her, but she shook her head. She knew only too well what her mother would say if she found them. She would accuse her of whining to her father, or manipulating, or trying to turn him against her mother. 'Don't you want to come downstairs to breakfast?' The truth was, she didn't want to see her mother. She wasn't hungry anymore, might never be again. She didn't care if she never ate, and every time she breathed it seared her like fire, and twisted a knife of pain in her rib cage. She couldn't imagine being able to get down the stairs, or sitting next to her mother at breakfast, let alone eating.

'It's okay, Daddy. I'm not hungry.' Her eyes were huge and more sorrowful than usual. And he told himself she was probably very tired. He refused to see the awkwardness with which she moved, the place where her hair was still matted with blood, the lip that was still more than slightly swollen. He told himself fairy tales about all of it, just as he had from the beginning.

'Come on, I'll make you pancakes.' As though he

43

had something to make up to her. As though he knew, which he would have insisted he didn't. If he allowed himself to think of what Eloise had done to her, it would have made him feel far too guilty.

He walked slowly into the room, and saw that Gabriella had a sweater on over her dress. That was usually the sign that her thin arms had been too badly bruised to expose them. It was a sign he always recognized, and one he never acknowledged. Even at seven, Gabriella understood that she had to cover herself so as not to offend them, especially her mother, with the outward signs of her 'badness.' Her father didn't ask her if she was cold, or why she wore the sweater. Sometimes she even wore a sweater, a long-sleeve shirt, or a shawl, at the beach for the same reasons. And no one said anything, they just let her do it. It was a silent vow, a tacit agreement between them.

'Where's Meredith?' he asked, as he glanced around the room, aware for the first time that the doll wasn't there. She was always close at hand in Gabriella's room, and this time he didn't see her.

'She went away,' Gabriella said with lowered eyes, trying not to cry again, thinking of the sound it had made when her mother battered her against the wall and destroyed her. It was a sound she knew she would never forget, a sight she would never forgive her for. Meredith had been her baby.

'What does that mean?' he asked innocently, and then, backing off almost instantly, he decided not to pursue the matter further. 'Come on downstairs and have something to eat, sweetheart. We have an hour before we have to go to church, we've got plenty of time for breakfast,' he said pleasantly, and then hurried back downstairs, relieved to escape the intensity of her eyes, the depths of her sorrow. He knew now that something had happened in his absence, but he didn't want to ask, and didn't want to know the details. Today was no different from any other. He never wanted to know what had happened, if he wasn't forced to see it. And even then, he did nothing about it.

Gabriella crept down the stairs quietly, taking one step at a time, gasping for air, and clutching the banister. Her ankle hurt, her arms, her head, and not just two but all of her ribs felt as though they had been broken. She felt sick from the pain as she slipped quietly into her seat at the breakfast table. She had put her sheets in the laundry bag after rinsing parts of them carefully, her bed had been changed, and she thought there was a chance her mother might never discover her 'accident' of the night before. She hoped not, with her entire being.

'You're late,' her mother said without ever taking her eyes off the paper.

'I'm sorry, Mommy,' Gabriella whispered. Talking hurt incredibly, but she knew what would happen if she didn't answer.

'If you're hungry, pour yourself a glass of milk and make a piece of toast.' She paused, not wanting to get up again, but without saying a word, her father did it for her, and as soon as her mother became aware of it, she looked up and stared at him in annoyance. 'You're always spoiling her. Why do you do that?' She looked at him pointedly, angry about crimes that had nothing to do with making Gabriella's breakfast. But she hated it when he made any effort for her, or offered any

45

kind gesture.

'It's Sunday.' As though that answered her question. 'Would you like another cup of coffee?'

'No, thank you,' she said curtly. 'I have to get dressed for church in a minute. And so do you.' She looked angrily at Gabriella. But the thought of changing again, having to get in and out of her sweater and her clothes almost made the child weep at the thought of what it would cost her. 'I want you in your pink smocked dress with the matching sweater.' The directions were clear, as was the penalty if she did not wear them. 'And stay in your room until we're ready to leave. Try not to get filthy dirty, as usual, in the meantime.' Gabriella nodded, and silently left the table a moment later without breakfast. She knew that today it would take her longer than usual to follow her mother's orders. And her father watched her go without saying a word. It was a complicity of silence between them.

She walked slowly up the stairs again, with more difficulty than she had come down them, but she made it to her room finally, and looked for the dress her mother had requested in her closet. She found it easily, but putting it on was another story. It took her nearly the full hour to change her clothes, and get into the dress as she winced in agony, and wiped away the tears that fell copiously as she did it. The sweater was the final blow in an already wretched morning. But she was dressed and waiting when her father came to tell her it was time to go, and she followed him down the stairs in her black patent leather shoes, and little white socks, and the pink smocked dress and matching sweater. She looked, as she always did, like a little

46

angel.

'My God, did you comb your hair with a knife and fork?' her mother asked angrily the moment she saw her. She had been unable to raise her arms to comb her hair that morning, and foolishly hoped her mother wouldn't notice.

'I forgot' was the only thing she could think of to say, and at least her mother couldn't say that she was lying. At least she hadn't pretended that she'd done it.

'Go back up and do it now, and wear the pink satin ribbon.' Gabriella's eyes filled with tears at the command, and for once her father came to the rescue. He took a comb out of his jacket pocket for her, and instead of handing it to her, he ran it through the silky curls himself, and she looked presentable in less than a minute. The blood had dried in her hair by then and he pretended not to see it.

'She doesn't need the ribbon,' was all he said to his wife as Gabriella looked up at him gratefully. In his dark suit, white shirt, and blue-and-red tie, he looked more handsome than ever. Her mother was wearing a gray wool suit with a fur around her neck, a small elegant black hat with a veil, and white kid gloves that, as usual, were spotless. She had on beautiful black suede shoes as well, and carried a black alligator handbag. She looked like a model in a magazine, Gabriella knew, except that, as she always did, she looked so angry. But for once Eloise decided not to argue with John about the ribbon. It simply wasn't worth it.

They were very nearly late for church, but arrived right on time, by cab, and slipped into a pew, with Gabriella seated between her parents.

47

She knew instantly what that meant. Every time her mother didn't like the way she behaved, or if she moved even a millimeter in her seat, her mother would squeeze a leg or an arm until it bruised, or grab her beneath her dress and pinch her.

Gabriella sat as still as she could, she barely moved today, and she could hardly breathe from the pain in her ribs. She sat in a daze of agony through most of the service. Her mother sat with her eyes closed most of the time, seemingly praying with total concentration. And now and then, she would open her eyes again and glance at Gabriella. But fortunately today, each time she did, Gabriella was sitting completely still, holding her breath so her ribs wouldn't be even more painful.

She followed her parents outside afterward, while they mingled with people they knew, and chatted with friends. Several people commented on how pretty Gabriella looked, and her mother ignored both their compliments and the child. And each time Gabriella was introduced to someone new, or met someone she had seen before, she had to shake their hand and curtsy. It was no small feat for her, in light of the damage of the night before, but knowing that she had no choice, she did it.

'What a perfect child!' someone said to John, and he agreed, while Eloise appeared not to hear them. Perfection was exactly what she expected of her. And Gabriella did her best to deliver it, though today it was anything but easy.

It seemed hours before they left the church, and went to the Plaza for lunch. There was music, and elegant silver trays being passed with tea sandwiches on them. And her father ordered her a hot chocolate. It arrived with a whole bowl of whipped cream, and Gabriella's eyes grew wide with delight, just as Eloise reached for it, and set it down on the far side of the table.

'You don't need that, Gabriella. It's not healthy. There's nothing more unattractive in the world than fat children.' She was in no danger of becoming fat, as all three of them knew. If anything, she looked like one of the starving children in Hungary she had heard so much about when she didn't finish her dinner. But nonetheless the whipped cream never came her way again. And she knew better than anyone that it was because she didn't deserve it. She had driven her mother to a frenzy the night before. There was no doubt in her mind that the ravages of the night before were probably her own fault, no matter how little she understood it.

They stayed at the Plaza until late that afternoon, greeting friends and observing strangers. It was a fun place to go for lunch, and normally Gabriella would have enjoyed it, but today she couldn't. She was in too much pain, and she was relieved when they left finally, to go home. Her father had already gone outside to find a taxi and Gabriella hung back a little bit, moving slowly, watching her mother stroll elegantly across the lobby. Heads turned as she walked past, as they always did, and Gabriella watched her in awe and silent hatred. If she was so beautiful, why couldn't she be nice as well? It was one of those mysteries to which Gabriella knew she would never have the answer. And as she walked out of the hotel, thinking about it, she stumbled for just an instant and accidentally stepped ever so lightly on the toe of her mother's black suede shoe. Gabriella shuddered inside as she did it, and her mother reacted even more quickly. She stopped dead in her tracks, stared at Gabriella with contempt, and pointed to her shoe in silent outrage.

'Fix that,' she said in a growling undervoice that made her sound like the voice of the devil, at least to Gabriella. Her mother was pointing at her shoe, with an imperiousness that would have startled anyone who heard her, but as usual, no one seemed to notice.

'I'm sorry, Mommy.' Her eyes were bottomless pools of regret and sorrow.

'Do something about it,' her mother snarled, but Gabriella had nothing to fix the black suede with except her fingers, and she began rubbing frantically in order to eliminate the offending dust spot. She thought of using her dress, but that would make her mother even angrier . . . or her sweater . . . There had to be something, but there wasn't. There didn't appear to be an available handkerchief, or even a bit of tissue. So Gabriella did the best she could with her nimble little fingers. And on closer inspection, it appeared that the smudge was gone, but Eloise refused to believe it when Gabriella said so. She made her clean the shoe again and again, kneeling on the pavement outside the hotel to do it. 'Don't ever do that again. Do you understand?' she said harshly to Gabriella, as the child said a silent prayer of thanks that she had been able to remove the spot. If she hadn't, there would surely have been another beating, or perhaps there still would be. The day was young yet.

They took a cab back to their house after that, and Gabriella's intense pain grew worse with each

50

passing moment. She was as white as a sheet, and her hands trembled as she folded them quietly, hoping her mother wouldn't see them before they got home. But for some reason, Eloise was in good spirits for a change, and although she wasn't pleasant to Gabriella, considering the scene of the night before, she was surprisingly civil to her husband. She didn't apologize for anything, she never did. As far as she was concerned, she didn't have to. In her mind, their argument of the night before was entirely his fault, and nothing she had to apologize for or explain.

She sent Gabriella to her room almost as soon as they got home. She hated finding her afoot, or wandering around the house for no apparent reason. She preferred to see her confined to a small space, sitting on a chair in her room, keeping out of trouble. And Gabriella meant to do just that. She didn't want to provoke her any further. So Gabriella went to her room, and stayed there. She had nothing to do, but she was in so much pain, she couldn't have done anything, if they'd asked her. But as she sat in her room, she couldn't help thinking about Meredith, the doll that had been demolished the night before. She genuinely missed her. Meredith had been her only friend, her confidante, her soul mate. And now she had no one.

She was still thinking about it when she heard laughter in the hall, outside her door, and was surprised to realize that she was hearing the voices of her parents. Her mother seldom laughed at anything, but as Gabriella listened, she sounded almost girlish. Their voices drifted away eventually, and she heard their bedroom door close heavily.

51

She had no idea what was happening in there, and wondered if they were fighting. But it didn't sound like it. They sounded happy as they laughed and giggled. And for a long time, Gabriella just sat there waiting. They'd have to come back eventually if only just to feed her.

But by the end of the afternoon, they still hadn't reappeared, and she knew that there was nothing she could do about it. She couldn't knock on their door, or speak to them through it. She could hardly demand an explanation as to why they had been ignoring her, or why they had left her to her own devices, and neglected to give her dinner.

In the end, they never came back to her that night. They had come to some kind of temporary peace, and were happily consummating it in the privacy of their bedroom. Eloise had forgiven him for the night before, which was rare, and he was so startled by it and she looked so pretty that day that he was actually attracted to her. That and the fact that he'd had several drinks at the Plaza at lunch helped to soften him to a woman he normally detested. For some reason, they were both feeling unusually mellow. But none of their newly found warm feelings extended to their daughter. John knew it would only be a temporary peace, as did Eloise, but it was enjoyable anyway, for however long it lasted. And Eloise decided not to take a single moment away from their time in bed to bother feeding Gabriella.

Gabriella knew she could have gone downstairs. There were still leftovers from the night before, but she had no idea what would happen if she dared to touch them. It was best to just stay in her room, and wait. They couldn't be that long. They were only talking, after all, with the door closed. But as she sat and watched first six and then seven and eight o'clock come, and finally nine, and even ten, it was obvious to her that she had been forgotten. She went to bed finally, grateful that the day was done and nothing particularly untoward had happened to her. But it could still happen, just as it had the night before, if her father angered her mother, or abandoned her, walked out and left her, as he did so often, however much or little she deserved it. Anything was possible, and Gabriella would have to pay the price for all his weaknesses and failings. But this time nothing happened. He didn't go anywhere, and the two lovebirds remained in their room, and Gabriella fell asleep finally, without her dinner.

CHAPTER FOUR

By the age of nine, having survived two more years of her parents' unthinkable behavior, Gabriella had retreated into a world where she could occasionally escape them. She wrote poems, stories, letters to imaginary friends. She had begun to develop a world where for an hour or two at least, her parents and the tortures they inflicted on her seemed to vanish. She wrote about happy people in pretty worlds, where wonderful things happened. She never wrote about her family, or the things her mother still did to her whenever the mood struck her. Her writing was her only escape, her only means of survival. It was a respite from a cruel world, despite seemingly comfortable

53

surroundings. Gabriella knew better than anyone that neither her address, nor the size of her father's income, or the distinction of the families from which her parents came, protected her from the kind of realities that other people's nightmares were made of. Her mother's elegance, and the jewels she wore, and the pretty clothes that hung in her own closet, meant nothing to her. She knew the meaning of life better than most, and the bitter contradictions in her own. Gabriella had understood early on what was important, and what wasn't. Love meant everything to her, she dreamed of it, thought of it, wrote of it. It was the one thing in her life that had eluded her completely.

People still talked about how pretty she was, how well behaved, how immaculate, how she never misbehaved or answered back, or challenged her parents. As did her teachers, her parents' friends talked about her lovely hair, her huge blue eyes, how rarely she spoke. Her grades were excellent, and although her teachers lamented the fact that she seldom spoke up in class, and only answered questions in class when directly pressed to do so, she was nonetheless far ahead of most of the other children her age. She read constantly, and had learned early. Just as her early writing did, the books she read transported her to another world, light-years away from her own. She loved reading, and now when her mother wanted to torment her, she threw away her books, and took her pencils and paper away from her. She was always quick to discover what meant the most to her, and to seal off all of Gabriella's avenues of escape. But when that happened, Gabriella sat lost in thought, dreaming. In the ways that mattered, at least, they could no longer touch her, though they never noticed. And for reasons Gabriella herself couldn't explain, she knew instinctively now that she was a survivor.

Eloise often had Gabriella help in the kitchen, scrubbing, or washing dishes, or polishing silver. She complained that Gabriella was still intolerably spoiled, and owed it to them to make herself useful somewhere in the house. She did her own laundry, changed her sheets, cleaned her own room, and bathed and dressed herself. She was never allowed to be idle for a single moment, unlike other children her age, who were left to play outdoors, or in their own rooms, and given books or toys to entertain them. Gabriella's life was still a constant battle for survival, and as she grew older, the ante was upped frequently, the rules changed on a daily basis. Her skill lay in deciphering her mother's threats, determining her mood of the hour, and striving constantly not to annoy her, doing everything possible not to incur her fury.

The beatings still occurred just as frequently, but she was in school for longer now, which mercifully kept her away from home for more hours every day. And inevitably, the sins she was accused of committing were more serious as she grew older. Forgotten homework, lost articles of clothing, breaking a plate when she was doing dishes in the kitchen. She knew better than to make excuses for her crimes. She just braced herself and took what came. She was artful at hiding the bruises in school, from teachers and the few children she played with. She kept to herself most of the time. She couldn't see the children after school anyway, her mother would never have allowed another child in the house to visit. It was bad enough, as far as Eloise was concerned, having Gabriella underfoot to destroy the house, she had no intention of inviting other children in to help her. One child to endure was bad enough. Yet another was inconceivable torture to her.

Only twice in her three years in school had teachers observed something wrong with Gabriella. Once her uniform had slipped up her thigh while jumping rope at recess, and they had seen the appalling bruises on her legs. When questioned, she had explained that she'd fallen off her bike in her parents' garden, and after sympathizing with her over the enormity of the bruise and how much it must have hurt when it happened, they let it go and forgot about it. The second time had been at the start of the current school year. Both her arms had been badly bruised and one of her wrists had been sprained. Her face, as was almost always the case, was remarkably untouched, her eyes innocent as she explained a bad fall from a horse over the weekend. They had excused her from doing homework until her wrist got better, but she couldn't explain that to her mother when she got home that night, so she did the homework anyway, and turned it in at school in the morning.

Her father remained as uninvolved as he had always been. And in the past two years, he seemed to spend most of his time away. He was traveling for the bank, and Gabriella knew that something untoward had happened between her parents, although it had never been clear to her exactly when it had occurred, or what it was. But for the past six months, they had had separate bedrooms, and her mother seemed angrier than ever

56

whenever Gabriella's father was home.

Eloise went out in the evenings alone a lot now. She got dressed up, and left Gabriella alone when she went out with friends. Gabriella wasn't entirely sure her father knew that, since he was gone so much, and her mother stayed home whenever he was in town. But the atmosphere between them had clearly deteriorated. Eloise made a lot of rude remarks about him, and no longer seemed to hesitate to insult him to his face, whether Gabriella was in the room or not. Most of the comments were about other women, whom she called harlots or hookers. She talked about him 'shacking up,' which was an expression Gabriella heard a lot, but she never knew quite what it meant, and she never dared to ask. Her father never answered her mother when she said it, but he drank a lot more these days. And when he did, eventually he left the house, and Eloise came to take it out on her.

Gabriella still slept at the bottom of the bed to escape her, but it was more out of habit than out of any success she'd had in convincing her mother that she wasn't there. Eloise always knew exactly where to find her. Gabriella didn't even waste time hiding now. She just took what she knew was coming to her, and tried to be brave about it. She knew that her only mission in life was to survive.

She also knew that somehow she must have caused the coldness between them, and although her mother never mentioned her name when she berated him, she knew that somehow, in some way, she was to blame for all their troubles. Her mother told her frequently that all her problems were because of Gabriella, and she accepted that now, along with the beatings, as her fate.

By Christmas that year, her father almost seemed not to live there. He hardly ever came home anymore, and whenever he did, Eloise flew into an uncontrollable rage. She seemed, if possible, angrier than ever. And now there was a name she screamed at him constantly. She shouted at him about 'some little tart,' or 'the whore you're shacked up with.' Her name was Barbara, Gabriella knew, but she had no idea who she was. She could never remember meeting any of their friends by that name. She didn't understand what was happening, but it seemed to make him even more remote, and he seemed to want nothing to do with her mother. He scarcely ever spoke to Gabriella, and most of the time when he was home now, he was drunk. Even Gabriella could see that, and he made no attempt to hide it anymore.

On Christmas Day, Eloise never came out of her room. John had been gone since the day before, and didn't return until late that night. There was no tree that year, no lights, no decorations. There were no presents for her, or any of them. And the only Christmas dinner she ate was the ham sandwich she made herself on Christmas Eve. She thought of making something for her mother, but she was afraid to knock on her door, or draw attention to herself. It seemed wiser to keep to herself and stay well out of the way. She knew how angry her mother was that her father wasn't there, particularly on Christmas Day. She was nine by then, and it was easier to understand what had happened, though the reason for her parents' hatred for each other was not entirely clear. It had something to do with the woman called Barbara, and undoubtedly something to do with her as well.

58

It always did, always had, according to her mother. Gabriella understood that very well.

When he came home late on Christmas night, the argument they had was not confined to their bedroom. They pursued each other around the house, shouting, and throwing things at each other, and knocking things down. Her father said he couldn't take it anymore, and her mother said she was going to kill them both. She slapped him, and he hit her mother for the first time. But instinctively, Gabriella knew that whenever the fight ended, she would be the one to take the brunt of it. She wished for the first time in a long time that there was a safe place to hide, a place to go for protection, people she could turn to. But there was no one, and she knew that all she could do was wait and see what happened. She had known for years that there were no rescuers, no saviors in her precarious life.

Eventually, her father left the house, and it was then that her mother found her. It was all too predictable, as she descended on her like a large, furious black bird. Her hair was down and flying out behind her. Her fists were powerful and relentless. Gabriella was aware of a sharp pain in her ear right from the first, a blow to her head, and a battery of blows to her chest, and this time her mother used a candlestick to hit one of her legs. Gabriella was sure she would hit her in the face or on the head with it, but miraculously she didn't. And after the shock of the first few minutes, the rest was a blur. Eloise was angrier than she had ever been, and Gabriella could sense easily that whatever she did now, whatever she said, might cost her her life.

She did nothing to avoid the blows that rained down on her that night. She simply waited, as she always did, for the storm to abate. And when it receded finally, and her mother left her alone on the floor of her room, Gabriella couldn't even crawl onto her bed. She simply lay there, drifting between consciousness and darkness, and was surprised to find that this time nothing hurt. She felt nothing this time, and all through the night she saw what seemed like halos of light around her. She thought she could hear voices once, but she couldn't hear what was being said. It wasn't until morning that she realized someone real was speaking to her, the voice was familiar, but just like the voices the night before, she couldn't distinguish what she was hearing. She didn't even realize it was her father. She never saw his tears, or heard his gasp of horror when he saw what Eloise had done to her. Gabriella was lying in a pool of blood this time, her hair matted to her head, her eyes glazed and unseeing, a terrifying wound on the inside of one leg. He wanted to call an ambulance but he was afraid to. Instead, without even waiting to talk to Eloise, he wrapped Gabriella in a blanket, and hurried outside to hail a cab.

When he arrived at the hospital, he wasn't even sure she was still breathing, but he rushed inside and deposited her on an empty gurney, called for help through his tears, and explained that she had fallen down the stairs. It was almost a believable tale, considering the extent of the damage, and no one questioned him. They put an oxygen mask on her small pale face and rushed her away, surrounded by nurses with worried faces, while John stared at them in disbelief.

He sat there looking stunned for several hours, and it was four o'clock in the afternoon before they came to reassure him that she would in fact survive. She had a concussion, three broken ribs, a broken eardrum, and a serious wound on one leg. But they had stitched her up, taped her ribs, and after a few days in the hospital, they felt sure that the worst of her injuries would be repaired. They asked him how long he thought it had been from the time she fell until he found her, and he said he thought several hours, although he admitted he wasn't sure when she had 'fallen.' He didn't tell them he'd been out.

'She'll be fine,' a young intern reassured him, and the nurses promised to take good care of her. He peeked in at her once, but she was sleeping, and without approaching her again, he left. He felt dazed as he rode home in the taxi, unsure of what to say. He had no idea how to stop Eloise now, how to end this, how to do anything except escape himself. At least Gabriella was in good hands now. It seemed like nothing short of a miracle that she'd survived the beating of the previous night.

He entered the house with overwhelming trepidation, and was relieved to discover when he went upstairs that Eloise wasn't there. He had no idea where she was, and he no longer cared. He went to the library and poured himself a stiff drink, and then sat there waiting, not even sure what to say to her when he saw her at last. What could he possibly say to her? She wasn't human. She was an animal of some kind, a being from another planet, a machine that destroyed everything it touched. He wondered now how he could ever have loved her, how he could have deluded himself that she could be a wife to him, or a mother to their child. He wanted nothing now except to get as far away from her as possible. He wanted to be with Barbara that night, but for once he didn't dare. He knew he had to wait for Eloise and confront her, even if it was only for this one last time. He had to do it now.

She came home shortly after midnight, in a dark blue evening gown, and as he looked up at her all he could think of was that she looked like an evil queen. The Queen of Darkness. And seeing the state he was in, she glanced at him sprawled across the couch in the library with utter disdain.

'How nice of you to visit, John,' she said with icy contempt that wasn't lost on him even in his drunken state. 'You're looking well. To what do I owe the honor? Is Barbara out of town, or is she servicing one of her other clients?' She walked slowly into the room swinging a small beaded purse in her hand, and he was aware of an overwhelming urge to throw his drink in her face or hit her, but he refrained. He knew that whatever he said or did to her, inhuman as she was, he could never hurt her. She was well beyond his reach in every possible way.

'Do you know where our daughter is tonight, Eloise?' His words slurred, but he knew exactly what he wanted to say now. It had finally become crystal clear to him, after far too many years. He was only sorry it had taken him this long to do it. But Barbara had finally given him courage. And seeing the state Gabriella had been in had strengthened his resolve.

'I'm sure you're going to tell me where she is, John. Did you leave her somewhere, or perhaps give her away?' She seemed amused rather than concerned, and it was easy to see her now for the monster she was. The only thing he didn't understand was how he could have been fooled by her for so long. He had wanted to be, wanted to believe that she was someone she wasn't, but that was another story, and something he was still unable to face, even now.

'You'd like that, wouldn't you? If I gave her away, I mean. Why didn't we just drop her off at an orphanage when she was born, or leave her on the steps of a church? You'd have loved that, wouldn't you, and it would have been so much better for her.' He was fighting back tears as he spoke, remembering the sight of Gabriella's small broken body on the gurney. It was a sight he knew he would never forget.

'Spare me your maudlin theories, John. Is she at Barbara's? Are you planning to kidnap her? If so, you know I'll have to call the police.' She set her evening bag down on a table, and sat down elegantly across from him in a chair. She was still a beautiful woman, but rotten to the core. She had no soul. She was an iceberg, and cruel beyond measure. The woman he was with now was far less beautiful, but she seemed to care a great deal more about him. Her ancestors were far less aristocratic, but she loved him, and she had a heart. And all he wanted to do now was forget this woman, and the life he'd shared with her, and get as far away from her as he could. He had been hesitating for a year because of Gabriella, but he couldn't help her now anyway, couldn't stop this monster anymore. All he could do now, he was certain, was save himself.

'Gabriella is in a hospital,' he said ominously. 'She was nearly unconscious when I found her this

63

morning.' Just looking at Eloise, he was trembling with rage. Yet in some part of him, she still terrified him. He knew what she was capable of now, and he was afraid he would lose control of himself and kill her. The only thing she deserved was to be destroyed.

'How fortunate that you came home then, isn't it? What a blessing for her,' Eloise said coolly.

'She might have died if I hadn't. She has a concussion, broken ribs . . . a broken eardrum . . .' But it was obvious from the look on his wife's face that she didn't care. It was of absolutely no importance to her. And she felt anything but guilty about what she'd done to their child.

'Are you expecting me to cry? She deserved it.' She looked completely in control and utterly indifferent as she lit a cigarette and stared at him.

'You're insane,' he whispered hoarsely, running a nervous hand through his hair. This was harder than he thought it would be. With her unshakable calm and guiltless cruelty, she was a formidable opponent. And she was much stronger than he was. He had known that for a long time.

'I'm not insane, John. But you look it. Have you seen yourself in the mirror? You look quite mad.' Her eyes only laughed at him, and he suddenly wanted to cry.

'You could have killed her.' His eyes blazed as he spoke hoarsely from his own emotions.

'But I didn't, did I? Perhaps I should have. Most of our problems are thanks to her. If I didn't care about you so much, I wouldn't be as angry at her. None of this would have happened if she hadn't come between us, if you hadn't been as besotted with her as you are.' It was obvious as he watched

64

her that she believed that, that in some twisted part of her mind, she had convinced herself that Gabriella was to blame, and deserved everything they'd done to her ever since. It would have been impossible to make her see the insanity of what she was saying, and he knew that now.

'She has nothing to do with what happened between us, Eloise. You're a monster. You're insanely jealous, and you hate that little girl. Blame me, for God's sake, don't blame her. Hate me if you have to, because I failed you, because I've been unfaithful to you, because I'm not strong enough to give you what you want . . . but please . . . please . . .' He started to cry, pleading with her to hear the truth of his words. 'Don't blame her.'

'Can't you see what she's done to us? She turned you around completely. You loved me before she was born. We loved each other . . . now look at us . . .' There were tears in her eyes for the first time in years as she looked at him. 'She did this . . .' She even blamed Gabriella for the fact that he was in love with another woman. As far as Eloise was concerned, Gabriella was responsible for it all.

'*You* did it,' he accused her, unmoved by her tears. 'I stopped loving you when I realized how much you hated her, when I saw how you beat her . . . and, oh God, one day she will hate us for what we did to her.'

'She deserves it.' Eloise retreated to her earlier stance, convinced of the wisdom of her words. 'I don't care what I did to her. She cost me everything . . . cost us our marriage and our love . . .'

'You hated her from the day she was born. How could you?

'I could see what was coming even then.'

'You have to stop, Eloise, before you kill her,' he implored her. 'You have to . . . You'll spend the rest of your life in jail.'

'She's not worth it,' Eloise said firmly. She had thought about it before, and she was careful never to go too far, for her own sake, not for the child's. But the night before, she had come dangerously close. He understood that better than she did. He had seen Gabriella in the hospital, and heard what the doctors said. No one had accused him of beating her, fortunately. It would have been inconceivable to them, particularly given his good manners, respectable name, and expensive address. Asking him a question like that would have been offensive, and even if they suspected it, which he hoped not, they wouldn't have dared to accuse him of abusing his child.

'I won't kill her, John,' Eloise reassured him, but it was an empty promise from a woman with no soul. 'I don't have to. She knows what I expect of her. She knows the difference between right and wrong.'

'The trouble is, you don't.'

'I'm tired,' she stood up then, 'and you're boring me. Are you going up to bed, or are you going back to your little harlot? And when is that going to end?' Never, he promised himself. Never in a thousand years. He was never coming back to this woman. But he knew he had to be here now, to calm her down again, until Gabriella came home. No matter how much he hated her, he knew he owed that much to Gabriella. He couldn't give up the rest of his life for her, but he could smooth things over for her, at least until she came home.

'I'll go up in a while,' he said calmly, pouring himself one last drink. He was grateful they had separate bedrooms. He would have been afraid to sleep in the same bed with her now, for fear that she might kill him. Knowing what she was capable of terrified him. He had warned Barbara of that, and tried to tell her how dangerous Eloise was. But Barbara foolishly insisted she wasn't afraid of her. She couldn't conceive of the monster she truly was. No one could. Except he, and Gabriella, who knew it only too well.

'I assume you're sleeping in your own room tonight,' she said as she walked out of the room, and he watched the train on her evening gown trailing behind her. But he didn't answer her, he was thinking of Gabriella again, and he didn't have the strength to say another word. He just watched her as she walked slowly up the stairs.

*   *   *

When Gabriella woke up in the hospital that night, she had no idea where she was. Everything was white and clean and looked very stark. There were shadows on the ceiling, and a small light in the corner of the room. A nurse in a starched cap was looking down at her, and as soon as Gabriella's eyes fluttered open, the young woman smiled at her. It was an unfamiliar sight to Gabriella. The nurse's eyes looked very kind.

'Am I in heaven?' she asked softly, convinced, and relieved to think, that she had died.

'No, you're at St. Matthew's Hospital, Gabriella. And everything is fine. Your daddy went home a while ago, but he said he'd come back tomorrow to see how you are.'

She wanted to ask if her mother was angry at her for being here, and if she ever had to go back there again. If she never got well again, couldn't she just stay? There were a thousand questions in her head, but she was afraid to do anything more than nod, and when she did, it hurt. A lot.

'Try not to move around too much.' The young nurse had seen her wince. She knew the concussion was giving her a severe headache, and there was still blood draining from her ear. 'Your daddy said you fell down the stairs, and you're a very lucky girl that he found you when he did. We're going to take good care of you while you're here.' Despite the pain, Gabriella nodded gratefully again, and closed her eyes.

She cried in her sleep after that, the shifts changed, and an older nurse came to watch over her for several hours. She checked her vital signs and changed the dressing on the wound on her leg. She stood and stared at it for a long time, and then back at the little girl's face. There were questions in the nurse's mind that she knew would never be answered, questions that should have been asked, but no one would have dared. She had seen injuries like this before on children, but usually children with wounds like these were poor. They went home anyway, just as this one would. And most of the time, they came back again. She wondered if Gabriella would too, or perhaps they had frightened themselves enough this time, and it wouldn't happen again. It was hard to say.

Gabriella slept fitfully till morning, and most of the time for the next few days. Her father came to see her twice, and explained to the doctors and the nurses that her mother wasn't able to come because she was ill. They understood and sympathized with him, and complimented him on his little girl. She was so good, so sweet, so well behaved. She never gave them any trouble, never asked for anything, and was grateful for everything they did. She never even spoke to them. She just lay there, watching, but she smiled whenever she saw him.

He came to take her home on New Year's Day, and brought some clothes for her to wear. She left the hospital in a navy coat, a gray wool dress, white knee socks, and red shoes. He had forgotten to bring her hat and gloves, and she looked so small and pale when she left the hospital after thanking everyone for how nice they'd been to her. And just before the elevator doors closed, she smiled and waved. They all agreed on what a nice child she was, and were sorry there weren't more like her. She had even told them the night before that she was sorry to be going home.

'That's a first!' one of the nurses said with a grin as she hurried off to take care of a child with whooping cough, and another with severe burns. Gabriella had been the darling of the pediatric ward, and they were sorry she was leaving too. But not nearly as sorry as Gabriella was herself. She hated leaving their safe haven, and returning to her life in hell.

Her mother was waiting for her when she got home, frowning darkly, with eyes filled with accusation. She had never gone to the hospital to see her, and had told John repeatedly that all that pampering was unnecessary and an outright disgrace. He didn't argue with her, but anyone could have seen how pale Gabriella was when he brought her home, and from the damage to her ear, she was still a little unsteady on her feet.

'Well, did you get enough attention playing sick for all the nurses and doctors?' Eloise asked unkindly as John went to Gabriella's room to drop off her things and turn her bed down for her. The doctor had told him she should rest.

'I'm sorry, Mommy.'

'You should be. Whining little brat,' she said, and then turned on her heel and disappeared.

Gabriella had dinner with both her parents that night, and predictably it was a silent and awkward ordeal. Her mother was clearly angry at her, and her father was lost in another world, and had had too much to drink by the time they sat down to eat. Gabriella spilled some water on the table, and her hands shook as she quickly mopped it up.

'Your table manners haven't improved in the last week. What did they do, feed you?' Eloise asked meanly, and Gabriella lowered her eyes, and thought it best not to speak. She never said a word during the entire meal. And as soon as she'd eaten the last bite of her dessert, her mother ordered her to her room. Gabriella could sense that a battle was brewing and it was a relief to leave.

She got into her bed immediately, and listened in the dark as her parents argued, and it was no surprise when she heard footsteps in her room late that night. She was sure it was her mother, and braced herself for what was to come. This time the covers were peeled back slowly, and she tensed her entire body and squeezed her eyes shut, waiting for the first familiar blow to strike her. But for a long moment, there was none. She could feel someone standing over her, but she couldn't smell her perfume, there was no sound, and nothing happened. After waiting an interminable moment she couldn't stand the suspense and opened her eyes.

'Hi . . . were you sleeping? . . .' It was her father, he was whispering, and all she could smell now was the whiskey on his breath. 'I came to say . . . to see . . . if you were all right.' She nodded, confused. He never came into her room like that.

'Where's Mommy?'

'Asleep.' She exhaled slowly at the news, deeply relieved, although they both knew it wouldn't take much to wake her. 'I just wanted to see you . . .' He sat down gently on the bed. 'I'm sorry . . . about the hospital . . . and everything . . . The nurses said you were very brave . . .' But he already knew better than anyone how brave she was, far braver than he was.

'They were nice,' she whispered, watching his face in the darkness. She could see him clearly now in the moonlight from her window.

'How do you feel?'

'Okay . . . my ear still hurts . . . but I'm fine . . .' The headache had been gone for the past two days, and her ribs were still taped, as they would be for the next two weeks.

'Take care of yourself, Gabriella . . . always be brave, you're very strong.' She wondered why he said that to her, what he was really trying to say. And she couldn't help asking herself why he thought she was strong. She didn't feel it. Most of the time, she just thought about how bad she was.

He wanted to tell her he loved her, but he didn't

71

know what to say. And even he knew that if he had loved her, truly, he wouldn't have let her mother beat her to within an inch of her life. But Gabriella had no idea what was on his mind. He stood there looking at her for another moment, and then pulled the covers up around her again, and left her, without saying another word.

He paused in the doorway for just the fraction of an instant, as she watched him, and then closed the door as softly as he could. Neither of them wanted to wake her mother, and he was so quiet, she couldn't even hear him tiptoe away. She burrowed down in the bed again after that, and she was still asleep the next day when her mother threw open the door to her room, and shouted at her.

'Get out of there!' the familiar voice screamed at her, as Gabriella bounded out of bed still half asleep. Her rapid movements brought the headache back instantly, challenged her ribs, and caused her to lurch a bit from the damage to her ear. 'You knew, you little bitch, didn't you! Did he tell you? *Did* he?' She was shaking Gabriella by both arms by then, with total disregard for where she'd been for the past week, or the injuries that had caused her to be there.

'Know what? I don't know anything, Mommy . . .' She was out of practice suddenly, and in spite of herself began to cry. She knew from her mother's face that something terrible had happened, but she couldn't begin to imagine what it was. For the first time Gabriella could remember, her mother looked frantic and disheveled.

'Yes, you do . . . Did he tell you in the hospital? Is that it? Just what did he say?' She was shaking her so hard, Gabriella could hardly answer.

'Nothing . . . he didn't tell me anything . . . what happened to Daddy?' Maybe he was hurt, or something had happened to him. She couldn't imagine it, but her mother spat the words in her face before she could ask again.

'He's gone, and you knew it. It's your fault . . . you were so much trouble to both of us, that he left us. You thought he loved you, didn't you? Well, he didn't. He left you just like he left me. He doesn't want either of us anymore . . . you little bitch . . . you did it, you know. You did it! He left because he hates you, just as much as he hates me.' She said it with a resounding slap across Gabriella's face. 'He left because of you . . . and there's no one to protect you now.' And as she descended on the child with a vengeance, Gabriella began to understand. Her father had left them. That was why he had come into the room last night. He had come to see her one last time . . . he had come to say good-bye . . . and now he was gone . . . and all she had left was this. The blows that never ended, the beatings that were her life. He had told her to be brave the night before . . . told her she was strong. His words were all she had now, and as she remembered them, and her mother's fists flailed at her harder than ever this time, Gabriella fought valiantly not to cry, but she couldn't stop herself. All she had left now was this nightmare. Her mother said he hated her, and she knew that wasn't true. Or did he? He had never protected her, never helped her, never saved her from any of it. And now, whatever his reasons, he had left her. And all she could feel, rising up in her throat like bile, was fear.

CHAPTER FIVE

The rest of the year until Gabriella turned ten was a kaleidoscope of darkness, the patterns moving and shifting, but the theme always the same, the terrors always as acute no matter how varied the colors.

Gabriella's father disappeared as effectively as if he had vanished off the face of the earth, never to be seen again. He never called, never wrote to her, never came to see her, never explained how or why it had happened, what he had done, or why.

And the day her mother got her first notice from his attorney she was so enraged that, predictably, she nearly beat Gabriella senseless. Only her own exhaustion finally stopped her. But in the days following, she showed Gabriella no mercy. She blamed her for everything, as she had since Gabriella was born, and told her that he hated Gabriella as much as he hated her. She said he no longer needed her, the woman he was going to marry had two little girls who had replaced her. 'They're not like *you*,' her mother raged at her venomously every time she mentioned them, which was as often as she could. 'They're beautiful and good and well behaved, and everything you aren't. And he loves them,' she whispered cruelly. And once when Gabriella foolishly tried to argue with her, defending the feelings she attributed to him but no longer felt quite so sure of in the face of his defection, her mother took out a scrub brush and the laundry soap and washed her mouth out until the soapsuds oozed down her throat and she vomited, as much from the soap as from the bitter taste of her own sorrow and loss. She knew her father had loved her, she told herself, she knew it ... or thought so ... or perhaps only wanted to believe it. Until, finally, she no longer knew what to think.

She spent most of her time alone, in the house, reading, and writing her stories. She wrote letters to her father sometimes, but she didn't know where to send them, so she tore them up and threw them away. He had left her no address, and when she tried to look for it when her mother was out, she never found it. She wouldn't have dared ask her mother for it. She knew where he worked when he left, and when she called she was told that he had left the bank, and had moved to Boston. It might as well have been in another galaxy, for all Gabriella knew. And when she didn't hear from him on her tenth birthday, she knew she had lost him forever.

She still felt rising waves of panic sometimes, when she thought about it, remembering back to that last night in her room, when they had whispered in the moonlight. There was so much she would have liked to say to him ... maybe if she had ... if she had told him how much she loved him, he might have stayed, he might not have left her for the two little girls her mother talked about ... the ones who were so much better than she was, the ones he loved now. Maybe if she had tried harder, or got better grades in school, though she could hardly have done much better ... or perhaps if she hadn't had to go to the hospital at times ... if she hadn't made her mother hate them both so much, maybe then he wouldn't have run away ... or maybe he was dead, and it was all a lie. Maybe he'd been in an accident and she didn't know it. The very thought of it made it impossible to breathe . . . What if she really never did see him again? What if she forgot what he looked like? She stood and stared at pictures of him sometimes. There were two on the piano, and several in the library, but when her mother saw her doing that one day, she took all of his photographs out of their frames and tore them into a million pieces. Gabriella had an old one of him in her room, from when she was five, in Easthampton one summer, but her mother found that one too, and threw it away.

'Forget him. He doesn't care about you. Why waste your time thinking about him? He won't save you now,' she said, laughing at her, making fun of her, watching Gabriella's eyes fill with tears. The one thing that reached her now, with greater force than her mother's blows, was the knowledge that she would never see her father again, as her mother reminded her constantly, and that he had never loved her. It was hard to believe at first, and then eventually, she knew it had to be true. His silence confirmed it. But if he did love her, she knew she would hear from him one day. All she could do was wait.

And one year after he left she spent Christmas alone in the house on Sixty-ninth Street. Her mother spent the day with friends, and the evening with a man from California. He was tall and dark and handsome, and looked nothing like her father. He spoke to her once or twice when he picked her mother up to take her out to dinner, but whenever he did, Eloise made it clear to him that it was neither necessary nor welcome for him to speak to the child. Gabriella was wicked, she explained to him vaguely more than once, so much so that she was reluctant to share the details with him. And he understood early on that befriending Gabriella was not the way into Eloise's good graces. If anything, it was wiser to avoid her, so after a while, he said nothing to her at all.

There had been a constant parade of men who came to see Eloise to take her out, but the man from California was the most frequent visitor. His name was Frank. Franklin Waterford. And all Gabriella knew about him was that he was from San Francisco, and living in New York for the winter. She wasn't sure why, and he talked about California a lot with her mother, and told her how much she was going to love it when she came out. And then her mother began to talk about going to Reno for six weeks. Gabriella had no idea where that was, or why her mother wanted to go there, and they never explained any of it to her. All she knew was what she overheard as they walked past her room, chatting animatedly on their way out, or what she could hear when they sat in the library late at night, drinking and talking and laughing. And she couldn't help wondering what she would do about school when she and her mother went to Reno. But there was no way to ask her about it. She knew that if she asked her anything, her mother would fly into a rage.

Gabriella just went on with her life, waiting for news and explanations, checking the mail every day when she got home from school, hoping to find a letter from her father, telling her where he was. But it was never there, and when her mother saw her rifling through the mail one day, the inevitable happened. But the beatings were a little less energetic these days, and slightly less frequent. She

77

was too busy with her own life now to worry about 'disciplining' Gabriella. Most of the time, she informed Gabriella that she was hopeless. Her father had figured it out after all, hadn't he? And she herself could no longer be expected to waste her life trying to make something of Gabriella. It wasn't even worth her time to do that. So she left Gabriella to her own devices, to fend for herself and, most of the time, make her own dinner, if there was enough food in the house to do it at all, which more often than not, there wasn't.

Jeannie, the housekeeper, left promptly at five o'clock every afternoon, and whenever she thought she could get away with it, she left a little something on the stove for Gabriella. But if she fussed over her, or 'spoiled' her, or talked to her too much, the child paid a high price for it, and she knew that, so she feigned indifference, and forced herself not to think of what would happen to Gabriella after she left. She had the saddest eyes of any child Jeannie had ever seen, and it pained her just to look at her. But she knew better than anyone that there was nothing she could do to help her. Her father had disappeared and left her to work out her own fate with her mother, and Eloise was a hellion. But Gabriella was her child, after all. What could Jeannie possibly do to help her, except leave a little soup on the stove sometimes, or put a cool compress on a bruise the child said she had gotten in the schoolyard. But even Jeannie knew that schoolyard bruises didn't happen in those sizes and locations. There was a handprint on Gabriella's back once that looked like someone had drawn it on her, and Jeannie didn't have any trouble figuring out how it got there. At times, she

78

almost wished the child would run away, she'd have been better off alone in the streets, than with her mother. All she had here were warm clothes and a roof over her head, but she had no warmth, no love, scarcely enough food to survive, and no one in the world to care about her. But Jeannie knew that even if Gabriella ran away, the police would only bring her back. They would never interfere between parent and child, no matter what Eloise did to her. And Gabriella had long since known that as well. She knew that grown-ups didn't help you. They didn't interfere, or come riding up on a white horse to save you. Most of the time, they pretended not to see things, closed their eyes, or turned their backs. Just like her father.

But as the months passed from winter into spring, Eloise's rages seemed to dwindle to indifference. She seemed to care nothing about what Gabriella did now, as long as she didn't have to see or hear her. And the only time she had beaten her recently was when she claimed Gabriella 'pretended' not to hear her. The 'pretense' was simply that Gabriella's hearing was no longer what it had once been. She seemed to hear well most of the time, but from certain angles, or if there were other confusing noises in the room, she could no longer distinguish the words quite as clearly as she once could. It was simply a remnant of earlier beatings, and Gabriella never complained about it, though it hampered her in school at times, but no one seemed to notice, except her mother.

'Don't ignore me, Gabriella!' she would shriek, and descend on her like a banshee with fists flailing. But Frank was around more than ever these days, and she was careful around him. She never laid a hand on Gabriella during his visits, but now only when they were alone, or he disappointed her in some way by not showing up when he promised or forgetting to call her, which she always blamed on Gabriella. 'He hates you, you little wretch! You're the only reason he's not here tonight!' Gabriella didn't doubt it for a moment, she only wondered what would happen if he stopped coming over. But for now anyway, that seemed less than likely, although he was talking about going back to San Francisco in April, and Gabriella could tell that made her mother very nervous, and her nervousness translated into something far more dangerous for Gabriella.

And in March, every time he came over, the door to the library was closed so they could talk in private, or they went upstairs to her mother's bedroom and stayed there for hours. It was hard to imagine what they were doing, and they were always very quiet. He would smile at Gabriella when he walked by her room, but he never stopped to chat, or even say hello anymore. It was as though he understood that that was forbidden. Gabriella was treated like a leper in her own house.

And in April, he left as promised, and returned to San Francisco. But much to Gabriella's surprise, Eloise didn't seem particularly dismayed by it. If anything, she seemed busier and happier than ever these days. She scarcely spoke to Gabriella, which was a blessing. And she seemed to be making a lot of arrangements. She spent a lot of time on the phone, talking to her friends, and always lowered her voice when Gabriella came into the room, as though she were telling secrets. But Gabriella couldn't hear them anyway.

80

It was three weeks after he had left that she began dragging suitcases out of the basement, and asked Jeannie to help her get them upstairs. Eloise seemed to be packing everything she owned, and Gabriella wondered when she would tell her to pack her things. It was days after she had started when she finally told Gabriella to pack a suitcase.

'Where are we going?' Gabriella asked with cautious interest. It was rare for her to ask a question, but she wasn't sure what kind of clothes to put in the suitcase, and didn't want to infuriate her mother by packing the wrong ones.

'I'm going to Reno,' she said simply, which told Gabriella nothing. She didn't dare ask where it was, or how long they would be staying, and prayed she'd make the right guesses about what clothes to pack. She went quietly to her room and began packing, and she couldn't help wondering if, when they got there, Frank would be there. She didn't even know if she liked him. She scarcely knew him. All she knew was that he was handsome and tall, and very polite to her mother. They didn't shout at each other the way her mother and father had, but he didn't say anything to Gabriella either. It was hard to tell if she'd like him, or if she would disappoint him as she had everyone else. It was something she had come to expect now, a fear she lived with. She knew that if she loved someone enough, they would eventually come to hate her, and possibly leave her, just as her father had. And if her own father felt that way about her, who wouldn't? But maybe Frank would be different. It was hard to guess that. And just to relieve her own worries on the subject, she began writing stories about him, but when her mother found them, she

81

tore them up and said she was a little slut, and she was after him herself. She had no idea what her mother meant, or why she was so angry. She had described him as Prince Charming in one of her stories, and she'd been beaten for it. It would undoubtedly have sickened Frank, if he knew that, but of course he didn't. He was already in California by then.

And on a bright Saturday morning, two weeks after Easter, her mother looked at her over breakfast, and smiled at her for what seemed like the first time in her life. It almost frightened Gabriella. There was something glittering in her eyes that warned Gabriella that, if she wasn't careful, there would be trouble. But all Eloise said was, 'I'm leaving for Reno tomorrow.' And she seemed happy about it. 'Are your bags packed, Gabriella?' Gabriella nodded silently in answer. And after breakfast, her mother checked her room and the suitcase, and nodded. Gabriella was relieved to see she hadn't made any unpardonable mistakes in her packing. She saw her mother glance around the room, as though checking to see if she'd forgotten anything, but she seemed satisfied with what she saw. There were no pictures on the walls, there never had been, and the single photograph she'd had of her father on her dresser had been thrown away by her mother shortly after he left. There was nothing to adorn the room, just her bed, the dresser, a chair, plain white curtains at the window, and a linoleum floor, which Jeannie helped her scrub every Tuesday afternoon.

'You won't need any fancy clothes, Gabriella. You can take the pink dress out of the suitcase,' was her only comment as Gabriella quickly removed it and hung it back in her closet before it could displease her further. 'Don't forget your school clothes.' The instructions were confusing, but she had packed some of them anyway because they were comfortable and warm and she wasn't sure how long they'd be staying in Reno. Her mother turned and looked at her then with a look of sarcasm that wasn't unfamiliar to Gabriella. 'Your father is getting married in June. I'm sure you'll be happy to know that.' But all Gabriella felt was relief, along with the crushing disappointment of the realization that he was never coming back again. She had known it anyway, but now it was certain. But she was relieved to know he was alive, and hadn't died in a terrible accident, which would have explained his persistent silence. She had written a story about it, and it seemed so real as she wrote it that she had begun to fear that he really had died, and not just left them. 'You won't be hearing from him again,' her mother confirmed for the ten thousandth time. 'He doesn't care about either of us. He never did. He never loved you, or me. I want you to remember that, Gabriella. He *never* cared about you.' Eloise stared down at Gabriella with a spark of anger kindling in her eyes and she seemed to be waiting for an answer as Gabriella stood there. 'You do know that, don't you?' Gabriella nodded in silence, wanting to say that she didn't believe her, but doing that might have cost her her life and she knew that as well. She was far too wise now to risk her own survival for the sake of defending her father. And perhaps he never had loved them, though she still found it hard to believe that. Perhaps if she had been better, and less troublesome, he might have loved

83

them more, and stayed ... but she still remembered the look in his eyes on that last night in her bedroom. His eyes had told her he loved her, no matter what her mother said now. That's what made it all so confusing.

Her mother went out with friends that night, and Gabriella made a sandwich, and ate it in the kitchen by herself. The house was quiet and peaceful, and she sat for a long time, contemplating the mysterious trip they were undertaking the next day. What awaited them in Reno, or their reasons for going there, was still a mystery to her, and she knew she would have to wait until they got there to discover the answers to her questions. It was a little unsettling not knowing anything at all, and she felt sad, in an odd way, leaving home. This was the house where she had lived with her father, and she could still envision him there as she walked from room to room, or slowly up the stairs, remembering the sound and the smell of him, when he had just put on his aftershave. But they wouldn't be gone long, and maybe it would be an adventure. Maybe Frank would be there, and he would talk to her this time. Maybe he would be nice to her, and if she was very, very good, and did everything possible not to make him angry at her, he might even like her. She promised herself to try hard, as she walked slowly up the stairs.

She was asleep when her mother came in that night, and she didn't hear her as she walked down the long hall to her bedroom. Eloise was smiling to herself as she undressed, a whole new life was about to begin, filled with new promise, and the opportunity to close the door on all her old disappointments. She could hardly wait to leave the next day. She was taking the train the following evening, but she hadn't explained that yet to Gabriella, who still had no idea what time they were leaving.

And so as not to be late, and anger her mother before they left, Gabriella got up at dawn the next day, and when her mother came downstairs for breakfast at nine o'clock, Gabriella had coffee waiting for her. She set the cup down in front of her mother, excruciatingly careful not to spill it. She rarely did now. By this time, she had learned most of her lessons to perfection. The coffee was exactly the temperature her mother liked it. And Eloise said nothing, which was a sign to Gabriella that at least she hadn't upset her. Yet. But that could change in an instant, like a flash of summer lightning.

It was a full half hour before her mother spoke to her, and then she asked Gabriella if she was ready. She was. She had closed her suitcase before coming downstairs, and she was wearing a gray skirt and a white sweater, and she had a navy blue blazer carefully folded over the chair in her bedroom, along with her navy beret and the white gloves she wore whenever they went out together. Her black patent leather Mary Janes were impeccable and without scuffs, and the white ankle socks she wore were immaculate and folded over just the way her mother liked them. With her blond hair pulled back in a neat ponytail, and her huge blue eyes, she was a vision that would have melted any heart but her mother's. At ten, she was still an adorable little girl. Not yet gangly, and no longer a baby, there were already signs that she would be a beauty one day, which won her no favor with her mother.

Eloise stood waiting in the doorway as Gabriella went upstairs to put on her hat, her gloves, and her jacket and pick up her suitcase, and when she came back downstairs, she saw that her mother hadn't brought her own bags down yet. She wondered instantly if her mother expected her to do it for her, and started back up the stairs to get them.

'Where are you going now?' Eloise asked in an exasperated tone. She had a thousand things to do and didn't want to waste another moment.

'To get your bags for you,' Gabriella said solemnly, turning to look over her shoulder.

'I'll do that later. Hurry up now.' The directions were confusing, but there was no way Gabriella could ask her for an explanation, even now, at the eleventh hour, as they seemed to be ready to leave the house. She noticed then that her mother was wearing a gray skirt and an old black sweater she usually only wore in the house, or to do errands. Unlike Gabriella, she didn't seem to be dressed for travel. And she hadn't even bothered to put on a hat that morning, which was rare for her mother. But without saying a word, Gabriella preceded her out of the house, carrying her small suitcase, and suddenly as she glanced back into the house where she had known so much pain, she felt a brief stab of terror. Something was wrong and she knew it, but it seemed crazy to think that. But suddenly all she wanted to do was run back inside and hide in the back of the hall closet. She hadn't done that in nearly two years now. She had learned long since that hiding only made the beatings worse, she was better off just subjecting herself to them, and yet

86

suddenly now anything would have seemed better than following her mother blindly down the stairs to an unknown fate, which might possibly be even worse than the familiar agonies she had known here.

'Don't drag your feet, Gabriella. I don't have all day,' she said with a scowl as she walked across the sidewalk briskly in high heels and hailed a taxi. But she had no suitcases with her whatsoever, and Gabriella knew now without a doubt that wherever she was going, her mother wasn't going with her. But where could she possibly be taking her, with a valise, on a Saturday morning? Gabriella had no idea, and her mother told her nothing.

Eloise gave the cabdriver an address Gabriella didn't recognize, in the East Forties, and Gabriella could feel her heart pound as they silently drove the twenty blocks downtown. The uncertainty of their destination filled her with terror, but she knew that if she asked a single question now, she would pay for it dearly later. Her mother did not look inclined to talk as she stared out the window of the Checker cab, lost in her own thoughts, with nothing to say to her daughter. Eloise glanced at her watch once or twice, and seemed satisfied that her tight schedule wasn't being jeopardized too badly. And by the time they reached a large gray building on Forty-eighth Street near the East River, Gabriella's hands were shaking and she felt nauseous. Maybe she had done something really terrible this time, and her mother was taking her to the police, or somewhere similar, to be punished by someone else. Anything was conceivable in a life as filled with terror as hers was. There was never any security for Gabriella, anywhere.

87

Her mother paid the cab, and got out ahead of Gabriella, who seemed to be moving with irritating slowness as she wrestled awkwardly with her suitcase, but nothing on the outside of the building gave her the least clue as to what it was or why she had come here. Her mother rang the bell, and banged a heavy brass knocker. It was an impressive building, and it seemed unusually austere to Gabriella, as they waited interminably for someone to open the door. Her eyes sought her mother's for a long moment, and then she looked down at her feet, so her mother wouldn't see the tears she was trying not to succumb to, as she felt her legs shake in raw fear. And then finally, with agonizing slowness, the door opened just enough for a small, frail face to peek through.

'Yes?' Gabriella couldn't see far enough past her mother to determine even if it was a man or a woman. The face, or what little she could see of it, appeared to be both ageless and sexless.

'I'm Mrs. Harrison, and I'm expected,' Eloise said curtly, annoyed at the painfully slow procedures. 'And I'm in a hurry,' she added, as the heavy door closed with a resounding thud, as the unidentifiable face went to research the matter further elsewhere.

'Mommy . . .' Gabriella began, fueled by her own terror, despite the fact that wisdom should have forced her to keep silent. But she just couldn't anymore. 'Mommy . . .' Her voice was a trembling whisper, as Eloise turned to her sharply.

'Keep quiet, Gabriella! This is no time for bad manners, and certainly not the place for it. They're not going to put up with the nonsense I have.' It was true then . . . she was being taken to jail . . . or

88

the police . . . or a place of punishment for her ten years of misdeeds that had ultimately cost them both her father. She was going to pay for it now. Her eyes filled with tears at the sound of her mother's words. She felt as though she were waiting for a death sentence, standing here, and couldn't understand what had happened to their trip to Reno. Or was this Reno? Was that what they called it? Where was she? And what were they going to do to her here?

And just as she thought that fear could get no greater grip on her, the heavy door began to open in front of them, and it opened to reveal a yawning black cavern behind a small, ancient, gnarled woman in a black habit. To Gabriella she looked like a witch, and she was wearing an old black shawl over her habit and walked with a cane, as she gestured to them to step into the darkness with her. Gabriella gasped as she beckoned, and against her will, a sob escaped her, as her mother grabbed her arm and yanked her inside the building, as the door closed resoundingly behind them. And the only sound they could hear was Gabriella crying.

'Mother Gregoria will see you in a moment,' the old woman said to Eloise, without even glancing at Gabriella, and Eloise looked down at the child in fury, as she shook her by the arm.

'Stop that right now!' she commanded, and shook her harder to emphasize the statement, but she didn't dare do more than that here. 'I'm not going to listen to you wailing. You can cry all you want here when I'm gone, and I'm sure you'll do a lot of it, but at least spare me that nonsense. I'm not your father, and I'm not going to put up with your whining, and neither will the Sisters here. Do

89

you know what nuns do to children when they misbehave?' She never answered her own question, but as Gabriella lifted her eyes in terror, all she could see was an enormous crucifix with a bleeding, dying Christ hanging from it, and she only cried louder at all that it implied. This was truly the worst day of her life, and all she wanted now was to die as quickly as possible before they did anything to her for the innumerable sins she had committed in her short life. She had no idea why she was here, or how long she was staying, but the suitcase she had brought was clearly not a good sign.

Her small, breathless sobs had rapidly become uncontrollable, and no amount of warnings from her mother seemed to stop them. She simply could not stop, and she was still crying when the old nun returned and announced that the Mother Superior would see them now. They followed her down a long, dark hall, lit only by tiny, dim lamps and small clusters of sputtering candles. The general impression of the decor was that of a very daunting dungeon, and in the distance, Gabriella could hear people singing mournfully. Even the sound of their voices seemed frightening to her now, and the music that accompanied them was lugubrious and depressing. And all she knew was that she'd rather be dead than be here.

The old nun stopped at a small door, and gestured them inside, before hobbling away on her cane, her feet seeming to glide soundlessly on the stone floors despite her infirmity and her age, and as Gabriella watched her, she shook as though she were freezing. Her mother grabbed her arm then, and pulled her into the room where they were expected, and Gabriella's sobs only grew louder as she looked around. There was a nun with eyes like ice and a face like granite who stood up from behind a small battered desk to greet them. She had a crisp band of starched white across her forehead, and the rest of her was swathed in black, as they all were in the Order, and Gabriella was surprised to see that she was very tall. And more terrifying still, she seemed to have no hands at all as she looked down at Eloise Harrison and her daughter. Her arms were crossed, and her hands were invisibly tucked into the full sleeves of her habit, and the only decoration she wore were the heavy wooden rosary beads which hung from her waist. There were no visible signs of her importance in the Order, or the fact that she was the Mother Superior, but Eloise knew it. They had met twice in the past two months to discuss her plans for Gabriella. But the Mother Superior hadn't expected the child to be so upset. She had assumed that she would be forewarned about her mother's plans before she got here.

'Hello, Gabriella,' she said solemnly. 'I'm Mother Gregoria, and you're going to be staying with us for a while, as I'm sure your mother has told you.' There was no smile on her lips, but her eyes were kind, although Gabriella could not yet see that, and all she did was shake her head vehemently as she cried, as much to signal that she didn't want to stay as to explain that her mother had told her nothing at all about the visit.

'You're going to stay here while I'm in Reno,' Eloise said now in a flat voice, as the Mother Superior watched the exchange with interest, understanding easily that this was the first Gabriella had heard of it, and silently disapproving

91

of the way Eloise had handled her child.

Gabriella looked up at her mother in obvious terror. 'How long will you be gone?' As much as she had hated her all her life, she was all she had now. Gabriella couldn't help wondering as she looked at her mother if this was her punishment for silently hating her for so long. Maybe her mother had known all along, and now she was leaving her here to be tortured and punished for her evil thoughts.

'I'll be in Reno for six weeks,' Eloise said clearly, offering not a single word of comfort, and standing apart from the distraught child as Mother Gregoria watched them both.

'Will I go to school?' Gabriella asked, her voice still catching on the tears that continued to overwhelm her. She was hiccuping between sobs and having trouble breathing.

'You will study with us,' Mother Gregoria said in a quiet voice that did not reassure her. Suddenly nothing was familiar to her, and it scared her just being here. Being beaten by her mother at home seemed infinitely better to her. And had she had the choice at that moment, she would have gladly gone home and let Eloise do anything to her that she wanted. But she was not being offered that option. Her mother was going to Reno, wherever that was. 'There are two other children here as well,' the Mother Superior explained. 'They're older than you are, and sisters. One is fourteen and the other seventeen, and I think you'll like them. They've been very happy with us.' She didn't explain that the girls were living at the convent because they were orphaned. Their parents had died in a plane crash the year before, and the grandmother they had gone to live with, their only living relative, had died unexpectedly at Christmas. They were cousins of one of the Sisters in the Order, and for the time being, until something else could be arranged, it was the only solution for them. And for Gabriella, it was only a temporary measure. Two months, her mother had said, three at the most, but she said nothing about that to Gabriella now, as Mother Gregoria watched them. There seemed to be an extraordinary awkwardness between them, which the wise old nun observed with considerable interest. In fact, she might even have said that the child seemed frightened of her mother. She knew that the child's father had abandoned them, and was himself planning to remarry shortly, but Eloise had said nothing of her own plans, only that she needed a place to leave the child while she went to Reno for a divorce. It was certainly not a plan that met with the Mother Superior's approval, but she was not judging the morals of the mother, she was only interested in providing shelter for Gabriella.

Gabriella continued to sob as the three of them stood awkwardly looking at each other, and Eloise glanced at her watch with a look of surprise. 'I really have to go,' she said, as a small hand shot out suddenly to clutch her. Gabriella grabbed a handful of her skirt and clung to it, and begged her not to leave her.

'Please don't go, Mommy ... please ... I'll be good ... I swear ... please let me come with you ...'

'Don't be ridiculous!' Eloise said, shrinking backward, away from the child, in obvious revulsion. Just being that close to her, and having Gabriella clutch at her, made her want to run

93

screaming out the door.

'Reno is not a happy place for a child,' Mother Gregoria interrupted firmly, 'or for adults either,' she said in a disapproving tone. The Mother Superior had no idea that Frank had made reservations for Eloise at one of Reno's most luxurious dude ranches, and planned to be there with her the entire time. He was going to teach her how to ride, Texas style. 'Your mother will be back soon, Gabriella. You'll see, the time will pass very quickly,' Mother Gregoria said kindly, but she could see that Gabriella was engulfed by panic, and her mother did not seem to care, or even notice. The Mother Superior nodded ever so slightly at Eloise, allowing her to go, and within seconds, Eloise had picked up her handbag, shook Mother Gregoria's hand, and stood staring down at her daughter. There was a small smile on her lips, as though she could not suppress her pleasure at leaving, and in the face of Gabriella's overwhelming grief, she obviously had nothing to offer her. All she wanted was her freedom.

'Behave yourself,' was all she said. 'Don't give them any trouble. I'll hear about it if you do,' and they both knew what that meant, but Gabriella didn't care now. She put her arms around her mother's waist and cried, as much for the mother she had never had, as for the father she had loved and lost. There was a well of terror and loneliness in her that defied all the words she had to describe them, but whereas it meant nothing to Eloise, the look in the child's eyes had touched Mother Gregoria's heart. She waited to see if Eloise would kiss her, or say something to comfort her, but she simply pried Gabriella's arms from around her waist and pushed her away firmly. 'Good-bye, Gabriella,' she said coldly, as Gabriella stared up at her with wise old eyes that understood far more than she should have. Gabriella knew now, and perhaps always would, precisely what it meant, and how it felt to be abandoned. And suddenly she stood very still, the sobs still wracking her, despite her efforts to stop them, and looked up at her mother. She didn't say another word as Eloise left the room, and never looked back as she closed the door firmly behind her.

For an instant, just the smallest slice of a life, Gabriella knew precisely how alone she was, and perhaps always would be, as the tall, wise old nun's eyes met hers. They were two souls that had traveled far, and seen too much of life, and in Gabriella's case, far too early. She simply stood there, making those small heartbreaking sounds as Mother Gregoria moved slowly toward her. And without saying a word to her, she took her in her arms and held her.

She wanted to keep Gabriella safe from a world that had wounded her almost beyond repair. Everything Mother Gregoria knew and felt and believed in was in the strength of her embrace, and everything she wished for the child was implied in the way she held her. Gabriella looked up at her in astonishment and closed her eyes, knowing without words what had just passed between them, and what she had found here. And as she stood nestled in the gentleness of the embrace, the floodgates opened and she sobbed for all the losses, all the pain, all the sorrow, all the terror and disappointment life had inflicted on her. And whatever else happened after that, she knew with

95

all the wisdom of her ten years that she was safe here.

CHAPTER SIX

Gabriella's first meal at St. Matthew's convent was a ritual that at first seemed extremely strange to her, and ultimately brought her surprising comfort. It was one of the rare times of the day when the nuns were allowed to converse, and after joining Mother Gregoria in church with the entire community for an entire hour before the meal, Gabriella had been overwhelmed by their numbers and their austerity as they sat in the chapel, praying in silence. But in the dining room, what had seemed like a huge flock of faceless women in black only moments before, became a room filled with laughing, smiling, talking, happy people.

Gabriella was startled to realize how young many of them were. There were nearly two hundred nuns in the convent, more than fifty of them postulants and novices, mostly in their very early twenties. There were a number of nuns Gabriella's mother's age, and then another group the same age as the Mother Superior, and a handful of very old ones. Most of the nuns taught at nearby St. Stephen's School, and the others worked at Mercy Hospital, as nurses. And their conversation during dinner ranged from politics to medical issues, to anecdotes from the classes they taught in school, and funny little household hints that touched on everything from the garden to the kitchen. They told jokes and teased each other, used nicknames, and by the end of the meal, it seemed as though every nun in the convent had stopped and said a kind word to Gabriella, even the old scary one who had opened the door to them and terrified her only that morning. Her name was Sister Mary Margaret, and Gabriella learned quickly that everyone in the convent loved her. She had been a missionary in Africa when she was young, and had been at St. Matthew's for more than forty years. She had a broad, toothless smile, and Mother Gregoria chided her gently, as she always did, for forgetting to put her teeth in. 'She hates wearing them,' one of the younger nuns explained to Gabriella with a girlish giggle.

Gabriella was more than a little overwhelmed by all of them, it was like having been dropped in the middle of a family of two hundred loving women. And for the moment, at least, there didn't seem to be a sour one among them. She had never before met or seen so many happy people. And after ten years of walking through a minefield with her mother, trying to avoid her constant bad temper and devastating rage, it was like falling into a cloud of gentle cotton. So many of them stopped to introduce themselves and talk to her, and she tried valiantly to remember their names, but it was impossible ... Sister Timothy ... Sister Elizabeth of the Immaculate Conception ... Sister Ave Regina ... Sister Andrew, or 'Andy,' as they called her ... Sister Joseph ... Sister John ... and the one whose name she remembered instantly was Sister Elizabeth ... Sister Lizzie ... She was a beautiful young woman with creamy fair skin and huge green eyes that laughed from the first moment she met Gabriella.

'You're a little young to be a nun, Gabbie, don't you think? But God can use help from all quarters.' No one had ever before called her 'Gabbie,' and the laughing eyes that played with her were the gentlest and the happiest she had ever seen. She wanted to stand next to her and talk to her forever. She was only a postulant, and was soon to become a novice. She said she had had the calling since she was fourteen and had seen a vision of the Blessed Virgin when she had the measles. 'That probably sounds a little crazy to you, but it happens that way sometimes.' She was twenty-one by then, and she was a nursing assistant in the pediatric ward at Mercy, and she was immediately drawn to the child with the huge blue eyes so filled with sorrow. It was easy to see that there was a long story there, one she might never be able to share with them, but one that had cost her dearly.

But the encounter that had meant the most to her was her meeting with Mother Gregoria that morning when her own mother left her. She didn't have the words to explain what had happened to her, but she knew that she had found the mother she had never had before, and she was just beginning to understand why the others wanted to be here. And the Mother Superior watched her carefully as she interacted with the other nuns. She was a shy child, and in some ways seemed very frail, yet in other ways there was a quiet strength about her, and a depth to her soul that belied her age, and the cautious way she had of dealing with people. It was easy for the Mother Superior to see that in some vastly important way, Gabriella had been deeply wounded. And having seen her mother speaking to her, Mother Gregoria suspected the source of the grief she wore like a veil between her and the others. This was a child who had survived the torments of hell, and for some reason perhaps known only to God, had managed to reach beyond it. And the Mother Superior was intrigued to see if the soul she sensed within was one that was destined for a life of reaching out to others. There were others in the community who had come to them nearly as damaged as she was. And in spite of what the wise nun sensed in her, the broken pieces that had yet to heal, there was a wholeness and an inner force about Gabriella that was deeply compelling. For a child so young, she had a powerful presence.

They introduced their two other 'boarders' to her, the two girls that had been orphaned and with them since Christmas. The younger one was fourteen, and a pretty child who longed for the world, and chafed a bit at the restrictions of the convent. Her name was Natalie, and she dreamed of a world of boys and clothes, and she was mad about a young singer named Elvis. Her older sister, Julie, was seventeen, and was relieved to be removed from the world, and clung to the safety she found here. She was desperately shy, and still seemed to be in shock from the circumstances that had left them orphans. She longed to be one of them one day, and had begged Mother Gregoria for months to let her stay there, and seek no other arrangements for them. Julie seemed to have little to say to Gabriella when they met, and Natalie was full of whispers and secrets and giggles, though Gabriella was too young to really appreciate the full measure of her friendship. And after a few minutes of talking to her, Natalie whispered to

Sister Lizzie that Gabriella was 'just a baby,' but they promised to be kind to her anyway. She was only to be there for a short time, and everyone was sure she would be desperately homesick without her parents.

But it wasn't of them that Gabriella was thinking that night, but of the woman who had held her in her arms that morning and consoled her. She remembered the powerful arms that had held her tight and made her feel safe from the agonies she had endured, and that for ten years she had fled from. She had never known anyone like the Mother Superior, and like Julie she was already wondering what it would be like to stay there forever.

She shared a room with the two other girls. It was small and bare, and had a tiny window that looked out into the convent garden. And as she lay in bed, not making a sound, she could see the moon high in the sky, framed by the tiny window. She wondered where her mother was that night, still at home, or on the train, and how soon she would be back from the mysterious place called Reno. But however long she chose to be gone, Gabriella knew with absolute certainty that, for the first time in her life, she was completely safe here. She could hardly imagine what her life would be like, but for the first time in ten years, she knew she had nothing to fear, no beatings, no punishments, no accusations, no hatred to flee from. She had been so certain when they stood at the front door that day that she had been brought here to punish her, and now, just as certainly, she knew that her coming here had been a blessing.

She fell asleep that night, thinking of all of them,

the nuns who had circled her like gentle birds in the dining hall that night . . . Sister Lizzie . . . Sister Timothy . . . Sister Mary Margaret . . . Sister John . . . and the tall woman with wise eyes who had brought Gabriella into her heart, without a sound, without a word, but kept her nestled there, a small bird with a broken wing, and already now, as she lay hidden at the bottom of her bed as she always did, she could feel the broken parts in her soul slowly mending.

They came to wake them the next day, as they always did, at four o'clock in the morning. The three young girls spent the first two hours of the day in church, with the nuns, praying silently, and then finally, just before the sun came up, the entire community began singing together. Gabriella thought she had never heard anything as beautiful as their voices raised in unison, praising a God she had implored for years, and whom she often had reason to doubt ever listened. But here, in the power of their faith and love, his love for them seemed so obvious and irresistible, the safety he offered them seemed so certain. And by the time she entered the dining hall with them again for their first meal of the day, she felt strangely at peace among them.

Breakfast was a silent meal, it was a time for contemplation, and preparation for what they would bring to the world beyond these walls throughout the day, in the hospital and school where they worked, bringing solace and healing to those they touched and moved among as they sought to live and express God's blessing. They left each other with nods and smiles, and went to their cells and dormitories, depending on their age and status in the convent. The older nuns had individual cells of their own, the novices and postulants lived in small dormitories, just as Gabriella did now with the other two boarders. And like them, she would study here with two of the old nuns who were retired teachers. A small schoolroom had been set up for them, and she and the other two girls were settled into it and hard at work by seven-thirty that morning. They worked hard until noon, doing work that was appropriate for each of them, and then took their noon meal in the dining hall with the handful of nuns who did not work outside the convent.

Gabriella didn't see Mother Gregoria all day. In fact, she didn't see her again until that night at dinner, and Gabriella's eyes lit up, as did Mother Gregoria's, the moment she saw her. She walked shyly over to her, and Mother Gregoria asked her with a warm smile how her first day was.

'Did you work hard in school?' Gabriella nodded with a cautious smile. It had been much harder than her normal classes, and there had been no breaks for games or recess, but she was surprised to find that she liked it. There was something very peaceful about being here, and sharing the things they did. It seemed as though everyone had a job, a purpose, a goal. It was not merely the absence of the world one noticed here, but the presence of something more, a way of giving, rather than just surviving and taking. In their own way, in their own time, they had each come here for a reason, and they were each expected to empty their souls each day, for the benefit of others. And rather than depleting them, it seemed to fill them. Even the children were aware of it, like Julie, Natalie, and

'Gabbie,' as half the convent already seemed to have named her, and she was surprised to find that she liked it.

Everything about this was so different from the life she had known before. The women here were the exact opposite of her mother. There was no vanity, no egocentricity, no anger, no rage. It was a life entirely devoted to love, and harmony, and serving others. They were all amazingly happy and safe here. And for the first time in her life, so was Gabriella.

Two priests came to hear confession that night. They came four times a week, and the nuns lined up in silence in the chapel after dinner, and Sister Lizzie asked if she would like to join them. She had made her first communion four years before, and was able and expected to take the sacraments, though not necessarily as often as the Sisters, all of whom took communion daily. Most of their confessions were brief, some long, all prayed quietly for a considerable amount of time afterward, contemplating their failings and sins as nuns, and doing the penance they had been given.

Gabriella's confession was very short, but interesting to the priest who listened. After telling him how long it had been since her last confession, she admitted to him the sin of often hating her mother.

'Why, my child?' he asked her gently. Of the two priests hearing confession that night, he was by far the elder, a kindly man who had been a priest for forty years and had a deep love of children. He could hear through the grille how young her voice was, and knew from Mother Gregoria that there was a new child among them, although he had not

103

yet met her before her confession. 'Why would you allow the devil to tempt you to hate your mother?'

There was an interminable silence before she answered. 'Because she hates me,' the smallest of voices told him, but she sounded certain.

'A mother never hates her child. Never. God would never allow that.' But God had allowed a lot of things to happen to her that she felt sure he had never inflicted on others, perhaps because she herself was so bad, or perhaps God hated her too, although here, at St. Matthew's, it seemed hard to believe that.

'I know that my mother hates me.'

He denied it yet again, and then moved on through the rest of the confession, urging her to say ten Hail Marys and think of her mother lovingly with each of them, and know that her mother loved her. Gabriella didn't argue with him, but realized only that she was a bigger sinner than he knew for hating her mother as much as she did. She couldn't help it.

She said her penance silently with the nuns, and then went back to her room, where Natalie was reading a magazine she had bought on the sly, all about Elvis, while her sister Julie threatened to tell Sister Timmie about it. Gabriella left them to their squabbling and thought about what the priest had said to her in the confessional, and wondered if she would spend eternity in hell because of her hatred for her mother. What she didn't realize, nor did they, was that she had already been in hell for her entire lifetime. Surely had anyone seen what her life had been, she would have been assured a place in heaven.

She slept at the bottom of the bed, as she always

did, that night, and in the morning, as they dressed for church, the other two girls teased her about it, but not with any malice. They just commented on how funny it looked when they looked over at her bed and thought no one was in it. That had been the point, of course, though it had never really saved her. But it had long since become a habit.

She went to school with them again that day, and life at St. Matthew's slowly became a routine for her. Living with the nuns and the two other girls, going to church and school with them. She learned their hymns, their ways, the prayers they said morning and night and mid-afternoon, and she fell to her knees on the stone floor in the halls, without even thinking about it, when the church bells rang, just as the nuns did. By mid-May, she knew all of them by name, and the things they liked and did, and she smiled most of the time, and chatted easily at dinner with all of them, and whenever possible she sought Mother Gregoria out, without saying much to her, she just enjoyed being near her.

It was the end of May when the Mother Superior called her into her tiny office. It was odd for Gabriella to see her there, it reminded her of the first day when she had come here with her mother. That seemed so long ago now. It had been six weeks since she'd arrived and Gabriella hadn't had so much as a postcard from her mother. And although she hadn't heard from her, she knew her mother would be home soon.

She wondered if she had done something wrong and was about to be scolded when she stepped into Mother Gregoria's office. Sister Mary Margaret had come to the schoolroom to ask her to come here, and for some reason the request sounded

105

alarmingly official.

'Are you happy here, my child?' Mother Gregoria asked, smiling easily at her. There was something deeply compelling about Gabriella's blue eyes, they belied her years and the innocence one expected to find there. She smiled more openly now, but in spite of it, one sensed a distance between Gabriella and those she still feared might hurt her. Even here, there were times when she was still very guarded. And Mother Gregoria had noticed that she went to confession often, and worried that there were still demons that plagued her, demons she had not shared yet. Gabriella was still extremely private. 'Do you feel at home here?'

'Yes, Mother,' Gabriella answered simply, but her eyes were worried. 'Is something wrong? Did I do something I shouldn't?' She would rather know immediately what punishment would be meted out to her, for what offense, and how quickly. The anticipation of knowing was terrifying.

'Don't be afraid, Gabbie. You have done nothing wrong. Why are you worried?' There were so many questions she would have liked to ask, but even after six weeks, she did not dare yet. She knew it was still too soon to approach her, and perhaps always would be. She knew that Gabriella was entitled to her private griefs, and secrets, even at her age.

'I was afraid you were angry at me. When Sister Mary Margaret came to get me, she said you wanted to see me in your office, and I thought . . .'

'I only wanted to talk to you about your mother.' A tremor of fear instantly ran through her. The mere mention of her name filled Gabriella with dread, yet she knew she would see her again soon,

106

and in some ways she missed her. But she had been praying constantly to quell the hatred she felt, and had said countless Hail Marys. She wondered suddenly if the priests who were hearing her confessions had said something to Mother Gregoria about her. The wise old nun saw the shadows darting across the child's face and could only guess at the terrors they represented. 'I heard from her yesterday. She called me from California.'

'Is that Reno?'

'No.' She smiled. 'We're going to have to work on your geography. Reno is in Nevada. California is a different state.'

Gabriella looked confused. 'Isn't she supposed to be in Reno?'

'She was in Reno. And now she's divorced, and has gone to California. She said she was in San Francisco.'

'That's where Frank lives,' Gabriella said, by way of explanation. But Mother Gregoria already knew that. It had been rather a lengthy conversation, and she had felt strongly that Eloise should talk to the child herself, but she had been emphatic about wanting the Mother Superior to do it.

'Apparently...' She took a long, slow breath, wanting to choose her words well, and not shock Gabriella unduly. 'Apparently, your mother and Frank, whom you seem to know...' She smiled warmly at the child, watching her eyes for signs of suspicion or discomfort, but so far there were none, other than her initial look of terror. 'Your mother and Frank are getting married tomorrow.'

'Oh,' Gabriella said, looking at first blank, and then startled. She had never said more than ten words to him, and he had always more or less ignored her. And now her mother was marrying this stranger. And God only knew where her father had disappeared to. She still thought she would hear from him again one day, but it had been a long time now. And she got a sinking feeling when she realized again that she was alone now.

But now came the hard part, the rest of the story the child's mother had entrusted her with telling her only daughter. 'They're going to live in San Francisco.' Gabriella felt the briefest stab of disappointment as she heard the words. It meant she would have to leave and go to a place she didn't know. It meant she would have to fight for her life again, and struggle every moment, every hour, every day, for survival. It meant a new school, and new friends, or none at all. And it also meant living with a stranger, and the mother she both feared and hated. And leaving the women she had come to love in the convent.

'When do I have to go there?' Gabriella asked bluntly, and Mother Gregoria could see that something had died in the child's eyes again. It was the same look she had seen the first time Gabriella had come to her office.

There was another long, silent pause, while the Mother Superior weighed her words carefully, never taking her eyes from Gabriella's. 'Your mother thinks you would be happier staying here with us, Gabbie.' It was the kindest way to translate what her mother had really said, about not being able to put up with the child any longer, not wanting to jeopardize her own happiness, or burdening her new husband with a child she herself had never even wanted. She had been brutally frank with Mother Gregoria on the phone, while offering to pay her board there for as long as they would keep her. Forever, possibly, was how Mother Gregoria had interpreted it, and she had not read her incorrectly. Eloise had no plans whatsoever to bring the child to San Francisco, and seemed to have no remorse about it. And when she had inquired about the child's father, and the possibility of Gabriella staying with him, Eloise had assured her that he didn't want her either. Mother Gregoria knew that this was the sorrow she read in the child's eyes, or some of it at least. She herself was well aware that her parents didn't love, or want, her.

'My mother doesn't want me, does she?' Gabriella said bluntly. There were shards of pain in her eyes, and relief, at the same time, which confused the woman who watched her.

'You can't look at it that way, Gabriella. She's confused. She's still very hurt by your father leaving both of you, and now she has a chance for a new life. I think she wants to make sure it's a good one before she brings you to it. That's sensible of her, and although it's hard to be away from her, it's very loving of her to leave you here with people who care about you and want to make you happy.' It was a nice thought, but Gabriella knew it was more complicated than that, and she understood the subtleties better than she should have.

'My parents hated each other, and she says they never loved me.'

'I don't believe that. Do you?' Mother Gregoria said gently, praying that she didn't, but fearing that they had been far too open with her, just as Eloise had been on the phone with the Mother Superior. She had said it in no uncertain terms the day

109

before: 'I don't want her with me.' Mother Gregoria would have cut her tongue out before repeating that to Gabriella.

'I think my father used to love me . . . sort of . . . he never . . . he never did anything to . . .' Her eyes filled with tears remembering all the times he had stood in doorways, watching helplessly, or listened to her screams from the next room while her mother beat her. How could he have loved her? And he had left, hadn't he? He had never looked back, never written, never called. It was hard to believe he still loved her, if he ever had, which for a long time now, she doubted. And now her mother was doing the same thing. She was glad in a way. It meant the beatings would never happen again, she would never have to hide, and pray, and beg, and go to a hospital because she had been beaten so badly, and wait for the moment when her mother would finally kill her. It was over. But it also meant facing all that her mother had never felt for her, and never would. In spite of the nun's gentle words, Gabriella knew that her mother would never come back now. The war was over. But the dream of being loved by her one day, of doing it right, of winning her love at last, died with it.

'She's never coming back, is she?' Gabriella's eyes bore straight into the Mother Superior's, and the child's eyes were so direct and so clear, the question in them so powerful that Mother Gregoria knew she could not lie to her.

'I don't know, Gabriella. I don't think she knows. Maybe she will one day, but maybe not for a long time.' It was as honest as she could be without telling her the whole truth. Essentially, she had been abandoned by both her parents, and no matter what Mother Gregoria said now, Gabriella knew it.

'I don't think she's ever coming back . . . just like my father. My mother said he's going to be married to someone else, and he has new children.'

'That won't make him love you less.' But there was no denying he had never contacted her, and she suspected that Eloise wouldn't be in touch with Gabriella either. They were despicable people, and it was hard to understand how they could abandon a child like this one. But Mother Gregoria knew it happened, she had seen it. She had cried over children like Gabriella before. She was only very glad that they could be there for her. And perhaps this was God's way of making His wishes known. Perhaps her place was here with them, perhaps in time she herself would hear Him, and somewhat cautiously she said so. 'Maybe one day you'll decide to stay with us, Gabriella. When you're grown up. Maybe this was God's way to bring you to us.'

'You mean like Julie?' Gabriella looked startled by what Mother Gregoria had suggested. She couldn't even begin to imagine being a nun like they were. They were much too good, and she was much too bad, they just didn't know it. And she was still trying to absorb the shock of hearing that her mother had moved to San Francisco and left her. She couldn't help wondering if her mother had known that when she left her there. But unlike the last time she had seen her father, she had sensed none of the tenderness or sorrow or regret she had understood afterward, when she thought about it. There had been none of that when her mother had dropped her off at St. Matthew's. As usual, there had only been threats and anger, and she'd been in

111

a hurry to leave her.

'One day you will know, Gabbie, if you have a vocation. You must listen very, very carefully. And if you do, it will come to you very clearly. God speaks to us as loudly as He needs to, so we hear Him.'

'I don't always hear things,' Gabriella said with a small, shy smile, and the Mother Superior laughed gently. 'I think you hear everything you need to.' And then her eyes grew sad as she looked at the child. She had taken it well, but it was a hard thing to tell her, harder still to live with, knowing your parents didn't want you, which was what it amounted to for Gabriella. Impossible to understand how people in her parents' circumstances, particularly, could do this. But it wasn't the first time it had happened. And perhaps, in some way none of them could understand, perhaps it was a blessing. And despite the confusing emotions she felt, Gabriella knew that. She had never cried once when Mother Gregoria had told her. She just felt a sick feeling in her stomach, when she realized she might never see either of them ever again. It was hard to understand that, and in some ways Gabriella didn't.

'You're a strong girl,' the Mother Superior said to her mysteriously, and Gabriella shook her head in answer. She wasn't, she knew she wasn't, and she wondered why people always said that to her. Her father had said the same thing the night before he left. He told her how strong she was. She didn't feel strong. She felt very lonely, and much of the time, very frightened. Even now, it was scary. What if she couldn't stay here? Where would she go? Who would take care of her? All she wanted to know was that she had a place to be forever, a place where she didn't have to hide, where she was safe, and no one would ever hurt her, or leave her. And Mother Gregoria understood that. She came around her desk, as she had once before, and silently put her arms around the child who was so brave, so strong, so dignified as she stood there, but the nun could feel her tremble as she held her. Gabriella didn't sob this time, she didn't beg, she didn't rage against her fate, but she clung tightly to the only person who had ever offered her love and comfort, and a lone tear rolled slowly down her face, as she looked up into the older woman's eyes with something so terrible and so powerful there that the wise old nun nearly shuddered.

'Don't leave me,' Gabriella whispered, so softly she almost couldn't hear her . . . 'Don't make me go away . . .' The single tear was slowly joined by another, and then two more, but she maintained her dignity as she stood with her arms around the woman who offered her all she had now.

'I won't leave you, Gabbie,' she said softly, longing to give her something more, but not even sure how to do it. 'You will never have to leave here. This is your home now.'

Gabriella nodded silently, burying her face in the black habit that had already become so familiar. 'I love you,' she whispered, and Mother Gregoria held her as tears filled her own eyes.

'I love you too, Gabbie . . . we all do.'

They sat together that afternoon for a while, quietly holding hands, talking about Gabriella's mother, and why she had decided to leave Gabriella there. But it didn't make sense to either of them, no matter how reasonable the words, and

113

in the end, they both decided it didn't matter. She had done it. And Gabbie had a home here. Mother Gregoria walked her slowly back to her room then. It was too late for school, and she left Gabriella there with her own thoughts, her memories, and her visions of her mother ... the places she had hidden from her ... the times she had been unable to hide ... the brutality ... the pain ... the bruises ... she remembered all of it, and she was glad it would never happen again. But it was hard to believe it was over. What she would have loved most was another chance, a chance to be better than she had been, to do it right this time, and win her love. She would have loved to make her mother happy instead of angry. But she had made her so angry, and been so bad, that her mother had had to leave her. They both had. Gabriella couldn't say that to Mother Gregoria, she didn't want her ever to know how bad she was, how terrible, how much she deserved this. And knowing how bad she had been, and how much they had hated her, it was impossible to believe anyone would ever want her. The nuns did. Maybe God. But He knew how bad she was, how wrong she had been, and how much at times she hated her parents ... but he also knew, as she lay on her bed alone in the room for once, as she began to sob, how much she missed them ... she would never see either of them again ... and she knew it. She had driven both of them away ... with her badness. And there was no hiding from the truth now. There was no hiding from the fact that they had never loved her. How could they, she asked herself, as she lay there and cried ... how could they ... how could anyone? It was her destiny, her fate, her life sentence ... her

114

punishment for having been so bad for so long . . .
her curse, and she believed in it to her very core.
She knew as she lay on her bed that day that not
only had they not loved her, but no one ever could,
not if they really knew her. And no amount of Hail
Marys and confessions and rosaries could change
that.

She went through the motions for the rest of the
day, thinking of what Mother Gregoria had said . . .
and about her mother in California. She was quiet
at dinner that night, went to confession afterward
as usual, and went to her room with Natalie and
Julie. She was in bed before either of them, and she
burrowed down to the bottom of the bed, as she
always did, and lay there thinking about all of it.
Her parents were both marrying other people, her
father had 'new' children to replace her . . . her
mother didn't want any children at all, or maybe
she would now . . . good ones . . . not bad ones this
time . . . They had new lives, new husbands and
wives . . . and Gabriella had to live with knowing
why they had left her . . . and knowing that if she'd
been better, things might have been different. She
had a lifetime to make up for it, to give herself to
God, and other people, to atone for her sins, regret
all that she had done, and forgive all that had been
done to her. The priest had told her in the
confessional later that night that the responsibility
was hers now, and what she had to strive for, for
the rest of her life, was forgiveness. She repeated it
over and over to herself that night as she fell asleep
. . . forgiveness . . . forgiveness . . . she had to
forgive them . . . it was all her fault . . . she had to
forgive them . . . forgive them . . . and halfway
through the night, they heard her screaming . . . her

115

screams resounded down the long, dark halls, echoing off the walls . . . It took three of them to wake her, and they finally had to call Mother Gregoria to calm her . . . the memories of the beatings had been too clear, too real, she could feel the blood on her head again, the blinding pain in her ear, the shattering of her ribs, the aching in her limbs where she had been kicked so often . . . and she knew she would never forget it. And as she lay sobbing in the Mother Superior's arms that night, all she could say again and again was, 'I have to forgive them . . . I have to forgive them . . .' Mother Gregoria held her until she slept again, and watched her silently until she saw peace on the small face at last, and she understood better than anyone, or thought she did, how much Gabriella had to forgive them. And she knew, as Gabriella did, that it would take her a lifetime to do it.

CHAPTER SEVEN

The next four years were peaceful ones for Gabriella, living in the quiet safety of St. Matthew's. She continued studying with the nuns who taught her there. Julie became a novice, and her sister Natalie left on a scholarship to college. By then she was not only fascinated by Elvis, but passionately in love with all four of the Beatles. She wrote to the Sisters often from upstate New York, where she was happy in school, dating boys, and doing all, or at least most, of the things she had dreamed of while she was at St. Matthew's.

Two new boarders had arrived at the convent by

then, two little girls from Laos, sent there by one of their missionary Sisters. They were much younger than Gabriella, but shared a room with her, just as she had shared hers with Natalie and Julie.

For four years Gabriella never heard from her mother, but she still thought of her from time to time, as she did her father. All she knew of him was that he had gone to Boston and had been planning to get married, to a woman with two daughters. She had no idea what had happened to him after that, and had no way to pursue it. Her mother, she knew, still lived in San Francisco, and a check came to Mother Gregoria once a month, precisely on time, paying for her room and board, but there was never a letter with it, a note, an inquiry as to how Gabriella was, or if she was well and happy. There were no cards or gifts on Christmas or birthdays. Gabriella's life centered now entirely around life at St. Matthew's, and everyone there loved her. She worked harder than almost anyone, would scrub any floor, any table, any bathroom, she would do chores even the other nuns would balk at. And she did brilliantly at her schoolwork. She still wrote stories and poetry, and all of her teachers agreed that she had real talent.

She still slept at the bottom of the bed, still had nightmares at night far too frequently, and never explained them. And Mother Gregoria still watched her from afar, concerned at some of what she saw there. The pain in Gabriella's eyes was dimmer now, she had grown even more beautiful, though she herself had no sense of it, nor any interest in what she looked like. She lived in a world without vanity. There were no mirrors in the convent, and she still wore the cast-off clothes of the girls who came in as postulants, and never seemed to think anything of it. As she had set herself the goal at ten, her life was one of sacrifice, and doing for others. But she still insisted, when they talked about it from time to time, that she had no vocation. When she compared herself to girls like Julie, or the ones who came in from elsewhere, she could see the difference between them. They were so sure, so certain, so unfailing in their devotion to their calling. All Gabriella could see in herself were the faults, the failings, the mistakes she made, or the times she insisted she had thoughtlessly hurt others. In truth, her humility was far greater than those who held up their vocations like so many trophies. And Mother Gregoria tried year after year to make her see it. But she was so intent on denying her virtues and pointing to her flaws that she couldn't imagine herself becoming a nun at St. Matthew's, nor could she see herself ever leaving. Hers was a completely sequestered life, living among the love and protection of the nuns, and she knew without a doubt that she would die without that.

'I guess I'll just have to stay here and scrub floors for the rest of my life,' she joked with Sister Lizzie on her fifteenth birthday. 'No one else wants to do it. And I like it. It gives me time to think about my stories while I'm scrubbing.'

'You could still write your stories if you join the Order, Gabbie,' Sister Lizzie insisted, as they all did. Everyone in the convent knew how strong her vocation was. Gabriella was the only one who didn't know it. And sometimes they just smiled at her, and ignored the silly things she said. They knew that eventually she'd hear the calling. It was impossible to think that she wouldn't, and she still had a lot of growing up to do in the meantime.

At sixteen, she had completed all her high school work, and in spite of all their efforts to keep her with them, they had to admit she was ready for college. She insisted that she didn't want to go. She was happy here, with them, doing small things for the nuns, errands and chores, and thoughtful gestures for which she took no credit. But with the writing talent she had, Mother Gregoria refused to allow her to neglect her education. The poignant stories she wrote showed extraordinary talent, perception, and insight. They were filled with pathos, and a tenderness that tore at the heart just to read them, but there was a strength about them too. Her writing style was that of a much older person, and certainly not one who had spent their entire adolescence in a convent.

'So what are we going to do about school?' Mother Gregoria asked her when she turned sixteen, after speaking to all of her teachers. They had agreed in unison that Gabriella was entirely ready for college and it was a crime not to send her.

'We're going to ignore it,' Gabriella said firmly. She was terrified of the outside world by then, and had no interest in venturing back into a life that had so desperately hurt her. She never wanted to leave the safe haven of St. Matthew's, not for a single moment. And they teased her about being like the old nuns who complained every time they had to leave the convent to go to the doctor or the dentist. The younger ones still enjoyed going out from time to time, to see relatives, or go to the library, or a movie. But not Gabbie. She preferred to sit in her room and write stories.

'Being here is not for the purpose of shunning the world, Gabriella,' Mother Gregoria said firmly. 'We are here to serve God by giving Him our talents, by bringing them to a world that needs what we have to give, not depriving it of ourselves because we are too frightened to venture out of the convent. Think of the Sisters who work at Mercy Hospital every day. What if they chose to sit in their rooms and daydream, because they were too afraid to take care of the male patients? Ours is not a life of cowardice, Gabriella, but of service.' She was met by eyes filled with fear, and silent resistance. Gabriella had no intention of leaving the convent to go to college. Natalie was a junior at Ithaca by then, but even her enthusiastic letters, or the prospect of joining her, did nothing to sway Gabriella.

'I won't do it.' For the first time in her years there she defied the Mother Superior, and was surprisingly stubborn about it.

'You will have no choice when the time comes,' Mother Gregoria said, her lips narrowing into a thin line. She didn't want to have to force her, but if that was the only way to get her to go, she would be willing to do it. 'You are part of this community, and you will do as I tell you. You're not old enough to make these decisions, Gabriella, and you're being extremely foolish.' She then ended the subject, annoyed at how resistant Gabriella was. Mother Gregoria knew it was based on a terror of entering the world again, but she wasn't going to allow her to give in to it. Gabriella knew it wasn't healthy, but she wasn't going to give an inch. She felt safe here, she didn't want to be part of a world that had once hurt her so greatly. In all ways, spiritually and physically, at sixteen, she had removed herself from it, and she had every intention of remaining a recluse at St. Matthew's.

Mother Gregoria told her teachers to apply to Columbia for her, and they insisted Gabriella fill out the application. It was a remarkable battle between them, but in the end, complaining bitterly and swearing she wouldn't go, Gabriella did it. And she was accepted, naturally, and given a full scholarship, which thrilled everyone but Gabbie. The reason they had chosen Columbia, other than the obvious prestige of the school, was the fact that she could attend classes and still live at the convent.

'Now what?' she asked miserably when Mother Gregoria told her about the scholarship. It was June and she was nearly seventeen, and for the first time in her years with them, she was acting like a spoiled baby.

'You have until September to resign yourself to it, my child. You can live here while you go. But you must attend classes.'

'And if I don't?' she asked with rare belligerence, which almost made the Mother Superior want to throw up her hands in frustration.

'We line up the entire community on September first, and spank you, and believe me, you'll have deserved it. You're being very, very ungrateful. This is a wonderful scholarship, and you can do important things with your writing.' It sounded absurd to Gabbie.

'I can do the same things here,' Gabriella said darkly, rampant fear more evident in her eyes than ever, though the Mother Superior was never entirely sure what she was so desperately afraid of.

'Are you telling me that you are so wise, and so brilliant, and so talented that you have nothing to learn about writing? My, my, we do have a little work to do on our sense of humility, don't we? Perhaps a little quiet meditation is in order.' Gabriella had the grace to laugh at that, and the subject came up frequently in the next three months and was always an argument, but in the end, with the prodding of two hundred nuns, she finally went to college in September. And in spite of herself, within a week, she admitted grudgingly that she enjoyed it. And within three months, she not only enjoyed it, but loved it.

For four years she never missed a class. She took every creative writing class she could, soaked up her lit classes, and drank in every word of her favorite professors. But she rarely spoke unless asked, and made a point of staying away from all her fellow students. She avoided boys and girls alike, attended her classes diligently, and the moment they were over, hurried back to the convent. From a social standpoint, at least, the experience was entirely wasted. She wrote papers endlessly, took on extra projects, and when she was a senior, started a novella. And in the end, she graduated magna cum laude. The Sisters in the community drew straws to see who would attend her graduation, and twenty won them, and attended with Mother Gregoria, like so many doting mothers. She was nearly twenty-one when she graduated, and rode home triumphantly in one of the two vans they'd rented. They were thrilled with the awards she'd won, and not nearly as surprised as she was. Her years at Columbia were a great victory for her, and they never doubted for a moment that one day she would write a book and be a very successful writer, although she still had her doubts about it. Even her professors had told her that she was far too unsure of her talent. In their opinion, she was very gifted.

And the night of her graduation, as she walked around the garden with Mother Gregoria on a warm June night, she talked hesitantly about her future as a writer.

'I'm still not sure I can do it,' she admitted, as she always did. The guilt and humility of her youth had become an acute lack of confidence as an adult. Mother Gregoria was well aware of it, and argued with her about it often.

'Of course you can. Look at the novella you wrote as your senior thesis. Why do you think you graduated magna?'

'Because of all of you. They didn't want you to be embarrassed, and besides, the dean is Catholic.' Even she chuckled at that one.

'As a matter of fact, he's not. He's Jewish. And you know perfectly well why they gave you all those awards. It wasn't charity. You deserved it. The question is what you do with it now. Do you want to try your hand at a book yet? Do some sort of freelance work, get a job for a magazine, or a newspaper? There are so many areas open to you now. You could even teach at St. Stephen's, and try to work on a book in your off-time.' She wanted to help her get started. And she knew better than anyone that Gabbie needed a strong push in that direction.

'Could I still live here while I do it? Any of it? . . . all of it?' she asked anxiously, as Mother Gregoria frowned at her in consternation. It still dismayed the Mother Superior at times that Gabriella was so determined to remain separate from the secular world. She had never allowed herself even the smallest taste of freedom. She had made no friends, knew no men. In some ways, the Mother Superior knew that she needed to know a little bit more of the outside world before she rejected it completely.

The thought of leaving the convent or not being part of it would have killed Gabriella, and Mother Gregoria knew it. 'I could pay you room and board from the money I earn, to stay here,' she said, looking determined. 'If I earn any at all, which could take time.' She had been worrying about it for months, and dreading this conversation. She had lived at St. Matthew's for more than ten years, more than half her life, and she couldn't imagine leaving it, and she had no desire to even think about it. But she had had another idea for some time now, and had been waiting for the right time to discuss it with Mother Gregoria. She knew the time was right now.

'To answer your question, Gabriella, of course you can continue to live here. And you can contribute something when you can afford it. You contribute more than enough now with all the work you do here, and have ever since you came here. You've always been like one of the Sisters.' The checks from her mother had stopped on the day she turned eighteen. There had been no note, no letter, no explanation, no phone call. They simply stopped. As far as she was concerned, Eloise Harrison Waterford had fulfilled her obligation, and she wanted no further contact with her

124

daughter. There had been none since the day she left her at the convent, and Gabriella had realized for years that more than likely her father had no idea where her mother had left her. But then again, he hadn't contacted her when she was with her mother either, when he still could have. The truth was, neither of them wanted to be part of her life. And during all her years at Columbia, Gabbie had told people she was an orphan, and lived at St. Matthew's convent, though it was rare for people to ask her, it was usually only her professors. The other girls in her class found her painfully withdrawn and shy. And although the young men she met found her attractive, at the first sign of interest on their part, she rebuffed them. By her own choice, she was completely isolated, and even in her college years, her only social life was the one she shared with the nuns at St. Matthew's Convent. It had been in many ways an unhealthy life for a girl her age, but for some time Mother Gregoria had seen what was coming, and she didn't want to push her, one way or the other. Gabriella had to heed her own voices, as they all did. But what Gabriella said next did not surprise her.

'I've been thinking a lot lately,' she began, feeling suddenly shy and awkward with the woman who had been like a mother to her, the only mother she had known and loved since the nightmare of her childhood. She talked about it now occasionally, though rarely, and said only that she had been very unhappy with her parents, and they had been 'unkind' to her. She never spoke of the beatings, or the horror she had lived through. But from the nightmares, and the scars the wise old nun had noticed here and there over the years,

125

Mother Gregoria had deduced a great deal about her early life, and pieced some of it together. X rays when she'd had bad bronchitis two years before had shown where her ribs had been broken repeatedly, and there was a small scar near her ear that told its own tale, and explained her sometimes less-than-perfect hearing. There was much that the Mother Superior knew without actually knowing. And Gabriella sighed deeply as she tried to explain what she'd been thinking, but Mother Gregoria had a premonition of what was coming. It was time now. 'I think I've been hearing things, Mother . . . and having dreams. I kept thinking I was imagining it at first, but it seems to be getting stronger and stronger.'

'What kind of dreams?' Mother Gregoria asked with interest.

'I'm not sure. It's almost as though I'm being pushed to do something I never thought I would be able to do . . . or good enough to do . . . I don't think . . . I'm not sure . . .' Her eyes filled with tears as she looked helplessly at the woman who had been both mother and mentor to her. 'I don't know. What am I supposed to hear?' Mother Gregoria knew exactly what she was asking. To some it was so clear, to others, mostly those who were truly meant for it, they were never sure they were good enough for it. And it was so like Gabriella to be uncertain, to question herself, and doubt what she herself knew she was hearing.

'You're supposed to hear your heart, my child. But you're supposed to believe in yourself enough to listen. You can't keep doubting what you hear, and what you know to be right. I think you've known it for a long time now.'

126

'I thought I did.' Gabriella sighed again, relieved at what the Mother Superior was saying. She had wanted so desperately to make the right decision, but most of the time she didn't feel good enough to offer herself to the others. They were all so much better than she was. 'I was so sure of it last year, I almost said something to you last summer, and then again at Christmas. But I thought I just wanted to hear it. I wasn't sure what you'd say.'

'And now?' Mother Gregoria asked calmly, her hands tucked into opposite sleeves as they continued to walk peacefully around the garden at twilight. It was almost dark now. 'What are you saying, Gabbie?' She wanted to hear her say the words. She didn't want to take the moment from her. It was too important in her life for anyone to rob her of it.

Gabbie's voice was barely audible as they stopped walking and looked at each other.

'I'm saying I want to join the Order.' She looked worried, and the deep blue eyes reached out to the woman she considered her mother, for confirmation. 'Will you let me?' It was a moment of total humility, total selflessness, total giving. She wanted to offer herself to God, and the people who had given her so much—safety, freedom, love, comfort. She owed them so much. And she wanted to devote her life to them now. They had more than made up to her for everything her parents had taken from her.

'It's not up to me,' the Mother Superior said to her gently. 'It's up to you, and God. I'm only here to help you. But I've been hoping you would come to this decision. I've been watching you struggle for two years now,' she said warmly.

'You knew?' Gabriella looked surprised as she smiled at her, and tucked an arm in hers as they walked slowly through the garden.

'Perhaps before you did.'

'And? What do you think?' She was asking her as the Mother Superior of the Order she wanted to join now.

'There's a class of postulants beginning in August. I think your timing is perfect.' They stopped and smiled at each other, and Gabriella reached out and hugged her.

'Thank you . . . for everything . . . for my life . . . you'll never know what you saved me from when I came here.' Even now, she couldn't bring herself to tell her. It was still much too painful.

'I suspected that from the beginning.' And then, humanly, she couldn't resist asking her a question she had always wondered about. 'Do you still miss them?' It was the question of the adoptive mother about the birth parents the child might still long for.

'Sometimes. I miss what they should have been, or what I wanted them to be, and never were. Sometimes I wonder where they are now . . . what their lives are like . . . if they had other children. It's not important.' But it was, and they both knew that. 'Even less so now.' Gabbie lied to herself more than to the woman she had always called Mother. 'I have a family now . . . or I will in August.'

'You have had a family ever since you came here, Gabbie.'

'I know that,' she said quietly, and then tucked her arm into the nun's again as they walked back into the house they lived in, and where Gabriella would stay forever. For her, it was an important decision. It meant she would never have to leave them, and could never lose them. It meant she would never be abandoned. It was all she wanted. The certainty that she would belong to them forever.

'You'll make a very good Sister,' Mother Gregoria said quietly, smiling down at her.

'I hope so,' Gabriella answered with a smile of her own. She looked blissfully happy. 'It's all I want now.'

The two women walked arm in arm down the hall, as Gabriella felt a wave of relief wash over her. This was truly her home, and always would be.

And the next day, when Mother Gregoria told the other nuns of Gabriella's decision at dinnertime, there were shouts of jubilation. Everyone congratulated Gabriella and embraced her, and told her how happy they were, and how they had known all along she had a vocation. It was a celebration of major proportions, and as she went back to her familiar room that night she knew with utter certainty that nothing but death could ever take her from them. It was all she had ever wanted. And that night, she slept peacefully, until the nightmares came, with all the sounds and the terrors she still remembered so clearly, the memories of her mother's face, her blows, her hatred ... the smell of the hospital ... and the sight of her father standing helplessly in the doorway. It came back to her, as it always did, as she huddled at the bottom of her bed, as she had for years, trying to escape them. But even if she never did, if they haunted her for eternity, when she woke and looked around the room that was home to her now, she sat up in bed, trying to catch her breath, and knew that she was safe.

One of the Sisters poked her head into the room, and she saw Gabriella sitting there, looking shaken after the seeming reality of the nightmare. As they so often did, the others had heard her screaming. It no longer alarmed them as it once had, but they felt sorry for her.

'Are you okay?' the Sister whispered, and Gabriella nodded, smiling at her through her tears, trying to return to the present.

'I'm sorry I woke you.' But they were used to it by then. She had had the same dreams ever since she'd come here. She never talked about them, never explained them to anyone, and they could only guess at the horrors that haunted her, or what her life had been like before she'd come here. But here, in the safety of the convent where she had been left, and would stay now for the rest of her life, she knew that the demons could no longer touch her. She lay down on her bed again, thinking about her parents, and Mother Gregoria's questions yesterday evening, about whether or not she missed them. She didn't miss them anymore, but she still thought of them, and remembered them, and she still wondered on nights like this why it was that they had never loved her. Was she truly as bad as they had said? Was it their fault, or her own? Had they done it to her, or she to them? Had she ruined their lives, or they hers? And even now, she didn't know the answers to her questions.

CHAPTER EIGHT

Gabriella joined the class of postulants at St. Matthew's convent in August. She did everything she had always seen the others do, gave up the clothes she wore, had her hair shorn, and donned the short, simple habit that they wore until they would become novices a year later. She knew that she had a long road ahead of her after her first year, two years as a novice, then another two years of monastic training before she could take her final vows. In all, she had five years ahead of her before her final vows would be taken. To her, and to the others who began with her, it would be longer, yet far more exciting, than college. This was the moment they had all dreamed of.

She was assigned endless chores to do, but to Gabriella most of them were neither distasteful nor unfamiliar. She had done so many menial things in the convent over the years that nothing they asked her to do now seemed repugnant to her. Instead, she embraced whatever humiliation they offered with good grace, and unfailing good humor. And it was quietly discussed among the Mistress of Postulants, the Mistress of Novices, and Mother Gregoria that Gabriella had made the perfect decision about her vocation. She had chosen the name of Sister Bernadette, and among the postulants, they called her Sister Bernie.

She had a good time with most of them. There were eight postulants in the class, and six of them were clearly somewhat in awe of Sister Bernie. The eighth was a girl from Vermont, and she had a dour way of arguing with everything Gabriella said, and trying to make trouble for her with the others. She told the Mistress of Postulants that she thought Gabriella was arrogant, and lacked respect for the older nuns. The Mistress of Postulants explained that Gabbie had lived at St. Matthew's nearly all her life, and it was comfortable here for her. The young postulant from Vermont then complained that Gabriella was vain, and she swore that she had seen her looking at her own reflection in a window, for lack of a mirror.

'Perhaps she was just thinking about something.'

'Her looks,' the girl said glumly. She was an unattractive girl who had decided to join the Order six months after a broken engagement, and the Mistress of Postulants was still somewhat in doubt about the girl's vocation, though not in the least about Gabriella's. No one in the convent ever doubted it for a moment. And Gabriella had clearly never been happier in her life. She was obviously thriving in her new life at the convent. And all of the nuns who had known her all her life beamed each time they watched her.

Gabriella wrote a Christmas story for them all that year, and made little books of it for each of them, working on them late at night in Mother Gregoria's office, and each of the nuns found one at their place in the dining hall on Christmas morning. It was a story she had worked on for months, and which the Mistress of Novices insisted ought to be published.

'She's showing off again!' Sister Anne, the girl from Vermont, complained again, showing very little generosity of heart, and even less Christmas spirit. She left the table and went to her room, tossing the little book Gabriella had handmade for her into the garbage. And later that afternoon,

Gabriella went to see her, and tried to explain that this had been her home for many years, and it was hard for her not to be jubilant about joining the Order. 'I suppose you think everyone here is in love with you because they know you. Well, you're no better than the rest of us, and if you weren't so busy showing off all the time you might make a better nun. Have you ever thought of that?' She spat the words in Gabbie's face, and reminded her suddenly of her mother. Being told how inept and how wrong she was cut into her heart like a dagger, and later that afternoon, she talked to Mother Gregoria privately about it.

'Maybe she's right. Maybe I am arrogant . . . and show off without knowing it.' But the Mother Superior tried to explain the obvious to her, that the young nun from Vermont was jealous.

And for the next three months, it became a kind of holy vendetta. She reported on Gabriella constantly, and confronted her with her failings every time the opportunity arose. It became an agony of worry for Gabriella, who constantly feared that the girl saw flaws in her that were really there and would keep her from serving Christ with true humility and the appropriate devotion. Gabriella went to confession constantly, and began doubting her own vocation. By spring, she was beginning to think she'd made a mistake, and that the girl saw faults in her that were clearly there and had to be excised before she could make a final decision about joining the Order. There was something so painful and familiar about the way the young girl went after her that it rattled her to her very soul, and in confession one night she admitted to the priest on the other side of the grille that she had

133

serious doubts about the vocation she had once been so sure of.

'What makes you say that?' The unfamiliar voice sounded puzzled, and Gabriella was startled to realize that she wasn't confessing to one of the priests she had known since her childhood.

'Sister Anne accuses me constantly of vanity and pride, and arrogance, and self-justification, self-importance, and maybe she's right. How can I possibly be of any use to God if I can't express humility and simplicity and obey Him? And what's more,' she blushed in the darkness as she confessed, but it didn't matter anyway, since she didn't know him, 'I think I'm beginning to hate her.'

There was a moment of silence on the other side, and then a gentle question. He had a kind voice, and for some odd reason she found herself wondering what he looked like.

'Have you ever hated anyone else before?'

She answered without hesitation. 'My parents.'

'Have you ever confessed that before?' He sounded intrigued by her and she told him she had, frequently, for many years, ever since she had come to St. Matthew's. 'Why did you hate them?'

'I hated them because they beat me,' she said simply, sounding humbler than he had expected, and far more open. He knew only that she was one of the postulants, but this was only the second time he had come to hear confession there, and he knew nothing about her. The other priests all knew Gabriella, but he didn't. 'Actually, my mother beat me,' she went on to explain. 'My father only let her ... but when I thought about it as I grew up, I hated him for it.' It was the most outspoken she

134

had ever been in any confession, and she wasn't sure why she was doing it now, except that she needed to make a clean breast of everything so as to free herself of her feelings about Sister Anne. She had been utterly tormented by her but was ashamed of her dislike for her.

'Have you ever told your parents how you felt?' he asked, sounding very modern, trying to heal the wounds and relieve her of them, and not just hearing her confession.

'I've never seen them again. My father deserted my mother when I was nine and I never saw him after that. He moved away to Boston, and a few months later my mother left me here, and never came back. She told me she was going away for six weeks to Reno, and she got married again and decided that I didn't fit into her new life. In a lot of ways, it was a blessing. If I'd gone back to her, eventually she'd have killed me.' There was shocked silence on the other side of the grille again.

'I see.'

She decided to tell him the rest of it then, and make a good confession. 'Sister Anne is starting to remind me of my mother, and I think maybe that's why I hate her so much. She shouts at me all the time, and tells me how bad I am . . . my mother used to do that . . . and I believed her.'

'Do you believe Sister Anne?' Gabriella's knees were beginning to hurt from the length of the confession, and it was terribly hot in the confessional for both of them. It was like kneeling on the floor of an overheated phone booth, and the total darkness made it seem even warmer. 'Do you believe what she says about you, Sister? About how

135

bad you are?' He sounded deeply interested in her problem.

'Sometimes. I always believed my mother. I still do at times. If I hadn't been bad, why would they have left me? Both of them. There must have been something pretty awful about me.'

'Or them,' he said gently in a deep voice, as she tried to imagine the face that went with it. 'The sin was theirs, not yours. Perhaps the same is true of Sister Anne, although of course I don't know her. Perhaps she's jealous of you for some reason, because you seem so confident and so at home here. If you've lived here for most of your life, she may simply resent it.'

'And what do I do about it?' Gabriella asked, sounding desperate, and this time he chuckled.

'Tell her to knock it off, or get out her boxing gloves. When I was in the seminary, I had a boxing match with another seminarian I'd had a series of disagreements with. It seemed like the only way to resolve it.'

'What happened?' she whispered, smiling at the unconventional confession. It had been more like a session with a therapist than an ordinary confession. But whoever the unknown priest was, she liked him, and she felt as though he had helped her. He seemed to have compassion, wisdom, and humor. 'Did the boxing match help?' she asked with interest.

'Actually, it did. He gave me a fantastic black eye, and almost knocked me out cold, but we were great friends after that, for some reason. I still hear from him every Christmas. He's a missionary priest with the lepers in Kenya.'

'Maybe we could arrange for an early novitiate

and Sister Anne would like to join him,' she whispered. Even in college, she had had no exchanges like this one, bantering with her fellow students or professors. And the priest with the youthful voice was chuckling discreetly.

'Why don't you suggest it to her? In the meantime, say three Hail Marys and an Our Father, and mean them,' he said pointedly, sounding serious now that they had shared their little joke. She was surprised at how little penance he had given her before giving her absolution.

'You let me off pretty easy, Father.'

'Are you complaining?' He sounded amused again.

'No, I'm just surprised. I haven't gotten off that light since I got here.'

'Sounds like you're due for a break, Sister. Go easy on yourself, and why not just try to let it roll off your back for a while? It sounds like it's more her problem than yours, or should be. Don't confuse her with your mother. She's not the same person. Neither are you anymore. No one can torment you, except yourself. Love thy neighbor as *thyself*, Sister. Work on that until your next confession.'

'Thank you, Father.'

'Go in peace, Sister,' he whispered, and she left the confessional and slipped into a pew at the back of the chapel to say her penance. And when she looked up, she saw Sister Anne go into the confessional shortly after. She was in it for a long time, and came out with a red face and looked as though she had been crying. Gabriella hoped charitably that he hadn't been too hard on her, and then felt guilty for saying so much to him. But she

137

felt better than she had for a while when she stopped for a moment to chat with the Mistress of Postulants on her way out of the chapel. And they talked for so long about one of the older nuns who had been ill for a while that Gabriella saw the light come on in the confessional, and the priest she had spoken to emerge, and she was startled when she saw him. He was very tall and athletic-looking. He had broad shoulders, thick sandy-blond hair almost the same color as her own, and he smiled as soon as he glanced up and saw the two nuns chatting.

'Good evening, Sisters,' he said easily as he stopped for a moment where they were talking. 'What a beautiful chapel you have here.' He was looking around and admiring the church they were all so proud of, as the Mistress of Postulants smiled at him, and Gabriella tried not to stare at him. There was something very powerful and very compelling about him. And in an odd, more athletic, even better-looking way, he reminded her vaguely of her father, as he had looked to her when she was a child and he had just returned from Korea.

'Is this your first time here, Father?' the Mistress of Postulants asked him.

'My second. I'm taking over for Father O'Brian. He's on sabbatical in Rome for six months, visiting the Vatican and doing a project for the archbishop. I'm Father Connors, Joe Connors.' He smiled at them.

'How wonderful.' The older Sister was impressed about Father O'Brian's trip to the Vatican, and for a long moment, Gabriella said nothing.

'Are you one of the postulants?' he finally asked

138

her directly, and she nodded, worried that he might recognize her voice after their long, chatty confession. She was trying to envision him with a black eye, and engaging in a boxing match with the seminarian he had hated.

'This is Sister Bernadette,' the Mistress of Postulants introduced her proudly. She had loved Gabriella since she was a child, and now she was her star student. It had been a personal joy to her when Gabbie had decided to join the Order. 'She's lived here since she was a child,' the Mistress of Postulants explained, 'and now she's decided to join the Order. We're all very proud of her.'

There was a question in his eyes as he held out a hand to her, and Gabriella smiled as she took it. 'I'm very happy to meet you, Sister,' he smiled warmly at her, and relaxing slightly, Gabbie smiled at him.

'Thank you, Father. I'm afraid we all kept you very late this evening.' She could see from his eyes that he recognized her voice instantly, but made no comment about it . . . 'Oh, so you're the one who hates Sister Anne' would hardly have been appropriate, and she could barely repress a smile as she thought of it.

'I'm given to long-winded confessions,' he admitted with a grin that would have melted the hearts of a thousand women, if his circumstances had been any different. Gabriella guessed him to be about thirty years old, although she was usually a poor judge of those things, having lived out of the secular world for most of her adulthood. 'Short penances, though,' he grinned with a wink, and she blushed. He knew exactly who she was, and she couldn't help laughing at him.

139

'I'm very relieved to hear that. It's so embarrassing when you have to stay on your knees for an hour doing four hundred acts of contrition. Everyone can guess just how bad you've been. I like short penances a lot better.'

'I'll keep that in mind. I'll be back at the end of the week. Father George is covering for me in between. I have to go to Boston for the day for the archbishop.'

'Have a good trip, Father,' the Mistress of Postulants said with a friendly smile, as he thanked her and left them. 'What a nice young man,' she commented to Gabriella easily as they walked slowly out of the chapel. 'I had no idea Father O'Brian had gone to Rome. I never hear anything anymore, you girls keep me so busy.' They wished each other a good night, and Gabriella walked slowly up to her dormitory, hoping she wouldn't run into Sister Anne lurking in the hall somewhere, waiting for her to complain about her or berate her. But she was nowhere in sight as Gabriella walked upstairs, thinking about the young priest who had heard her confession. He was certainly a good-looking young man, and intelligent. He had made her feel a lot better about the hostility with Sister Anne. Suddenly it didn't seem very important. And for the first time in weeks, Gabriella was in good spirits when she got into her bed in the room she shared with two other postulants. Fortunately for her, Sister Anne was not among them. And for once, she didn't even have nightmares. They had been worse than ever lately, particularly since she had noticed how much Sister Anne reminded her of her mother.

'Good night, Sister Bernie,' one of the other

140

postulants called out to her in the darkness.

'Good night, Sister Tommy . . . 'night, Sister Agatha . . .' She loved being with them, being one of them, wearing her habit every day. Suddenly she realized how much she loved all of it, and all of them, everything they did and cared about and shared here. It was what she had wanted to be all her life, and never knew it. Until now, she had always resisted the idea of joining the Order, and now it was all she lived for. And as she fell asleep that night, she realized how much Father Connors had helped her with his good-humored and thoughtful attitude about her confession. She'd have to try and do her confession with him again. She was glad he was coming back later in the week. He was so much more reasonable, and helpful, than Father O'Brian. Everything seemed to be working out for her suddenly, and she smiled as she fell into a deep, peaceful sleep and never woke again until morning.

CHAPTER NINE

The rest of the week sped by easily. The postulants had a lot of chores to do. Gabriella had volunteered to do some extra gardening, and she wanted to plant a lot of vegetables for the Sisters before summer. It gave her some peaceful time to think and pray, and she always found it relaxed her to do manual labor. And in the evenings, after she said her prayers, she tried to get in a little writing. But she had had very little time for it lately. And Sister Anne had put a damper on it for her. She said that it was vain of her to be so proud of her writing. And the truth was, Gabriella wasn't proud of it, she just loved it. She was never really sure she had written anything someone else would want to read, it was just a window for her soul to peek through, an avenue she traveled with ease and without even thinking about it. It was the other nuns who loved reading her stories. But as usual, the young postulant from Vermont was jealous.

Gabriella tried to stay away from her that week, and she tried to remember the suggestions Father Connors had made when he heard her confession. He came back at the end of the week, as he said he would. He said Mass for all of them, and heard their confessions. And when he recognized Gabriella's voice in the darkness, he asked her comfortably how things were going. He had an easy way, and a warm, friendly style that made confession seem less austere, and much less daunting, although it was a ritual that had always brought Gabriella comfort. It was the only time and place where she knew she might be forgiven for the terrible, unspoken sins she had been blamed for, and felt so guilty for, since her childhood. It was one of the rare times when, in the darkest recesses of her soul, she didn't feel truly evil.

Gabriella assured him in the confessional that things were going better with Sister Anne, and she had been praying a great deal about her. He gave her five Hail Marys to say for the minor assortment of venial sins she'd confessed, and sent her on her way, and then later saw her again when he stopped in to see the nuns at breakfast. He was having coffee at Mother Gregoria's table, and waved casually at her, as she smiled from where she sat. It seemed odd to her again how much he looked like her father. He had a larger frame, and a warmer smile, but there was something very familiar about him. And it caught her up short when Sister Anne made an ugly comment to her later that afternoon when they were working in the garden.

'Have you spoken to Sister Emanuel about Father Connors yet?' Sister Emanuel was the Mistress of Postulants, and Gabriella couldn't imagine what Sister Anne meant as she looked up from her planting.

'Father Connors?' she asked blankly. 'What about him?'

'I saw you talking to him the other day, and flirting with him in the dining hall this morning.' At first, Gabriella thought she was joking. She had to be. She couldn't be serious in her accusation, and Gabriella laughed as she went back to planting a row of basil.

'Very funny,' she said, and forgot the comment almost immediately, but when she glanced up again she saw a look in the other nun's eyes which upset her.

'I'm serious. You should confess to Sister Emanuel about it.'

'Don't be ridiculous, Sister Anne.' A tone of annoyance crept into Gabriella's voice. She always had some new idea with which to torture Gabriella, and try to make her feel guilty, but this time at least, she didn't. 'I've only spoken to him in confession.'

'That's a lie, and you know it,' the young postulant from Vermont said harshly. She was a girl for whom life had not gone well, and bitter

143

disappointment had brought her to the convent. She was homely, and her childhood sweetheart had broken their engagement barely a week before their wedding. And it was easy for even Gabbie to see now that she had an enormous chip on her shoulder. 'I saw him watching you in the dining hall. And I'm going to tell Sister Emanuel, if you don't.'

Gabriella stood to her full height then, and looked down at Sister Anne with sudden anger. 'You're talking about a priest, a man who has given himself to God, and comes here to say Mass for us and hear our confessions. It must be a sin to even think something like that about him. You're not only insulting me, but you're questioning his vocation.'

'He's a man, just like all the rest of them. They only think about one thing. I know more about these things than you do.' She knew full well that Gabriella had led a sheltered life, hidden away for the past ten years at Saint Matthew's Convent. She had been engaged, married almost, and the man she'd loved had cheated on her and run off with her best friend from high school. She felt far wiser in the ways of the world, and was much more cynical than Gabriella, who still had a rare innocence about her.

'I think what you're saying, and thinking, is disgusting, and I think Sister Emanuel would tell you exactly the same thing. I don't know what you're talking about, but I would never say a thing like that about a priest. Maybe it's time you talked to Sister Emanuel about the kind of things you're thinking. A little more faith and charity might be in order.' Gabriella was still angry when she turned

144

back to her work, and the two young nuns did not exchange another word for the rest of the afternoon as they continued working in the garden. Eventually, Sister Anne went back inside to set the long refectory tables in the dining room, and Gabriella stayed in the garden until she finished. And by the time she went back to her room to wash her hands and say her afternoon prayers, she had regained her composure and was in better spirits. But if she'd allowed herself to dwell on it, she would have been furious at Sister Anne again about her accusations about Father Connors. He was the very spirit of Christ-like devotion, and he exuded the warmth and kindness they should all emulate. Gabriella had nothing but admiration for him, and the idea that he'd been 'flirting' with her was utterly repulsive.

They all spent the rest of the weekend peacefully, and Gabriella didn't think of Father Connors again until she saw him at the altar saying Mass for them, and then had lunch with them in the garden afterward. It was Palm Sunday, and she was still carrying the palm fronds she had picked up in church when he walked up to her casually after lunch in the garden.

'Good afternoon, Sister Bernadette. I hear you've been busy planting vegetables all week. I understand you have a real gift with herbs and enormous tomatoes. Don't forget to send us some at St. Stephen's.' His eyes were as blue as the April sky, and there was laughter in them as she looked up at him and smiled as innocently as he did.

'Who told you that?'

'Sister Emanuel. She said you grow the best vegetables in the convent.'

145

'I guess that's why they let me stay for so many years. I knew there had to be a reason.' She said it with good humor, as they began to stroll through the garden without any particular destination.

'There may be other reasons as well,' he said kindly. In just the few times he had come to St. Matthew's, he had discerned easily how fond the older nuns were of her. He knew she had been a protégée of Mother Gregoria's since her childhood, and he could see why she meant so much to them as they walked slowly toward the section of the garden where she had planted her vegetables, so he could see what she'd been doing. There was an air of poise and grace about her that went beyond her looks and the way she carried herself. There was a natural elegance about her, and at the same time a quiet warmth and gentleness that touched everyone around her. She had become very beautiful in the years she'd been here, and she was completely unaware of it. Her looks were something she never thought of. But even as a priest it was easy to admire her. She was like looking at a priceless painting, or a lovely statue, almost like a piece of art one wanted to stare at. And yet what one really saw was the light in her that shone so brightly. She seemed to be lit from within with a force he found irresistible, and he told himself it was the strength of her vocation that enhanced her beauty.

She showed him what she'd done that week, and explained the broad assortment of vegetables and herbs she was growing for the convent. 'I can plant some more for all of you, if you like, although we'll have plenty of extra to share with you next summer, if I can keep my Sisters from getting too enthused and picking them before they're ready. We have a whole patch of strawberries over there.' She pointed it out to him. 'Last summer they were delicious.' He smiled at her then, suddenly remembering memories from his boyhood in Ohio.

'I used to pick blackberries when I was a kid. I'd come back to St. Mark's all scratched up from picking them and with blackberry juice all over me.' He grinned. 'I ate so many on the way back, I had a stomachache for a week once. The Brothers told me God was punishing me for being greedy. But I kept on doing it after that. I figured it was worth it.'

'Did you go to a boarding school?' She had heard the mention of St. Mark's, and the Brothers, and it was so rare for her to talk to someone new, that she was naturally curious about him. Despite her normal shyness with people from beyond her world, she was surprised by how comfortable she felt with him. And Sister Anne's ugly comments of two days before had been totally forgotten.

'I guess you could call it a boarding school.' He smiled. 'My parents died when I was fourteen, and I had no other relatives, so I lived at the orphanage in the town where I grew up. It was run by Franciscans. They were terrific to me.' It still made him smile warmly to think about it.

'My mother left me here when I was ten,' Gabriella said quietly, looking out over her garden. But he already knew that.

'That's unusual.' But he already knew from what she'd said in the confessional that there had been nothing ordinary about her mother. He distinctly remembered her mention of the beatings, and wondered if her being left here had actually been a blessing. 'Was it a financial problem that made her

147

leave you?'

'No,' Gabriella said quietly. 'She remarried, and I guess I didn't fit into the picture. My father had deserted us the year before, and run away with another woman. For some reason, my mother always used to blame her troubles on me, and she always felt it was my fault.' She spoke very softly, as he watched her with silent compassion.

'Did you? Feel it was your fault, I mean?' He liked talking to her, and wanted to better understand why she had stayed here. He thought it was important to understand the people he tried to help, and worked with.

'I suppose I did. She always blamed everything on me, even as a child . . . and I always believed her . . . I figured that if she'd been wrong, my father would have interceded on my behalf, and since he never did, I just accepted the guilt for whatever it was they blamed on me. After all, they were my parents.'

'Sounds pretty painful,' he said gently, and she looked up at him then and smiled. It had been, but it seemed less so now, after more than ten years of peace and safety.

'It was. But being orphaned at fourteen can't have been easy either. Did they die in an accident?' she asked. They spoke like two friends, and it was so easy and open that neither of them were aware of time passing. It was so pleasant talking to him and she felt entirely comfortable with him, which was rare for Gabriella.

'No,' he explained. 'My father died of a heart attack, very suddenly, he was only forty-two, and my mother committed suicide three days later. I wasn't old enough to understand everything that

148

was happening, but I think she must have been overwhelmed with shock and grief. A little grief counseling might have worked wonders. That's why those things are so important to me. They make so much difference.' Gabriella nodded, wondering what kind of counseling would have helped her mother. 'It took me years to forgive her for what she did. But I talk to so many people now in those same situations, people who feel trapped, or frightened or alone, or overwhelmed, and just don't see any way out of their problems. It's amazing how many people don't have anyone to talk to, and they just panic in the face of problems the rest of us think aren't all that bad, or all that important.'

'Like Sister Anne.' She smiled at him again, and this time they both laughed. They had shared some important things about themselves with each other. And they had a lot in common. They had both lost their lives in the outside world, and their families, suddenly, and forever. And they had found their salvation in a life where they would never again encounter the kind of problems that had nearly destroyed them as children. 'When did you decide to become a priest?' she asked, curious, as they started to walk slowly back to the main part of the garden.

'I went into the seminary straight from high school. I made the decision when I was about fifteen. It just seemed right for me. I can't imagine a better life than this one.'

She smiled at him naively. He was so good-looking that in some ways it seemed incongruous to see him in the familiar Roman collar. 'I'll bet a lot of girls you knew were disappointed.'

'Not really. I never knew any. There were only boys at St. Mark's. Before that I was too young, and I was pretty shy as a kid. It just seemed like the right choice for me. I never doubted it for a minute.'

'Neither have I, once I was sure,' she admitted to him seriously. 'I thought about it for years, living here. The nuns I grew up with always talked about the "calling" and my "vocation," but I never thought I was good enough. I kept waiting to hear voices or something, and then finally I just knew that I never wanted to leave here. I belong here.' He nodded, understanding her perfectly. To both of them it seemed that this was the life they had been born for.

'You still have time to be sure,' he said gently, sounding like a priest again, and not just her friend, but she shook her head at his suggestion.

'I don't need time. I knew when I went to college that I never wanted to live in the world again. It's too hard for me. I don't know how to do it. I never went on dates, never wanted to meet men. I wouldn't have known what to say to them.' She grinned up at him, forgetting that he was one. 'And I never, ever want to have children.' It was the only thing she said that struck him as odd, and she said it with such vehemence that it caught his attention.

'Why not?' he asked, curious about her reasons.

'I decided that when I was a little girl. I was always afraid I would turn out to be like my mother. What if it's part of me, and I did the kind of things she did?'

'That's silly, Sister Bernadette. You don't have to be cursed with the same demons that plagued your mother. A lot of people suffer through terrible

150

childhoods, and go on to be extraordinary parents.'

'And if that doesn't turn out to be true, then what? You drop the kids off at the nearest convent and desert them? I wouldn't want to take that chance with someone else's life. I know what it's like to live through it.'

'It must have been terrible when she left you,' he said sadly, remembering the day he had found his mother. With a lifetime of prayer and service to God, he had never been able to forget it. She had been in the bathtub, with her wrists slashed. It had been the first and only time he'd ever seen her naked. She had nearly cut her hands off with his father's razor.

'It was,' Gabriella answered him soberly, 'and a kind of relief too, once I understood that I was safe here. Mother Gregoria saved my life. She's been like a mother to me.'

'From what I've heard, she's very proud that you decided to stay and join the Order. You'll make a fine nun, Sister Bernie. You're a good person.' And he looked as though he believed it.

'Thank you, Father. So are you. It was nice talking to you,' she said, blushing slightly, her natural shyness slowly returning as they rejoined the others. For the past hour, as they talked, it had been as though no one else had been there.

'Take care of yourself, Sister,' he said gently as she smiled at him and walked away, and he wandered into the main building to gather up his things and go back to St. Stephen's. It had been a nice Sunday for him. He liked coming here and talking to the nuns. They were such an important part of the life he led, the spirit they all represented, and he had always admired the tireless work they did in the hospitals and schools, and in the missionary posts that were often so dangerous for them. He couldn't help wondering what Sister Bernadette was going to do eventually. It was easy to imagine her bringing great comfort to others, especially children. And he was still thinking of her when he left, after stopping to say good-bye to some of the older nuns he knew, and walked slowly back to St. Stephen's. By then, Gabriella was busy scrubbing the kitchen floor with two other postulants, and she never saw the look of hatred in Sister Anne's eyes as she walked by and glanced at her, just as she hadn't seen Mother Gregoria watching her stroll through the garden with the young priest an hour earlier. The Mother Superior had stood at her office window, watching them, a look of concern in her eyes as she saw Gabriella smile up at him. They both looked so young, and so innocent, and so striking together. There was something so similar about them.

Mother Gregoria had walked slowly back to her desk after she saw Gabriella walk away from him, and sat for a long time lost in thought, but she said nothing when she saw Gabriella that evening. She was so gentle and so loving, and so alive, and so happy with all her Sisters. It seemed foolish to worry about her. Yet there was something about what she had seen that day that struck fear in Mother Gregoria's heart, but she told herself she was being foolish.

Father Connors didn't come back to the convent again the next week. Another priest was covering for him. He was traveling again, and he didn't get back to St. Matthew's until Easter Saturday, when he heard confessions all afternoon. The nuns in the

152

convent were happy to see him, he had a terrific sense of humor and he seemed to have a light touch when listening to confession. Sister Emanuel was talking about him to the Mistress of Novices, when he stopped and chatted with them on his way out.

'Are you joining us for lunch tomorrow, Father Connors?' Sister Immaculata, the Mistress of Novices, asked with a shy smile. She had been beautiful once, but she had been a nun for more than forty years now.

'I'd like that very much,' he said, smiling at both of them. He loved the old nuns, their bright eyes, their shy smiles, the sharp wit, which so often took him by surprise. Their faces were so free of the stresses of the world. They had escaped the horrors that he knew only too well plagued so many lives. Most of them looked younger than they were, the sheltered lives they lived spared them so much anguish.

'The postulants and novices are making Easter lunch for us this year. They've been hard at work on it since last night,' Sister Emanuel explained, proud of the group she was bringing along now. They were doing very well. And they'd been preparing turkeys and several hams. There was corn from the garden, mashed potatoes, fresh peas, and several of the older nuns had been in the kitchen, baking since early morning.

'I can't wait.' There were three other priests coming with him the next day, and some of the nuns' families came to visit on holidays. And this year the weather had been so fine that Mother Gregoria had agreed to set up picnic tables outside. 'Should I bring anything? One of our parishioners has given us several cases of very nice wine.'

'That would be wonderful,' Sister Immaculata beamed, knowing how pleased some of the visitors would be. It was rare for Mother Gregoria to allow any of the nuns to drink wine. It was understood that they drank wine when they went home to their families, or out to dinner with them, but in the convent itself they seldom, if ever, drank alcohol, even wine. The priests who visited them drank liberally, but it was a privilege Mother Gregoria preferred to extend only to them. 'Thank you for the thought.' Both Sisters smiled at him, and the next day when he arrived for Easter Mass, he had several cases of very good California wine in the back of his car to give them.

He lifted them out easily, and brought them to the kitchen, where he entrusted them to the elderly Sister in charge. He could see the novices buzzing everywhere, and the smells of the food they had prepared were mouthwatering. He could hardly wait for the picnic they had promised him after Mass.

All four priests celebrated Mass together that day, and the chapel was filled with the nuns, and their families. There were little children everywhere, and the crucifix behind the altar and the stations of the cross had been unveiled after the long season of Lent. It was a time for rejoicing everywhere, and spirits were still high after the Mass, when everyone gathered in small, friendly groups outside in the garden.

Mother Gregoria was busy greeting everyone, and shaking hands with old friends, and the young nuns had already begun bringing food out on trays. Gabriella was one of them, and she and Sister

Agatha were carefully carrying one of the hams out of the kitchen on an enormous platter when Father Connors spotted them and offered to help them. He took the platter from them with ease, and set it down on a long table, next to another ham and the four turkeys they had worked so diligently to prepare. There were biscuits and buns, corn bread, vegetables of every kind, mashed potatoes, several salads, and half a dozen different varieties of pie, and home-made ice cream.

'Wow!' he said, feeling like a kid again, as he looked at the vast array of food on the table with wide eyes and a broad smile. 'You ladies certainly know how to make an Easter picnic unforgettable, don't you?' And as Sister Emanuel looked over at them, and saw the expression on the young priest's face, she was very proud of her students.

The guests stayed for most of the afternoon, and Gabriella was eating a piece of apple pie when Father Connors finally made his way back to her again. He had spent the afternoon chatting with Mother Gregoria and some of the older Sisters. They had introduced him to their families, and he was having a wonderful time talking to them. He had loved chatting with Mother Gregoria, she was so well informed, so intelligent, and so wise. And she had enjoyed getting to know him. He had only been at St. Stephen's for a short time. He had been in Germany before that, and had spent six months working at the Vatican in Rome, and he was very well versed in what was going on there.

'You should try some vanilla ice cream on that.' He gestured to Gabriella's apple pie, as he obviously enjoyed the huge dollop of homemade ice cream on his own piece. 'Mmmm ... fantastic

155

lunch. You ladies should open a restaurant. We'd make a fortune for the church.'

Gabriella grinned at the look of ecstasy on his face, and laughed at what he had said. 'We could call it Mother Gregoria's. I'm sure she'd love that.'

'Or maybe just call it something catchy like The Nuns. I hear there's a nightclub that just opened downtown somewhere, in an old church. They're using the altar as a bar.' Just talking about it seemed sacrilegious to both of them, but it still made them laugh. 'I used to love to dance when I was a kid,' he admitted to her, starting in on the second piece of pie on his plate. It was blueberry, and reminded her of the story he'd told about picking blackberries when he was a child. 'Did you like to dance, Sister Bernadette?' he asked, as though they were old friends, and she smiled and shook her head.

'I've never tried. I've been here since I was ten,' but he already knew that. 'I used to love to watch people dance at my parents' parties when I was a little girl, but I never got to go downstairs. I used to sit at the top of the stairs, and peek at them. They all looked so beautiful, like fairy queens and princes. I always thought I'd be one of them when I grew up.' She had no idea what had happened to their house, or the furnishings that had been in it. She didn't know if her mother had taken them, or if everything had been sold. It had all been gone for a long time, and she had no way of knowing.

'Where did you live when you were a child?' he asked with interest as he looked at her, putting a small dollop of the delicious ice cream on what remained of her pie.

'Thanks . . .' She closed her eyes as she tasted it,

156

and then grinned up at him. 'That is good . . . yum . . . We lived in New York, about twenty blocks from here. I don't know what happened to the house.'

'You've never gone back to look?' That seemed odd to him. He would have gone back, just out of curiosity, and found it strange that she hadn't.

'I thought about it when I was going to Columbia, but . . .' she shrugged, looking up at him with her enormous blue eyes that were so similar to his own . . . 'too many memories . . . I'm not sure I want to see it again. It's been a long time.' And her life was very different.

'I'll drive by it sometime for you, if you want, just to see if it's still there. Give me the address, and I'll take a look.'

'That would be nice.' He could face the demons for her, and report back to her. She was almost sure Mother Gregoria wouldn't mind. 'Do you ever go back to St. Mark's?'

'Once in a while,' he said, with a warm look at her as he finished his second piece of pie. 'My parents' house has been turned into a parking lot. I don't have any relatives. All I have left of my childhood is St. Mark's.' They were both people with troubled histories, and very little left of their past. Painful memories, and broken dreams that could no longer be repaired, but they were both grateful for the fact that they had survived. They had sought refuge in the church, and were comfortable where they were, just as they were comfortable sitting side by side now in the garden of St. Matthew's. The sun was warm as she looked up at him again, and was struck by how handsome he was. It still seemed hard to believe that he

157

preferred being a priest to being out in the world, but as he looked at the young postulant he was coming to know well, he had the same feelings about her.

They sat and chatted for a while, watching the other nuns talk animatedly to their guests, and it struck both of them at the same time, that neither of them had another soul in the world except the nuns and priests they lived with.

'It's odd, isn't it?' he said quietly. 'Not having a family. I used to miss it terribly on holidays, for the first few years at least, and then I got used to it. The Brothers at St. Mark's were so good to me. I always felt like a hero coming home from the Seminary to visit. Brother Joseph, the director of St. Mark's, was like a father to me.' It was a common experience they shared, which went beyond the Masses he said for them, or his kindness to her in the confessional. It was something each of them understood perfectly, and which no one else seemed to share. It was a kind of solitude and loneliness which formed a silent bond between them.

'I was just glad to be away from the beatings when I first came here,' she said softly. He couldn't even imagine it, except that he had seen that and worse when he worked as a chaplain in the hospital as a young priest. It used to make him cry to see the damage people did to their children.

'Did they hurt you very badly?' he asked gently. She thought about it silently, then nodded and looked into the distance.

'Sometimes,' she said in barely more than a whisper. 'I wound up in the hospital once. I loved it there, people were so kind to me. I hated to go

158

home, but I was afraid to tell them. I never told anyone. I always lied about it to everyone. I thought I had to protect them, and I was afraid that if I didn't, my mother would kill me. If she had stuck around for a few more years, she probably would have. She hated me,' she said as she looked up at the young priest who had become her friend now. They had shared a multitude of confidences about their childhoods, and it suddenly seemed like a kind of glue between them.

'She was probably jealous of you,' Father Connors said reasonably. He had asked her to call him Father Joe by then, and she had told him that her name was Gabriella, even though all the other postulants, and some of the old nuns, now called her Sister Bernie.

But his suggestion didn't make sense to Gabriella. 'Why would she be jealous of a child?' She looked at him with eyes filled with memories and questions.

'People just are sometimes. There must have been something very wrong with her.' Gabriella knew better than anyone that it was an overwhelming understatement. 'What was your father like?'

'I'm not sure. Sometimes I think I never really knew him. He looked a lot like you,' she smiled up at him again, 'or at least I think he did, from what I can remember. He was scared of her. He never stood up to her, he just let her do it.'

'He must feel terribly guilty about it. Maybe that was why he ran away from her. He probably just couldn't face it. People do strange things sometimes, when they feel helpless.' It reminded them both of his mother's suicide, but Gabriella didn't want to bring up painful memories for him and ask him about it. It was a nightmare she couldn't even begin to imagine. 'Maybe you should try to find him one day, and talk to him about it.' She had fantasies about that sometimes, and it was odd that he should mention it. But she didn't know where to begin looking for him. All she knew was that twelve years before, he had moved to Boston.

'I don't suppose he ever knew that I came here. I don't think she would have bothered to tell him. I was going to talk to Mother Gregoria about it once, but she always says that I have to let go of the past, and leave it far behind me. She's right, I guess. He never called or wrote after he left.' She said it with a sad look in her eyes. Talking about them still pained her greatly.

'Maybe your mother wouldn't let him,' Father Joe offered, but it gave her small comfort, and maybe Mother Gregoria was right after all. She had a very different life, and the ghosts of her past had to be released, though they still haunted her in darker moments. 'Where is she now?' he asked, referring to her mother.

'San Francisco, or she was up until she stopped sending money for my room and board here.' It still amazed him to think that her family had completely abandoned her, never wrote to her, never visited, never saw her. He couldn't understand how they could do that. It was entirely beyond him.

'Well, Sister Bernie, you have a good life here, and St. Matthew's needs you. The nuns all love you. I think Mother Gregoria thinks you're going to step into her shoes one day. That would be quite an honor. We've done all right for ourselves,

160

haven't we?' he said, smiling at her. But as their eyes met, they both knew how hard-won it had been, how far they had come, and how much of themselves they'd left behind them. He patted her hand gently with his own, and for an instant she looked startled when he touched her. His hand was so firm, so strong, and once again reminded her so much of her father's. It had been so many years since she'd been that close to any man, that it couldn't help but bring back memories of the only other man she'd ever known or been this close to. And as though he sensed the shock of her memories, Father Connors stood up slowly. 'I'd better see how drunk my pals are after drinking your wine all afternoon, and get them back to St. Stephen's.' She couldn't help laughing at the vision of drunken priests, falling down amidst the nuns in the convent garden.

'They look all right to me.' She stood up next to him, glancing around, and then laughed at the image he'd created of them. Two of the priests were talking to the Mother Superior, and another was talking to a family he knew. Sister Emanuel looked as though she was trying to round up the postulants to clean up the kitchen, and most of the children and visitors were looking happy but tired. It had been a lovely Easter for all of them, and especially for Gabriella, talking to Father Connors. 'I never talk about this stuff with anyone,' she confessed as she prepared to leave him and join the others. 'It still scares me a little.'

'Don't let it,' he said wisely. 'They can't hurt you now, Gabbie. They're all gone. You're safe here, and you have been for a long time. They'll never come back to hurt you again, and you never have to go back there.' It was as though he had released her, with his kindness and his words, and with his gentle presence. It was as though just being there next to her for a while, he could protect her. 'I'll see you in the confessional,' he said with a lopsided smile. 'Try to stay out of trouble with Sister Anne,' he said, looking amused. Sometimes he felt so old when he was talking to her. She was twenty-one, and knew so little of the world beyond these walls, and he was a full ten years older than she was, and in his own eyes, a great deal more worldly, and far wiser.

'I'm sure she'll have a lot to say about my talking to you this afternoon.' Gabriella looked a little tired and somewhat exasperated as she said it. It was so annoying to have to deal constantly with the angry young postulant's accusations.

'Will she?' He looked startled. 'Why would she say that?'

'She always has a bee somewhere in her bonnet. Last week she was complaining about the stories I write. She claimed I was writing one when I was supposed to be saying Matins . . . or Vespers . . . or Lauds, or something. There isn't much I do that she doesn't complain about.'

'Just keep praying for her,' he said simply. 'She'll get tired of it.' Gabriella nodded, not particularly worried, and she left Father Joe with Sister Emanuel as she hurried off to the kitchen. There were a mountain of pots waiting to be scrubbed, a stack of platters, the pans the hams and turkeys had been cooked in, and the floor was a complete disaster. But for once, Sister Anne was so busy when Gabriella walked in, that she didn't even see her. Gabbie put an apron on, rolled up her sleeves,

162

and dug into the stack of greasy pans with a handful of steel wool and a bottle of liquid soap. And it was hours before they had finished. By then the older nuns were sitting quietly in the main hall talking about what a good job the novices and postulants had done with lunch, the families had all gone home, and Father Joe was back at St. Stephen's, in his room, looking strangely serious, and staring out the window.

CHAPTER TEN

For the next two months, Gabriella was busy with the other postulants, doing her chores, attending Mass, studying all that she needed to know, and working happily in her garden. She'd been working on a new story for a while, and it was so long that when Mother Gregoria read part of it, she said it was rapidly becoming a novel. But she was proud of her, she had done well, and even Sister Anne had stopped complaining about her for the time being.

It was already hot in New York and well into June when some of the older nuns left for their retreat at their sister convent in the Catskills. The younger nuns stayed in town, to continue working at Mercy Hospital and teaching summer school, but the postulants and novices rarely left the convent, and summer was no exception. Mother Gregoria also stayed to supervise all of them, and diligently run her convent. It had been years since she'd taken a vacation. She felt that was a privilege best reserved for the elders.

A group of missionary Sisters came to town, to

stay with them, and the stories they told of Africa and South America were fascinating, and made Gabriella wonder if one day she might want to be one of them. But she said nothing to Mother Gregoria, for fear it would upset her. Instead, she listened intently to the tales they had to tell, and after they left, wrote wonderful short stories about them. And when Sister Emanuel read them, she insisted that they really ought to be published. But Gabriella only wrote them for the pleasure of it. Writing always released something in her. It never felt as though she were doing the writing herself, but rather as though there was a spirit that moved through her. She had no sense of her own importance as she wrote them, but felt instead as though she didn't exist at all, as though she were a windowpane that another spirit looked through. It was difficult to describe, and the only person she said that to was Father Joe, when he found her scribbling away one day, eating an apple and sitting at the back of the convent garden. He asked if he could look at what she'd done, and when he did, he was deeply moved. It was a story about a child who had died, and returned to earth to seek injustices and bring peace to others.

'You really ought to publish that,' he said, looking impressed as he handed it back to her. He had a deep tan, and said he had been playing tennis with friends on Long Island. Listening to him say it reminded her instantly of her parents. She hadn't heard anyone talk about playing tennis since her childhood, although she was sure that some of the people she knew had played while she was in college. But she had never talked to any of them, she just went silently back and forth to St.

Matthew's. 'I'm serious,' he said, going back to the subject of her writing. 'You have real talent.'

'No, I don't. I just enjoy doing it.' And then she told him the feeling she had, about the spirit that seemed to just pass through her. 'When I'm conscious of it, of what I'm doing, I can't write anything. But when I just let go, and forget myself, then it just seems to come through me.'

'Sounds pretty spooky,' he teased with a grin, but he understood what she was saying and was impressed by it. 'Whatever's doing it, you ought to stick to it. How've you been otherwise?' He'd been on vacation for a week, and felt as though he hadn't seen her in ages.

'Fine. We've been busy planning the Fourth of July picnic. Are you coming?' They had a barbecue every year. Mother Gregoria was good about doing big holiday celebrations. It was their way of staying in touch with friends and relatives and people who were important to their community, and a relaxed way to see them. And as Gabriella looked at him, she felt as though she were talking to her brother. They were becoming good friends, and with very little effort, had developed an easy friendship.

'Is that an official invitation?' he asked, feeling almost exactly the same as she did.

'You don't need one,' she said casually. 'Everyone from St. Stephen's comes, all the priests and secretaries, and altar boys. A lot of people from the hospital come too, and from the school. Some of the families come, but a lot of people are away then.'

'Well, I won't be. They have me working six days a week this month. They're keeping me pretty busy, saving sinners.'

'That's good.' She smiled up at him, and handed him a sprig of mint and a handful of strawberries. 'If you don't mind their not being washed, they're delicious.' He tried one of the strawberries and seemed to be in ecstasy as he ate it.

'Terrific.' From the look in his eyes, anyone watching him wouldn't have been sure if he meant her or the berries. He seemed happy to see her. And eventually, he walked her back to the main hall where she had to place an order for more seeds with the sister in charge of buying supplies for their garden. He told her he'd be saying Mass the next day, and would be delighted to come to the picnic.

The next time they met was in the confessional the following day. They recognized each other's voices and they chatted all the way through her confession. She was used to his easy style now, and she didn't have much to tell him. He gave her absolution, and stopped for just a moment to say hello to her after she'd completed her penance.

'How about if some of the Fathers and I do your barbecue for you at the picnic?' he asked, and she looked delighted at the suggestion. It was the one job she truly hated. The smoke got in her eyes, and their habits made it awkward for them to deal with the fire and the charcoal. The priests had it a lot easier, since they always came to the picnic in jeans or khaki pants and sport shirts.

'I'll ask Sister Emanuel, but I think she'd love that,' Gabriella said gratefully. 'Barbecue is not really our forte.'

'What about baseball?'

'What?' She looked at him, not sure if he was joking, serious, or just making idle conversation.

166

'How about a baseball game? St. Matthew's against St. Stephen's? Or we can mix up the teams if you think you'd be at too much of a disadvantage. I just thought about it this morning.'

'What a great idea. We did it two years ago, with two teams of nuns, and it was pretty funny.'

He looked down at Gabriella with a mock serious air, and pretended to be insulted. 'We're not talking "funny," Sister Bernie. This is serious. The priests at St. Stephen's have the hottest team in the archdiocese in all five boroughs. What do you think?'

'Why don't you ask Mother Gregoria? I can't speak for her, but I think she'll love it. What position do you play?' she asked, teasing him, but the Fourth of July picnic was beginning to sound seriously exciting.

'Pitcher, what else? This arm was once recruited for one of the best minor league teams in Ohio.' It was a small claim to fame, but it was obvious from the way he looked at her, that he had a sense of humor about it, and it amused him. But he did love to play baseball.

'What happened? How come you're not playing for the Yankees?'

'God made me a better offer,' he said, smiling at his young friend, and happy to be talking to her about something as mundane as baseball. Much of the time they dove into serious discussions, about their lives, their histories, their vocations, or her writing. They always had a lot to say to each other. 'What about you? What do you play?'

'I think I have a real talent as bat boy,' she said demurely. She had never played any sports as a child, for obvious reasons. She'd been here with the

167

nuns, and hadn't even attended a real school from the time she was ten until she went to college, and the only exercise she'd gotten was walking around the garden at St. Matthew's.

'We'll put you in the outfield,' he said confidently, and promised to talk to Mother Gregoria before he left the convent.

And within days, word of the Big Game, as it was being called, had spread all over the convent. When Father Connors had proposed it to her, Mother Gregoria had loved it. All the nuns were laughing and giggling and whispering. Some hadn't played since they were kids, others were bragging about how good they had been, and the postulants were all arguing amicably about what positions they wanted to play. Chubby Sister Agatha insisted that she wanted to play short-stop. It was all in precisely the right spirit.

And when the big day came, everyone was ready for it. The food at the picnic was plentiful as usual, and appropriate for the occasion. The priests from St. Stephen's made good on their offer to do the barbecue, and there were hot dogs, hamburgers, barbecued chicken, ribs, french fries, and the first corn on the cob of the summer. There was homemade ice cream, and more apple pie than anyone thought possible. As one of the priests said, it looked as though the Sisters had gone crazy in the kitchen. But it was obvious that everyone loved it. Other than Christmas, it was everyone's favorite holiday, and the convent's favorite picnic. And when the food was gone, or most of it at least, and the last ice cream bar had been smeared all over the last child's face, the talk turned to baseball.

Not surprisingly, Father Joe was the captain of

the St. Stephen's team, and he organized it very professionally, and with great fairness. The priests and nuns had put it to a vote, and decided that it would make for a better game if there were both sexes on both teams, and as promised, Father Joe put Gabriella in the outfield, playing for St. Stephen's. Even Sister Anne seemed to relax that day. She was playing first base for St. Matthew's. The priests had an advantage, of course, in their jeans and T-shirts. The nuns wore their habits, but pulled back their coifs, and tied them up as best they could. And they amazed everyone by running nearly as well in their long habits as the men in their blue jeans. Some of the nuns had even found sneakers to play in. And everyone cheered when Sister Timmie slid into third base without even exposing her legs, although the Sister in charge of getting habits cleaned said her habit would never be the same. But when Sister Immaculata made a home run for St. Matthew's, both teams cheered so loudly that it almost frightened the children.

It was a great day, and great fun. St. Stephen's won by a single point, seven to six, and Mother Gregoria surprised everyone with lemonade and cases of beer, and the novices had made delicious lemon cookies. It was the best fun Gabriella could ever remember, and when she and Father Joe stood rehashing the game, he praised her for how well she'd done, and she laughed at him, sipping lemonade and munching on a cookie.

'Are you kidding?' She grinned, finishing off her cookie. 'I was just standing there, praying the ball would never come my way, and thank the Lord, it didn't. I don't know what I would have done if it did.'

'Duck, probably,' he teased her. They'd all had a great time, and were sorry to see it end. The families went home just before dinner, and the priests and nuns stayed to eat what was left of the barbecue. There was enough for everyone, and they sat in the convent garden afterward watching the fireworks that lit up the sky. It was a real holiday for all of them, and felt more like an entire vacation.

'What did you do on the Fourth of July when you were a kid?' he asked, in the deep voice that was now so familiar to her.

She could only laugh at the question. They were both still in high spirits. 'Hide in the closet mostly, praying my mother wouldn't find me and beat me.'

'That's one way to spend the holiday, I guess,' he said, adding a little levity to what they both knew was a painful subject, and probably always would be.

'It was a full-time job for me staying alive in those days. The only real holidays I remember were here. I've always loved the Fourth of July picnic.'

'So do I,' he said, looking at her with a tenderness that surprised her. 'When I was a little kid, we used to go camping with friends. My brother and I used to try and buy sparklers as kids, to take with us, but no one would ever sell them to us.'

She looked surprised then as she glanced over at him. 'You never told me you had a brother.' In the four months she had known him, he had never once mentioned a sibling.

Father Connors paused for a long moment, and then met her eyes firmly. 'He drowned when I was seven. He was two years older than I was . . . We

170

went swimming down by the river, and he got caught in a whirlpool. We weren't supposed to be there . . .' Tears filled his eyes as he talked to her, and he didn't even know it, as without thinking, she reached out and touched his fingers, and something almost electric passed between them. 'I watched him go down the first time, and I didn't know what to do . . . I tried to find a branch to hold out to him, but it was summer, and everything was green, and I couldn't find anything long enough. I just stood there while he went down again and again, and then I ran for help as fast as I could . . . but when I got back . . .' He couldn't go on and she wanted to take him in her arms and hold him, but she knew she couldn't. 'He drowned before we got back to him . . . There was nothing I could do . . . nothing I could have done . . . but I always felt my parents blamed me for it. They never actually said it, but I always knew it . . . His name was Jimmy.' There were tears slowly rolling down his cheeks as she touched his hand again and this time held it gently.

'Why would they blame you? It wasn't your fault, Joe.' It was the first time she hadn't called him 'Father,' but neither of them noticed.

He hesitated before he answered, and then took his hand away from hers to wipe the tears from his cheeks. 'I begged him to take me to the river. It was my fault. I shouldn't have asked him.'

'You were seven years old. He could have said no.'

'Jimmy never said no to me. He was crazy about me . . . and I was crazy about him. It was never the same after he died. My mom just kind of lost her spirit.' Gabriella wondered if that explained why

171

she had taken her own life after her husband died so suddenly. Maybe it had just been too much for her, after losing her son seven years before. But it had been a cruel thing to do to Joe, and left him an orphan. To Gabriella, it seemed unthinkably selfish, though she didn't say it to Joe as she listened.

'It's hard to understand why things like that happen. We should know that better than anyone.' There were so many times when all of them had to defend God when people asked questions about situations like this one.

'I hear about things like this all the time,' he admitted, 'but that doesn't make it any easier for the people I talk to, or for me. I still miss him, Gabbie.' It had happened twenty-four years before, and the pain was still fresh whenever he talked about it. 'In some ways, it affected my whole childhood. I always felt so responsible for what happened.' Not to mention the loss of his parents dimming the bright light of the rest of it. But she understood perfectly what he meant about feeling responsible. She was all too familiar with those emotions.

'I always felt as though everything that happened in my family was my fault,' she admitted, 'or at least that was what they always told me. Why are children so willing to take on those burdens?' She had never doubted for a moment that her parents abandoning her, and everything that had happened before that, was entirely her own fault. 'You didn't do it, Joe. It wasn't your fault. It could have been you, instead of him, who drowned. We don't know why these things happen.'

'I used to wish it had been me, instead of him,'

172

he said in a small, sad voice. 'We were all so crazy about him. He was the star of the family, the best at everything, their first-born, their favorite,' he admitted. Lives were so complicated, and the things that happened in them so impossible to explain, so difficult to live with. They both knew that. 'Anyway, I'll see him again one day,' he said, smiling sadly at Gabriella. 'I didn't mean to tell you all that. I just think of him a lot on holidays. We used to love to play baseball. He was one heck of a fantastic player.' He had been a nine-year-old kid, just a little boy, Gabriella realized, but to his little brother, Joe, he had been, and still was, a hero.

'I'm sorry, Joe,' she said, and meant it from the bottom of her heart. She was so sorry for him, and all that he had been through.

'It's okay, Gabbie,' he said, looking at her gratefully, and then one of the priests from St. Stephen's came over to rehash the game with them, and congratulated Father Joe on his victory for St. Stephen's.

'That's quite an arm you've got, son.' He really was a very good pitcher. The mood lightened again after that, and when the priests went home that night, Father Joe walked over to say good-bye to Gabriella. She was standing with Sister Timmie and Sister Agatha, and they were laughing and teasing each other. Everyone was still in good spirits.

'Thanks for a great game, Sisters,' he said jovially, and then with a last look at Gabbie that the others seemed unaware of, 'thanks for everything,' he said, and they both knew what he meant. He was thinking about telling her about Jimmy.

'God bless you, Father Joe,' she said gently, and

173

meant it. They both needed blessings in their lives, and forgiveness and healing, and that was her most fervent wish for him. In her opinion, he deserved it, even more than she did.

'Thank you, Sister. See you at confession. Good night, Sisters,' he called out with a wave as he went to join the others and gather up their equipment before they went back to St. Stephen's. It had been a great day, a great Fourth of July. And as Gabriella walked slowly back inside with the other postulants, she was startled to realize that one of the things she remembered most clearly about the day was when she had reached out and touched his fingers.

'Isn't that right, Sister Bernadette?' One of the other Sisters had asked her something, and she hadn't heard it. She had been thinking of Father Joe, and his brother, Jimmy.

'I'm sorry, Sister . . . I didn't hear you.' They all knew that at times Gabriella didn't hear things, particularly now with the habit covering her ears, but they were always patient with her about it and it never occurred to anyone that she would be thinking about the young priest and his lost brother.

'I said Sister Mary Martha's lemon cookies were fantastic. I want to get her recipe for next year.'

'Delicious,' Gabriella agreed, walking up the stairs, just behind them, but her thoughts were a million miles away, thinking of two little boys, one caught in a whirlpool, and the other left sobbing by the river. Her heart went out to him, and all she wanted to do as she thought of him, was drift back in time and put her arms around him. She could still see Father Joe's eyes in the half light that night, and the look of devastation in them. And her own eyes filled with tears again now, just thinking of him. All she could do now was pray for him that night, that he might finally forgive himself. She prayed for the man she knew and had come to love as a friend, and the soul of his brother, Jimmy.

CHAPTER ELEVEN

Gabriella didn't see Father Joe again for several days after the Fourth of July picnic. Everyone was still talking about it, and the baseball game had made convent history. They could hardly wait to do it again next year. But Gabriella was particularly surprised in light of that, and given the high spirits that had persisted at St. Matthew's, when she saw Father Joe, and he was less than friendly with her. He seemed almost cool, and the word that came to mind as she spoke to him was *grouchy*. She wasn't sure if he was annoyed with her, or simply in a bad mood, or worried about something. But he was anything but pleasant, and he seemed distant with her. She wondered for a fraction of an instant if he was embarrassed or sorry that he had told her about Jimmy.

She wanted to ask him if he was all right, but she didn't dare. There were other people around, and after all he was a priest and ten years older than she was. He never pulled rank on her, but she didn't know what to make of his behavior changing so radically since the Fourth of July picnic.

He heard her confession that day and was so curt and distracted with her in the confessional that she almost wondered if he was listening and had even heard her. He gave her two Hail Marys, and a dozen Our Fathers, which also wasn't like him. And then he added five Acts of Contrition as a last thought. And finally, just before she left the confessional, she couldn't stand it any longer. She hesitated, and then whispered into the darkness.

'Are you okay?'

'I'm fine.' He sounded so brusque that she didn't dare pursue it any further. Something was very wrong with him. He had none of his usual jovial ways, and he sounded very distracted. It was obvious that something had happened to him. Maybe he'd had an argument with another priest, or been reprimanded by a superior. There were also a lot of political things that happened in religious orders, and from long years of living there, she knew that.

She left the confessional, said her penance, and then went off on an errand for Sister Emanuel. Gabriella had promised her that she would look for a series of ledgers that seemed to have disappeared. They were last seen in an office no one used anymore, just down the hall from the chapel, but Gabriella was sure she had seen them there once before. She was standing, bending over a box of books, as she heard footsteps walk past, stop, and then come back toward her. She hadn't bothered to look up. She wasn't doing anything she wasn't supposed to, and she was engrossed in what she was doing, hunting everywhere for the ledgers she had promised to find.

She knew the person that had walked past wasn't a nun, because their footsteps were always soundless, and the footsteps she had heard had echoed loudly on the stone floor. She didn't give it any thought, but if she had, it would have been obvious to her that they'd been the footsteps of a man.

Sensing someone standing nearby, watching her, she stopped what she was doing, turned, and looked around. And she was surprised to see Father Joe standing in the doorway. He was watching her with a pained expression on his face.

'Hi,' she said quietly, only mildly surprised to see him. The room she was in was on his way out, after he left the church. He often walked through the central garden because it was so peaceful there, and the route was shorter, but this time he had gone the long way around. 'Is something wrong?'

He shook his head, watching her in silence, his deep blue eyes mirroring her own. But he looked deeply worried.

'You look upset.'

He didn't answer her at first, and then walked slowly into the room, his eyes never leaving hers, and they both knew that there was no one else around. The rooms on this corridor hadn't been used in a long time.

'I am upset,' he said finally, without further explanation. He didn't have any idea where to start, or how to tell her what he'd been thinking.

'Did something happen?' She spoke to him as she would have to a small child, although she didn't have much experience with children. But there was something about him which made her think of him as one now. He seemed very boyish and looked very worried and very young all at the same time. She almost wanted to ask him if someone had been mean to him at school today, but he didn't look as

177

though he was in the mood to laugh, which was rare for him.

He walked quietly into the room, and picked up one of the books she had discarded. So far, the lost ledgers hadn't surfaced. 'What are you doing in here, Gabbie?' He didn't call her Gabriella, or even Sister Bernie, and when their eyes met again, it was clear to both of them that they viewed each other now as good friends, in fact, she thought of him almost as a brother.

'Sister Emanuel is looking for some old ledgers that got misplaced. I thought someone might have stored them in here.' There was dust on her habit, and she looked lovelier than ever. It was hot and she looked a little disheveled. Going through the old boxes was dirty work. He stood very near to her, took the books she held from her hands and put them quietly on the desk.

'I've been thinking about you,' he said almost sadly. She wasn't sure what he meant by it, but there was nothing ominous about his manner or his words. 'Too much,' he added, 'after the other night.'

'Are you sorry you told me about Jimmy?' she asked softly, her voice was so gentle in the quiet room, it was almost a caress. He closed his eyes and shook his head, and without saying a word, he reached out and took her hand. It was a long time before he opened his eyes again. And Gabriella was still groping for the right words to offer him in comfort.

'Of course I'm not sorry, Gabbie. You're my friend. I've been thinking . . . about a lot of things . . . about you . . . about myself . . . about the lives that brought us here, the people who hurt us . . .

178

the ones we loved and lost.' He had loved and lost more than she had. She wasn't sure she had ever known love before, not until she came here. 'Our lives here mean a great deal to both of us, don't they?' He asked as though desperately seeking an answer to a question he couldn't bring himself to ask her.

'Of course they do. You know that.'

'I would never do anything to risk that, to jeopardize either of us ... to spoil anything ... that's not what I want.' She still had no idea what was on his mind. She had never been alone with a man before this moment.

'You haven't done anything to do that, Joe. We haven't done anything wrong.' She said it with such quiet certainty that it felt like a knife through his heart. And he confessed his sins to her now, as she had done to him so often.

'I have.'

'No, you haven't.' Not that she knew of anyway.

'I've been having dangerous thoughts.' It was the closest he could come to saying what was in his heart, and on his mind.

'What do you mean?' she asked, her eyes and her soul wide open. She moved a little closer to him, without knowing it, but the magnet that was slowly drawing them toward each other was more powerful than anything either of them had ever been exposed to before that moment.

'I don't know how to tell you ... what to say ...' There were tears in his eyes as he looked at her, and she put a gentle hand on his face. It was the first time she had ever touched him like that, or any man. 'I love you, Gabbie.' There was no way to hide it from her anymore, or from himself. 'I don't

179

know what to say to you, or what to do about it . . . I don't want to hurt you, or ruin your life. I want to be sure this is what you want, before I run away from here forever, or give up my job at St. Stephen's and go away. I'm going to ask the archbishop for a transfer.' He had been wrestling with the idea all morning.

'You can't do that.' She looked frightened as he said it. The thought of losing him terrified her far more than the rest of what he had just said. 'You can't go away.' He was her friend now and she didn't want to lose him.

'I have to. I can't stay here, close to you like this. It's driving me crazy . . . Oh, Gabbie . . .' The words were lost as he pulled her close to him and she buried her face in his powerful chest, his arms held tightly around her. It was the strongest force she had ever felt in her entire life, the safest place she had ever been, even more so than the convent. 'I love you so much . . . I want to be with you all the time . . . I want to talk to you . . . hold you . . . take care of you . . . I want to be with you forever . . . but how can we do this? I've been going crazy for the past four days. I love you so much,' he said, sounding agonized as she looked up at him in wonder, and all he wanted to do was keep her in his arms for the rest of time. So far, she hadn't said a word, and there were tears in her eyes now as she looked at him, tears of regret, and pain, and longing.

'I love you too, Joe . . . I wasn't sure what I was feeling . . . I think I knew it was wrong . . . I thought we could just be friends.' She looked both happy and devastated.

'Maybe we can be friends one day, but not now

180

. . . not yet . . . We both belong here. I can't ask you to leave the convent. I'm not even sure what to do myself.' He was so troubled, so wracked with guilt, so anguished, that suddenly it made everything clearer to her, and she put her arms around him and held him there, her own strength drawing him still closer as she held him, and gave him all she had to give him.

'Just be quiet . . . we have to pray about it . . . shhh . . . it's all right, Joe, I love you.' She was the strong one now, and he was the one who desperately needed her. He felt all the power and the warmth and the love she felt for him, and without saying another word, he pulled her closer still and kissed her. It was a moment neither of them would ever forget, a moment when universes collided, and two lives were changed forever with a single breath.

'Oh, my God, Gabbie . . . I love you so much.' He was suddenly glad he had told her. After the agony of the past week, he had no regrets. He had never in his life felt as he did at this moment.

'I love you, too, Joe.' She sounded suddenly so grown up, so brave, and so sure. It was a risky thing they were doing, a still more dangerous game they would have to play. 'What are we going to do now?' she asked him quietly, as he sat down next to her on the corner of the old desk.

'I don't know,' he said honestly. 'We both need time to figure this out.' But they both knew that if they went too far, it would be impossible for them to continue their lives here. It was not too late yet, they could still turn back. They were Adam and Eve in the Garden of Eden, the apple was untouched and they were still holding it in their

181

hands, staring at it. But the temptation would grow greater very quickly, and if they moved too fast, they would destroy each other's lives. It was an awesome responsibility as they looked at each other, and he drew her toward him and kissed her again. 'Can we meet somewhere?' he asked after he kissed her. 'Just for coffee, or a walk. Out in the real world, with real people. We need to be alone for a little while, just to talk about this.'

'I don't know,' she said, thinking. 'I don't see how I can do that. Postulants normally never leave the convent.'

'I know, but you're different. You're like a daughter of the house, you've lived here all your life. Can't you get them to send you on an errand, or do something for someone? I'll meet you anywhere you want.'

'I'll think about it tonight.' She was trembling as he held her. Suddenly, in half an hour, her entire world had turned upside down. But she didn't want to resist it. She knew she could still turn back, but nothing could have made her do that. She wanted to be near him more than she had ever wanted anything in her life. For all these months, she had never known it, and with a sudden flash of understanding, she realized that Sister Anne had been right. And she said as much to him.

'Maybe she was smarter than we both were,' he said wisely. 'I swear I never saw this coming.' But he had never been involved with a woman in his life, nor had Gabriella ever been close to any man. She had never dated, never flirted, never made friends with her fellow students at Columbia, let alone really talked to a man there. In her heart, in her life, in her behavior, ever since she was a child,

182

she had always been a nun. And now, in the blink of an eye, all of that had changed. She was suddenly a woman, and very much in love with him. 'They just asked me to say Mass and hear confessions here every day.' He had been alternating with Father Peter, but the older priest hadn't been well, and had just decided that he already had too much on his plate at St. Stephen's. And Father Joe seemed to get on well with the nuns, so he asked him to take over for him. 'You can tell me what you've figured out tomorrow morning.'

'It may take me a couple of days,' she said, and then she grinned at him mischievously, and he had a wild urge to remove the headpiece she wore, which concealed all but the front of her golden hair. He wanted to see how long it was, how much there was of it. He wanted to see more of her than he was allowed to, to hold her, to kiss her until they were both desperate for air. But he also knew that he couldn't keep her in the abandoned room forever, and in a minute he would have to let her go back to the others. But he hated to give her up, even for a few hours, until they were able to meet again.

'Maybe I should start hearing confessions here twice a day,' he said with a boyish smile, and feeling the same magnetic force pull them simultaneously, they kissed each other again, with increasing passion.

'I love you,' she whispered, wanting more of him than she dared.

'I love you too. I'd better let you go now. I'll see you tomorrow morning,' he said, kissing her yet again. 'I hate to leave you.'

'You'd better. We can meet here again. No one ever comes here, and I know where Sister Emanuel keeps the keys to this office.'

'Be careful,' he warned her, 'don't do anything crazy. I mean that.' He sounded very firm, and she laughed as she met his eyes again.

'Look who's talking. This is about as crazy as it gets.' But if they met outside these walls, they both knew it would get crazier yet.

'Are you mad at me for telling you, Gabbie?' He looked suddenly worried as he stood to his full height and faced her squarely. He had taken an enormous risk by telling her, but now he had put both of them in danger. But she looked as though she had no regrets. None whatsoever.

'How could I be angry at you, Joe? I love you.' And then with a shy smile, 'I'm glad you told me.' But the situation was easier for her in some ways, she was only a postulant and had taken no final vows. She wasn't even a novice. Joe had been a priest for more than six years, and the consequences of what they had done were far more dramatic for him. His whole life was in jeopardy.

'I'm not sure what we should do now, Gabbie. I don't even know how I'd support you,' he said, looking worried.

'We'll see what happens. We can always work it out later.' There was a strength in her that she had never felt before, and in some ways, she seemed stronger than he was. 'It's too soon to think about all that yet. Just know that I love you, Joe. That's enough for now.'

'That's all I wanted to hear. I thought you'd never speak to me again if I told you . . . I was so afraid . . .' She touched his lips with her fingers,

184

and he kissed her hand. 'Don't forget how much I love you,' he whispered, and forced himself to leave her. He stood in the doorway for one last moment, smiled at her, and then disappeared. She could hear his footsteps echoing in the hallway for a long time. She stood there, listening to them, and thinking of everything he had just said. She still couldn't believe it, didn't understand how this had happened to them. In so many ways, it seemed like an enormous blessing, in others, it was a dragon waiting to devour them. She wondered how long they could keep it a secret. Maybe for a long time. She knew they would have to, for a while at least, until they decided what to do about their future. And it was obvious to her that in spite of her delicate circumstances at St. Matthew's, it was Joe who had to make the biggest decision.

She looked through the rest of the dusty boxes, and only found one of the ledgers. But it would be enough to satisfy Sister Emanuel today, and it would give Gabriella an excuse to come back here again. They could meet in secret in the abandoned office, at least for a while. She left the room, and locked the door behind her, and as she walked back to find Sister Emanuel, she felt as though she were in a daze. He loved her . . . he had kissed her . . . he wanted to be with her . . . It was impossible to absorb everything that had happened, or even to begin to understand. But the sound of his words was still drifting through her head when she rejoined the others, and there was a smile on her lips that no one noticed, or understood, except Sister Anne, who stared at her intently.

CHAPTER TWELVE

Gabriella stood in line for the confessional the next morning. The others still looked half asleep, but she was wide awake, and had been since three A.M. It seemed like hours before she could see him, and she had begun to wonder if she had imagined it all, if he would be sorry, if he would tell her that he had come to his senses and never wanted to see her again. It was entirely possible, and there was a look of terror on her face when she finally stepped into the confessional after one of the oldest nuns in the convent, and said the familiar words to begin her confession. The comforting ritual was only a front now.

He recognized her voice instantly, he had been waiting for her, and without a sound, he opened the grille between them, and she could see the outline of his face, almost as though it were a dream.

'I love you, Gabbie,' he whispered, so softly she could hardly hear him, but she sighed with relief the moment she heard his words.

'I was afraid you'd change your mind.' She looked anxious in the darkness.

'So was I, that you would.' He kissed her through the tiny window, and there was a brief silence, and then he asked her if she could meet him outside the convent.

'Maybe. They take the mail out tomorrow, but one of the other Sisters usually does that. I can offer to do it for her. It's kind of a big job. Mother Gregoria lets me do it for her once in a while. But I wouldn't know till the last minute.'

'Call me at St. Stephen's. Tell them you're the
186

secretary for my dentist, and you had a cancellation. Just tell me the place and time. What post office do you go to?' She told him, and he promised to be there anytime she called him.

'What if you're out?' Gabriella sounded worried.

'I won't be. I've had a lot of paperwork lately, and I've been meeting with parishioners at the rectory. I'll be there, and I can leave quickly if I have to. Just do what you can.'

'I love you,' she whispered.

'I love you too.' They were in total collusion now, and determined to be together, if only briefly, no matter how high the price. They had both lain awake almost the entire night after their meeting in the abandoned office, and they knew that despite the danger of it, for them what they were doing was right. Neither of them had any doubt. 'Say as many Hail Marys as you want to. And pray for me, Gabbie. I mean that. We both need it right now. I'll pray for you. Call me when you can.'

'I'll see you here tomorrow morning if I can't.'

She left the confessional with her head bowed, looking very solemn, and hoping that no one could see the excitement in her eyes. She was very glad that Mother Gregoria had been busy the night before, and had never stopped to speak to her at dinner. It would have been hard to face her now, and Gabbie feared that the Mother Superior knew her too well, and would see the look in her eyes, and discover her secret.

She watched him say Mass that morning, and found herself looking at him differently than she had before. He no longer seemed so remote to her, so mystical. Suddenly he seemed more like a man. It frightened her a little, and when she thought about it too intensely, she felt a little finger of fear race up her spine. But she also knew that she couldn't turn back now. She didn't want to. She wanted more of his kisses, and to feel the powerful hands and arms around her.

She left the church with the other nuns, and was grateful for her work in the garden. It kept her busy, and away from prying eyes. She mentioned to Mother Emanuel after breakfast that if they needed her help for the mail run that day, she'd be happy to do it. Her work in the garden was going well, and she had time to help them.

'That's sweet of you, Sister Bernadette. I'll tell the others. I don't think we have much going out today. But maybe another time.'

In the end, it was a frustrating week for them. There was simply no reason, and no way, for her to get out of the convent. But they met in the abandoned office two more times. There was a definite risk to it, and they were both aware of it. He was quieter when he came here now, and she had found the last of the ledgers, but she kept it hidden there so she continued to have a reason to come back and search for it. They locked the door while they were in the room, and they kissed and whispered and held each other as tightly as they dared. They sat on the floor in the heat of a July afternoon, and talked about their lives. Neither of them had figured it all out yet. All Joe was asking for now was just a little time. Time when they could behave like real people, speak openly, and walk down a street or through a park hand in hand. But even if they met outside, they knew they'd have to be careful, and she couldn't stay out for very long without alarming the Sisters.

For the moment, going out for a walk, and a few minutes of each other's time, was all they dreamed of, a small pleasure other couples took for granted, and one they would have to wait for until they were blessed by chance.

The moment came finally a full week after his first declaration. It came suddenly and unexpectedly when Sister Immaculata handed her the car keys to an old station wagon they used to pick up supplies. Some fabric had come in for their habits, and the nuns in charge of making them were anxious to get to work while they had time. There was no one else to pick it up, and she had to go all the way downtown to get it. The warehouse it had come into was on Delancey Street, and Gabriella knew how to get there. She had done the same errand for them before many times. And as long as she was going out, two of the other nuns had other errands for her as well. She had a lot to do for them, but she knew that if she hurried, she could eke out a little time with Joe somewhere on her rounds.

She took the lists they gave her with trembling hands, and hoped no one saw it. She had the car keys, the money they handed her in an envelope, and as soon as she could leave gracefully, she hurried out the door of St. Matthew's. The station wagon was parked just outside. She waved to Mother Gregoria as she left, and the Mother Superior smiled at her as she always did. She was happy to see Gabbie in such good spirits these days. There was a lovely joyful light in her eyes. Everyone assumed her postulancy was agreeing with her. She was working hard in the garden, and Mother Gregoria hoped, as she always did, that

Gabbie was still finding time to write, and reminded herself to ask her.

As Gabbie pulled away from the curb, she stepped on the gas as hard as she dared, and sped around the corner. She drove two blocks, stopped at a pay phone, and then, with trembling hands, she called him. The young Brother on the phone answered on the third ring, and she said, as Joe had told her to, that it was Father Connors' dentist calling, they'd had a cancellation, and wondered if he had some free time that morning.

'Oh, I'm sorry,' the young Brother answered politely, 'I don't believe he's in.' Her heart sank at the words. 'I'll check for you, but I saw him getting ready to leave a few minutes ago, and he might be out for quite some time.' There was a long pause while he kept her on hold, and she railed silently at the bad luck that had caused her to miss him, and wished she had had the wisdom to leave half an hour before. For an instant, she wondered if she should feel guilty, if this was God's way of seeing that it didn't work out. They had both talked so much about what it would mean if they left the church together. She knew she should feel guilty about it, but she didn't yet. It was still too new and too exciting, and they had waited so anxiously for just a little time together. Maybe in the end, nothing would ever come of it, and they would come to their senses before it was too late. But if they did, they would have had this love they shared for a few moments, a few days, and she didn't want to give that up now. She had the rest of her life to repent for it, and give her life to God, if that was what He wanted for her.

The Brother came back on the line breathlessly,

as Gabbie waited to hear what he'd found, and she almost whooped with glee when he told her he'd caught him, and if she was willing to wait, he'd come right on the line.

A moment later she heard Joe's voice, and he sounded as though he'd been running. He had. He'd been halfway out the door, and hurried back upstairs to take her call. 'Where are you?' he asked, grinning from ear to ear. Neither of them had thought this day would ever come. It seemed to have taken forever.

'I'm around the corner from St. Matthew's. I have to go downtown to pick up some things. They gave me a few errands, but I don't think anyone will worry about how long I'm gone,' she explained to him.

'Can I come with you? Or is that too dangerous? I'll meet you somewhere if you want. Where are your errands?'

'Delancey Street, and some stores where they give us discounts on the Lower East Side.'

'What about Washington Square Park? I don't think anyone there will know us. Or Bryant Park behind the library?' He had always liked it there, despite the pigeons and the drunks. It was peaceful and pretty.

They settled on Washington Square Park in an hour, which gave her time to pick up the fabric, and if she hurried, she could get everything else done.

'I'll meet you at ten o'clock,' he promised. 'And Gabbie . . . thank you for doing this, sweetheart. I love you.' No one had ever called her that before, in her entire life, or sounded as he did now.

'I love you, Joe,' she whispered, still afraid that someone would hear them. It took a while to sink

191

in that there was no one else around.

'Go do your errands. I'll see you in an hour.'

They were quick for once at the warehouse. They helped her load the car with the huge bolts of fabric. It took five yards for each habit, and there were two hundred nuns at St. Matthew's. What they gave her this time, just for some of them, filled most of the back of the car. She did the rest of the errands in record time, and it was five after ten when she drove up Sixth Avenue, and turned toward the park until the familiar arch came into sight. The park looked a little like the pictures of Paris she had seen. Joe was already there, waiting for her, when she arrived. She found a place to park the car, and locked it, and then as an afterthought, she unlocked it again, carefully pulled off her coif, and left it on the front seat of the car. She didn't even bother to look in the mirror, but ran her fingers through her hair, as she locked the car again, and went to meet him, hoping that in spite of the somber black dress, she looked like everyone else. She was grateful that she still wore the short dress of the postulants. There would have been no way to disguise her habit if she had already taken her final vows, or become a novice.

She ran across the square when she saw him, beaming at him, and without saying a word to her, he pulled her into his arms and kissed her. He also had taken his Roman collar off and left it and his jacket in the car. He looked like a man in a short-sleeve black shirt and matching pants, and attracted no attention.

'I'm so glad to see you,' he said breathlessly, walking slowly beside her, and excited to be out in the world with her for the first time. It was a world

192

full of colors and excitement and people, even at that hour. There were children with balloons, couples on benches talking and holding hands, old men playing chess, and the canopy of trees overhead softened the summer sunshine. He bought her an ice cream from a passing cart, and they sat down on a bench together. He was smiling at her, and she had never seen him as happy, as they kissed and held hands and ate their ice cream. It was like a dream for them, a dream that could easily become a nightmare, but neither of them could think about that now.

'Thank you for meeting me here, Gabbie.' He looked at her gratefully, and knew only too well how hard it was for her to get out. But their long wait for these few hours made them even more precious to them. They didn't waste a single moment, but talked about everything, shared as many thoughts as they could in the short time they had, and kept themselves focused on the present rather than the future. He wanted to know how soon she thought they could meet again, and she had no idea what to say to him. This seemed like such a miracle to both of them that it was difficult to imagine doing it again, but she knew she had to. The moments they shared at St. Matthew's now seemed like crumbs. It was so wonderful to be out in the world together, and feel so free with each other.

'I'll do what I can. I think Mother Emanuel will let me do errands for her again. I don't think anyone will object, as long as I get everything done, and don't disappear for too many hours.' The nuns always broke the rules for her, they always had, and she had always been extremely helpful to them.

There was no reason for that to stop now, as long as she did what she had to with the other postulants. She hadn't written a word all week, but she had still managed to work for hours in the garden.

'I'd love to go to Central Park with you sometime, or walk by the river.' There were so many things he wanted to do with her, and they had so little time in which to do them.

He walked her back to the car at eleven-thirty, and the moments they had shared had been so well filled they seemed like hours to them. Their time together had been everything they hoped it would be, and it made them hungrier still to meet again. They both knew what the dangers were, the risk to them potentially, yet it was too late for either of them to turn back. He kissed her one last time, and she could feel his body so close to her that it startled her at first, and then she relaxed and seemed to melt into his arms.

'Take care of yourself, Gabbie. Be careful. Don't say anything to anyone,' he warned unnecessarily, and she smiled at him.

'Not even to Sister Anne?' she teased, and he grinned. He wanted to take her back, to be with her, to call her that night. He wanted to do all the things men in love did, and he never had. At thirty-one, he had never loved a woman, never allowed himself to even think of it. He had never had a crush, never flirted, never allowed himself the kind of fantasies he had now. But for him, it was like the opening of a dam. And once open, it was impossible to stop the avalanche of feelings that overtook him.

He stood next to the car and watched her put

her coif back on. She looked like a little girl to him, as she looked up at him with her huge blue eyes. Just seeing her like that made him want to run away with her right then. And neither of them had the vaguest idea when they would be able to meet this way again.

'I'll see you in the confessional tomorrow,' she said cautiously, and he nodded at her, wanting so much more of her. He hated to let her leave him.

'Do you still have the keys to the locked room?' he asked hopefully, and she smiled at him.

'I know where they are.'

It was dangerous, but better than the whispers they shared in the confessional. He already wanted more of her than he had now.

They kissed one last time, and as she drove away, she waved at him, and drove back through the midtown traffic as fast as was allowed. She got back to St. Matthew's easily, and one of the other postulants came out to help her unload the car. The bolts of fabric were heavy, but Gabriella felt as though she had the strength of ten after the time she had just spent with Joe, and the tenderness they'd shared.

She had lunch with the other nuns, worked in the garden that afternoon, arrived at dinner on time, after saying her prayers with the rest of them, and that night she went to her room in her spare time, and began to write. Mother Gregoria came to visit her, and asked if she had written any new stories. She felt as though they hadn't talked in a while. But she was pleased to see that Gabbie was looking well, and all the reports she'd had recently told her that Sister Bernadette was thriving. She could hardly wait for her to take her final vows. It

195

wouldn't be for a long time, but she was well on her way. And when Mother Gregoria left her room, Gabbie felt the first serious stab of guilt she'd felt since the whole odyssey with Joe began after the Fourth of July. It had been only two weeks since then, but it was hard to believe, it seemed like a lifetime to her.

She couldn't help thinking about how disappointed Mother Gregoria would be in her, how devastated she would be. And yet Gabbie knew she couldn't stop now. All she wanted in her life was to be with Joe Connors.

She saw him in the confessional the next day, and they met in the abandoned office late in the afternoon, but it seemed so confining to them after the time they'd spent in Washington Square Park. And she had no hope of getting out and doing more errands for a while. In the end, it was a full two weeks before she could get out again, and waiting for the time to come almost drove them both mad.

As he had hoped they would, they met in Central Park. They walked around the model pond, and watched the children and adults playing with their boats, and then they walked slowly uptown. The park was lush and green, there was a steel band playing in the distance somewhere, and as it always did when she was with him, it felt like a dream to her, an entire holiday compressed into a single hour. They had so little time to be together, and all they wanted now was more. Of each other and their lives. Every moment they shared was precious to them. A few days later, they were able to go back to Central Park. They lay on the grass under a tree this time, and he put his head in her

196

lap, as she stroked his hair and listened to him intently as they talked. There was so much to say, so little time in which to say it. And he bought her an ice cream again as they walked back to the car. They were seeing each other every day, hidden away in the confessional and the dusty office they felt was theirs, and they had only been out in the world together three times.

There was still so much to say, so many things to work out. Neither of them had any idea where to begin. It was a difficult journey to undertake, although they felt sure of each other. It had been done before, in circumstances similar to theirs. Priests usually left with nuns, he would not be the first, or the last. But they both knew what an explosion it would cause, how many people would feel betrayed. And there were times he was afraid for himself. Joe especially was worried about leaving the church, and had said as much to Gabbie, although he was certain that he loved her.

'We need more time,' Gabriella said sensibly. 'You can't do something like that, Joe, without giving it a lot of thought.' And he had. He thought of it all the time, especially at night when he was alone, waiting to see her again, desperate for their stolen kisses in the confessional. He was doing something he could never have conceived of, until he met her.

She had begun writing a journal to him, about their love, and her dreams for them. She hoped to give it to him one day. It was a never-ending love letter to him, and she kept it concealed with her underwear in her only drawer, where she knew no one would find it. It was a way of being with him, even when she was not, and talking to him when she couldn't.

'When do you think you can get out again?' he asked, looking sad one afternoon, as he walked her back to the car.

'Whenever I can. Maybe next week.' The older nuns were all going away to Lake George. Someone had lent them a house there, and Mother Gregoria was going to join them for a few days to help them get settled. It might mean more freedom for Gabriella, or not, those things were always hard to judge in the convent.

But the day they left, Gabriella found herself with an entire afternoon at her disposal. The rest of the postulants had gone to the dentist that day, and they were planning to be out for several hours. Gabriella had been to the dentist only two months before, so they left her at home, with no obligations and no plans. She told the nun in charge that she was having a problem with some of her vegetables and needed some sprays. The old nun had had a bad headache for days, asked her no questions at all, and handed her the keys to the car without comment. Gabriella said vaguely that she'd be back in a while. She drove around the corner, as she always did, and called Joe, and luckily, he hadn't gone out. He hadn't expected to hear from her, but he hated leaving St. Stephen's now, he was always afraid to miss one of her rare calls, and an opportunity to see her.

'How long do you have?' He always asked her that, but this time he was startled when she told him several hours. He had been waiting for this day, but he was stunned that it had come. They had been meeting this way for more than a month. 'Meet me all the way east on Fifty-third Street.' He

198

gave her an address, and she had no idea what it was. But it was only a few blocks away from her. She got there before him this time, and waited in the car, without her coif, anxiously awaiting his arrival.

He parked across the street from her, and put an arm around her as they walked slowly down the block. He seemed quiet and thoughtful.

'Don't you want to go to the park?' She seemed surprised.

'I thought it was a little too hot.' He turned to her then and looked down at her. He seemed concerned, as he took her in his arms. He knew that no one they knew would see them there, which was why he had suggested she come here. And he explained to her then what he'd done. He told her an old friend of his from St. Mark's had just moved to New York. He was in advertising and had done well, and he and Joe had had a long talk recently. Joe had told him that he was having serious qualms about his life, though he hadn't explained why. And his old friend had given him the keys to his apartment, and told Joe to use it anytime, just to get away from everything, and think and relax away from St. Stephen's. Joe knew his friend was out of town that week. He was staying with friends in Cape Cod for his summer vacation.

'Would you like to spend a little time in the apartment, just so we can be together for a while? I didn't know if you'd be afraid, or if you'd like to get off the streets for the time we have together.' He didn't want to pressure her, and he had no master plan. But he had brought the keys with him, and he was prepared to let her do whatever was comfortable for her. 'It's up to you,' he said gently,

199

and she smiled at him.

'I think it would be very nice,' she said quietly, and followed him inside. Joe had never been there before, and they were both impressed by what they saw. There was a large, comfortable living room with big leather chairs, and a long, brown leather couch. It was very modern, very male. There was a large, airy kitchen, and a big, handsome bar. And in the back, overlooking a small garden, were two bedrooms, one that was obviously his, and another he used as a guest room.

Joe put the air-conditioning on, and whistled admiringly at the stereo. He put on a selection of things he liked, after consulting her, and then helped himself to a glass of wine from the bar. It was a kind of time they'd never shared before, and Gabbie looked more than a little overwhelmed, as they sat down side by side on the couch. She was more nervous with him than she'd been before, but mostly because this was all so new to her. But as they listened to the music, and she took a small sip of his wine, she began to unwind. It was still Joe, the man she loved, even if the circumstances were different this time, and he asked her if she'd like to dance with him.

She smiled at the thought. She'd never danced with anyone before, but they moved together easily, as he held her close. He thought he'd never been as happy before, and she seemed to dissolve into his arms as they kissed and moved slowly to the music. He had put on a tape of Billy Joel.

This was different than anything they'd ever shared before, but it was what they had both longed for, for so long, a chance to be alone, to be who they were, to do anything they wanted

200

together. And as they danced, he looked down at her, and their passion slowly mounted. He could feel her heart beating too fast as he held her next to him, and he couldn't stop kissing her. They were both excited and out of breath as they stopped dancing.

'I know what I'd like to do,' he said quietly, wanting her desperately, but unsure if she was ready to take a step of that magnitude with him. It had been five weeks since he declared his love to her, but they were hungry for each other in ways that neither of them were fully able to understand. He had never been with a woman before, and she had never been with a man. It was all so new, yet it felt so right to both of them, and she understood what he meant. She looked up at him with loving eyes.

'I'd like that too,' she whispered, as he felt the pounding of her heart as he held her.

'Don't be afraid, Gabbie . . . I love you so . . .' He swept her easily into his arms, and walked slowly into the guest bedroom with her. The room looked inviting, and he set her down gently on the bed. She was still wearing her postulant's dress, and he fumbled with it. She helped him with the buttons and folds and pins, as they kissed, and suddenly he sat looking at her, her flesh like cream, her breasts the first he'd ever seen, her limbs longer and far more graceful than he'd ever dreamed they would be.

She had no fear of him, as he began to undress, and he slipped into the bed and took off the rest, as did she. Their clothes lay in a small heap on the floor as he began to explore her, aching with desire for her. Neither of them had ever felt this way before. It was a time of discovery, and trust, neither of them quite sure what to expect, yet both of them certain they wanted to be here, needed to be with each other. It was a road they had to travel, side by side, to move on to their new life together.

He kissed her everywhere, as she trembled beneath his hands, and began to look slowly for him. She found what she was seeking, and her eyes widened in surprise. No one had ever prepared her for this. She had no idea what to do, but nature took over gradually, and he knew instinctively what to do for her. She was startled when he entered her, and he was careful with her, despite his mounting desire, which was harder to control with each moment. He knew it would be painful for her, and it was at first, but he restrained himself for as long as he could, and then he couldn't stand holding back anymore. He came, shuddering violently, calling her name, and she held him tightly to her as she moaned in a strange mixture of pain and pleasure that seemed to transport her. He caressed her afterward, and looked down at her, there were tears in her eyes, but they were for the new life they shared, the sorrows they had left behind, the tie that would hold them together now for the rest of their lives. She knew that she could never leave him now, nor he her. They had come far for this, and he kissed her lips and her hair and her eyes, and then just lay there with her and held her tight. And when finally he could bear to be parted from her, he looked at her, in awe of the beauty that had been hidden so carefully in the ugly habit.

'You're so beautiful . . .' He had never dreamt it would be anything like that, and he wanted her again, but he was afraid to hurt her. But as he kissed her passionately once more, she wanted him too, and it was different for her this time. They lay wrapped in ecstasy, lost in each other's gifts for what seemed like an eternity, and then afterward, he took her into the bathroom with him, and they took a shower. She was surprised at how easy they were with each other despite their lack of experience, and their natural shyness. She stood in the shower with him, the water running down on them, washing them clean, as they kissed again, and she smiled. It was obvious to both of them what they had to do now, what they would do after this. The die had been cast. And they no longer had any doubts about the future.

They changed the bed together, and put the sheets and towels through the washing machine, and then they walked back into the living room to wait for them to dry and sat on the couch again, discussing what they were going to do about their lives now.

'We can't do this forever, sweetheart,' he said practically, and they both knew that afternoon had changed their lives forever. She couldn't even imagine what she'd say to Mother Gregoria eventually. She couldn't begin to think about that now. All she could think about was him, and what they'd done that afternoon. She knew that she was his now for the rest of her life, whatever their future brought them.

It would be hard to be satisfied with a walk in the park, or a quick kiss in the confessional, after all they had shared here.

'We can do whatever we have to, for a while,' Gabriella said, worried about him. He had so much on his mind.

'Could you live in abject poverty?' he asked, looking worried. He knew she never had before, and it troubled him. She had lived without luxuries in her convent days, but all her needs had been met, and she had total security. If he married her, he knew they might have to starve for a while, or close to it.

'I can work too, you know.' She had a college degree, she could teach, or work for a magazine. She could always try to write and sell her stories. She had no idea how much money she'd make at it, but Mother Gregoria and the other nuns had always wanted her to try and sell them.

'I can get a job teaching school,' he said nervously. St. Stephen's paid him a salary, but if he left the church, none of the skills he needed there would be of any use to him outside. He had never before had to worry about making a living.

'You can do a lot of things,' she said reassuringly, 'if that's what you want.' She didn't want him to feel he'd been pushed out of the priesthood. He had to walk out because he wanted to, otherwise he might hate her for the rest of his life, particularly if their road got rocky. And she knew it would for a time. It was a huge adjustment.

'You know I want to be with you more than anything in the world,' he said, kissing her again, transported again by the emotions of the past two hours. He was glad now that there had never been anyone else. He had never realized how much it would mean to him to have saved himself for her. And what they lacked in experience, they made up for amply in passion.

'I'd better go back,' she said with regret finally.

It was hard to believe she still had to go back to the convent, but Joe still had a lot to work out in his own mind. They had agreed to wait for a while, to give him time to sort things out, but they had both made their decisions. It was just a question of time now. But they both knew they couldn't continue the charade indefinitely, and to Gabriella, at least, that part of it seemed very wrong. They had to admit it now, confess their sins, and eventually move on toward their future. If they were going to be together, she didn't want to lie to Mother Gregoria for a long time.

She adjusted her dress carefully again, and he took her in his arms one last time before they left the apartment together. 'I'm going to miss you terribly,' he said in a voice still gruff with passion. 'I'll remember this day for the rest of time.'

'So will I,' she whispered, her love for him mixed with the guilt she felt for the women she had betrayed when she gave herself to him. But in her heart, she already felt married to him.

They left the apartment, and he walked her slowly back to the car, and watched her put her coif on. She was a postulant again, a nun in the eyes of the world. But as he looked at her, he knew better. He remembered every inch of her, all the sheer, raw beauty of her, and their passion for each other as he leaned down and kissed her.

'Take good care of yourself,' he said gently to her. 'I'll see you tomorrow morning.' He heard confessions and said Mass every day now. It wasn't much for them to share, but it was all they had beyond the world of their borrowed apartment.

'I love you,' she said, and they kissed again, and then with a heavy heart, she drove away. She hated

205

to leave him. And it was even more depressing when she got back to the convent. She wanted so desperately to be with him, and seeing the nuns around her everywhere reminded her of what she'd done, and how far behind she'd left them. And yet, she still had to be here. Until they decided what to do about it, she had nowhere else to go, and neither did Joe. They had a lot of practical issues to work out before they made any kind of announcement. And she still wanted Joe to be sure about his decision to leave the priesthood. But she also knew that if he left her now, she had no doubt whatsoever in her mind that it would kill her.

She lay awake in her bed for hours that night, and several of the postulants had noticed that she scarcely spoke at dinner. She seemed lost in her own thoughts, and the Sister in charge of them that week was worried that she might be getting sick. In fact, the next morning she urged Gabbie to go see the doctor. She looked tired and pale, but she insisted that she was fine, and as usual went to both Mass and confession.

Joe was waiting in the confessional for her, and he opened the grille immediately to kiss her.

'Are you all right?' he asked, sounding worried. He had been anxious about her all night, as well as hungry for her. She had awakened an insatiable appetite, and after he'd gone back to the apartment to clean up, it had seemed so empty without her. 'No regrets?' He held his breath as he waited for her answer.

'Of course not. It was so sad coming back here yesterday. I was so lonely without you.'

'So was I.' He wanted to go back to the apartment with her again, but she had no idea when she could do that.

They met in the empty office at noon instead, and for once they both seemed very nervous. They had been lucky here so far, but Gabriella was beginning to worry that one of these days someone might see them.

She worked in the garden for the rest of the afternoon, thinking of him, and longing to be with him. She even took the chance of calling him from Mother Gregoria's office. They had a quick chat, and were careful not to reveal their names or their secret. But they both knew the risks were high and the stakes were mounting. They would have to make a clean breast of it soon, but Joe still hadn't decided when to do it.

She managed to meet him in the apartment again one more time before Mother Gregoria came back, but this time she couldn't stay away for as long, and they were both still hungry for each other when she left. The time they spent in bed in each other's arms seemed much too short, their hours together, infinitely precious.

And when Mother Gregoria returned from Lake George, she was worried by what she saw. Gabriella seemed far too quiet to her, and there was something in the young postulant's eyes that concerned her. She had known her for a long time, and she knew instinctively that Gabriella was deeply troubled about something. She tried to talk to her about it the night she came back, but Gabriella insisted that it was nothing. She perked up a bit the next afternoon after she'd written to Joe in her journal, but she was lonely for him all the time now, and she felt that she no longer belonged at the convent.

She went to the post office the following day, and met with Joe for a walk in the park. She knew she wouldn't have time to go to the apartment, and she was too afraid that Mother Gregoria would notice something.

'I think she senses it, Joe,' Gabbie said with a worried frown as they listened to a group of wandering musicians and shared an ice cream. 'She knows things about people, even when she doesn't really know them.' And then she looked up at him with grave concern and a mild look of terror. 'Do you think someone has seen us?' They'd taken a lot of walks, and met more frequently than she should have dared, and they'd gone to the apartment. Someone could have seen them on Fifty-third Street.

'I doubt it,' Joe said calmly. He was far less worried than she was. He had a lot more freedom than she did. Priests were never as carefully watched as nuns, and had the right to go places she would never dream of. No one questioned his comings and goings. He was conscientious, responsible, and highly trusted. 'I think she's just keeping an eye on her little chickens.'

'I hope so.' It was August by then, and the summer seemed to be speeding by very quickly. Soon the teaching Sisters would be back at school, the older nuns would be back from their retreats at Lake George and in the Catskills. The kitchen staff were already planning a Labor Day picnic, but all of it seemed less important to Gabbie now as she contemplated their future.

And when Labor Day finally came, she came down with a bad case of flu, and Mother Gregoria began to worry seriously about her. There was something wrong with more than just Gabbie's flesh, there was something seriously amiss with her spirit, and Mother Gregoria knew it.

Joe came to the Labor Day picnic with the other priests, as he always did, but he seemed to avoid Gabbie this time. They had discussed it the previous morning and agreed that it was wiser to stay away from each other, in case someone noticed the ease with which they talked now. There was something private and intimate about all their exchanges. And halfway through the day, Gabbie left and went back to her room. She felt too ill to eat, or even be with the others. Mother Gregoria noticed it, as did Sister Emanuel, and they discussed it quietly with each other.

'What do you suppose is wrong with her?' the Mistress of Postulants asked with genuine concern. She had never seen Gabbie like this.

'I'm not sure,' Mother Gregoria said with an unhappy expression. She had already decided to talk to her about it, and that afternoon she went to her room, and found Gabbie writing furiously in her journal. 'Something new?' she asked pleasantly, as she sat on the single chair that stood in the corner of the stark room, for occasions such as this one. 'Anything for me to read?'

'Not yet,' Gabriella said wanly, as she shoved the thin volume under her pillow. 'I haven't had much time lately,' and then she looked at her apologetically, for more than the Mother Superior knew. 'I'm sorry I left the picnic.' It had been blazing hot outside, and Gabriella had looked green by the time she left them.

'I'm worried about you,' Mother Gregoria said honestly, and Gabbie looked nervous as she answered.

'It's nothing. Just the flu. Everyone had it while you were away.' But Mother Gregoria knew that wasn't true. Only one very old nun had been ill, and that had been due to her gallbladder. No one else had been ill recently at St. Matthew's.

'Are you having doubts, my child? It happens to all of us at one time or another. Ours is not an easy life, nor an easy choice to make, not even for someone like you, who's been here seemingly forever. At some point we must all wrestle with it and come to a final decision. After you do, you will be at peace for a long time, perhaps forever.' And as she said it, she wished that Gabriella had taken greater advantage of her years in college. Perhaps she was regretting giving up a world she had never known, one which, in her childhood at least, had never been kind to her. 'Don't be afraid to tell me.'

'No, Mother, I'm fine.' It was the first time she had ever lied to her, and she hated herself for it. This was rapidly becoming an untenable situation for her. She wanted to tell her she was in love with Joe, that she had to leave. As awful as it would have been, she would almost have preferred it.

'Perhaps you should take a last look at the world again, while you are still free to do it. You could get a job somewhere, and still live here, Gabriella. You know we'd allow you to do that.' It was precisely the opening she needed, and yet she knew that even that liberty would be abused if she was meeting with Joe in borrowed apartments. If she left, she had to do it honestly and cleanly.

'I don't want to do that,' she said firmly. 'I love being here with my Sisters.' That much was true, she did, but now she loved Joe more, that was the problem. And he still had a final decision to make about the priesthood. They both had to be sure. She was, and he said he wanted to leave, but so far he had offered no clear plan as to how he was going to do it. It was still too soon for him, no matter how much he said he loved her, and she knew that. It had only been two months since it all began between them.

But the next weeks rapidly became a nightmare for her. She did errands whenever she could, but Mother Gregoria was so worried about her that most of the time she wouldn't let Gabbie do them. She and Joe still met in the spare room, and in the confessional, but most of the time they were together now was spent discussing their plans, and his obvious guilt at leaving the priesthood. She kept telling him to take his time about his decision. She never wanted him to regret it, once he did it. And they had only been able to meet two more times in the borrowed apartment. His friend was back in town by then, but Joe was still able to use it while his friend was at the office.

And to make matters worse, by mid-September Gabbie was feeling deathly ill much of the time. She tried to conceal it from the others, but everyone noticed how pale she was, how little she ate, and there was real panic when she fainted in church once. Joe had been there, he'd been saying Mass, and he looked up sharply when he saw the stir in the row of postulants, and then nearly panicked when he saw her carried outside. He had to wait a full day before he could meet her in the confessional and ask her what had happened.

'I don't know, it was just very hot in church yesterday.' They had been having an endless heat

211

wave, but as he pointed out to her with anguish in his eyes, none of the other nuns had fainted, not even the old ones. He was desperately worried about her.

She waited another two weeks to be sure. It was the end of September by then, and there was no doubt in her mind, although she had no scientific way to confirm it. But she was sure anyway. She had all the signs, and inexperienced as she was, she was still able to figure out that she was pregnant. Finally she managed to leave the convent and she called Joe to meet her at the apartment. They met in the apartment that afternoon, and he knew there was something wrong as soon as he saw her. But when she told him, Joe looked terrified, and he held her in his arms and cried. He felt terrible about it. In his eyes, it was no way to start a marriage. And it was certainly going to force their hand very quickly. From all she could determine, she must have gotten pregnant the first time, and she was now nearly two months' pregnant. She couldn't wait much longer to make her own decision. And whatever he did now, she had to leave the convent. She wouldn't do anything to jeopardize the baby, and he didn't expect it. In fact, he would have done anything to stop her. They both had deep religious feelings on the subject.

'It's all right, Joe,' she said quietly, sensing his distress over it, and the enormous pressure it added to an already untenable situation. 'Maybe it was meant to be this way. Maybe it's what I needed to make my decision.'

'Oh, Gabbie, I'm so sorry . . . it's all my fault . . . I never thought . . . but I should have.' But how could a priest even think about buying condoms?

212

And there was certainly nothing available to her in their circumstances. They had had no choice and no options. They had been forced to take their chances. And naive as they were, it had never occurred to either of them that something like this could happen so quickly.

Now he had two people to think about, a wife, and a baby, and no way to support either of them. The prospects facing him seemed suddenly devastating, and the pressure almost beyond bearing.

'I'm going to leave St. Matthew's in a month,' Gabbie said. She had already made her decision once she realized what had happened to her. 'I'll tell Mother Gregoria about it in October.' That gave him a month to figure out what he was doing. In these circumstances, it was all she could give him. She could give him longer than that, but she had to make a move herself before they all figured it out and it became the scandal of the convent.

He held her in his arms for a while that afternoon, afraid to touch her now, to damage her or the baby, and he began to cry again as he held her. 'I'm so afraid to fail you in the world, Gabbie . . . what if I can't do it?' It was his worst fear now.

'You can do it, Joe, if you want to. We both can. You know that.' She seemed remarkably certain, given how unproven they both were.

'All I know is how much I love you,' he said, knowing that now he had not only her to think of, but their baby. He wanted to leave the church, for both of them. He wanted to be with her, and take care of her, but he still wasn't sure he could do it. 'You're so strong, Gabbie, you don't understand. I've never known anything but the priesthood.'

213

And she had never known anything but St. Matthew's, and a lifetime of beatings before that. And why was it that they all thought she was so strong? Her father had said the same thing to her the night before he left her. It touched a chord of memory for her now, and a deep, silent place of terror. What if Joe left too? What if he abandoned her, and their baby? The mere thought of it filled her with panic, but she didn't say a word to him as he held her. She merely clung to him silently, trying not to frighten him further.

He kissed her before she left, and she drove back to the convent lost in her own thoughts. She didn't even see Mother Gregoria watching her as she came in, or Sister Anne leaving an envelope outside her office. And she had no way of knowing later on when the Mother Superior called St. Stephen's. She met with the monsignor there that night, and came back to St. Matthew's with a heavy heart. No one knew anything for sure, but there had been rumors, and a number of phone calls from a young woman who left different names at different times. Father Connors had been out a lot lately, and, Mother Gregoria realized now, at St. Matthew's far too often. And she and the monsignor had come to an agreement that night. Father Connors would not be back again for some time to hear confession or say Mass at the convent.

Gabriella had no way of knowing that, and when she slipped into the confessional the next morning and said, 'Hi, I love you,' the voice that answered her was not one she recognized. There was a long moment of silence, and then he continued the confession as though everything were normal. Her heart was pounding as she left, and she couldn't

214

even remember hearing her penance. She wondered if something had happened to Joe, if he were ill, or if he had told them he was leaving, or worse yet, if they had been discovered. She knew he wouldn't have said anything to them without consulting her first, but maybe after her announcement the previous afternoon, he had decided to move ahead and tell them he was leaving very quickly.

She was still frantic over it when Mother Gregoria called her into her office later that morning. She said nothing for a short time, and then looked across her desk sadly at Gabriella.

'I think you have some things to say to me, don't you, Gabriella?'

'About what?' Gabbie's face was as white as paper as she looked across the desk at the woman whom, for twelve years, she had called 'Mother,' and loved as though she had been born to her.

'You know what I'm talking about. About Father Connors. Have you been calling him, Gabriella? I want you to be honest with me. One of the priests at St. Stephen's thought he saw you with him in Central Park, in August. I don't know for sure if it was you, and neither does he, but everyone at St. Stephen's seems to suspect it. It's still not too late to avoid a scandal, if you tell me the truth now.'

'I . . .' She didn't want to lie to her this time, but there was no way she could tell her the truth. Not yet, at least. Not until she talked to Joe about it, and found out what he'd told them. She was sure that they had already questioned him about it. 'I don't know what to say to you, Mother.'

'The truth would be your best course of action,' Mother Gregoria said grimly, feeling her heart

215

ache as she looked at the young woman she loved like a daughter.

'I . . . I've called him, yes . . . and we met in the park once.' It was all she was willing to give her. The rest belonged to them, and was far too private.

'May I ask why, Gabriella? Or is that a foolish question with a far-too-obvious answer? He's a handsome young man, and you're a beautiful young woman. But although you have not taken final vows yet, you have told me that you're sure of your vocation, and I believed you. I am no longer quite so certain. And in his case, he has been a priest for a number of years. Neither of you are free to behave this way, or to violate your commitments.'

'I understand that.' There were tears in her eyes, but she refused to cry now, or beg for mercy.

'Is there more to this ugly story, Gabriella? If there is, I want to know it.' It was not an ugly story, and hearing it described that way nearly broke Gabriella's heart as she listened. All she could do was shake her head. She refused to tell her any more lies now. 'I'm sure you won't be surprised to hear that there is going to be an investigation at St. Stephen's. The archbishop will be called today. And we won't be seeing Father Connors here for quite some time.' She paused for breath, looking deep into Gabbie's eyes, searching for answers Gabriella wouldn't allow her to see there. 'I am going to suggest to you that you spend some time seriously examining your conscience, and your vocation, at our sister house in Oklahoma.' It sounded like a death sentence to Gabbie, and she almost shrieked when she heard it.

'Oklahoma?' It came out as a single croaking

sound that seemed unfamiliar to her. But it was all she could say now. 'I won't leave here.' It was the only time Gabriella had defied the Mother Superior since their initial battle over her going to college. But Mother Gregoria was more than firm now. Beneath her calm exterior, she was livid. At Gabriella, and the priest who had offered her temptation and nearly broken her spirit. It was an unpardonable sin as far as the Mother Superior was concerned, and she would have to do a great deal of praying herself, she knew, to forgive it. He had had no right to do this to her. He had been in a situation of extreme trust here. She was a young, innocent girl, and he should have known better.

'You have no choice in this matter, Gabriella. You are leaving here tomorrow. And you will be carefully watched until you go, so don't try to reach him. If you choose to stay with us, and that choice is still yours, you must carefully think about what you've done, and decide if you really want to be here. I offered you every opportunity to go back to the world for a time, to be part of it, if that's what you wanted to do, and you refused it. But at no time did that include consorting with a priest in clandestine meetings.'

'I didn't,' Gabbie said, looking agonized, and hating herself for the lies she was telling, but she felt she had to, if only for his sake.

'I wish I could believe you.' The Mother Superior stood up then, and signaled in no uncertain terms that the meeting was over. 'You may go back to your room now. You will not speak to the other postulants for the rest of the day, or until you leave. One of the Sisters in the kitchen will bring a tray to your room, but you may not

217

speak to her either.' Overnight, she had become a leper. And without a word she left the room, and went back upstairs, desperate to call him, but there was no way she could do it. All she knew was that she could not go to Oklahoma. She would not leave him.

She lay on her bed all that day, thinking of him, and by nightfall she was in a total state. She had written to him in her journal all day, and when she wasn't writing or lying down, she paced, wishing she could at least get out to the garden, but she knew she couldn't. She could not defy Mother Gregoria's orders any further. And all day she wondered what they were doing to him, and what he was saying to the archbishop. But neither of them had ever thought for a moment this would be easy. They had both known that from the beginning. Now all they had to do was survive the pain and humiliation until they could be together.

She never touched the food that came to her that day, and it was after dinnertime when she felt a strange pain low in her belly. It took her breath away at first, and then disappeared, and in a little while, it was followed by another. Gabriella had no idea what it meant, but she was in such a state worrying about Joe that she scarcely noticed. And by the time the other two postulants returned to the room, she was in bed, in agony, but she said nothing to them. She knew that whatever it was, it was from sheer terror.

The others said nothing at all to her, they had been warned that Gabriella was deeply troubled and they were not to speak to her. They had no idea what she had done, or what punishment was being meted out to her, but they whispered about it

218

constantly whenever Sister Emanuel left the room, trying to guess what had happened. Only Sister Anne remained strangely silent.

Gabriella never slept that night, thinking about him, worrying about what he had said, or what they were saying to him. She imagined something much akin to the Spanish Inquisition going on at St. Stephen's, and at two o'clock that morning, she was in so much pain, she almost called out to the others, but she couldn't. What could she tell them? She could hardly say she was afraid she might lose her baby. Instead, she nearly crawled, hunched over, to the bathroom, and there she saw the first telltale signs of what she suspected was a serious problem. But there was no one she could turn to for help, not even Mother Gregoria this time, and surely not the others. And she had no way of reaching Joe. She had to wait to hear from him. She felt sure he would come for her, and that the whole situation would explode by morning. If he had told them he was leaving the priesthood for her, when they confronted him, it was only a matter of time before he came to find her at St. Matthew's. And then, she promised herself, she would tell Mother Gregoria everything that had happened, or as much of it as she needed to know. But she would not leave here with a trail of lies, like tin cans, rattling behind her.

But by morning, Gabriella was nearly blinded by pain and terror. And she had no idea what time they would come to try and make her go to Oklahoma. But that, at least, she knew she was not doing. She would refuse to leave here, and they could hardly carry her out in her nightgown.

She heard the others get up silently, and waited

219

until they were gone, and when she stirred finally from her own bed, she saw that there was blood on the sheets, and she had no idea what to do about it. She went back to bed, crying softly, and lay there. And as the first light of day came up, after she had heard them singing in the chapel, she heard the door to her room open again, and saw Sister Emanuel looking down at her with immeasurable sorrow. She thought the old nun had even been crying.

'Mother Gregoria wants to see you now, Gabbie,' she said sadly. This was a sad day for all of them, saddest of all for Gabriella, who had so terribly betrayed them.

'I'm not going to Oklahoma,' she said hoarsely, not even sure she could get up. The pains had continued getting worse as she lay there.

'You'll have to come downstairs and talk to her about it.' She was afraid to say she couldn't, and waited instead until Sister Emanuel left the room, and then struggled into her clothes with enormous difficulty. It reminded her of the days when she'd been beaten, had been wracked with pain, and had to dress for her mother. And much to her own amazement, she found this was harder.

And as she dressed, the pains were worse than ever. She could barely get down the stairs, and she nearly had to crawl into the Mother Superior's office. But she forced herself to stand upright as she walked into the office, and was so blinded by pain she nearly fainted. And as she entered, Gabbie gave a visible start to see that there were two priests standing beside Mother Gregoria. They had been there for nearly an hour, discussing what they were going to say to Gabriella.

When the Mother Superior looked up at her, she had never seen Gabriella look worse. She was clearly in hell now, and it took all her restraint to keep from getting up and going to her.

'Father O'Brian and Father Dimeola have come to speak to you, Sister Bernadette,' she said, using the name of her postulancy so it would seem less personal to both of them, and not hurt her quite so much as she listened to what they had to say to her. But in spite of herself, her entire heart and soul went out silently to the child she had known and loved as Gabbie.

'Mother Gregoria will decide your fate later today,' Father O'Brian said, with a look of grief in his eyes, which took in nothing of Gabbie's situation. She seemed to be gasping for air, as the room closed in around her, and with each passing second she got paler. But as far as they were concerned, whatever agonies she suffered now, she deserved them. 'But we have come to speak to you about Father Connors.' He had told them then, Gabbie thought with relief as she watched them with unseeing eyes. She was in such pain, she could barely hear them. 'He has left a letter for you,' Father Dimeola said sadly, 'explaining how he felt about the situation you lured him into.'

'Did he say that?' Gabbie looked shocked as she stared at him. Joe would never have said that about her. It was clearly their interpretation of the situation, and they had decided to blame her. She could hear a clock ticking on the wall somewhere and she wished they'd get through with it, so she could leave them.

'Father Connors did not say that precisely, but it's obvious from what he did say.'

'May I see the letter, please?' Gabbie held out a shaking hand with surprising dignity, and had they been able to admit it to her, or themselves, they admired her for it.

'In a moment,' Father O'Brian answered. 'We have something to tell you first. Something you must live with now, and understand clearly your part in it. You have condemned a man to hell, Sister Bernadette. For eternity. There will be no redemption for his soul. There cannot be, after what he's done . . . after what you brought him to. Your hell will be in knowing that you did this.' She hated the ugly sound of their words, and their cruel lack of forgiveness, for either of them. No matter what they had done, they did not deserve this, and all she could think of now was how Joe must have suffered at their hands, and she hated them for it. She only wanted to see him now, to tell him how much she loved him, and bring him comfort. They had no right to torture him, as well as condemn him.

'I want to see him,' she said in a strong voice that surprised even her. She was not going to let them do this to him. And they could not keep her from him. They no longer had a right to.

'You will never see him again,' Father O'Brian said in a voice so terrifying, Gabriella actually shuddered.

'You have no right to decide that. It is Father Connors' decision. And if that is his decision, I will respect it.' She looked beautiful and strong and dignified as she said it, and in spite of herself, Mother Gregoria loved her for it. And as pale as she was as she spoke to them, Gabriella looked almost angelic.

'You will not see him again,' Father O'Brian intoned again, and Gabriella looked immovable this time as she faced him. And then he dealt her the final blow, the only one she had in no way expected, and they meted it out to her so cruelly it nearly destroyed her faith forever. 'He took his life early this morning. He left you this letter.' Father Dimeola waved it at her menacingly as the room spun slowly around her.

'He ... I ...' She had heard the words, but she did not fully understand them. Not yet. That would come later. She looked up at them imploringly, begging them with her eyes to tell her they had lied to her. But they hadn't.

'He could not live with what he had done ... he could not face leaving the church ... or taking on what you expected of him. He took his life rather than do what you wanted. He hanged himself in his room at St. Stephen's last night, a sin for which he will burn in hell eternally. He chose to die rather than to abandon the God he loved more than he loved you, Sister Bernadette ... and you will live with this on your conscience forever.' She looked at him clearly then, and stood up with a strength she didn't know she had. She stood very still for a moment, looking at each of them with eyes that refused to believe what he had just said, and then with a small, startled sound, the life went out of her entirely, and she fainted, knowing only as she fell that Joe had abandoned her, he was gone. He had left her alone, like all the others.

But before she could say a single word to them, she had disappeared into the merciful arms of darkness. As she fell, they stared at her, and saw for the first time, the pool of blood spreading rapidly around her.

CHAPTER THIRTEEN

Gabriella was aware of a high-pitched wailing somewhere in the distance. It was an endless sound, the howling of banshees, and sounded to her like the death screams of her spirit. She tried to speak, but found that she couldn't. She tried to open her eyes, but could not see. Everything was dim and gray, alternating with silent blackness. She had no idea where she was, and did not understand that the sound she heard was the siren of the ambulance she rode in.

It seemed like years before she finally heard a voice speaking to her, but she could not decipher what it was saying. Someone kept calling her name, pulling her back from somewhere, dragging her back forcefully to a life she no longer wanted. She wanted only to drift away, toward the blackness and the silence, but the dim voices she heard sporadically would not let her.

'Gabriella! . . . Gabriella! . . . Come on! Open your eyes now . . . Gabriella!' They were shouting at her, and clawing at her, and someone with a knife was tearing her heart out. She had begun to feel the pain now. It was like a dragon fighting from within her, tearing her from top to bottom. She didn't want to wake up to this, couldn't bear what she was feeling, and beyond the pain, she knew that something terrible had happened. She opened her eyes finally, but there were lights everywhere, blinding her, searing through her

224

mercilessly, just as the pain was. People were doing something to her, but she had no idea what they were doing, only that the pain devouring her was beyond bearing. She could not even seem to breathe now. And then suddenly, as a pain so terrible it could not be borne ripped through her, she remembered why she had come here . . . her mother had beaten her . . . and broken her doll . . . she killed Meredith, and nearly killed her . . . and she knew that her father must be here somewhere, watching.

'Gabriella! . . .' They were shouting her name again, and the people around her sounded angry. All she could see was still light and dark, and no matter how hard she tried, as the demons of pain devoured her, she could not see their faces. And as she fought to see them again, and listen to what they said, a single horrifying pain seemed to tear her body apart, as she fought desperately to free herself from it. But it would not loose her from its clutches. And then suddenly, with total clarity, she saw not her father, but Joe smiling down at her. He was holding out a hand and beckoning to her, saying something she could not hear . . . the other voices seemed to drown out what he was saying. But when she looked at him again, trying to ask him where she was, he was laughing.

'I can't hear you, Joe . . .' she kept saying to him again and again. And then he started to move away, and she shouted at him to wait for her, but she found her feet would not move as she struggled to go to him. Everything about her was too heavy. He stood there, waiting for her, and then he shook his head and disappeared, and suddenly she was free and running toward him. But he was moving too fast for her, she couldn't keep up with him, and the people who were behind her now sounded very angry as they followed. They were still calling her name, and this time when she looked at them, she saw why she could not follow Joe. They had tied her down, with her legs strapped high in the air, and her body and arms strapped down, and everything around her was too bright now. 'No ... I have to go ...' she shouted weakly at them ... 'He's waiting for me ... he needs me ...' Joe turned and waved, and he looked so happy that it frightened her. But in the room where she lay, the people around her were very angry, and she knew that they were doing something terrible to her. They were ripping out everything inside her, tearing her soul away, and keeping her from him. 'No!' she kept shouting at them. 'No!' But they wouldn't listen to her.

'It's all right, Gabriella ... it's all right ...' There were women and men, and they all seemed to have knives and were stabbing her, and when Gabriella looked at them, she saw that none of them had faces.

'Her blood pressure is dropping again,' a voice said from somewhere, and she had no idea who they were talking about, and to Gabriella, it no longer mattered.

'For God's sake,' a different voice said, 'can't you stop it?' And like the others, he sounded angry at her. She had done something terrible, obviously, and they all knew what it was, but she didn't. She closed her eyes again, howling in pain this time, and in the distance she could hear the same sound she had heard before, and this time she knew it must be sirens. There had been an accident,

226

someone was hurt, and in the darkness that engulfed her again, she could hear a woman screaming. And then more people came, they seemed to be everywhere, surrounding her, but she couldn't help them. Every part of her was too heavy, except the part of her where the demons of pain were raging. She tried to move her arms, to push them away, but they were still tied down, and she didn't doubt for a moment now that they were going to kill her.

'Shit . . .' a voice in the darkness said, 'get me two more units.' They had been pumping blood into her to no avail, and it was clear to all of them now, they were not going to win this one. There was no way they could save her. Her blood pressure was almost gone, and when her heart began fibrillating, they knew they had lost her.

For a long time, the voices stopped, and Gabriella lay quietly, at peace finally. They had left her alone at last, and the demon within her was silent. Joe came back to her then, walking slowly back from the shadows, but this time he did not look happy. He said something to her, and she heard him clearly this time. Her arms were free again, and she held a hand out to him, but he wouldn't take it.

'I don't want you to come with me,' he said clearly, and he no longer seemed angry, or even sad. He looked very peaceful.

'I have to, Joe. I need you.' She began walking next to him, but he stopped and would go no farther.

'You're strong, Gabriella,' he said, and she struggled to tell him that she wasn't.

'I'm not . . . I can't . . . I won't go back without
227

you.' But he only shook his head and drifted away, as she felt a crushing weight drop down on her again, and a final searing pain that tore her away from him like a riptide. And suddenly, she knew she was drowning, just like Jimmy. She was fighting for air, and being pulled into the whirlpool with him, but when she tried to find him, she saw that she couldn't. He had abandoned her, just as Joe had, and she was alone in the roaring waters, and a force greater than any she had ever known pushed her suddenly toward the surface. She came up, gasping for air, spluttering and crying and screaming.

'Okay, we've got her . . .' She could hear the voices again, and hands seemed to pull at her from everywhere. She could feel each one of her broken ribs when she breathed, her eyes were filled with pain, they had tied her arms down again, and the place where the demons had been, burned with a white heat now.

'No! No! Stop!' She was trying to scream at them, but she couldn't, and all she knew was that they were tearing something from her. It was the place where her heart had been, and she knew they were trying to take Joe from her, but they couldn't. She had never before known such agony, and all she could think of now was her mother, wondering if she had done this to her.

'Gabriella! . . . Gabriella!' They were talking to her, more gently now, but all she could do was cry. There was no way to escape the pain they had caused her. They kept calling her name, and she felt someone stroking her hair. It was a gentle hand, but she couldn't see the face that went with it. Her eyes were still blurred, and the lights shining

228

on her blinded her, but someone had begun to pull the demon from her.

'Christ, that was a close one,' a man's voice somewhere in the room said softly. 'I thought we'd lost her.' They had for a while, more than once. But she was still alive, in spite of all her efforts to leave them. She had stayed because of Joe. It was Joe who had refused to take her with him. She knew, as she opened her eyes again, that he was not coming back again. They never did. They all went away and left her.

'Gabriella, how do you feel now?' She could see a woman's eyes as the voice talked to her, but they still had no faces. They all wore masks, but their voices were gentler. And when Gabriella tried to answer her, she found that she still couldn't. No sound came from where the screams had been. Every part of her body and her soul seemed empty.

'She's not hearing me,' the voice complained, as though, once again, she had failed them, and she wondered if now they would beat her. It didn't matter to her, they could do anything they wanted, as long as the demons did not come back again with their knife-sharp tails that cut through her soul like rapiers.

They left her alone then for a while, and she drifted off, but to a different place than she had been, and when she woke, there was a mask on her face. It smelled terrible, and she was very drowsy. And then, without saying anything to her, they rolled her away, and she saw people and hallways and doors drifting past her, and someone told her they were taking her to her room now. She wondered if she was in jail, if they were going to punish her finally for the terrible things she had done to all of them. They knew, they all did, that she was guilty. But no one said anything to her as they wheeled her into a room, and left her there, dozing on the gurney.

Two women in white walked into the room finally, wearing starched caps and somber faces, and without saying a word to her, they lifted her carefully from the gurney to the bed, and adjusted the IV that was still giving her a transfusion. They said very little to her, and left her to sleep for the rest of the day. Gabriella still didn't know why she was here, though she still remembered the sound of the woman she had heard screaming. It had been a wail of agony, a keening of pain, and sorrow. And later, when the doctor came in to talk to her, she cried again, but this time she understood what had happened. She had lost Joe's baby.

'I'm very sorry,' the doctor said solemnly. He did not know she was a postulant, but he assumed because of the convent where she lived that she was an unwed mother, and had been placed there by her parents. 'There will be other children one day,' he said optimistically. But Gabriella knew better than he did, that there wouldn't. She had never wanted children because she was too afraid that she would become a monster like her mother. She would never have risked it. But with Joe at her side, she thought it might have been different. It had been a chance for another life, with a man she loved, and the child born of their love for each other. It had been a dream she had cherished all too briefly and didn't deserve, and now it had become a nightmare without him.

'You'll have to be very careful for a while,' the

doctor admonished her. 'You've lost a lot of blood, and,' he added ominously, 'we almost lost you. If you'd come in here twenty minutes later, we would have.' Her heart had stopped beating twice in the delivery room, and it was the worst miscarriage he'd ever seen. She had lost more than enough blood to kill her.

'We're going to keep you here for a few days, just to watch you, and to keep up the transfusions. You can go home after that, as long as you promise me you'll rest and take it very easy. No running around, no parties, no visits, no dancing.' He smiled at her, imagining a life different than any she had ever known, but she was young and beautiful and he assumed she would be anxious to get out and see her friends again, and probably the man who had gotten her pregnant. Then he asked her if she wanted him to call anyone for her, and Gabriella looked up at him with grief-stricken horror.

'My husband died yesterday,' she said in a hoarse whisper, endowing Joe posthumously with the role she had wished for him, and the doctor looked at her with wisdom and compassion.

'I'm very sorry.' It was a double blow for her, he knew, and explained something to him. For most of the surgery and delivery he had had the odd feeling that she was fighting them and didn't want to make it, and now he knew that for certain. She had wanted to die and be with the man she called her husband, although he still doubted they'd been married. If they had been, she would never have come to them from St. Matthew's. 'Try and rest now.' It was all he had to offer her, and after a few more minutes of observing her, he left her. She was a pretty girl, she was young and had a long life ahead of her. She had survived this, and would survive other things. It would all be a dim memory one day, he knew, but for now she looked and felt as though her world had ended.

And in Gabriella's eyes, it had. She was absolutely convinced she had nothing left to live for. She didn't want to live without him. And as she lay there, she thought about him constantly, and the journal she had written to him, the time they had shared, the talks, the confidences, the whispered laughter, the walks in Central Park, the stolen moments, and the brief hours of passion in the borrowed apartment. She couldn't even remember where it was now, and as she lay there, thinking of him, she struggled to remember every word, every inflection, every moment. And then each time, she came to the end of it, the two priests sitting with Mother Gregoria only that morning and telling her that he had taken his life, and she would live with it on her conscience forever. And now she believed that it was her fault. She remembered seeing him that morning, in her dreams, while they were working on her, and knew that she had almost gone to join him, and hated the fact that she hadn't. She would have done anything to be with him. And she tried to bring him back now as she dozed fitfully, but he would not come to her. She could not bring him to mind again, or make him seem real. He had left her, like the others. And all she could think of now was what he must have felt before he died, the agony that had brought him to a decision like that, the sorrow and pain he must have felt. It reminded her of his mother. She had made the same decision seventeen years before, and left her son an orphan. But this time, Joe left no one, except her, all alone now. She didn't even have their baby. She had nothing. Except sorrow.

Mother Gregoria came to see her that night. She had spoken to the doctor twice that afternoon and was well aware of how close Gabriella had come to dying. He mentioned what Gabriella herself had said, about the father of the child dying the day before, and he said he felt very sorry for her. And although she didn't say so, so did Mother Gregoria when she saw her. Gabriella looked deathly pale, her cheeks were as white as the sheets where she lay, and her lips seemed bluish and almost transparent. It was easy to believe they had barely been able to save her. She had had yet another transfusion by then, but so far, they seemed to have made no difference. She had hemorrhaged so violently, the doctor had told Mother Gregoria that it could take her months to recover. And for the Mother Superior, that posed a serious problem.

She sat next to Gabbie's bed for a while, and said very little to her. Gabbie was almost too weak to speak, and everything she tried to say made her cry, and cost her an enormous effort.

'Don't talk, my child,' Mother Gregoria said finally. She just sat there, holding her hand, and was grateful when Gabriella drifted off to sleep again. And it made the Mother Superior shudder to see that she looked dead as she lay there.

News of Father Connors' death had already reached the convent that morning. There had been frantic whispers all day, and Mother Gregoria had made a solemn announcement in the dining hall at dinner. She said only that the young priest had died unexpectedly, there would be no services for him, and his remains were being cremated and returned for burial with his family in Ohio. It had been the archbishop's decision.

Joe's own mother, having committed suicide, was not buried in a Catholic cemetery, and Archbishop Flaherty's decision seemed to be the humane one. He had to be disposed of somehow. And no further explanation was being offered, but the nuns themselves knew that the fact that he was being cremated was suspicious. It was forbidden by the Catholic Church, and only a special dispensation would have made it possible for him to be cremated. As Mother Gregoria asked for a moment of silent prayer for the peace of his soul, their eyes were filled with questions. And later, when she looked around the room at them, she could see that Sister Anne had been crying.

It was several hours later when Sister Anne appeared at the door of the Mother Superior's office, looking stricken. As she waved to her to come in, the Mother Superior asked, 'Is something wrong?'

At first the young nun said nothing, and then she came in and sat down at Mother Gregoria's invitation, and burst instantly into tears. 'It's all my fault,' she wailed. She knew that something terrible must have happened, and she was filled with remorse now.

'I'm equally certain that you had nothing to do with it,' Mother Gregoria said calmly. 'Father Connors' death is a shock to us all, but it has nothing to do with you, Sister Anne. The circumstances are rather complicated, and he apparently had a health problem none of us were aware of.'

'One of the altar boys told the man at the grocery store that he hanged himself,' she sobbed openly, having heard the horror story third-hand from the mailman, who stopped at the grocery store to buy a soda before he delivered the mail at St. Matthew's. And Mother Gregoria was not pleased to know that.

'I can assure you, Sister, that's nonsense.'

'And where is Gabriella? Sister Eugenia said she was taken away in an ambulance and no one knows why. Where is she?'

'She's very well. She had an attack of appendicitis last night, and came to tell me about it early this morning.' But Sister Anne had seen the somber-faced priests from St. Stephen's leaving Mother Gregoria's office. The convent was a small community, an enclosed world, and like others of its kind, even here in the arms of God, it was filled with gossip and rumors. And there had certainly been plenty of them that morning, but Mother Gregoria was far from happy to hear it. All she wanted to do now was reassure the young postulant who felt so guilty.

'I wrote you an anonymous letter,' she confessed haltingly, sobbing between words, 'about them, because I thought she was flirting with him. . . . Oh, Mother . . . I was jealous. . . I didn't want her to have what I lost before I came here . . .'

'That was wrong of you, my child,' Mother Gregoria said calmly, remembering the letter only too well, and the concern it caused her. 'But the letter was harmless. I paid no attention to it at the time, and your fears were groundless. They were merely good friends, and they only admired each

235

other in the life in Christ they shared. None of us here need to involve ourselves in the worries of the world. We are free of them. And now you must forget all this, and go back to your Sisters.' She comforted the girl for a while, and sent her back to Sister Emanuel with a little note, urging her to come to the Mother Superior's office as soon as the postulants were in bed. She sent the same to Sister Immaculata, and spoke to the others herself to come to a meeting that night after they had completed their duties.

There were twelve faces looking at her expectantly across her desk at ten o'clock that night, and she urged each of them to quell the rumors that were flying. It was a time of great grief for all of them, particularly the priests at St. Stephen's, but she felt that it was their responsibility as well to protect the others in the community from them. It served no purpose to seek further information about the details, or fan the flames of a potential scandal. On the contrary, they had every reason to want to silence the whispers of the devil. She was firm, and hard, and very powerful in what she said, and when they asked about Gabriella's whereabouts, she told them nothing more than what she had told Sister Anne. She had had an attack of appendicitis and would be back in a few days when she was better.

'But are the rumors true then, Mother? Is it true what they are saying?' Sister Mary Margaret was the oldest nun in the convent, and had no hesitation in questioning her superior, who was far younger. 'They say that she and Father Connors were in love with each other.' But not, Mother Gregoria silently thanked God for small indulgences, that she was pregnant. 'Is that possible? Did he kill himself? The novices were all buzzing with it this morning.'

'And we won't be, Sister Mary Margaret,' Mother Gregoria said sternly. 'There are circumstances surrounding Father Connors' death of which I am not aware, nor do I wish to be, nor do I wish you to worry about it any further. He is in the hands of God, where we will all be one day. We must pray for his soul, and not to discover the details of how he got there. I am certain that whatever happened between him and Sister Bernadette was entirely without merit. They were both young, intelligent, and innocent. If they were drawn to each other in any way, I'm sure that neither of them was aware of it. And I do not wish to hear any more about it. Is that clear, Sisters? All of you? The rumors are over. And to be certain that my wishes on this subject are carried out, and those of the Fathers at St. Stephen's, the convent will maintain silence for the next seven days. There is to be no conversation whatsoever, not a word spoken among any of us, as of the moment we rise tomorrow morning. And when we speak again, let it be on hallowed subjects.'

'Yes, Mother,' they said in unison, mollified by the force with which she said it. But this was more than just a directive from the Mother Superior. She could not bear to hear the things they were saying about Gabriella. She still loved her far too much to hear her name linked with the scandal that had caused a young priest to take his life. And she was grateful that no one had discovered she'd been pregnant. Fortunately, the priests who had seen her collapse were as anxious to keep the matter quiet as she was. But they had also agreed on the inevitable resolution before leaving Mother Gregoria that morning. Gabriella's rapid departure in the ambulance had made a huge impression on them all, and it was nothing short of miraculous that almost no one had seen what had really happened. The story of her appendectomy seemed to cover the situation for the moment.

Mother Gregoria dismissed the other nuns summarily, and remained in her office briefly after they left, and then went to the church and fell on her knees, praying to the Blessed Virgin to help her, as she slowly gave way to the wracking sobs that had been begging to be released since morning. She couldn't bear what had happened to them, couldn't bear losing Gabriella, couldn't stand what might happen to her in a cruel world that had so badly ravaged her before, and which she was in no way prepared for. If only they had listened to the wisdom in their hearts, if only they had stopped before it was too late ... but they were both so young, and so innocent ... and so unaware of the risks they were taking. She knelt in prayer, thinking of the child Gabriella had been when she came to them. She prayed for Joe Connors' soul as well, knowing only too well how tortured he must have been the night he died, and how bereft Gabriella must feel now. And she was sure, as she prayed for both of them, that there could be no hell for either of them worse than that one.

CHAPTER FOURTEEN

Mother Gregoria did not go to see Gabriella in the hospital again, but she called frequently to see how she was, and was encouraged by the reports from the nurses. They had stopped giving her transfusions finally. They had given her all they could, without risking an adverse reaction, and now her body had to repair itself, in time. But Mother Gregoria knew only too well that the body would heal faster than the heart would.

She was grateful, too, that the ambulance had taken her to a city hospital, and not to Mercy. Had she been there, it would truly have been impossible to quell the rumors. The story of her emergency appendectomy had spread quickly the night before, and now with silence imposed on all of them, they could not discuss it further. But Mother Gregoria knew she still had to deal with Gabriella. She had met with the priests from St. Stephen's again, and the archbishop came to see her the next morning. They had come to a difficult decision, but Mother Gregoria knew that there was no other way to handle what had happened. To bring her back into their midst again would be to plant a seed with a fatal flaw in it in a holy garden. Or at least that was what they told her.

She argued with them at first, begging for mercy for her, yet she knew herself that had it been any other girl than the child she loved, she would have come to the same conclusion as they had. It was obvious that Gabriella wasn't in a proper state to rejoin the Order, and maybe she never would be. Perhaps one day, in another place, another time, they said . . . but for now . . . Archbishop Flaherty was immovable in the conclusion he'd come to. And now it remained for Mother Gregoria to tell her.

She sent one of the Sisters to the hospital for her the morning she was released, and reminded her once again before she went of her vow of silence, and that they were not to engage in conversation. And as soon as they returned, Gabriella was to come to the Mother Superior's office. There was no doubt in her mind that the Sister she sent would follow her orders.

But she was in no way prepared for how Gabriella looked when she returned. She was so deathly pale, and appeared so frightened, that she looked like an apparition. She sat uncomfortably in the stiff chair where she had sat the morning they had told her that Joe Connors had hanged himself in his room at St. Stephen's. The morning she had nearly died, and still wished she could have. Her eyes met the Mother Superior's now, and there was something broken and empty in them.

'How are you, my child?' But she didn't need to ask the question. It was easy to see how she was. She was dead inside, as dead as Joe Connors, and their baby.

'I'm all right, Mother. I'm sorry for all the trouble I caused you.' Her voice sounded weak, and she looked frail, and the black coif she wore with her postulant's dress made her look even more somber. But *trouble* seemed a small word for the two lives that had been lost, and the one remaining that had been ruined.

'I know you must be.' And she meant it, she knew that Gabriella must be torturing herself, but no one could help her. She had to find her own

240

peace, and eventually, forgiveness. And Mother Gregoria knew it would not come easily to her, if ever.

'I am entirely responsible for Father Connors' death, Mother. I understand that,' she said, as her lips quivered and her chin trembled. She could barely finish the sentence. 'I will do penance for it for the rest of my life.'

For a moment, the Mother Superior stepped aside, and Gabriella glimpsed the woman. 'You must remember one thing, my child. His mother did the same thing at an early age. It's a very wrong thing to do, not only in the eyes of God, but to the people one leaves behind. Whatever your part in this, there was something in him, more powerful than he was, that allowed him to do it.' It was her own way of giving Gabriella absolution, of reminding her that perhaps some fatal flaw in him had led him to do it. And in Mother Gregoria's eyes, it was a terrible sign of weakness. 'You are very strong,' she said, fighting for composure herself, 'and whatever life metes out to you, whatever it is, I want you to remember that you are equal to it. God will not give you more than you can handle. And when you think you can bear no more, you must remember that you will survive it. You *must* know that.' It was a message delivered from the heart, but one that Gabriella could bear no longer. They all told her how strong she was. It was always the sign they gave just before they hurt her.

'I'm not strong,' Gabriella said in a broken whisper. 'I'm not. Why do people say I am? . . . Don't they know I'm not?' Tears swam in her eyes as she said it.

241

'You have more strength than you know, and much more courage. One day you will know that. These people who have hurt you, Gabriella, are the weak ones. They are the ones who cannot face it.' Like Joe, and her father, and her mother. 'But you can.'

Gabriella didn't want to hear it, nor did she want to hear what Mother Gregoria was about to say to her, almost as much as the Mother Superior didn't want to say it. 'I'm afraid I have some difficult news for you.' It was going to be quick and hard and cruel, but Mother Gregoria had no choice now, and she could not question their wisdom, no matter how much she questioned their mercy. But hers was a life of obedience, and she could not break her vows now, even for Gabriella. 'The archbishop has decided that you must leave us. Whatever happened between you and . . . Father Connors,' the older woman felt as though she were fighting for air, but she knew she could not turn back now, despite Gabriella's sudden look of horror. 'Whatever happened, or didn't, there is a crack now in the walls we built around you. It will never be the same again, it will never be repaired. The crack will only grow wider. And perhaps what you did, what you shared with him, is a sign that you did not belong here. Perhaps we pushed you to it, perhaps you stayed here out of fear, my child—'

'No, Mother, no!' Gabriella was quick to interrupt her. 'I love it here, I always have. I want to stay here!' Her voice had risen alarmingly, she was fighting for her life now. But Mother Gregoria forced herself to stay calm and to go on talking. They had to reach the end of the road now, and she wanted to do it quickly.

'You cannot stay here, my child. The doors of St. Matthew's are closed to you forever. Not our hearts, or our souls. I will pray for you until the day I die. But you must go now. You will go to the robing room after you leave here, and change your clothes. You will be given two dresses, and the shoes you are wearing. The archbishop is allowing us to give you a hundred dollars,' and her voice trembled alarmingly as she said it, but she steeled herself to go on, remembering the day Gabriella had come here, with eyes filled with terror. Mother Gregoria saw the same look in her eyes now, but she could no longer help her, only love her. 'And I am giving you four hundred dollars of my own. You must find a place to live, and a job. There are many things you can do. God has given you intelligence and a good heart, and He will protect you. And you have a tremendous gift in your writing. You must use it well, and perhaps one day you will bring great pleasure to others. But you must take care of yourself now. Make wise decisions, keep yourself out of harm's way, and know that wherever you go, my child, you take our prayers with you. What you did was wrong, Gabriella, very wrong, but you have paid a high price for it. You must forgive yourself now,' she said in barely more than a whisper, holding a hand out to her to touch the girl she loved so much for the last time now. 'You must forgive yourself, my child . . . as I do . . .'

Gabriella put her head down on the desk and sobbed, clutching the old nun's hand, unable to believe that she had to leave her. This was the only real home she had ever known, the only real mother she'd ever had, the only place where she had found safety. But she had betrayed them, she had broken their trust ultimately, and now, the apple having been eaten to the core, the snake had won, and she had to leave the Garden of Eden.

'I can't leave you,' she sobbed, begging for mercy.

'You must. We have no choice now. It is only fair to the others. You cannot live among them as you did before, after all that has happened.'

'I swear I'll never tell them.'

'But they know. In their hearts, they all know that something terrible has happened, no matter how we try to protect them from it. And if you stayed, it would never be the same for you again, you would always feel that you had betrayed them, and one day you would hate them and yourself for it.'

'I already hate myself,' she said, choking back sobs. She had killed the only man she'd ever loved, and lost his baby. And now she had to lose all the rest. Mother Gregoria was forcing her to leave, and the realization of all she had lost and was about to lose again, filled her with a terror so uncontrollable, she wanted it to kill her. But the worst fear of all was that it wouldn't.

'Gabriella,' Mother Gregoria said quietly, rising to her feet as she had the first time they met. It was a terrible day for both of them, as she looked down at Gabriella now, shaking visibly as she stood there. 'You must go now.' Gabbie was stunned into silence as Mother Gregoria handed her an envelope with the money she had promised her, most of it from the small bank account she kept, with small gifts sent to her by her own brothers and sisters. And with it, she handed Gabriella the slim journal she had kept for Joe. They had found it

244

under her pillow, but the young nun who had found it suspected what it was and hadn't read it. Gabriella recognized it instantly and her hand shook as she took it from her.

The two women stood looking at each other for a long moment, and Gabriella's sobs filled the air as she reached out to her, and Mother Gregoria took her in her arms, just as she had when her mother left her.

'I will always love you,' she said to the child she had been, and the woman she would become when she reached the other side of the mountains life had put before her. Mother Gregoria had no doubt that she would arrive safely on the other side, but she knew that she had a long journey ahead of her, and the road would be far from easy.

'I love you so much... I can't leave you...' Gabriella sounded like a child again as she clung to her, feeling the stiff wool of the habit against her cheek, knowing her own was about to be taken from her.

'You will always have me with you. I will be praying for you.' And then, without another word, she walked Gabriella to the door and opened it, and signaled to the nun waiting outside to take her to the robing room where she would change her habit and be given two ugly, ill-fitting dresses left there by someone else, and a battered suitcase. The rest of what she needed, whatever it was, she would have to purchase with the money they gave her.

Gabriella stepped out into the corridor on trembling legs, and turned to look at Mother Gregoria for one last time, as tears ran down her cheeks in rivers. 'I love you,' she said softly.

'Go with God,' Mother Gregoria said, and then

245

turned slowly around and walked back into her office without looking back, and closed the door gently behind her. Gabriella stood staring at it in disbelief. It was like watching the door of someone's heart close, except that on the other side, the old nun had buried her face in her hands and was silently sobbing. But Gabriella would never know that.

She followed the nun to the robing room silently, both of them still bound by the silence Mother Gregoria had imposed on them. And the young nun pointed to the two dresses that had been left for Gabriella, one an ugly navy blue floral print polyester that was two sizes too large for her, particularly after last week, and an even uglier shiny black one that had stains down the front that hadn't come out no matter how often the Sisters washed it. But it fit Gabriella better than the first one, and the somber color suited her circumstances. She was in deep mourning for Joe, and she exchanged one black dress for the other, and slowly took off her coif, remembering the many times she had done it for him, and left it in the car when they went for walks in the park, or to the borrowed apartment. This was the price she had to pay now. She had lost the coif, and all it represented to her, forever, and all the people who went with it.

She stood in front of the nun who had been assigned to assist her with her departure, and their eyes met and held, and without a sound they embraced as tears ran down their cheeks in silence. It was a sad day for both of them, and the one remaining knew she would never be able to tell anyone what she'd seen, or the sorrow she had seen so clearly on Gabriella's face as she left them. It was a lesson to all of them. She was being cast into the world, alone, with nothing, and no one to help her.

Gabriella put the money, the journal, and the blue flowered dress carefully into the cardboard suitcase, and then left the robing room behind the woman who for twelve years had been her sister and would soon be swept away by the tides that had overtaken Gabriella.

They reached the front door in the main hall all too quickly. She stood there for a moment, and the elderly nun in charge of letting people in and out came forward and opened the door very slowly, and for a long, silent moment, the three of them stood there. The old nun nodded then, showing Gabbie the way out, and with a single, trembling step, Gabriella stepped across the threshold. This was nothing like the days she had hurried out to meet Joe, pretending to do their errands. This was a single step into darkness. And as she stood in the bright sunshine outside, she turned and looked at them, and as their eyes met, the old nun closed the door, and she was lost to them forever.

CHAPTER FIFTEEN

Gabriella stood outside the convent door, staring at it, for what seemed like an eternity, and she had no idea where to go, or what to do now. All she could think of was all that she had lost in the past four days, a man, a life, and a baby. The enormity of it was so overwhelming, she felt as though she were reeling.

And then, she picked up her suitcase, and slowly walked away. She knew she had to go somewhere, find a room, and a job, but she had no idea where to go or how to do it. And as she looked at the buses passing by, she suddenly remembered some of the girls she'd gone to school with at Columbia. Some of them lived in boarding houses and small hotels. She tried to remember where they were. Most of them were on the Upper West Side, but she had never really paid any attention.

She still felt numb as she got on a bus and headed uptown, with no particular sense of where she was going. And for a crazed moment, she thought about trying to find her father in Boston. When she got off the bus on Eighty-sixth and Third, she walked into a phone booth and called Boston information. They had no listing for a John Harrison, and she didn't know where he worked, or even if he was alive by then, let alone if he wanted to hear from her. It had been thirteen years since she had last seen him. She was twenty-two years old, and she was starting her life as though she were a baby. And as she came out of the phone booth outside a coffee shop, she suddenly felt very dizzy, and realized she hadn't eaten since breakfast that morning. But she wasn't hungry.

People were hurrying past, and there were children in strollers being pushed along by their mothers. Everyone seemed to be going somewhere, and Gabriella was the only one with no direction and no purpose. She felt like a rock sitting in the river, as the currents and everything they carried with them rushed past her. She walked into the coffee shop for a cup of tea finally, and as she sat

248

there staring into it, all she could think of was what Mother Gregoria had said to her when she left her. She wondered why everyone told her how strong she was. It was a death knell, she knew now, a sign that the people she loved were about to leave her. They were preparing her to be strong, because she would have to be, without them.

And as she finished her tea, she picked up a discarded newspaper. She needed to find a place to stay, and glanced down a list of small hotels and boardinghouses, and she noticed that there was a boardinghouse not far away, on East Eighty-eighth Street, near the East River. She didn't know the neighborhood, but it was a start. But without a job, she wasn't even sure she could afford it.

She paid for her tea, and walked slowly back into the sunshine. She still felt dead inside, and the tea had only slightly warmed her. She had been icy cold for days, after all the blood she had lost, and even the hot drink hadn't really helped her. She was still deathly pale, and her whole body ached as she walked east down the long blocks toward the East River, wondering how much a room would cost her. She knew she couldn't survive long on five hundred dollars, or at least she didn't think so. She had never had to take care of her own needs. She didn't know what anything cost, not food or restaurants or rooms or clothes. She had no idea what she could do, or how to manage her money, but she was grateful for what Mother Gregoria had given her. Without it, she knew her situation would have been even more desperate.

She walked past it the first time, missing the small sign. It was a tired old brownstone with a chipping facade, and all the sign said was ROOMS

249

FOR RENT in a dust-streaked window. Nothing about the place looked very inviting. And when she walked into the downstairs hall, it was clean but shabby and smelled of cooking. It was as far removed as anything could be from the stark, immaculate precision and order of St. Matthew's convent.

'Yes?' A woman with a heavy accent poked her head into the dark hallway when she heard Gabriella's footsteps. She had watched her come in, from her window, and wondered what she wanted. 'What do you want?'

'I . . . ah . . . are there rooms to rent? I saw the sign . . . and the ad in the paper.'

'There might be.' Gabriella recognized the accent as Czechoslovak or Polish. She still remembered the accents of the people who had come to her parents' parties, although this woman was very different. And she was looking Gabriella over. She didn't want any druggies or prostitutes, and Gabriella looked younger than she was. The woman didn't want any runaways or trouble with the police either. She ran a respectable house, and she liked old people a lot better. They got their social security checks and they paid their rent, and they didn't make a lot of noise, or give her a lot of trouble, except if they got sick, or died. She didn't want people cooking in their rooms either, and young people were always doing things they shouldn't. Smoking, eating, drinking, cooking in their rooms, bringing people in at all hours, making too much noise. They never followed the rules, or held down proper jobs. And the landlady didn't want any headaches.

'Do you have a job?' the mistress of the
250

boardinghouse asked, looking worried. Without a job, Gabriella couldn't pay her rent, and that would be a problem.

'No . . . not yet . . .' Gabriella said apologetically. 'I'm looking for one.' She didn't want to lie to her and pretend she had one.

'Yeah, well, come back when you get one.' This was no rich girl with a trust fund, or parents on Park Avenue who were going to pay her rent for her. But then again, if she had been, she wouldn't have been there. 'Where you from?' Gabriella could see the landlady was suspicious of her, and she didn't really blame her.

Gabriella hesitated for an instant, wondering how she could explain the fact that she didn't have a job and had nowhere to live. It sounded, even to her, as though she'd just gotten out of jail, and she could see that the woman wasn't impressed with her. And the ugly black dress with the stains down the front didn't exactly improve her image. 'I'm from Boston,' she settled on, thinking of the father she'd been unable to find that day, 'I just moved here.' The woman nodded. It was a believable story.

'What kind of work do you do?'

'Anything I can get,' she said honestly. 'I'm going to start looking tomorrow.'

'There's a lot of restaurants on Second Avenue, and all the German ones on Eighty-sixth Street. You might find something there.' She felt sorry for her. Gabriella looked tired and pale, and the landlady thought she didn't look healthy. But she didn't look like a druggie. She seemed very clean, and very proper. Mrs. Boslicki finally relented. 'I got a small room on the top floor, if you want to

251

take a look. Nothing fancy. You share a bathroom with three others.'

'How much is it?' Gabriella looked worried as she thought of her small budget.

'Three hundred a month, no food included. And you can't do no cooking. No hot plates, no double burners, no crock pots. You go out for dinner, or you bring home a sandwich or a pizza.'

It didn't look like a problem. Gabriella looked like she'd never eaten. She was rail thin, and her eyes were so huge in her thin face, it made the landlady think she was starving. 'You want to see it?'

'Thank you, I'd like that.' She was extremely polite and well spoken, and Mrs. Boslicki liked that. She didn't want any smart-aleck kids in her house. She had been renting rooms for twenty years, ever since her husband died, and she'd never had any hippies either.

Gabriella followed her upstairs while Mrs. Boslicki asked her if she liked cats. She had nine of them, which explained the smell in the downstairs hall, but Gabriella assured her she loved them. There had been one who sat with her sometimes while she did her gardening in St. Matthew's garden. And by the time they reached the top floor, the slightly overweight Mrs. Boslicki was breathless, but it was Gabriella who looked as though she might not make it. The room was on the fourth floor, and Gabriella wasn't up to that yet. The doctor had particularly told her to avoid stairs and too much exercise, or carrying anything heavy, or she might start bleeding, and she couldn't afford to lose another drop of blood after all she'd been through.

'You all right?' She saw that Gabriella was even paler than she'd been downstairs, she was almost a luminous green, and she was moving very slowly.

'I haven't been well,' Gabriella explained wanly as the old woman in the flowered housedress nodded. She was wearing carpet slippers, and her hair was neatly done in a small knot. And there was something comfortable and cozy about her, like a grandma.

'You gotta be careful with some of the flus around these days. They turn into pneumonia before you know it. You been coughing?' She didn't want any boarders with TB, either.

'No, I'm fine now,' Gabriella reassured her, as Mrs. Boslicki opened the door to the room she was willing to show her. It was small and dreary and barely big enough for the narrow single bed, the straight-back chair, and the single dresser with the hand-crocheted doily on it. She had rented it for years to an old woman from Warsaw, who had died the previous summer, and she hadn't been able to rent it since then. And even she knew that three hundred a month was a stiff price for it. The window shades were worn and the curtains were old and a little tattered, and the carpet was nearly threadbare. She saw Gabriella's face, who had been used to the spartan cells at St. Matthew's, but somehow they hadn't been quite this depressing. And for the first time, Mrs. Boslicki looked a little worried.

'I could let you have it for two-fifty,' she said, proud of her generosity. But she wanted the room rented, she needed the money.

'I'll take it,' Gabriella said without hesitation. It was grim, but she had nowhere else to go, and she was afraid to lose this one. And she was so exhausted just from coming up the stairs that she wanted it just so she could lie down for a while. She needed a place to sleep tonight, but thinking of this as her new home almost reduced her to tears as she handed the woman half of Mother Gregoria's money.

'I'll give you sheets and a set of towels. You do your own laundry. There's a Laundromat down the street, and a lot of restaurants. Most people eat in the coffee shop on the corner.' Gabriella remembered walking by it and she hoped it wasn't too expensive. She only had two hundred and fifty dollars left now, but at least she had a roof over her head for the next month.

They walked down the hall then, and Mrs. Boslicki showed her the small bathroom. It had a tub with a shower over it, and a pink plastic shower curtain. There was a small sink, and a toilet, and a mirror hanging from a nail. It wasn't pretty, but it was all she needed. 'Keep it clean for the others. I clean it once a week, the rest of the time you do it yourselves. There's a living room downstairs. You can sit there anytime. It's got a TV,' and then she smiled a little grandly, 'and a piano. You play?'

'No, I'm sorry,' Gabriella apologized. She remembered that her mother did, but they had never wasted lessons on her, and at the convent she did other things, like work in the garden. She had never had any talent for music, and some of the nuns had teased her about her singing. She loved it, but she sang too loud and a little off-key.

'You get yourself a job now, so you can stay here. You're a nice girl, and I like you,' Mrs. Boslicki said warmly. She had decided that Gabriella was all right after all. She had good manners and was very polite, and she didn't look like she was going to be a lot of trouble. 'You gotta take care of yourself though. You look like you been sick. You gotta eat right and get healthy.' She bustled down the stairs then, and promised to come back later with some towels, and Gabriella said she'd stop in to pick them up herself to spare her the stairs and the trouble. Mrs. Boslicki waved as she disappeared, still clutching Gabriella's money.

Gabriella walked into the small room again, and looked around. She sat on the uncomfortable chair, and wondered if there was anything she could do to cheer the place up. She could buy a few things when she made some money, but not for the moment. A new bedspread, some prints on the wall, some fresh flowers would work wonders.

With a small sigh, Gabriella set her small suitcase down in the closet, and hung up her other dress. There was something else in her valise, her journal to Joe, which she left in the suitcase without looking at it. And it made her sadder now to realize that he had never seen it. She took it out, finally, unable to resist it, and sat down on the bed and opened the little book. It was filled with her notes about their meetings, and her love for him. It was brimming with all the excitement of first love, and the exquisite terror of their first clandestine meetings . . . and then further on, the passion she had found in his arms in the apartment. It was all there, right up to the end, talking about the life they would share, and at the very end it talked about the hopes that she had for their baby. And as she read the last entry, a letter fell out on the bed next to her, and she realized that she had never seen it. The envelope said 'Sister Bernadette' in an unfamiliar hand, and then she realized with a start it was Joe's writing, and she trembled as she opened it. It took a minute to understand what it was. It was his suicide note, the last thing he had written to her before he died by his own hand. Father O'Brian had left it with Mother Gregoria and she had slipped it quietly into the journal before she gave it to Gabbie. But Mother Gregoria hadn't warned Gabriella that it was there, and she touched it now with tears in her eyes as she read it. It was so strange that he had touched this paper only days before, that he had held it in his hand, that it was the only thing she had left of him. Just these words, carefully written on two sheets of white paper.

'Gabbie,' he began, the 'Sister Bernadette' on the envelope had only been so that the letter would find her, and ultimately expose all their secrets. Without that, they might never have known, and she might still be at St. Matthew's. But that was done now, and there was nothing left to do but live with it. She couldn't go back now.

'I don't know what to say, or where to begin. You are so much better and more wonderful, and stronger than I am. All my life I have known how weak I am, what my failings are, how many people I have disappointed ... my parents when Jimmy died, because I could not save him.' No matter that his brother had been two years older and far stronger, it was the younger brother who blamed himself for the heroic miracle he had been unable to accomplish, and perhaps they had silently blamed him, and if they had, she hated them for it. 'I have disappointed everyone, people who knew me and loved me and counted on me. It is, ultimately, why I came to the priesthood. If I had not been such a disappointment to them.' He was talking about his parents again, and knowing him as she did, she understood that. Reading the letter was like listening to him, and it tore her at the heart now. She wanted to tell him how wrong he was, to convince him to stay . . . If only she had been there that night . . . if he had told her what he was thinking when she last saw him . . .

'Maybe if I hadn't been such a disappointment to them,' he went on, 'or made a difference in their lives, my mother wouldn't have done what she did when my father died. She would have known that I would be there to help her. But she didn't. She preferred to die than live without him.

'But when I went to St. Mark's, they gave me everything I'd never had, all the love, all the chances, all the understanding I needed. They had so much faith in me, they forgave me everything, and I know how much they loved me, just as I know how much I love you now, and you me. These have been the only certainties in my life, the blessings I cling to, even now, in my darkest hours.

'I went into the priesthood for them, for the Brothers at St. Mark's, because I knew it was the greatest joy I could give them. It was the only thing they wanted of me, and I gave them my whole heart and my life. I thought that maybe if I did, if I did something right for a change, it would make up for my mother and Jimmy, and maybe God would forgive me.

'It was right for me for a long time. I've been happy here, Gabbie. I felt good about doing the right thing. I liked the idea that I had traded my

257

life for theirs ... until I met you, and I knew just how badly I wanted my life back. I had never known real happiness, or real love, until I met you, never knew what life could be like. All I could think of from the first moment I met you was being a husband and lover to you. All I wanted was to be with you, and give you everything I had, of myself, of my life, of my soul. But my soul and my life were no longer mine to give you.

'I have tried every way I could to imagine being with you, living with you, marrying you, being all that you deserve in life. But I know that if I did, I would only disappoint you. I don't know how to give you all that you deserve, and I cannot go back on a promise. I cannot now take my life back from God because I have found someone I love more, or want to be with more than I want to serve Him. I cannot do that to the Brothers at St. Mark's, or my fellow priests here at St. Stephen's. I traded my life for Jimmy's and Mom's, for failing them, and now if I take it back again, I will only fail you and myself and those I have already given my soul to. You will always have my heart, I will always love you, always be with you. I could not bear to live without you, nor to disappoint them all yet again. I cannot leave them now and prove to them how worthless I am. We would never have a decent life together if I did that. I know now that whatever it costs me, I must stay here. The deal was made a long time ago, and the things I have promised you were not mine to give you. But I also know now with every ounce of my heart and soul, that I cannot live without you. I cannot bear to be here another day, knowing that you are nearby and I can't be with you. Gabbie, I cannot live without you.

'I am going now, to Jimmy and Mom. It's time for me. I've done what I can here. I've done a little good for some people in my years in the priesthood. But how could I face them now, knowing how little I care about them, and how much I love you? I cannot be anywhere but with you, or nowhere at all. I cannot live up to the promises I made, neither to you, nor to them. I can't leave here, and can't leave you. I am torn apart, and as bad as I've been, how can I ever be a decent father to our baby?

'Gabbie, you're very strong,' the hateful words again, she winced through her tears as she read them, 'you're so much stronger than I am. You'll be a wonderful mother to our baby. And I will be much happier watching both of you from heaven, if I ever get there. Tell the baby one day how much I loved him, or her, and how much I loved you, that I was a decent man, that I tried ... and oh, God, Gabbie, tell him how much I loved you. Please always know that, please forgive me for what I've done, and for what I'm about to do now. May God protect you both ... pray for me, Gabbie ... I love you ... may God forgive me ...' The writing seemed to go off the page then, and he had signed it simply 'Joe.' She sat and stared at it for a long time, sobbing softly. It was all so clear to her now, it was all right there. He thought he had failed them all, he thought she was so strong, but only because he was so afraid to do what he wanted. He had been so much more frightened than she was. And the baby he talked about was already gone. If only he had had the courage to leave St. Stephen's, if only they could have tried to have a life together she could have shown him how wrong he was, that he had not failed anyone until now . . . when he failed them all, and abandoned her, while telling her to be strong because he wasn't. In so many ways, he reminded her of her father, and he had left her now, all alone, with nothing but a letter to hold on to. She wanted to scream as she read it, but all she did was cry. She sat on her bed for a long time, and read it over several times. It was all there, all his anguish, all his fears, all the guilt he felt for things he had never been responsible for, like his brother's death, and his mother's suicide.

And who was responsible now? Whose fault was it? She knew that it was her own, because she had led him to a place where he could not exist, she had led him right into the arms of yet another failure. She had done that to him, just by loving him. She had led him to the edge of a cliff he didn't know how to escape from, so he had jumped off, into the abyss, and taken her with him. But she had lived and he had died. He had condemned her to this now, a room in a boardinghouse far from anything comforting or familiar. He had left her all alone, with nothing but memories and a letter that told her how strong she was, and had to be now, because he had opted for weakness. And as she read it for the tenth time, she was suddenly angry at him for what he hadn't dared, hadn't tried, hadn't cared enough to live for. He had run away, to be with his mother and Jimmy. He had done the same thing his mother did. He had chosen to die rather than to fight and take the chance that they might win this time, that it would be right, and they might even be happy. He had left her no choice, no options. He had taken the only way out he saw, and left Gabbie to fend for herself without him. She wanted to scream at him, to shout, and shake him ... if only she had known what he was thinking. She could have talked to him, argued with him, even left him if it would have meant his staying alive. But he had shared none of it with her. He had simply left, at the end of a piece of rope in a dark closet.

It was a coward's way out, and part of her hated him for it, yet, she also knew that part of her would always love him. And as darkness fell, and she sat staring out the window long after dinnertime, she remembered Mother Gregoria's words about him, reminding her that his mother had done the same thing, that there was some fatal flaw Gabriella had nothing to do with. But even knowing that, she felt intolerably guilty. She knew in her heart of hearts that she was responsible for this, just as he knew it about Jimmy. And as she lay down on her bed in the darkness again, thinking about him, she knew that no matter how much she had loved him, and he her, she had killed him. She had paid a high price for it, but she also knew with utter certainty that whatever happened now, God would never forgive her.

CHAPTER SIXTEEN

For an entire week after she rented the room at Mrs. Boslicki's, Gabriella pounded the pavements. She looked for jobs everywhere she could think of. She tried department stores, the 5 & 10, coffee shops, restaurants, even the small, dirty restaurant across the street from where she was living. But no one wanted to hire her, despite her degree from Columbia, her experience at gardening, her gentle ways, or her talent at writing. All the restaurants said, dismissing her, was that she had never waited on tables. And the department stores and 5 & 10 said she had no experience with retail.

And she walked so much and so far, looking for jobs, that she hoped she wouldn't begin to bleed again, because she didn't dare spend any money on a doctor. She had all but given up hope, and her funds were dwindling alarmingly, when she stopped late one afternoon in a small konditorei on Eighty-sixth Street for a piece of pastry and a cup of coffee. She hadn't eaten anything since morning, and couldn't resist this one treat, but she was frightened of spending too much money.

She had an éclair and a cup of coffee with *schlag*, the delicious sweet whipped cream they served there. And she saw the old German man who owned the place put a HELP WANTED sign in the window. She knew how hopeless it was by now, but she decided to ask him anyway, when she paid for the pastry and the cup of coffee. She told him point-blank that she had no experience, but she needed a job, and she felt sure she could wait on tables. And then in desperation, she admitted that she'd lived in a convent and waited on tables there. He was the first one she'd ever said that to, she didn't want to have to answer a lot of questions, but she needed the job and was willing to say almost anything she had to, to get it. And he was obviously intrigued by what she said.

'Were you a nun?' he asked, looking at her with interest. He had a bushy white mustache and a shiny bald head, and all she could think as she

262

looked at him was that he looked like Pinocchio's father, Geppetto.

'No, I was a postulant,' she said, with eyes so full of sorrow that he wanted to reach out and touch her. She looked as though she needed a good meal, and a kind hand in her life. She was rail thin and frighteningly pale, and he felt sorry for her.

'How soon can you start?' he asked, still watching her. She carried herself well, she had an elegant carriage, and she was a beautiful girl. He sensed that there was more to her than met the eye, and he was startled to see the ugly dress she wore. She was still wearing the shiny black one with the indelible stains that they had given her in the convent, but she didn't dare waste her money buying another. The funny thing about her, he thought, was that she had very aristocratic looks, and somehow looked as though she came from money, but it was obvious from what she was wearing that she had fallen on hard times.

'I can start anytime,' she answered him. 'I live nearby. And I'm free now.'

'I'll bet you are.' He smiled. The state of her wardrobe told him she needed the money. 'Okay. Then you start tomorrow. Six days a week. Noon to midnight. We're closed on Mondays.' It was a twelve-hour shift and she knew she wasn't up to it, but she was so grateful for the job that she would have done anything he wanted, scrub floors then and there if he'd asked her. But that would come later.

She learned that his name was Mr. Baum, and he came from Munich. There were four other women working in his shop, all of them middle-aged, and three of them German. It was a family operation, a nice clean place, and they served hearty German meals, and in between all afternoon, and late at night, they served pastry. Mrs. Baum made the pastries and did the cooking.

Gabriella was grinning from ear to ear as she walked into the house on Eighty-eighth Street, and Mrs. Boslicki saw her.

'Well, did you meet Prince Charming, or did you find a job finally?' Mrs. Boslicki had been worried about her. She was out all day, looking for work, and stayed in her room alone at night with the lights out. For a girl of her age, it wasn't a happy existence, or even normal.

'I got a job,' she said, beaming. They were paying her two dollars an hour, and she knew she could pay her rent now. Mother Gregoria's money had been dwindling daily. 'I'm working at a konditorei on Eighty-sixth Street.' It was four blocks away, and despite the long hours, it seemed absolutely perfect. She just prayed that, for the next few weeks, being on her feet for so many hours wouldn't cause her to hemorrhage. It had been less than two weeks since the miscarriage . . . less than two weeks since Joe had been gone . . . only a week since she had been forced to leave the convent . . . so many awful things had happened to her, but now, finally, something good had happened.

'Congratulations!' Mrs. Boslicki said, grinning. 'Maybe now you'll come out of your room once in a while, and watch a little television, or listen to some music. Everyone thinks I rented your room to a traveling salesman.'

'I'll be gone most of the time, Mrs. Boslicki,' Gabriella explained. 'I'll be working noon to midnight. But I'll come down tonight. I promise.'

'*After* you go eat some dinner. Look at you, you look like a broomstick. You're never going to find a husband if you don't feed yourself once in a while. Boys don't like broomsticks.' She wagged a finger at her, and Gabriella laughed. She reminded her of some of the old nuns in the convent, although none of them had been pushing her to find a husband. Far from it.

Gabriella actually took her advice and went across the street to the greasy spoon that night, and ordered a plate of meat loaf. It was plain but nourishing, and reminded her a little of the food at St. Matthew's, which in the end made her homesick. She would have done anything to see Mother Gregoria again, just a glimpse of her, hurrying down the hall, with her arms crossed and her hands tucked into her sleeves, and her heavy wooden rosary beads flying. Or any of the other Sisters would have been a welcome sight too. Sister Agatha or Sister Timothy, or Sister Emanuel . . . or Sister Immaculata. She was thinking of all of them as she walked back to the boardinghouse again, and remembered her promise to Mrs. Boslicki to stop in the living room for a moment. She didn't feel like it, but she thought it might seem rude if she didn't. So she forced herself to go in for just a few minutes. And when she did, she was surprised how many people were sitting there. There were six or seven, chatting and playing cards. The TV was on, and an old man with white hair who looked like Einstein was tinkering with the piano. He said they needed a piano tuner to come look at it again, and Mrs. Boslicki was arguing with him and telling him it had never sounded better to her.

They all looked up in surprise as she walked into

265

the room, and Gabriella was suddenly embarrassed. She hadn't expected to see so many people. There were men and women, mostly in their sixties, except for the man at the piano, who seemed even older. The women had white hair, some with a blue rinse, and they smiled when they saw Gabriella. She was such a breath of youth in the room, and she was so startlingly pretty. She was wearing the blue flowered dress, and old, well-worn shoes, but her straight, shining blond hair framed her face and looked almost like a halo. Her huge blue eyes seemed full of innocence, and none of them were perceptive enough to see the sadness beyond it. She looked far too young to have seen much of life or even have suffered. And just seeing her there in their midst made them feel happy.

Mrs. Boslicki introduced her to everyone. Many of them were European, and one of them, Mrs. Rosenstein, proudly said she was a survivor of the camp at Auschwitz. She had lived at Mrs. Boslicki's for twenty years now. And she introduced the man at the piano as Professor Thomas. Gabriella wasn't sure if it was his first name or his last, but he made a little bow to her and clarified it by saying his name was Theodore Thomas, and explaining that he was no longer a professor, he was retired. She was intrigued to learn that he had been a literature professor at Harvard. His field of expertise had been eighteenth-century English novels.

'And where did you go to school?' he asked with a mischievous smile, abandoning his attempts to revitalize the piano. It never occurred to him that she might not have gone to college at all.

'Columbia,' she said quietly.

'That's a fine school.' He smiled at her. They

had heard about her from Mrs. Boslicki, though none of them had seen her even once in the week she'd been there.

'And what are you up to now, young lady?' he asked, looking a little wild and woolly with his fuzzy hair and droopy trousers. He definitely looked like an eccentric old professor. He was visibly older than the other guests there, and Gabriella correctly guessed him to be close to eighty, but his wits were still sharp, his eyes clear, and he seemed to have a good sense of humor.

'I just got a job working in a restaurant on Eighty-sixth Street,' she said proudly. It had been a real victory for her, and one she needed very badly. 'I start tomorrow.'

'One of those cozy places that sells pastry, I hope. Mrs. Rosenstein and I will have to come to see you, when we take a stroll in that direction.' He was fascinated by the stories she told about her past, and he had lived there for almost as long as she had. His wife had died eighteen years before, and he had moved to the boardinghouse when he gave up his apartment. He lived on a pittance now, and had no relatives, and he enjoyed the company of Mrs. Boslicki and her boarders. But this latest addition to the group he found both fascinating and lovely. And he commented to everyone in the room afterward that she had a face like an angel and a noticeable natural elegance and style.

But for now he asked her what sort of things she had studied at Columbia, and embarked on a long, interesting conversation with her about the novels she'd read while she'd been there. He was intrigued to discover that she did a bit of writing. But she was very modest about it and said that it was nothing anyone would want to read. She was sure, although she didn't say it to him, that only the nuns who knew her would like her stories. Joe had read some of them, of course, she had given them to him one afternoon when they met in the park, and he had told her he thought they were terrific. But like the nuns, he knew and loved her.

'I'd like to see some of your work one day,' the professor said, giving it an importance she knew it didn't deserve, and she smiled shyly.

'I don't have any of it with me.'

'Where are you from?' he asked, fascinated by her. It had been a long time since he'd had a chance to chat with a girl her age, and he found it incredibly refreshing. It reminded him instantly of his years at Harvard. There was something about youth and the excitement of their minds that still invigorated him, and he would have loved to sit and talk to her for hours.

'She's from Boston,' Mrs. Boslicki answered for her, and Gabriella looked suddenly nervous. If he had taught at Harvard, he knew the city well, and of course she didn't.

'My mother lives in California,' she said by way of a distraction. 'My father lives in Boston.' And she lived nowhere. Only here now.

'Where in California?' one of the women asked. She had a daughter in Fresno.

'San Francisco,' she said, as though she had seen her mother, or at least talked to her, only the day before, instead of the twelve years it had been since she'd seen her last.

'They're certainly both lovely cities,' Professor Thomas said easily, watching her eyes. There was something about her that touched him, something

268

deep and sorrowful, and excruciatingly lonely. Mrs. Boslicki would have put it down to homesickness, but it was far deeper, and something far more raw than that, and he sensed an aura of tragedy about her.

Her gentleness touched all of them, and she chatted with each one, and then went upstairs finally, with a set of fresh towels Mrs. Boslicki had handed her, and for which she thanked her politely.

'Lovely girl,' Mrs. Rosenstein said, and one of the other women said she reminded her of her granddaughter in California. 'Very well brought up. She must have nice parents.'

'Not necessarily,' Professor Thomas said wisely. 'Some of the best students I had, and the most decent ones, came from people who were slightly less well behaved than Attila the Hun, and some of the brightest ones had incredibly stupid parents. There's no telling what mysteries happen in the gene pool.'

Gabriella would have been relieved to hear it. All her life she had waited anxiously, in fear of seeing telltale signs of her mother's personality defects emerging in her, but so far, much to her relief, that hadn't happened. It was why, until she met Joe, she had never wanted children.

'But she is a very nice person. I hope she stays for a while,' he said warmly.

'I don't think she's going anywhere now that she has a job,' Mrs. Boslicki reassured them all. It was nice having someone young in the place, although she was certainly very quiet. 'She doesn't seem to have any friends here. And her parents haven't called all week. I thought they would, but she never asks for messages. She doesn't seem to expect

269

anyone to call her.' They noticed everything about each other at Mrs. Boslicki's, since they had nothing else to do with their time, being widowed or retired. Once in a while a young boarder came into their midst, but only to stay temporarily, until they saved some money and moved on. Until Gabriella the youngest resident of the house was a salesman in his early forties, who had just gotten a divorce. He had been more than a little intrigued by Gabriella, and her striking looks hadn't been lost on him, when she was introduced to him as he stopped by to say good night on his way in from a movie. But she hadn't even seemed to see him. She was far more interested in talking to Professor Thomas.

'I'd like to spend some time talking to her,' Professor Thomas said, and Mrs. Rosenstein smiled at him.

'If you were fifty years younger that would worry me, but I don't think it does now.' She had had a crush on him for years, but their relationship was strictly platonic.

'I'm not sure I'm flattered.' He looked at her over his glasses. 'I wonder why a girl with a degree from Columbia, and a mind like hers, is working as a waitress.'

'It's not easy to find a job these days,' Mrs. Boslicki said practically, but he sensed more than that, and had an odd impression that there was some mystery about her.

He saw her leaving the house the next day, and stopped to talk to her. She was on her way to work, and wearing the same blue dress she had worn the day before. It was so unattractive that it looked ridiculous on her and only heightened the contrast

270

between it and her good looks. As pretty as she was, he thought she could have worn sackcloth and ashes and still look lovely.

'And where are you off to?' he asked, taking a grandfatherly interest in her. She still looked tired and pale, and he couldn't help wondering if she slept well.

'Baum's Restaurant,' she said, smiling at him. His hair looked wilder and woollier than ever, as though he'd stuck a wet finger in an outlet.

'Good. I'll take a walk up there later. I'll be sure to sit at one of your tables.'

'Thank you.' She was touched by his obvious interest in her, and as she left the house, Mrs. Boslicki waved at her from the living room window. She was watering her plants, and one of her many cats was crawling all around her. It was an odd place, filled with funny old people, but Gabriella was surprised to find she liked them. It was a comfortable place to be, after the warm community she had shared for so long in the convent. And even if she could have afforded it, which she thought she never would, she would have been lonely in an apartment.

She arrived at Baum's ten minutes early for work, and put a clean apron on over her dress, while Mrs. Baum explained their procedures to her, and Mr. Baum checked the cash register, as he did constantly, and he was pleased to see that she looked nice. Her dress was unflattering but clean, her shoes had been shined, and her hair was immaculate, she had it pulled back from her face, and had gone to the 5 & 10 to buy a headband. She still needed to grow it, it was still fairly short from the convent, but it was clean and neat.

271

As far as the Baums were concerned, she was perfect. And by that afternoon, they were even more pleased. She was polite to all their customers, took their orders carefully, and hadn't made a single mistake in what she delivered to them. What's more she was quick, and seemed comfortable handling several tables. In some ways, it reminded her very much of serving meals to the Sisters in the convent. You had to be fast and neat and organized to serve that many people, and she was all of those things. By the time Professor Thomas came in, with Mrs. Rosenstein, Gabriella was feeling very much at home there.

They ordered strudel and plum tarts, and coffee with lots of whipped cream, and they left her a big tip afterward, which embarrassed her, but she thanked them both profusely. And on the way out, she saw them stop and chat with Mr. Baum, and heard them tell him how good the strudel was, and he promised to tell his wife that. They were still talking to him when she went back to the kitchen to pick up several other orders. And when she came back, they were just leaving. They told her they'd see her at Mrs. Boslicki's, and she waved and went back to delivering her orders.

They came in every day after that, at the same time. And it became a kind of ritual, but after the first day, she always refused to take a tip from them. She said that bringing her their patronage, and seeing them there, was payment enough. They didn't have to give her any money, all they had to do was pay Mr. Baum for the apple strudel.

And on Monday, on her day off, as she walked back from the Laundromat, she ran into Mrs. Rosenstein coming back from the dentist. She invited Gabriella to sit with them in the living room that night, and she commented later to Mrs. Boslicki that the girl was looking better. She seemed stronger and healthier, and not quite as pale as she had been. And Professor Thomas thought she looked a little less grief-stricken when he saw her in the living room later. They were sitting side by side, chatting amiably, while the others played cards, when he turned to her and spoke in a gentle voice no one else could hear, and Gabriella looked up at him in amazement.

'Mr. Baum tells me you were a nun,' he said quietly. It had never occurred to her that Mr. Baum would say that. She had only told him that so that she would get the job waiting on tables, and she knew it was the only experience she had that might convince him. But the professor wondered now if that accounted for her sadness, or if there was another, deeper story. He suspected the latter.

'Not really,' she explained, looking away from him pensively, and then up at him again. 'I was a postulant. That's not quite the same thing.'

'Yes, it is,' he smiled. 'It's just a tadpole instead of a frog.' He grinned and she laughed out loud at the description.

'I'm not sure the Sisters would be happy to hear you say that.'

'I always had a priest or two in my classes at Harvard. Mostly Jesuits. I always liked them, they were well educated, intelligent, and surprisingly open-minded.' And then without pausing for breath, he turned the conversation back to Gabriella. 'How long were you in the convent?'

She hesitated before answering him, there was a lot to explain, and she didn't really want to do that.

273

Even thinking about all she had lost so recently was still far too painful, and he could see sorrow in her eyes again as she answered. But she liked him enough to be honest with him.

'Twelve years,' she said quietly. 'I grew up there.'

'Were you an orphan?' he asked gently, and she had the feeling that he was asking her because he cared, not because he wanted to announce it to the others. He was a sensitive, kind man, and she was surprised by how much she liked him.

'I was left there by my parents. It's really the only home I've ever known.' Yet she had left there, and he was compassionate enough not to ask her the reason. And he could sense easily that she didn't want to tell him.

'It must be a difficult life, being a nun. I can't imagine it. Celibacy has never appealed to me much,' he said with a twinkle in his eye, 'until lately.' He glanced at Mrs. Rosenstein playing bridge intently across the room and they both laughed. He had been devoted to his wife for forty years, and although he had good friends here, he had never wanted to date, or remarry. 'I had a number of very interesting conversations with my Jesuits on that subject, and they never convinced me of the validity of the theory.' But what he said reminded her instantly of Joe, and he could almost see her pull back in anguish, and he was immediately sorry. 'Did I say something to upset you?' he asked, looking worried.

'No . . . of course not . . . I just . . . miss it a lot,' she said, turning sad eyes up to him, and he could see tears there. 'It was hard to leave them.' Something about the way she said it told him she had been forced to, and he decided it was time to

274

change the subject.

'Tell me about your writing,' he said warmly.

'There's nothing to tell.' She smiled gratefully at him. 'I just write silly stories occasionally. Nothing worth talking about, and certainly nothing of the caliber you're used to at Harvard.'

'The best writers say things like that. The really bad ones tell you how great their work is. Beware of the writer who tells you how much you're going to love his novel. I guarantee you, you'll be asleep before the end of the first chapter, and snoring!' he said, wagging a finger at her for emphasis as she laughed at the description. 'So, having said all that, when may I see your work, Miss Harrison?' He was gentle, but persistent, giving it an importance she knew it didn't deserve.

'I don't have any with me.'

'Then write some,' he said, waving a hand magically. 'All you need is pen and paper, and a little inspiration.' And time, and perseverance, and the soul to put into it, still feeling as though her own had been extinguished when Joe died. 'I suggest you buy a notebook tomorrow.' And then he hit a nerve again, without intending to, and he realized that talking to her was like tiptoeing through a minefield. 'Have you ever kept a journal?' he asked innocently, and was devastated when he saw her look of sorrow.

'I ... yes ... I have ... but I don't do that anymore.' He didn't ask her why she'd stopped. He could see it was a painful subject. For one so young, she had a great many scars, and many of them seemed fresh still.

'What do you enjoy most? Poetry or short stories?' He liked drawing her out, and talking to

275

her. And he liked sitting next to her too, she was so young, and so pretty. It reminded him of a thousand years before, with Charlotte, when they had both been at the University of Washington, and had been barely more than children. He married her the week after they graduated, and his only regret with her was that they had never been able to have children. But for forty years after that, his students had been his children. She had taught music, theory and composition. She used to write him songs sometimes, with wonderful lyrics, and he told Gabriella all about it while she listened, smiling at him.

'She must have been a lovely person.'

'She was,' he said wistfully. 'I'll show you a photograph of her sometime. She was very beautiful when she was young. I was the envy of all the young men who knew her. We got engaged when we were twenty.' He asked Gabriella how old she was then, and she said twenty-two. The memory of it made him smile, as he patted her smooth hand with his gnarled one.

'You don't know how lucky you are, my dear. Don't waste it with regrets of the places and people you have lost. You have a lifetime to fill, so many good times and good years and great people ahead of you. You must rush to meet it.' But she wasn't rushing lately. She was still barely crawling, and she knew it. But what he said to her touched her deeply.

'Sometimes it's difficult not to look back,' Gabriella mused to him, and in her case, she had a great deal to look back at, and not all of it pretty.

'We all do that at times. The secret is in not looking back too often. Just take the good times with you, and leave the bad times behind you.' But she had so many of them, and the good times had been so sweet and so brief, and there had been so few of them, except for her peaceful years at the convent. But now, even the memory of that was painful, because she had lost it. And yet, she had to admire him. His life was mostly behind him, and he was still looking ahead with enthusiasm and excitement and interest. He liked talking to her, and keeping up with the young, and he hadn't lost his energy or his sense of humor. She found it extremely impressive, and he set a worthy example to the others. The other people in the room were complaining about their health, their ills, the size of their social security benefits, their friends who had died recently, the condition of the sidewalks in New York, and the amount of dog poop they saw there. He cared about none of that. He was far more interested in Gabriella and the life she had ahead of her. He was offering her a road map to happiness and freedom.

She sat with him for a long time that night. He never played bridge with Mrs. Rosenstein and her friends, he said he hated it, but eventually he played dominoes with Gabriella, and she truly enjoyed it. He beat her every time, but she learned a lot from him, and when she went upstairs to her room finally, she had had a delightful evening. They were small pleasures that they shared, but she suddenly felt as though her life was filled with new adventures. She had spent the evening talking to an eighty-year-old man, but he was far more interesting to her than anyone half his age, or half that again. And she was looking forward to speaking with him again, and had even promised him she'd stop on the way to work the next day, and buy a notebook for her writing.

And when he came to Baum's the next day, this time without Mrs. Rosenstein, who had gone to the urologist, he asked Gabriella if she'd done it.

'Well, did you?' he asked portentously, and she didn't know what he meant by the question, as she wrote down his standard order for coffee and apple strudel.

'Did I what?' She'd been busy all afternoon, and she was a little distracted.

'Did you buy the notebook?'

'Oh.' She grinned at him victoriously, amused by his persistence. 'Yes, I did.'

'I'm proud of you. Now, when you come home from work tonight, you must start to fill it.'

'I'm too tired when I come home from work at night,' she complained, she was still exhausted from the blood loss she'd suffered in the miscarriage, though she didn't want anyone to know it. The doctor had said it would take months to improve, and she was beginning to believe him. But Professor Thomas was not accepting any excuses.

'Then do it in the morning, before work. I want you to start writing every day. It's good for the heart, the soul, the mind, the health, the body. If you're a writer, Gabriella, it's a life support system you can't live without, and shouldn't. Write *daily*,' he emphasized, and then pretended to glare at her. 'Now go get me my strudel.'

'Yes, sir.' He was like a benevolent grandfather, one she had never had, and had never even known enough to dream of, she'd always been far too busy concentrating on her parents, and what they

278

represented to her. But the presence of Professor Thomas in her life was a real gift, and she thoroughly enjoyed him.

He continued to come to see her every day, and on Mondays when she was off, he began taking her to dinner. He told her about his teaching days, his wife, his life in Washington as a boy, growing up in the 1890s. It was a time she could barely imagine it seemed so long ago, and yet he seemed so aware of what was happening in the present day, and so completely modern. She loved talking to him, and listening even more than talking. And more than anything, they talked about writing. She had written a short story finally, and he was extremely impressed with it, made a few corrections, and explained how she could have developed the plot more effectively, and told her she had real talent. She tried to brush off his compliments, and told him he was just being kind to her, and he got very annoyed, and wagged his famous finger at her. That had always been a sign of danger to his students, but she was anything but frightened of Professor Thomas. She was growing to love him.

'When I say you have talent, young lady, I mean it. They didn't hire me at Harvard to grow bananas. You have work to do, you still need some polishing, but you have an instinctive sense for the right tone, the right pace ... it's all a question of timing, of sensing when to say what, and how, and you have that. Don't you understand that? Or are you just a coward? Is that it? Are you afraid to write, Gabriella? Afraid you might be good? Well, you are, so face it, live up to it. It's a gift, and few people have it. Don't waste it!' They both knew she was no coward, and then she smiled sadly at him,

279

remembering the words she had always hated.

'Usually people tell me how strong I am,' she said, sharing one of her secrets with him. It was the first of many. 'And then they leave me.'

He nodded wisely and waited for her to say more, but she didn't. 'Perhaps they're the cowards then. Weak people usually congratulate others for their strength so they don't have to be strong, or they use it as an excuse to hurt you . . . it's a way of saying, "You can take it, you're strong." A great deal is expected of strong people in this world, Gabbie. It's a heavy burden,' and he could see it had been. 'You are strong though. And one day you'll find someone as strong as you are. You deserve that.'

'I think I already have.' She smiled at him, and patted the gnarled hand with the wagging finger which was at rest now.

'You're just lucky I'm not fifty or sixty years younger, I'd teach you what life is about. Now you'll have to teach me, or at least remind me.' They both laughed.

He took her out every week, to funny little restaurants on the West Side, or in their neighborhood, or the Village, and sometimes they took the subway to get there. But he always treated her to dinner, despite the fact that he appeared to live on a brutally tight budget, and in deference to that, she was always careful about what she ordered. He complained that she didn't eat enough, remembering what Mrs. Rosenstein had said about her being too thin, and sometimes he made her order more in spite of her protests. And now and then he scolded her for not making any effort to meet young people, but he loved having her to himself, and was happy she didn't.

'You should be playing with children your own age,' he growled at her, and she smiled at him.

'They play too rough. Besides, I don't know any. And I love talking to you.'

'Then prove it to me by doing some writing.' He was always encouraging her, pushing her, and by Thanksgiving, two months after they'd met, she had filled three notebooks with stories. Some of them were excellent, and he told her frequently that thanks to her diligence, he thought her style was improving. He had encouraged her more than once to send her work to magazines, just as Mother Gregoria had, but she seemed to have no inclination to do it. She had far less faith in her writing skill than he did.

'I'm not ready.'

'You sound like Picasso. What's "ready"? Was Steinbeck ready? Hemingway? Shakespeare? Dickens? Jane Austen? They just did it, didn't they? We are not striving for perfection here, we are communicating with each other. Speaking of which, my dear, are you going home for Thanksgiving?' They were at a tiny Italian restaurant in the East Village, and she was startled by his question.

'I . . . no . . .' She didn't want to tell him there was no home to go to. He knew she had grown up in the convent, but she had never told him clearly that she had no contact with her family at all, and she was no longer welcome in the convent. The only family she had was him now. 'I don't think so.'

'I'm happy to hear it,' he said, looking pleased. Mrs. Boslicki made a turkey for them every year, and he had been hoping Gabriella would be there.

Only a few of the boarders there still had relatives, and the young divorced salesman had already moved to another city. 'I was hoping to share the holiday with you.'

'So was I.' She smiled and went on telling him about her latest story. There was a flaw in the plot and she couldn't quite figure out how to solve it, with violence, or an unexpected romance.

'There's certainly quite a contrast in your options, my dear,' he mused, 'although the two are sometimes related. Violence and romance.' His words reminded her of Joe again, and her eyes clouded over but he pretended not to see it. He wondered if she would ever tell him what tragedies she had lived through. For the moment, he was still guessing, but wise enough never to ask her directly. 'Actually love is quite violent.' He went on, 'It is so painful at times, so devastating. There is nothing worse. Or better. I found the highs and lows equally unbearable, but then again, the absence of them is more so.' It was a sweet, romantic thing for a man his age to say, and she could almost imagine him as a young man, in love with his bride, the youthful hero. But clearly he had been. 'And you, Gabriella, I suspect you have found love painful as well. I see it in your eyes each time we touch on the subject.' He said it with the tenderness of a young lover, and touched her hand gently as he said it. 'When you can bring yourself to write about it one day, you will find it all less painful. It is a catharsis of sorts, but the process can be brutal. Don't do it until you're ready.'

'I . . .' She began to say something to him, and then thought better of it. She wanted to, but she was afraid to, and it still hurt too much to say it. 'I was very much in love with someone once.' She admitted it to him like a terrible secret, and in their case, it had been. But he suspected immediately that there was a great deal more to it than she was saying.

'At your age, Gabriella, once is pretty fair. You'll have a few more of those before it's over.' He had never loved anyone but Charlotte, but they had been both rare and lucky. Most people weren't. 'I take it it didn't go well.' It sounded to him as though the affair was over, and she nodded, and took a sharp breath before she continued.

'He died in September.' It was barely more than a whisper. She didn't offer to tell him more than that, and he didn't ask her. He only nodded. 'I thought it would kill me, and it very nearly did.' She remembered the miscarriage, or what she knew of it, all too vividly, and she still hadn't recovered completely, although she was feeling a great deal better.

'I'm very sorry to hear it.' He had known there was a tragedy in her life somewhere, perhaps even several. He could smell it. 'Love doesn't always end that way, and it never should. It leaves everything so unfinished. Even after forty years, I still had so much left to say to Charlotte.'

Gabriella nodded, understanding what he meant, but she couldn't go on talking, and he covered for her for a while, chatting about his wife, and Gabbie's writing. He wondered how the man had died, he assumed an accident, but he would never have asked her. He was gone, and she was heart-broken, that was all that mattered. But he couldn't begin to imagine the tragedy it had been, or the toll it had taken. Gabriella knew that even

283

he couldn't have written that story, it was far too ugly for his gentle imagination.

They took a cab back to the boardinghouse that night. It was cold and he was feeling flush, his social security check had just come in, and he knew it had cost her a lot to tell him about the man who had died two months before. He wanted to do something special for her, and she was grateful to him as they got out in front of Mrs. Boslicki's tired old brown-stone. And they both looked up at the sky at the same time. It was snowing. The first snow of the winter, and suddenly she remembered how beautiful the first snow had always looked in the convent garden. As a child, she had loved to play there, and the nuns had always let her. She said something about it as they walked inside, and she smiled at the memory, and he was happy for her. She needed something happy to cling to. They all did.

'I had a wonderful time tonight,' she said softly as she stopped outside his room. 'Thank you, Professor Thomas.'

'Not at all, the pleasure is always mine, my dear,' he said, executing a little bow as she smiled. She couldn't begin to imagine how he looked forward to these evenings, now more than ever. She was almost becoming a daughter to him ... or a beloved grandchild, especially after she had shared her confidence with him that evening. It was a sign of trust, which he cherished deeply. 'I'm looking forward to Thanksgiving,' he said gently.

'So am I,' she said, still smiling at him, and meant it. Before that, she'd been dreading it, but it didn't seem quite so bad now. She had lost a lot, but she had found something, like a diamond sparkling in the snow. And as she walked slowly upstairs, thinking of him, she thought of how sad it might have been if she had missed it.

CHAPTER SEVENTEEN

Thanksgiving was beautiful for all of them. There was a thick blanket of snow outside, and the entire city stopped moving. People skied in Central Park, and children played in the streets, made snowmen, and threw snowballs. And Mrs. Boslicki made a turkey no one would ever forget. It was so large she barely got it into the oven. And as he did every year, Professor Thomas carved it. And everyone seemed to have funny stories to tell about Thanksgivings that had gone wrong, appalling relatives, or silly things about their childhoods.

They all went for a walk afterward, and everyone said they felt as though they were about to explode. Baum's Restaurant was closed that day, and Gabriella was happy to be at home with all of them. She was like everyone's favorite daughter or niece or grandchild. In the two brief months she'd been with them, they had all come to love her.

And for the rest of the weekend, they talked about Christmas shopping, and there were suddenly decorations everywhere. Mrs. Boslicki and Mrs. Rosenstein went downtown to go shopping at Macy's and reported on the crowds with amazement. And for the entire weekend that she was off, Gabriella stayed in her room and worked on a story, and on Sunday night she dropped her notebook in the professor's lap with a smug expression.

'There! Now stop complaining!'

'All right . . . all right . . . let's see what you've got here.' But even he was amazed this time. Her story was brilliant. It was a Christmas story of sorts, filled with pathos and moments that brought tears to even his eyes, but it was beautifully done, elegantly written, and the surprise turn at the end was nothing short of brilliant. He let out a whoop of admiration and glee when he finished. She had been watching him with her arms crossed from a comfortable old club chair in the corner.

'Do you like it?' she asked nervously, but she could see he did. He was ecstatic about it, and he insisted it had to be published. This time he wouldn't allow her to deny it.

'Like it? I *love* it!'

'I still need to do some work on it,' she said anxiously when he talked about getting it published.

'Why don't you let me do some editing first?' he suggested, cleverly putting her notebook in his pocket before she could argue with him about it, and then offering her a game of dominoes to distract her. But she was so pleased he liked it that she would have done anything for him, particularly tonight. She had worked hard on it, and was very happy with the outcome. Even she had to admit, albeit grudgingly, that it was her best story. She even beat him at dominoes that night, and had a general feeling of victory when she went to bed, relieved to have completed the story. She had stayed up working on it until well past three that morning. It was the first time that she had felt a total mastery of her subject, and the feeling was both heady and addictive.

And the next day she was still excited about it when she went back to work. After being closed over the long weekend, Mr. Baum had decided to open on Monday. Professor Thomas still came in to see her there every day, sometimes with one of the others from the boardinghouse, or sometimes alone, and when he left that afternoon, Gabriella warned him to be careful going home. The slushy snow had become icy. But he was extremely independent.

All the customers that came in were in high spirits that day, and were all talking about getting ready for Christmas. Even the Baums were more expansive than usual, after spending Thanksgiving with all three of their daughters, and greeted their customers with a little more cheer than normal. They asked her how her holidays were, which was unusual because they only looked at her as a worker and never seemed interested in getting to know her.

And when Gabriella got back to the boardinghouse that night, Mrs. Boslicki stuck her head into the hallway when she heard her. She beckoned Gabriella to come closer, and Gabbie was instantly worried about the professor, but Mrs. Boslicki looked to be in too good a humor to be the bearer of bad tidings.

'We have a new boarder,' she said triumphantly. She had been trying for weeks to replace the traveling salesman.

'That's wonderful.' Gabriella congratulated her, relieved that her news had nothing untoward to do with the professor. He had become enormously important to her. In a short time, he had become

287

the only family she had, and sometimes she worried about him so much, she had nightmares about him. She still slept at the bottom of the bed, as she always had, even more so lately, since leaving the convent.

'He's very handsome,' Mrs. Boslicki added about her new boarder.

'That's nice,' Gabriella said blankly, not sure what that had to do with her. But Mrs. Boslicki seemed pleased, and Gabriella smiled, wondering if her landlady had a crush on her new tenant.

'He's twenty-seven, and very smart. He went to college.' Gabriella smiled at her, only mildly amused. She had no interest in any man, of any age, no matter how smart or attractive he was. The only man she needed in her life now was the professor.

'Good night, Mrs. Boslicki,' Gabriella said firmly. It had been a long night for her, but the tips had been good. She had been able to buy herself some new clothes recently, and she suspected the Baums were relieved too. They had made several comments about her two hand-me-down dresses from the convent. Most of the time now she wore skirts and sweaters. She had even bought a strand of fake pearls, and once when she looked in the mirror, she was afraid that she was beginning to look like her mother, but the Professor loved the way she looked and never hesitated to say so. He always said that she looked exactly like Grace Kelly.

Gabriella walked upstairs, relieved to know that the room that had been vacant was on the second floor, and she didn't have to share a bathroom with the new man. The bathroom she did share was only used by women. And she hoped it would be a while before she had to see him.

But she ran into him the next day for the first time, as she was leaving for work, bundled up against the cold, in her heavy gray coat, which was one of her purchases, and a pair of white earmuffs. He was standing at the door, helping Mrs. Boslicki with a bag of groceries, and he smiled pleasantly at Gabriella.

'Hi, I'm Steve Porter,' he introduced himself. 'I'm the new kid on the block.'

'It's nice to meet you,' Gabriella said coolly, unconsciously relieved that she didn't find him handsome. He had thick dark hair, and dark eyes, he was tall and slim, but he had powerful shoulders. He looked very clean-cut, but there was something she didn't like about him, and as she walked to work, she decided it was arrogance. He was too sure of himself, and entirely too familiar. He was nothing like Joe in any way, who had become, for her, as the only man she'd ever known biblically or otherwise, the standard of perfection. But she had known instantly that she didn't like this one. And she said so to the professor in no uncertain terms the next time she played dominoes with him.

'Oh, don't be such a grouch,' he said to her gruffly. 'He's a nice kid, Gabbie. He's a good-looking guy and he probably knows it. So what? That doesn't make him a villain.'

'I don't like him,' she said firmly.

'You're just afraid to get hurt again. You know, they don't all die, or walk away, they're not all going to hurt you,' he said gently, and she shook her head and refused to pursue the conversation

289

with him. She pretended to be intent on winning, but they both knew she wasn't. And something about her told the old professor that she was frightened.

Steve Porter's presence in the house was actually threatening to her. But it wasn't surprising after spending all of her adolescence and adult life in the convent. 'Don't worry about him,' the professor said comfortingly, 'he's probably not interested in you either.' And he could see that that relieved her, although he hoped that he was wrong and that Steve would become intrigued by her. He looked like a nice guy, and the professor thought it would be good for her to have a real date with someone. She seemed to have no desire whatsoever to see anyone but the professor, which was flattering for him, but not healthy for her. But he thought maybe if he left it alone, eventually the two young people would find each other.

But in the ensuing weeks, Gabriella seemed to do everything she could to avoid Steve Porter. If anything, she was rude to him, which was unusual for her. She was always so polite to everybody. But not to Steve. For him, she reserved her grumpiest behavior, but Steve seemed not to notice. He seemed to be in good spirits all the time, and he was particularly kind to all the old people. He bought a lovely Christmas tree for them, and set it up in the living room. He bought the decorations himself, because Mrs. Boslicki had never bothered, and she was always afraid to offend her boarders who were Jewish. But no one seemed to mind, they thought he was a lovely young man. He had just arrived from Des Moines, and he was looking for a job working with computers. He went out to interviews every morning and afternoon, and he was always nicely dressed, either in a sports coat or a suit. Everyone in the house, except Gabbie, approved of him. And they all thought it would be terrific if the two young people got together. And Steve was pleasant enough to her, but Gabbie made it clear that she had absolutely no inclination in that direction.

In fact, she was annoyed at him one afternoon on her way to work. He had bought little Christmas wreaths for everyone, and hung one on her door, without asking her. She didn't want to be indebted to him in any way or form, and she was very irritated that he had done it. But she thought it would be ruder still to take it down, so now she felt obliged to keep it. And she grumbled about it to herself all the way to work on Eighty-sixth Street.

'You look happy this afternoon,' Mr. Baum teased her as she walked in. It was rare to see Gabbie in a bad mood, but today she was definitely in one, and he didn't dare ask her what had happened.

Christmas was only a week away by then, and although some people were feeling stressed, most seemed to be in high spirits. The holidays seemed to bring out the worst and the best in everyone. He loved Christmas himself, and Mrs. Baum had been making beautiful gingerbread houses for weeks and selling them to people for their children. It was something she did every year, and they were always the prettiest ones on Eighty-sixth Street. Just seeing them in the window always brought people in, and today was no different. There were half a dozen people at the counter and the cash register, with their children standing near them, pointing to the specific house they wanted. There were little candies stuck all over them, and chocolate and spun sugar decorations. There were even tiny chocolate reindeer. Gabriella loved looking at them, and wishing she had had something magical like that in her childhood. But there had been no magic in Gabriella's childhood, no gingerbread houses, no visits to Santa. Christmas had always been a time when her mother was particularly malevolent and on edge, and never failed to beat her.

She was trying not to think about it, as she waited on a table and saw a woman come in with a little girl, who was pointing excitedly to one of the houses Mrs. Baum had made. 'That one! That one!' She was about five years old and so excited she could barely contain herself as her mother held her hand and told her to calm down, they were going to buy one.

They stood in line behind several other people, and when it was finally their turn, the child started to jump up and down, clapping her hands in her little red mittens. She was wearing a funny little hat with a bell on it, and when she hopped around, it made a tinkling sound that, to Gabriella, seemed to be full of the magic of Christmas. But suddenly as she jumped, she stumbled and fell down, and without hesitating, her mother reached down and yanked her to her feet by one arm, and the child began to cry and hold her arm, while her mother shouted at her.

'I told you to stop that, now you got what you deserved. And if you do it again, Allison, I swear I'm going to slap you.' Gabriella stopped what she was doing, and stood and stared at them, forgetting all about the customers whose orders she had just taken. She was mesmerized by what she had just seen, and the familiar words, and she was watching the expression on the woman's face. There was something particularly vicious about it, and the child standing next to her was still crying. The quick yank on her arm seemed to have dislocated it, and she was crying ever more loudly as she held it. It had happened that way to Gabriella once, her mother had pulled hard on her arm, and pulled her elbow right out of the socket, and she still remembered vividly what it felt like. Her father had gently put it back for her eventually, with a sharp twist and a turn. Later her parents had fought about it, and then her mother had gone after her in earnest. But this woman was furious now as the child continued to wail, and Gabriella walked slowly over to her to suggest that the arm, or the elbow more precisely, might have been dislocated.

'Don't be ridiculous,' the woman snapped at her as the Baums watched, 'she's just whining. She's fine.' But Allison looked anything but fine as she continued to clutch her elbow. 'Now, do you want a gingerbread house or not?' she shouted at her then, yanking on the arm again, and everyone who watched them winced in unison. It was obvious that this time her mother had really hurt her. 'Allison, if you don't stop crying, I'm going to pull your pants down right here and spank you in front of all these people.'

'No, you're not,' Gabriella said quietly, with a power she had never felt in her life, a rush of adrenaline that suddenly surged through her. But this was not going to happen twice, and she was not going to stand there and watch the woman do it.

293

'You're not going to do anything of the sort.'

'What right do you have to interfere with my disciplining my daughter?' The woman looked outraged. She was wearing a mink coat and she had walked over from Madison, on her way back to their Park Avenue apartment. But the scene was all too familiar to Gabriella. And the word *discipline* set off a bell in her heart that sounded like a death knell to her as she listened.

'You're not disciplining her,' Gabriella answered her in a voice she didn't recognize herself, 'you're humiliating her, and torturing her in front of all these people. Why don't you tell her you're sorry? Why don't you fix her arm? If you take her coat off, you'll see that it's dislocated.'

With that the woman turned to Mr. Baum with an aristocratic look of outrage. 'Who is this girl? How dare she speak to me that way?' And with that, as the child continued to cry, the mother gave another hard yank on her arm, and the child let out a yowl that almost ruptured Gabriella's remaining eardrum. And without thinking twice, she gently pulled the child away from her mother's hand, and began taking her little red coat off. It came off easily and she saw instantly that what she had suspected had in fact happened. The arm dangled uselessly and the child screamed the moment Gabriella touched it.

'Take your hands off my child!' the woman was screaming. 'Someone call the police,' and with that, Gabriella turned around, and spoke to her in a voice that almost sounded like the devil.

'Yes, let's call the police, and explain to them what you've been doing to her. And if you make another sound, I'm going to slap *you* right in front

294

of all these people,' and with that, as the woman stared openmouthed, Gabriella turned to the child, and quickly did what she remembered her father doing to her, praying it would work this time. There was a terrible snap and a frightening sound as she first pulled the arm away from the child and then sharply turned it, but within an instant, the crying stopped, and the little girl was smiling. The dislocated elbow had been put back in its socket. But the woman came alive again then, grabbed the child's coat from her, shoved it, trembling, onto the child again and yanked her halfway to the door, while screaming at Gabriella.

'If you ever touch my child again, I'll call the police and have you arrested.'

'And if I ever see you doing that to her again, I'm going to testify against you in court, and we'll see who gets arrested.' There were no thanks for what she had done, but she knew enough about situations like these not to expect that. Gabriella was just grateful that she'd been able to help the little girl and stop her from hurting. But the little girl was halfway out the door with her coat on now, and crying for the gingerbread house she'd been promised, and which her mother hadn't purchased.

'But Mommy, you said I could have one!'

'Not now, Allison. Not after what you've just done, we're going straight home and I'm going to tell Daddy what a bad little girl you were today and he's going to *spank* you! You embarrassed Mommy in front of all these people.' She was concentrating on the child and didn't see the horrified expression on the faces of all the other people. She was truly a monster, but nothing about what she was seeing was new to Gabriella.

'But you hurt my arm!' the child was saying imploringly, looking back over her shoulder at Gabriella, wanting to stay, wanting to seek protection from the only kind lady she'd ever met. It reminded Gabbie instantly of Marianne Marks, the woman who had let her try on her tiara, and how she had wished that she had been her daughter. There were always people like that crossing the paths of children in distress, and they never knew or saw the longing they spawned in these terrified children.

Gabriella watched Allison fly out the door, pulled sharply along by her mother. She got no gingerbread house that afternoon. She got nothing. And she was being told how terrible she was as they left, how it was all her fault, how her mother would never have to spank her if she weren't so naughty. It made Gabriella feel physically ill as she watched them, and she turned toward the Baums with a glazed expression. But what she saw there startled her even more than what she had seen happen to the child called Allison at the hands of her mother. They were furious with her. They had never been part of a scene like that before, and they were outraged that she had put them in an awkward spot, challenged a customer, no matter how wrong she was, and cost them the sale of one of their gingerbread houses. In fact, Mrs. Baum had decided, watching her, that Gabriella was probably crazy. And she had been for a minute. With very little additional provocation she would have gladly slapped the woman in the mink coat so she could understand what it felt like. Gabriella's memories were extremely clear on the subject. She could still remember the piercing sound when her mother had hit her so hard she ruptured her eardrum.

'Take your apron off,' Mr. Baum said quietly, as both customers and other employees watched them. 'You're fired!' he said, holding out a hand for the white apron, while his wife nodded her approval.

'I'm sorry, Mr. Baum,' Gabriella said quietly, not arguing for her job, but only for the salvation of one small child, who had no one else in the world to defend her. 'I had to do that.'

'You had no right to interfere. It's her child, she has a right to do anything with her she wants to.' It echoed the voices of an entire world, which believed that parents had a right to do anything they wanted to their children, no matter how cruel, or dangerous, or inhumane, or violent. But if no one were to stop them? What then? Who would ever defend those children? Only the strong, and the brave. Not the cowards like the Baums, or her father, who had let it all happen to her. No one had ever stepped in for her either.

'And if she kills her? What then? What if she stood here in your store and killed her? What if she goes home and does it now, Mr. Baum? What then? What will you say tomorrow when you read about it in the paper? That you're sorry, that you wish you'd helped . . . that you never knew? You knew. We all know. We see it, and most of the time people walk right by it, because they don't want to know, because it scares the hell out of them, and it's embarrassing, and it's just too damn painful. What about the child, Mr. Baum? It's painful for her too. It was her arm that was hanging out of the socket, not her mother's.'

297

'Get out of my restaurant, Gabriella,' he said clearly, 'and don't ever come back here. You're dangerous, and you're crazy.' And with that he turned to wait on his customers, who despite what they had seen and heard, just wanted to forget about it.

'I hope I am dangerous to people like that,' she said calmly, laying her apron on the counter. 'I hope I always will be. It's people like you, who turn away from it, who are the real danger,' she said, looking at the crowd as well as her employers, who were too embarrassed to look at her. And with that, she picked up her coat from a hook at the door, and saw for the first time that Professor Thomas was watching. He had just walked in when the child began to cry and he had seen everything that had happened. He had seen it all with utter and complete amazement. He helped her put her coat on without a word, and walked out of the restaurant with his arm around her, and he could feel how violently she was shaking, but she stood tall and proud and she was crying when she finally faced him.

'Did you see what happened?' she whispered. Now that it was over she could hardly speak, and in spite of the warm coat she couldn't stop shaking. He walked her away from the restaurant and thought he had never admired anyone so much in his entire life, and he wanted to say so, but for a moment, he was almost too moved to say it.

'You're a remarkable woman, Gabriella. And I'm proud to know you. What you did in there was beautiful. Most people just don't understand it.'

'They're too afraid to,' she said sadly, as they walked away, with his arm still around her shoulders. He wanted more than anything to protect her, from the past as much as the future. 'It's so much easier to pretend you don't see it. That's what my father always did. He just let her do it.' It was the first time she had talked about her childhood to him, and he knew there was more there, much more, and he had a feeling she was going to tell him about it when she was ready.

'Was it like that for you?' he asked sadly. He had never had children, but he couldn't imagine anyone treating them that way. It was beyond his realm of comprehension.

'It was much worse,' Gabriella said honestly. 'My mother beat me senseless, and my father let her. The only thing that saved me finally is that she left me. I'm almost deaf in one ear now, I've had most of my ribs broken, I have scars, I had stitches, I had bruises, I had concussions. She left me bleeding on the floor, and then beat me harder because I stained the carpet. She never stopped until she left me.'

'Oh my God.' Tears sprang to his eyes as he listened to her, and he felt suddenly very old. He couldn't imagine the nightmare that had been her childhood, but he believed her. It explained a lot of things to him, why she was so careful about people, and so shy, why she had wanted to stay in the refuge of the convent. But what he saw in her now was why people told her she was strong. She was more than strong. She had the power of a soul that had defied the devil, she had lived through worse nightmares than anyone could ever dream of. And with all her scars and the things she described to him now, she had survived intact. She was a whole person, and a very strong one. Despite all her efforts to destroy her, her mother had never been able to kill her spirit. And he said as much to Gabriella as they walked home to Mrs. Boslicki's.

'That's why she hated me so much,' Gabriella said, walking tall next to him. She was proud of what she had done for the child in Baum's Restaurant. It had cost her her job, but to Gabriella, it was worth it. 'I always knew she wanted to kill me.'

'That's a terrible thing to say about one's mother, but I believe you.' And then, with a worried frown, 'Where is she now?'

'I have no idea. I suppose San Francisco. I never heard from her again after she left me.'

'That's just as well. You should never contact her again. She's caused you enough pain for one lifetime.' And he could understand even less the father who had never stopped it. They sounded like animals, worse than that, to Professor Thomas.

They walked into the boardinghouse together, hand in hand, and Mrs. Rosenstein saw them as soon as they walked in. She knew it was too early for Gabriella to come home, and she looked instantly worried. She thought maybe something had happened to him, and Gabriella had brought him home, but it was Gabriella who had had the problem.

'Are you all right?' she asked both of them with anxious eyes, and they both nodded.

'I just got fired,' Gabriella said calmly. She wasn't shaking anymore. She was strangely calm, and Professor Thomas went to his room to pour both of them a brandy.

'How did that happen?' Mrs. Rosenstein asked, as he returned with a small glass for her too, but she declined it, and he volunteered to drink it for her. 'I thought everything was going so well for you there.'

'It was.' Gabriella smiled, feeling suddenly very free and very powerful, as she took a sip of the brandy. It burned her tongue and her eyes and her nose, but after it had burned her throat as well she decided that she liked it. 'Everything was going fine, until I shot my mouth off, and threatened to slap one of their customers tonight.' Gabriella suddenly smiled, it almost sounded funny to her, except she and the professor knew that it wasn't.

'Did someone get fresh with you?' She imagined it was a man, and she was outraged that someone would do that to Gabriella.

'I'll explain it to you later,' the professor said, as he downed the second shot glass, just as Mrs. Boslicki appeared, having heard the stir in her hallway.

'What's happening? Are you having a party out here, and did you forget to invite me?'

'We're celebrating,' Gabriella said, laughing. She was beginning to feel a little tipsy, and she didn't mind it. It had been a hard night for her, full of ugly memories, but she had come through it feeling stronger.

'What are you celebrating?' Mrs. Boslicki asked happily, anxious to share it.

'I just lost my job,' Gabriella said, and then giggled.

'Is she drunk?' she asked, with an accusing look at the professor.

'Believe me, she's earned it,' he said, and then remembered that they had real cause for celebration. It was why he had gone to the

301

restaurant to see her. And looking at Gabriella, he pulled an envelope out of his pocket and handed it to her. It had only taken two weeks. He had thought it would take much longer. 'If you're not too drunk,' he said to Gabriella lovingly, 'read that.'

She opened the envelope, and then the letter carefully, with the exaggerated gestures of someone who'd been drinking a little. She had never before tasted brandy, but it had actually calmed her, as well as warmed her. But as she read the letter he handed to her, her eyes grew wide, and she was instantly sober. 'Oh my God . . . oh my *God*! I don't believe this. How did you do it?' She turned to him with a look of amazement and then started jumping up and down like a child, holding the letter.

'What is it?' Mrs. Boslicki asked. They were all crazy tonight. Maybe they'd been drinking for a long time in the hallway. 'Did she win the Irish Sweepstakes?'

'Better than that,' Gabriella said, throwing her arms around her, Mrs. Rosenstein, and then finally the professor.

He had sent her most recent story to *The New Yorker* without telling her, and they had agreed to publish it, in their March issue. They were informing her that they were going to send her a check, and wanted to know if she had a literary agent. They were going to pay her a thousand dollars. Overnight, thanks to the professor, she had become a published writer. He had taken a liberty with her work, but he knew, as she did, that on her own, she would never have done it.

'What can I ever do to thank you?' she asked

302

him. It was proof of everything he had said to her, and Mother Gregoria before him. They were right. She was good. And she could do it. She couldn't believe it.

'The only thanks I want is for you to write more. I'll be your agent. Unless, of course, you want a real one.' But she didn't need one yet, although one day he was sure she would. She had the makings of a great writer, and he had seen that clearly the first time he had read one of her stories.

'You can be anything you want. This is the best Christmas present I've ever had.' Suddenly she didn't care at all that she'd lost her job. She was a writer now, and she could always find another job as a waitress.

They sat in the living room after the others went to bed, for long hours into the night, talking about what had happened in the restaurant, and what it meant to her, her own childhood, and her writing, and what she hoped to do with it one day. Professor Thomas said she could go far as a writer, if that was what she wanted and she was willing to work for it. And when she said she did, he believed her. But what's more, with the letter from *The New Yorker* clutched firmly in her hand, she now believed it.

She thanked him again profusely before she went up to bed that night, and as she stood in her small room, thinking about it, she thought of Joe, and how proud he would have been of her. If things had been different, they'd have been married by then, starving in a little apartment somewhere, but happy as two children. They would have been celebrating their first Christmas, and she would have been five months' pregnant. But life hadn't

303

worked out like that for them. He hadn't been willing to fight for it. He had been too afraid to cross the bridge into another life with her. And suddenly she knew what he had meant when he said how strong she was. Because therein lay the difference between them. She was willing to cross the bridge, to fight for anyone, or anything. She had been willing to be there for him, but no matter how much she loved him, or he her, he just couldn't do it. She wondered if he could have stopped the scene in the restaurant, and she couldn't see him doing that either. He had been a gentle man, and she knew she would never again love anyone as she had loved him. But whatever he had been, and however much he had loved her, he hadn't loved her enough to fight for it. He had turned back at the last minute, he had given it all up, and they had lost everything. And now little by little, she had to start over. She didn't hate him for it, but she was still very sad, and thought she probably always would be, whenever she thought about him.

And as she looked out her window that night, she could see his face in her mind's eye so clearly, she could almost touch him. The big smile, the blue eyes, the way he had held her in his arms . . . the way he kissed her. It made her heart ache thinking about him. But as much as she loved him, she knew something else now. She was a survivor. He had abandoned her, and she didn't die. And for the first time in her life, she was excited about what life had in store for her, and she wasn't frightened.

CHAPTER EIGHTEEN

Two days before Christmas, less than a week after she'd been fired, Gabriella walked into a bookshop to buy a gift for Professor Thomas. She wanted to get something wonderful for him, something he'd really want, and didn't already have on the crowded shelves in his bedroom.

She had decided to wait until after Christmas to get another job. She had enough money saved to pay for her January rent. And the money from *The New Yorker* was going to be a real windfall. She wanted to buy something really nice for the professor from it. She had already bought little gifts for everyone in the boardinghouse, she had something small and thoughtful for each of them, except for Steve Porter. She had decided that she didn't know him well enough to buy him a present.

And she had thought of buying something for Mother Gregoria too, but she knew that given her circumstances, the Mother Superior wouldn't be allowed to accept it. What she had decided to do instead was send her a copy of *The New Yorker* when her story was published. She knew how pleased she would be, and how proud of her. It would be gift enough just knowing how much she had helped her, and even if Mother Gregoria never answered her, Gabriella knew in her heart how much the Mother Superior still loved her. It was just very hard not being able to see her. It was the first Christmas she hadn't spent with her since she was a child. But that couldn't be helped now.

Gabriella walked into a handsome bookstore on Third Avenue and looked around. They had new books, and a section of old leather-bound books as well, and even some rare first editions. And she was shocked to see how expensive they were when she browsed through them. There were even one or two that cost several thousand dollars. But she settled on something finally that she thought would really please him. It was a set of very old books, by an author she had heard him use as an example to her very often. They were leather bound, and obviously had been much read and held by loving hands. There were three volumes, and when she paid for them, she doled out her money slowly and carefully. She had never in her life bought anything as expensive, but he was worth it.

'That's a great choice you made,' a young Englishman said, as he counted her money. 'I bought them in London last year, and I was surprised no one snapped them up immediately. They're very rare editions.' They chatted for a few minutes about the books, and then he looked at her curiously and asked her if she was a writer.

'Yes, I am,' she said cautiously, 'or I'm starting to be. I just sold a story to *The New Yorker*, thanks to the man I'm giving the books to.'

'Is he your agent?' he asked with interest.

'No, a friend.'

'I see.' He told her he wrote too, and had been struggling for the past year with his first novel.

'I'm still on short stories.' She smiled. 'I'm not sure I'll ever get up the courage to write a novel.'

'You will,' he said confidently, 'although I'm not sure I'd wish that on you. I started out doing short stories, and poetry. But it's awfully hard to make a living at it.' He was sure that she already knew that.

'I know,' she smiled at him again, 'I've been working as a waitress.'

'I did that too.' He grinned. 'I was a bartender in the East Village, then a waiter at Elaine's, and now I work here. I'm the manager, actually, and they let me do some of the buying. The people who own the store live in Bermuda. They're retired, and they bought this because they love books so much. They're both writers.' He mentioned two names that instantly impressed her, and then he looked at her curiously. 'I don't suppose you'd want to give up waiting on tables?' He knew the tips could be good, but the hours were long, and the conditions usually gruelling.

'It just gave me up, actually.' She laughed. 'I got fired this week. Merry Christmas.'

'The woman who usually works here with me is having a baby, and she's leaving for good next Friday. I don't suppose you'd be interested, would you? The salary is pretty good, and you can read all you want when business is quiet.' He smiled at her shyly then. 'And they say I'm not too dreadful to work for. My name is Ian Jones, by the way.' He extended a hand and she shook it and introduced herself to him, excited about the offer he'd made her. He told her what the salary was, and it was more than she'd been making at Baum's, including tips, working twelve hours a day. And this was exactly the kind of job she wanted. She offered him references and he said that wasn't necessary, he liked her look and the way she carried herself. She was well-spoken and intelligent, and a writer. As far as Ian was concerned, she was perfect. And she agreed to start the day after New Year's.

He wrapped her package for her, and she tucked it under her arm, and took the bus home with a broad grin on her face, and she practically exploded into the boardinghouse when she got there.

'Did you sell another story?' Mrs. Boslicki asked excitedly, as she ran into the hallway to meet her.

'No, better than that, almost. I got a great job in a bookstore! I start the day after New Year's.' She told Professor Thomas about it later that afternoon, and he was pleased for her, and delighted to see her so happy. He hadn't been feeling well all day. He was coming down with the flu, and he was starting to develop bronchitis. But he was happy for her, and they sat in his bedroom and talked, while he stayed warm and cozy in his old bathrobe. She could hardly wait to give him his Christmas present, but she was determined to wait until Christmas morning.

And on her way upstairs to her own room, she ran into Steve Porter. He was looking a little subdued and he couldn't help commenting on how happy she was. She told him she'd just found a job that afternoon, and he congratulated her and said he wished he'd been as lucky. He'd been in New York for a month, interviewing everywhere, and so far he'd had no luck at all, and he said he was running out of money.

'I hear you sold a story to *The New Yorker* too,' he said admiringly. 'It sounds like you're having a lucky streak these days. I'm happy for you.' He didn't know that she'd already paid her dues and had had enough bad luck to last a lifetime. But she was sorry he was looking so glum. It seemed unfair to be in such good spirits when he was having such a hard time, and she felt suddenly guilty for all the unpleasant things she'd said about him.

'Thank you for the wreath, by the way.' It was

the first time she'd really thanked him. He seemed to do a lot of nice things for everyone, and she'd been very critical of him, and now she was sorry. 'I'll keep my fingers crossed for you, Steve.'

'Thanks, I need it.' And then as he walked away, he turned and looked at her hesitantly and she saw it. 'I've been meaning to ask you something, but I wasn't sure if it would sound odd to you. I was wondering if you'd want to go to midnight Mass with me on Christmas Eve.' She was touched that he had asked her. She knew it was going to be a hard Christmas for her, with Joe gone, and having left St. Matthew's. But she also hadn't been to Mass since she'd left the convent.

'I'm not sure I want to go,' she said honestly, 'but if I do, I'll go with you. Thanks for asking.'

'Sure. Anytime.' He smiled and went back downstairs to pick up his messages. Understandably, since he was looking for a job, he made a lot of phone calls. And Gabriella realized suddenly how wrong she'd been about him. Professor Thomas was right. He was a nice guy. And so was Ian Jones, her new boss. She thought he was going to be fun to work with. He said he lived with someone, and it was obvious that his interest in Gabbie was professional and intellectual, and not romantic, which suited her to perfection. She wasn't interested in getting involved with anyone, or dating. She was still missing Joe, and she wondered if she'd ever be ready for someone else in her life. She couldn't imagine ever finding anyone even remotely like him. But it was sweet of Steve to ask her to Mass anyway. It would be nice if they could be friends. She was in such a good mood these days, that she was much more open to being friends with him than she had been. And she said as much to Professor Thomas that night after she brought him dinner from across the street, and they ate it in his bedroom.

'I think you might be right about him,' she admitted, talking about Steve. 'He seems like a nice guy after all. He says he's having a hard time finding work.'

'That's hard to believe for a bright young guy like him. I've talked to him a few times. He has a lot going for him. He went to Yale, and graduated summa cum laude. And he has an MBA from Stanford. Pretty impressive.' It was one of the reasons he would have liked to see him go out with Gabbie. He was bright, well educated, and once he got a job, the professor was sure he would do well. He just had to be patient. Listening to him, Gabbie realized again how lucky she'd been to find a job that suited her so well only days after she lost the last one. She still thought about the scene with the little girl in the restaurant, and she knew she'd always be glad she'd come to the child's rescue. Maybe it would tell Allison one day that somewhere in the world there were people who could care about her.

She and the professor talked for a while that night, but his cough sounded worse to her so she left him to get some rest and she went back up to her own room to do some writing. And she was surprised when she found a note from Steve there. It was polite, and neatly written.

'Dear Gabbie, thanks for the encouragement. Right now I need that. I've been having a lot of problems with my family, my mom's been sick for

310

the last year, and we lost my dad last winter. We could all use a bit of cheer, and I can't get back to Des Moines right now, so if you come to Mass with me on Christmas Eve, it would mean a lot to me. If not, we'll make it another time. Maybe even dinner. (I'm a great cook, if Mrs. Boslicki will ever let me use her kitchen! Steaks, spaghetti, pizzas! You name it!) Take care, hope this Christmas season ends as well as it started for you. You really deserve it. Best, Steve.'

She read it over carefully, and was touched by what he'd said about his family. He was obviously having a rough time, and she promised herself she'd be nice to him from then on. She didn't know why she'd been suspicious of him at first. He just seemed too slick to her, he tried too hard, and was too friendly. But you could hardly hold it against someone for being pleasant. She was ashamed of herself now for her suspicions, and she thought maybe she would go to Mass with him on Christmas Eve, if only for his sake. And maybe she owed it to Joe and Mother Gregoria anyway, to pray for them. It would be hard this year, but she'd survive it.

She put the note from Steve on the dresser, took out her notebook, and forgot about him. She didn't see him again until Christmas Eve, when she told him in the afternoon that she'd be happy to go to midnight Mass with him, and he looked ecstatic and thanked her profusely for her kindness. It made her feel even worse about the earlier things she'd said about him, and she said as much to Professor Thomas when she brought him another dinner.

'You should feel guilty,' he scolded her. 'He's a
311

nice guy, and he's having a hard time.' He got a million messages every day, but he never found a job. The professor wondered if he'd set his sights too high, and expected to be running General Motors. But in spite of what Gabbie had said about him initially, he didn't seem arrogant, just smart, and easygoing.

They met in the hallway at eleven-thirty, and Steve held the door open for her, as they walked out into the bitter-cold night. There was ice on the ground, and frost in the air each time they spoke to each other. They didn't say much because the air was so cold it felt like fire in their lungs each time they breathed, and Gabriella's face was tingling by the time they got to St. Andrew's. It was a small church, but it looked as though the entire parish had come and brought friends. It was filled to the rafters. And Gabbie felt a rush of familiar feelings as she slipped into a pew beside him. The incense was strong, the candles were lit everywhere, and there was the smell of pine boughs from the altar. It was like coming home for her, and she was overwhelmed by a wave of grief and nostalgia. She stayed on her knees most of the time, and once when Steve looked at her, he saw that she was crying. He didn't want to bother her, but he put a gentle hand on her shoulder just to let her know he was there, and then took it away so she didn't feel he had intruded on her.

The hymns were particularly beautiful that night, and she knew all of them. The entire congregation sang 'Silent Night,' and they both cried when the choir sang 'Ave Maria.' They both had tender memories. He had lost his dad, and his mother was sick, and he couldn't be with her.

312

And afterward Gabriella went to one of the side altars, and lit three candles to the Blessed Virgin, one for Mother Gregoria, one for Joe, and the third one for their baby. She prayed for all three of their souls, and she was very quiet when they left St. Andrew's. Steve waited awhile to say anything to her, and then he commented on how hard it was to be far from home and lose people you loved. She took a deep breath, said nothing, and then nodded.

'I get the impression this may not have been an easy year for you either,' he said to her. It had been impossible to ignore the fact that she was crying, although he didn't say anything about it.

'It wasn't,' she admitted, as they walked home side by side.

He was careful not to touch her, although in church she had felt the gentle touch of his hand on her shoulder while she was crying. 'I lost two people I loved very much this year . . . and there's a third one I can't see anymore. It was a very hard time for me when I moved to Mrs. Boslicki's.' She was trying to tell him that she understood what a hard time he was having.

'She's been very nice to me,' Steve said gratefully. 'The poor thing spends half her day taking my phone calls.'

'I'm sure she doesn't mind it,' Gabbie said. They were within a block of the house, and then, as though he'd just thought of it, he asked Gabbie if she'd like to stop for a cup of coffee. It was one o'clock by then, but the coffee shop on the corner was still open. 'Sure. Why not?' she said easily. She knew that if she went home now, she would think about Joe and wind up crying. It was Christmas

Eve, and it was impossible not to feel alone. Maybe they both needed company. He had his own griefs and worries to cry over.

He talked about growing up in Des Moines, and going to Yale and then Stanford, how much he'd loved it in California, but he had thought New York would be a better place for him. He thought he'd find a better job here, and he was worried that he might have made the wrong decision.

'Give it time,' she said quietly, and then he told her he had heard that she had been in the convent, and she nodded. 'I spent twelve years at a convent called St. Matthew's. I was a postulant. But I left for a lot of complicated reasons.'

'Most things are complicated in life, aren't they? It's a shame it has to be that way. Sometimes it seems like nothing can ever be easy.'

'Sometimes it's easier than we make it. I think we all complicate things for ourselves. Or at least, I'm beginning to see it that way. Things can be easier, if we let them.'

'I wish I believed that,' he said, as the waitress poured their third cups of coffee. They had switched to decaf. He told her then that he'd been engaged to a girl he'd met at Yale, and they'd been planning to be married last summer, on the Fourth of July. And two weeks before the wedding, she'd been killed in an accident, on the way to see him. He said it had changed his life forever. And then he decided to really take Gabriella into his confidence, and he had tears in his eyes when he told her that it was all the worse for him because she had been pregnant. They weren't getting married because of it, they'd been getting married anyway, they just moved up the wedding a few months, and he'd really been looking forward to having their baby. And as she listened, Gabbie looked at him in amazement. It was almost like the reverse of Joe. She had lost Joe, and their baby. She wanted to tell him about it now, but she didn't dare. A love story between a priest and a postulant was still a lot for most people to handle. She hadn't even admitted that to Professor Thomas.

'I felt the same way when Joe died,' she admitted. 'We were thinking about getting married, but we had a lot of things to work out.' And then, with huge sad eyes, she looked at him across the table, and decided to lay down at least one of her burdens. 'He committed suicide in September.'

'Oh my God ... oh Gabbie ... how awful.' Without thinking about it, he reached out and touched her hand, and she didn't stop him.

'Looking back at it now,' and it had only been three months, 'I don't know how I lived through it. Everyone felt it was my fault, and so did I. I'll never be able to tell myself it wasn't,' she said sadly. It was one more guilt added to all the others, but this was by far the worst one.

'You can't blame yourself. When people do things like that, there are a lot of reasons. They're usually under a lot of pressure. They stop seeing things clearly.'

'That's more or less what happened. His mother had committed suicide when he was fourteen, and I think he blamed himself. And his older brother died when he was nine, and Joe was seven, and he felt responsible for that. But I can't absolve myself completely. He basically did it because of me. He didn't think he could live up to my expectations.'

'That's a tough thing to put on someone.' It

315

didn't sound fair to him to blame her for that, but he didn't want to say that to her. She had had a hard time, they both had. And as they walked back to the boardinghouse, he put a gentle arm around her shoulders, and she didn't resist him. It was Christmas Eve, and they had shared a lot of confidences. It was amazing how much they had in common.

He left her on the stairs up to her room, he didn't want her to feel pressured by him, and he waved to her as he went into his own room. She thought about him for a while that night. He was a nice man, and he had been through many of the same agonies that she had. But as she still did too often now, she sat down on her bed and cried as she reread Joe's letter. If only she could have talked to him, if she could have been with him, everything might have been different. If she had, she might not have been alone tonight, sharing her sorrows with a total stranger, and telling him how much she and Joe had loved each other. It still seemed so unfair, so wrong of him to have done it. But she wasn't angry at him anymore, she was past that now, she was just sad. And when she went to bed that night, she dreamed that she saw him, still waiting for her in the convent garden.

CHAPTER NINETEEN

Mrs. Boslicki made one of her turkey dinners for them on Christmas Day, and this time Steve joined them. He told a lot of funny stories and made them laugh, and everyone exchanged small presents with each other. She had gone out and bought Steve a bottle of aftershave the day before, embarrassed that she didn't have a present for him, and he said he loved it. He said he had just run out and couldn't afford to buy another bottle.

And Professor Thomas was crazy about the books she'd bought him. He couldn't believe she'd found them for him, and she told him that was how she had found her new job, shopping for him. It all seemed very providential, as did her meeting with Steve. They spent a long time that night talking to each other, and the Professor noticed it and was pleased, although Gabriella spent a long time talking to him too, and as usual he beat her at dominoes. And after the first game, he invited Steve to join them.

Gabriella was worried about the fact that the professor wasn't looking well, he still had the flu, and had been dragging the same cough for weeks now. Mrs. Boslicki made him drink tea with lemon and honey, and he added a shot of brandy to it, and then offered Steve a glass, which he took gratefully. He said that if it hadn't been for all of them, it would have been his worst Christmas, but thanks to them, it wasn't. And he glanced across the room at Gabriella especially as he said it.

He walked her to her room that night, and hovered in the doorway for a while. He had given her a beautiful leather-bound notebook, which she knew he could ill afford. But he had given all of them lovely gifts, and a warm scarf to the professor.

'They're beginning to feel like my family,' he said, and Gabriella understood perfectly. She felt the same way about them. They talked about her new job, and her writing, and they stayed off the

317

subject of the past. They had enough to cope with as it was, without dealing with that too. But she had missed everyone at the convent that night at dinner. And she found herself wishing that she'd had a photograph of Joe that she could look at. They had never taken any, and now all she had were her memories, and she was always terrified that she might forget him, the exact look of his face, his eyes, the funny way he smiled. She found herself thinking of the baseball game he'd organized on the Fourth of July, and laughed remembering something he'd said. She was still so haunted by him, and Steve sensed that. He didn't want to push her, but he loved being with her, and he gently touched her face with his hand that night before he left her. She worried about it afterward. It was still too soon for her to get involved with anyone. She didn't know if she ever would again, and Steve was very different. He was so much a part of the world, he was a businessman, he didn't have Joe's innocence or naïveté, he didn't have the same magic about him. But he was a nice man, and he was alive and there with her, and Joe wasn't. Joe had abandoned her. He had taken the easy way out, because he wasn't brave enough to fight for her. There was no denying that now either.

And on the day after Christmas, Steve came upstairs and knocked on her door. He had gone for a walk and brought her a cup of hot chocolate. She was always impressed now by how thoughtful he was, and he was impressed when he saw that she was writing.

'Could I read something you wrote?' he asked, sounding a little awestruck. And she handed him a couple of her stories. He seemed bowled over by

318

them, and she was pleased. They sat and talked for a long time, and afterward they went out for a walk. It was cold again, and it felt like it was going to snow that night. And in the morning, when they all woke up, the city was blanketed with snow, and she and Steve went out and threw snowballs at each other like children. He said it reminded him of when he was a kid, and she said nothing to him about her childhood. She didn't feel ready to share that. But they had a nice time, and afterward, when they went inside, he admitted to her how worried he was about money. He was sending money home, to help his mom, and if he didn't find a job soon, he'd probably have to go back, or at least give up his room and find a cheaper one, maybe somewhere in one of the rougher neighborhoods on the West Side. That sounded awful to her, and she didn't want to embarrass him, and she had no idea how to broach the subject to him, but with the money from *The New Yorker*, she was going to have a little left over in her savings. She could easily lend it to him, until things got a little better for him. And after an agony of attempts, she finally said that to him, and he had tears in his eyes when he thanked her. She offered to pay the January rent for him. His room was almost the same price as hers, and he could consider it a loan, and pay it back whenever he could afford to. She had a job, she was in good shape, and she was very cautious with her money.

Gabbie gave it to Mrs. Boslicki for him the next day, and as she took it from her, Mrs. Boslicki raised an eyebrow.

'So? You're supporting him now? How did a poor boy get so lucky?' She didn't want anyone

319

taking advantage of her, even a nice boy like Steve Porter. After all, she said to Mrs. Rosenstein that afternoon, what did anyone know about him? All she knew was that he got a lot of phone calls. But Gabbie told her it was just a loan, and this one time only.

'I hope so,' Mrs. Boslicki said, and went to put away the money. She liked getting her rent paid, but she liked getting it from the people she was supposed to.

Gabbie talked to Professor Thomas about him the next day, and told him what she'd done, and he didn't seem to disapprove. He thought that Gabbie could trust him, and he was happy to see that they were getting closer to each other.

And on New Year's Eve, Steve asked her if she wanted to go to a movie. It was her first New Year's Eve out in the world, and she was a little hesitant about it, but he just seemed to want to be with her. They went to see the new James Bond movie, and they both thought it was fun. And afterward they went out for hot dogs, and came home in time to watch the ball drop in Times Square on the TV in the living room, and she was relieved when, at midnight, he made no move to kiss her. Instead, he talked about his fiancée, and she thought about Joe, and he walked her slowly up to her room, just happy to be with her. And then, as they stood in the doorway, he looked down at her, and without saying a word, he pulled her slowly to him. She could have stopped him then, and she wanted to, but there was something so compelling about the way he looked at her, that she knew she didn't really want him to stop, as he kissed her. She tried to force the memory of Joe from her mind, and she

320

was embarrassed to realize with how much fervor she had returned Steve's passion. He was getting excited just holding her, and they kissed again, and Gabbie felt swept away by him this time as he walked her into the room and closed the door behind them. There was something almost mesmerizing about him, and she felt his hand opening her blouse and touching her, and with great difficulty she stopped him.

'I don't think we should do this,' she whispered hoarsely.

'Neither do I,' he whispered back, 'but I can't seem to stop.' He looked very boyish and very handsome, and he was far more passionate than she had suspected. And then he kissed her again, and suddenly she found she wanted him, and she opened his shirt as he unhooked her bra and fondled her breasts and then bent to kiss her nipples. She wanted to tell him to stop, but she found she couldn't. And when she finally pulled away from him, they were both half dressed, and breathless with desire, and Gabriella looked worried and startled.

'Steve, I don't want to do anything we'll both regret,' she said finally, knowing that if she didn't stop him now she never would. They were both adults, and had no one to answer to, and they had both lost people they loved dearly, and their emotions were still raw, their nerves more than a little jagged.

'I don't think I'd ever be sorry for anything I did with you,' he whispered to her. 'Gabbie, I love you.'

But she couldn't say that to him, because she didn't. She still loved Joe, but Steve's hands seemed to work a thousand wonders. She wanted

321

him to go back to his room, and yet she didn't. She wanted to be with him, and lie with him, and not be alone just this once. It was New Year's Eve, and just tonight she didn't want to think about anything but the present.

'Gabbie, let me stay with you. I don't want to go back to my room, it's so lonely there . . . I promise, I won't do anything you don't want to do. I just want to be here.'

She hesitated as she looked at him, and she felt the same way now. She didn't want to be alone with her memories, and they could be together, and not do anything they'd regret later. They were both strong enough to do that.

She nodded finally, and kept her blouse and her stockings on as she climbed into bed with him. He wore his shirt, and his underwear, and they lay side by side under the covers and held each other. He felt very different to her. He wasn't as powerful as Joe, and she didn't love him, but he was a kind man, and she wondered if in time she would come to love him. It was certainly a possibility, and as he stroked her hair and whispered to her, she felt safe with him, and that meant a lot to her. They were both so very lonely.

They whispered in the dark for a long time, and finally she began to doze off in his arms. It was so comfortable being there with him.

'Happy New Year, Steve,' she whispered sleepily, and a moment later she was nearly asleep, when suddenly she felt him. He was lying next to her, as he had before, but somewhere he had lost his underwear and he had his shirt off, and he was gently pulling down her pants. Her stockings were already off, and she wasn't sure she wanted to resist him. He touched her gently, and without meaning to, she moaned softly in the darkness. He was sensual and adept, and awoke a passion in her that even Joe hadn't touched, in all his innocence. Theirs had been the passion of two hearts, two souls, given completely to each other without reservation. And what she began to share with Steve now was very different, it was a passion of a sexual nature of the highest order, and what he unleashed in her would have frightened her if he hadn't been so good at what he was doing. He kissed and touched and stroked, and drove her slowly into a frenzy, and she wouldn't have stopped him now for anything in life. In fact, she would have begged him not to. Their clothes lay in a heap on the floor, and he played her body like a harp as she arched her back and keened to have him within her, and finally, with agonizing slowness he gave her everything she wanted from him. She was overwhelmed by him, and driven crazy by him as he made her come again and again, until finally she begged him to stop, she couldn't stand it any longer. And afterward, they snuck into the shower, and he made love to her again standing with her, and then lay her down on the bathroom floor, still soaking wet, and took her with a force and renewed sensuality that surprised her and left her spent and breathless. She had never known anything like it with Joe, and suspected she never would again, but it was a night she would never forget, and when they went back to her bed and he pulled her into his arms finally, and held her pressed against him, their bodies sated and exhausted, she slept like a baby.

CHAPTER TWENTY

The affair that began between Steve and Gabriella on New Year's Eve was consummated again the next morning before they got up, and several times that afternoon, and within days of becoming involved with him, it seemed to be all they did now. They were polite and circumspect when they were downstairs amidst Mrs. Boslicki's other guests, and the moment they could get away, they raced upstairs separately, met silently in her room, and made love with each other. They made love every way and every place they could, and he taught her things she had never known or dreamed of. It was nothing like the pure, sweet love she had shared with Joe Connors. But what she shared with Steve was something very powerful and highly addictive. She could hardly bring herself to leave him to go to work every morning.

She had begun her new job on schedule after New Year's Day, and she loved working there. The bookshop was everything she had dreamed of. And then her nights were spent with Steve, reveling in the spell he had cast on her. And when they weren't in bed, they talked and laughed and teased, and most of the time didn't even bother to eat dinner. They devoured each other instead, and lived on potato chips and cookies.

'I can't afford to feed you anyway,' he teased her, but whenever they could force themselves to get out of bed, she treated him to dinner. She knew the tables would turn eventually, and he would repay her the money she'd paid Mrs. Boslicki for his rent in January. But for the moment, he just didn't have it. He talked about moving out on the first of February, and she hated to see him leave now. She paid his February rent for him as well, although this time she paid it directly to him, so no one would know she'd done it. Professor Thomas was pleased to see she liked Steve, and he still thought highly of him, and always talked about how educated he was, but she knew that some of the others had begun to suspect the affair, and were less enthusiastic about it. Steve had been out of work for four months, and people were beginning to make comments.

He still got as many phone calls every day, but none of his leads ever panned out, in spite of his good looks, fine mind, and expensive wardrobe. People just weren't hiring men with his qualifications, or so he said to Gabriella, and she believed him. He said people were nervous about him, because they thought he was overqualified, and some of them were just plain jealous, and she could see that. He had so much to offer.

She was doing less writing these days, and the professor had scolded her for it, and when her story came out in *The New Yorker* in March, he reminded her that it was time to write another story. He said she should strike while the iron was hot. But the only heat she wanted now was from Steve's body. She was discovering a world with him that was exciting beyond anything she had dreamed, and very heady. And the only dark note in her life was that the professor hadn't been feeling well since Christmas. Mrs. Rosenstein was urging him to get tests, but he always said he hated doctors, and said they invented trouble when there was none, and Gabriella was inclined to believe him. But there was no denying that he did not look well, and he still coughed constantly. It was a deep, wracking cough, and even if she hadn't been involved with Steve, the professor would not have been well enough to take her to dinner. He was happy she was busy with Steve, she looked better than she had in months. She seemed to be thriving with Steve's attention.

Steve came to visit her at work sometimes, and always had interesting exchanges with Ian. The two men seemed to like each other, which pleased Gabbie too, and on more than one occasion they went out to dinner with Ian and his girlfriend. And as she always did, Gabriella had to lend Steve the money. He just didn't have it. His bank account had been empty for three months now, and the only money he had was whatever Gabbie lent him. In effect, she was supporting him on the salary she made at the bookshop. It meant deprivations for her, but it seemed a small sacrifice to make in order to help him. And he was always very grateful, and repaid her by taking care of her, being nice to her, doing their laundry while she was at work, and more often than not making love to her for several hours the moment she came through the doorway. Sometimes he was already waiting for her in bed, naked. And she didn't want to tell him how tired she was, what a long day she had, or that she just didn't feel like it. He loved pleasuring her, it was the only gift he could give her, and he was more than generous with his body.

It was May before she even realized that he was no longer telling her about his interviews, or the companies he'd called. He seemed to have stopped looking for a job entirely, and was no longer as embarrassed to ask her outright to give him money.

And he no longer called it a loan now. And the only thing that bothered her was that there had been a subtle change in their relationship, and he seemed to expect it. She found him going through her handbag more than once, and helping himself to whatever she had there. After that, she found that she had started hiding her money from him. She never told him what day she got paid. And on the first of June, she realized that she had paid his rent at Mrs. Boslicki's for six months, and she asked him how he felt about giving up his own room. Of the two, she liked hers better, though his was cheaper. But he didn't warm up to the suggestion.

'I think that would be embarrassing,' he said proudly. 'Everyone would know you're supporting me. Besides, it's not good for your reputation.' But paying for his room every month was wreaking havoc with her budget. A salary that would have been adequate for her, though not overly generous, was vastly diminished by her having to pay his rent, his cab fare to appointments and interviews, and his daily food bills. She was ready to suggest he get a job waiting on tables, as she had. But when she tried to broach the subject with him after she'd paid his rent again, and couldn't afford to get her own clothes out of the dry cleaners, he got angry with her.

'Are you calling me a gigolo?' he accused her in a heated argument in her bedroom, and she was mortified that he would think so.

'I didn't say that. I'm just saying I can't afford to support you.' She had never covered this ground with anyone before, it was unfamiliar territory to her, and she didn't like it. It made her feel like a

327

monster, and he seemed to feel she owed him something, and he was easily insulted.

'Is that what you think you're doing?' he shouted at her, wounded to the core. 'Supporting me? How dare you!' But she was, no matter what he chose to call it. 'All you're doing, Gabriella, is advancing me money.'

'I know, Steve . . . I'm sorry. It's just . . . I can't always manage it. My salary just isn't big enough. I think you have to get some kind of job now.'

'I didn't go to Yale and Stanford in order to learn how to wait on tables.'

'Neither did I, and I went to Columbia. That's a good school too, but I had to eat when I left the convent.' And he did too, but he had her to pay for it. And he made her feel guilty every time the subject came up, so eventually she stopped asking him, and decided to try to write some stories. But this time, when she did, every one of them got rejected. And the day the last rejection came in, she found Steve once again plundering her handbag. He had most of her salary in his hands when she came back from the bathroom.

'What are you doing with that?' she asked, looking panicked. 'I haven't paid our rent yet.'

'She can wait. She trusts us. I owe someone some money.'

'For what? Who?' she asked, on the verge of tears. He was creating a situation she couldn't handle, and she had no other resources to draw on. It was rapidly becoming a nightmare, and when she tried to reason with him about it now, he got hostile, probably because he felt embarrassed, she explained to herself. But his answers had become vague, and this time he answered, 'People.'

'What people?' she asked him. He didn't know anyone in New York. But then again, for a man who didn't know anyone, he sure got a lot of phone calls. For months, Mrs. Boslicki had complained that she felt like she was running a switchboard. There were a lot of things Gabriella realized she didn't know about him, and he wasn't anxious to share his secrets.

'I'm sick and tired of your questions,' he raged at her when she pressed him, and he had taken to slamming out of her room, banging the door behind him, and disappearing. Sometimes he vanished for hours, and she had no idea where he went to, but he always made her feel that his disappearances were her fault. He was good at that, and it was a role she had played for her entire lifetime. She was always willing to blame herself, and assume the innocence of others. And she knew he was under a lot of pressure. He had been in New York for eight months, and was mortified about not working, or so he told her.

And when she talked to Professor Thomas about it, she felt disloyal to Steve, and the professor always told her to be patient. He couldn't be out of work for much longer. 'I'd hire him in a minute if he came to me for a job. Believe me, someone else will.' She hated to bother him with her problems, his health had been failing since the previous winter. He was beginning to look his age, and was very frail now. And that spring, they had discovered that Mrs. Rosenstein had cancer. They all had their troubles. And Gabriella's seemed small in comparison. She knew that her problems with Steve would end the moment he found employment.

329

But it was July when she realized that he was stealing her checks, and forging her name on them. He had cashed several by then, and her bank manager was going crazy. Steve had bounced checks all over town, and for the rest of the month, they were both out of money. It was only a week after that that Mrs. Boslicki took three phone calls in one afternoon from the Department of Probation in Kentucky. And not knowing what to make of it, she went to talk to the professor. But he was sure there was a reasonable explanation for it, and told her not to panic.

But it was by a series of strange coincidences that the professor opened some of Steve's mail after that and discovered that he had been using several other names, cashing checks everywhere, and was on parole in both Kentucky and California for being a forger. Professor Thomas made several phone calls of his own then, and what he uncovered was not a pretty story. Steve Porter was none of the things he had claimed. He had attended neither Yale nor Stanford Business School, and his name wasn't even Steve Porter. It was Steve Johnson, and John Stevens, as well as Michael Houston. He had a multitude of names and identities and a police record as long as his stories. He had come to New York on parole, not from Des Moines, but from Texas. And the professor felt terrible that he had been so wrong about him and had encouraged Gabriella to see him. The man was a monster.

Professor Thomas had no idea what to say to her, but after a great deal of thought and anxiety, he decided to confront Steve himself, and suggest he leave town immediately, or the professor would expose him. It seemed a simple plan, and in

330

exchange for his rapid departure, the professor would agree to keep his secrets from Gabriella. He didn't want her to know that she had been used shamelessly, and the man she thought was so in love with her was a con artist and a liar. After all the grief she'd been through in her life, the professor felt that Steve could at least give her that much.

He waited for him in the living room, and when he heard Steve come in, he got up and went to meet him. The professor was wearing a clean shirt, his best suit, and he was coughing badly, but he wanted this to be a meeting between reasonable men, a kind of gentlemen's agreement to protect Gabriella. And he had no doubt whatsoever that Steve would agree to it.

But the moment he saw Steve come in, he knew there was going to be trouble. He looked as though he were in a dark mood, and the professor correctly suspected he'd been drinking. He'd made a small deal on the Lower East Side to buy some marijuana he wanted to resell, and the deal had gone badly. He'd been ripped off by the dealer, and had wasted the last of Gabriella's money.

'Steve, I'd like to speak to you for a moment, if I may,' the professor said politely, and Steve nearly snarled at him as he walked past him. His manners were no longer quite so impressive.

'Not now, Professor, I've got some things to take care of.' He wanted to go through her room carefully, sometimes she hid money from him, and he knew all her hiding places. He wanted to get to them now before she did.

'This is important, Steve,' the professor said, looking stern. It was an expression that used to terrorize his students, but they were outclassed by Steve Porter, and so was the professor.

'What is it?' Steve turned and looked at the old man, as the professor handed him a stack of letters. They were the incriminating documents that the professor had used to begin his investigation. And he had done his homework. He had called Stanford and Yale, and the Department of Corrections in four states. He had the goods on Steve Porter, and glancing at the letters he handed him, Steve knew it. And he didn't like it. 'Where did you get these?' He advanced on the old man slowly, but the professor looked anything but frightened.

'They came to me by mistake, and I opened them in all innocence. But I think we'd both prefer Gabriella not to see them.'

'I'm not sure I understand you,' Steve said clearly. 'Are you planning to blackmail me, Professor?'

'No, I'm asking you to leave, so I don't have to tell her.' Everyone else in the house was out. Even Mrs. Boslicki had gone to her doctor. The two men were alone in the house, and Steve knew it.

'And if I don't leave?' He looked at the old man through narrowed eyes. But the professor knew he had the winning hand now.

'I expose you. It's that simple.'

'Is it?' Steve asked, giving the professor a gentle shove, which sent him reeling backward, but he regained his balance quickly. 'You expose me? I don't think so. I think you say nothing to Gabriella, my friend, or you have a serious accident the next time you walk down the street, and I don't think you or Gabriella would enjoy that. You know, one of those nasty little things that end up in a broken hip, or a crushed skull, or a hit and run. I have very effective friends here.'

'You're a rotten little bastard,' the professor said in a fury. Steve was evil to the core, and he had taken full advantage of the kindness and naïveté of Gabriella. It made the professor sick to think it. 'She doesn't deserve this. She was good to you. You've gotten all you could out of her. Why don't you leave her alone now?'

'Why should I?' Steve asked evilly. 'She loves me.'

'She doesn't even know you, Mr. Johnson, Mr. Stevens ... Mr. Houston. Who the hell are you, other than a small-time operator, a rotten little con man who preys on women? You're nothing.'

'It works for me, Grampa. You don't see me knocking myself out nine to five, do you? It's great work, if you can get it.'

'You hateful little shit,' the old professor said, advancing on him, but it was like facing a cobra. Steve was far too dangerous for the professor to win this one, but he did not yet know it. He still thought he could intimidate Steve into leaving, which was a fatal error. Without saying a word, Steve sprang forward and gave the old man an enormous shove and sent the professor reeling backward, until he tripped and knocked the side of his head against a table. There was blood at his temple as he fell, and he was more than a little dazed, as Steve bent down and picked him up by his collar.

'If you ever threaten me again, you pathetic old bastard, I'll kill you, do you hear me?' But in the face of his own rage, the professor began coughing fiercely, and suddenly he was fighting for air, as

Steve continued to hold him there, choking him as he pulled back his collar. He fought desperately to catch his breath and couldn't, and then as he hung there, suspended in space, his entire face contorted. It was precisely what Steve had wanted, as he continued to hold him. A heart attack would have served his purposes to perfection. But instead, something even worse seemed to be happening as the professor choked and spluttered. He lost consciousness in Steve's hands, as Steve dropped him to the floor and he lay there seemingly lifeless. Steve righted the table then, walked slowly around the room, making sure that all was in order, and then dialed the operator very slowly. When she answered, he explained frantically that an old man in the boardinghouse where he lived was on the floor, unconscious, and she promised to have an ambulance there in five minutes.

He picked the offending letters up off the floor, and put them in his pocket, and when the ambulance arrived, he told the attendants that he had found the professor on the floor, and the old man looked as though he had hit his head on a table. But they could see almost instantly that it was more than that. The problem they observed instantly was more likely the reason for his fall, rather than the reverse. They shone a light in his eyes, took his vital signs, and put him on a stretcher, wasting no time at all to talk to Steve about the details.

'Will he be all right?' Steve shouted after them. 'What is it?'

'Looks like a stroke,' they shouted back to him, but they were gone two minutes later, with sirens screaming, as Steve walked back inside with a slow smile, and closed the door behind him.

CHAPTER TWENTY-ONE

Gabriella was putting a stack of new books away when the phone rang at the bookshop. Ian was out picking up lunch, and she hurried down from a ladder to answer. She was still thinking about the books she'd been looking at when she heard Steve's voice, and she sensed instantly that something had happened. He sounded distraught and he was nearly crying.

'Is something wrong?' She had never heard him sound like that. Things had been a little strained between them recently. They were both upset that he hadn't found a job, and she didn't want him to think she was pressuring him, but having to make her income stretch to cover both of them had her constantly worried. 'What is it?'

'Oh . . . oh God, Gabbie, I don't know how to tell you this . . .' He knew how much she loved the professor, and a knife of terror sliced through her heart as she listened. She couldn't even imagine what he was trying to tell her. 'It's the professor.'

'Oh my God, Steve . . . tell me quickly . . .'

'I came home and found him on the floor in the living room . . . he looked as though he had hit his head . . . there was blood on the side of it, and he was lying near a table. I don't know if he got dizzy and fell, or tripped, or what happened.'

'Was he conscious?' she asked breathlessly . . . or worse yet, was he dead? She couldn't even dare to think it.

335

'Not really. He was incoherent when I found him, and then he passed out. I called the operator for an ambulance right away. The ambulance attendants thought he might have had a heart attack or a stroke. They didn't seem to know. He just left here, I called you the minute the ambulance left. They've taken him downtown to City Hospital.' It was a big public hospital and Gabbie wasn't sure he'd get the best care there. She'd been begging him for months to get some tests, as had Mrs. Boslicki and Mrs. Rosenstein. His health had been failing steadily since the previous winter. He never took her out anymore, he was hardly well enough to leave the house, even for short walks. And his wracking cough had been persistent.

'They said they'd call us the minute they know something. I'll wait here by the phone,' he said valiantly, and Gabbie was instantly grateful that he had called her.

'Thank God you were with him, or at least that you found him. I'll go down there as soon as Ian comes in. He just went out to get us lunch.' All she wanted to do was grab her handbag and go, but she didn't want to close the store while Ian was at the deli, without telling him what had happened.

'Maybe you should wait till they call us,' Steve suggested, but she wouldn't hear of it. She couldn't stay away from him. The professor was the only semblance of family she had, and she wanted to be with him.

'I couldn't stand waiting for the phone to ring,' she said anxiously. 'I'll go the minute Ian walks in,' and as she said it, she saw him come through the door, and signaled him to hurry. 'I'll call you from the hospital,' she said hurriedly, knowing that Steve would be as frantic for news as she was, as would be the others once they heard what had happened.

She told Ian the news hurriedly, and apologized for leaving him in the lurch, but he understood perfectly, and wished her luck as she ran out the door of the bookstore clutching her handbag. She hailed a cab right outside, and told him which hospital, and when she opened her wallet to pay him, she was surprised to see she had so little money. She was sure she'd had more than that the day before, and then with a nervous flutter, she wondered if Steve had once again helped himself to her wallet. He was so embarrassed to ask her most of the time, that now he just 'borrowed' it without telling her, but sometimes it left her badly strapped when she least expected it. She barely had enough for the cab fare.

As she hurried into the emergency room, she forgot about it, and had to ask several people for directions. She gave them the professor's name, and it was very confusing trying to find out what was going on. It was nearly an hour before they told her anything, but at least they didn't tell her he had died on the way to the hospital. But when she saw him, finally, she was shocked at his condition. His face was gray, his eyes were closed, there were monitors attached to him everywhere, and a full team was working on him, struggling to keep him going. In order to get in to see him at all, she had to tell them she was his daughter.

No one seemed to realize she had entered the room, and they were talking to each other in staccato phrases. He was getting oxygen and an IV, and they were doing an EKG on him as Gabriella

337

stood silently in the corner. It was a long time before any of them noticed her, and they asked what she was doing there. They had no idea how long she'd been there. And she just stood there with tears coursing down her cheeks, terrified that they were going to lose him.

'How is he?' she asked the nurse who approached her.

'Is he your grandfather?' the woman asked, curt but sympathetic.

'My father.' She decided she'd better stick to the same story, and knew that the professor would be flattered. He always said to her how much he and Charlotte would have loved to have a daughter like her.

'He's had a stroke,' the trauma nurse explained. 'He's got a fair amount of paralysis on the right side. He can't speak, and he has no motor control on the right side, but when he's conscious, I think he hears us.' Gabriella was shocked at what the woman told her. How could something so terrible have happened to him? And so quickly?

'Is he going to be all right?' She barely dared to whisper the words, but she wanted some kind of reassurance.

'It's a little early to say, his EKG isn't looking great, and he got quite a blow when he fell, which compounds it.'

'Can I talk to him?' Gabbie said, fighting panic.

'In a few minutes,' the nurse said, and then went back to the others.

But the minutes turned into hours as they did more tests, attached more machines, and by the time they wheeled him into ICU, Gabbie was frantic. She had seen what they were doing, and

338

they were obviously having a rough go of it trying to keep him breathing. But at last, in the ICU, they let her see him.

'Don't say too much to him, and don't expect him to answer you. Keep it short,' the nurse in charge said, as Gabriella approached his bedside. His hair looked wilder than usual, and his eyes were closed, but they fluttered open slowly the moment he heard her.

'Hi,' she said softly, 'it's me ... Gabbie ...' He looked like he wanted to smile at her, and his eyes recognized her instantly, but he couldn't move and he couldn't say anything to her. She gently took his left hand in her own, and lifted it to her lips, as a lone tear rolled down his cheek and onto his pillow. 'Everything's going to be okay,' she tried to encourage him, willing him to live. 'The doctors said so,' she lied, but he didn't look as though he believed her. And then he frowned as though he were in pain, and scowled at her. She had the feeling he wanted to say something to her, but there was no way he could do it. He was trapped behind a stone wall, and all he could do was hold her fingers. He made little grunting sounds then, and he looked agitated, and the nurse assigned to him spotted it immediately and said she'd have to go now.

'Can't I stay?' Gabriella begged her with imploring eyes, and he tightened his weak grip on her fingers.

'You can come back in a couple of hours. He needs to sleep,' she admonished her, wishing people could understand what the ICU was all about. Having visitors there at all was a hazard and a nuisance.

'I'll come back later,' she whispered, stroking his cheek gently with her hand, and he closed his eyes for just an instant, and then opened them as he made a deep guttural sound. It was obvious that he was trying to speak to her. 'Don't try to talk. Just rest.' She kissed his cheek, and then told him what he knew anyway, 'I love you.' She meant it from the bottom of her heart, and all she wanted now was for him to get better.

She cried all the way home on the subway. She didn't have enough money on her for a cab, and she reminded herself to ask Steve about the money in her wallet when she got back. But when she walked into the boardinghouse, everyone was so upset that she forgot all about it. Steve was waiting for her, and Mrs. Boslicki and Mrs. Rosenstein, and several other boarders. They had been sitting in the living room for hours, waiting for news, as Steve explained again and again how he had looked, and where he'd been lying, and what he thought must have happened when he found him.

'How is he?' they asked almost in unison the moment they saw her.

'I don't know,' she said honestly, 'he had a stroke, and he hit his head when he fell. He can't speak and his right side is paralyzed, but he recognized me. He keeps trying to talk, but he can't, and he seems very upset.' She didn't want to tell them how terrible he looked, but it was written all over her anyway, and Mrs. Rosenstein started to cry again as soon as she heard Gabbie's description. Gabriella went to her then, and hugged her, and tried to tell her he'd be all right, but none of them could be sure now.

'How could something like this happen so

quickly?' Steve railed at the fates, and everyone kept saying how fortunate it was that he had walked in and found him before it was too late. If he hadn't, the professor would be dead now. Of that there was no question. 'I guess there are some blessings to being unemployed,' he said cynically, and Gabbie looked sympathetic. She knew how embarrassing that was for him, but he'd had a lot of bad luck, and she understood that. She was sorry for all the complaining about it she'd done recently, and the pressure she'd put on him. She felt guilty now, seeing the condition the professor was in. It reminded her of how quickly life could change, and how easily one could lose the people one loved. But she had already learned that. It made the problems between them seem so unimportant.

He walked over to her and held her. 'I'm sorry, Gabbie.' He knew how much the professor meant to her, or he thought he did. But in fact, he didn't. The professor had become the final symbol of the family she never had, the one person she could turn to, and count on, other than Steve. He was the father she had never had, trusted confidant, beloved mentor. He had given her the praise and the hope and the unconditional love she had always longed for. He meant as much to her as Mother Gregoria had, though she had known him for a shorter time. And having lost so many and so much before, the thought of losing him now, she knew, would destroy her. He couldn't die. She wouldn't let him.

Gabriella called the hospital several times, while Mrs. Boslicki and Mrs. Rosenstein forced her to eat dinner. She could barely get the food down, as

341

Steve went upstairs to do some things. But she managed to eat a few mouthfuls of stew, just to please them, and two of Mrs. Boslicki's famous dumplings. And as soon as she'd finished, she jumped up from the table.

'I'm going to go back to the hospital now,' she announced, looking for her bag, and then she remembered that she had no money. She ran upstairs to her room. She had an envelope with some cash in a drawer, underneath her stockings, and she pulled it out of its hiding place quickly, and was shocked to see that it was empty. She had had two hundred dollars in it only yesterday morning, and it was no mystery to her where it must have gone to. She didn't want to confront Steve now, but she didn't want to take the subway at night either.

She hurried downstairs to Steve's room, and he was sitting there, reading some letters he had written. 'I need money for a cab,' she said without ceremony.

'I don't have any, babe. I'm really sorry. I had to order more stationery today, and xeroxing my résumés again cost a fortune.' He looked genuinely apologetic, but she wasn't in the mood now.

'Come on, Steve, you took two hundred dollars out of my envelope, and almost everything I had in my wallet.' They both knew that no one else could have done it.

'Honest, sweetheart, I didn't. I just took about forty bucks last night for the xeroxing. I'm sorry I forgot to tell you. I was going to tell you tonight, but with everything happening, I forgot. All I have left is two dollars.' He opened his wallet and showed her, and she was even more upset that he was lying. She knew he was embarrassed to be

342

taking money from her, and that he lied about it sometimes. But his stories wouldn't pay her cab fare.

'Steve, please, I need it. I don't have any money to get to the hospital, and I don't get paid again till Friday. You have to stop doing this.' Lately every time she opened her wallet to pay for something, she discovered that it was empty. But this was no time for his nonsense.

'I didn't do anything,' he said, looking instantly hurt and angry. 'You're always accusing me of something. Can't you see how hard this is for me? Do you think I like it?'

'I can't talk about this now,' she said, feeling panicked again. She just wanted to get back to the professor.

'Stop blaming me for everything. It's not fair.'

'I'm sorry.' She always tried to be fair with him, but the inequities between them made them both very touchy. 'Mrs. Rosenstein's not doing it,' she said, trying to sound calm to Steve. 'And somebody keeps taking all my money. I didn't mean to be rude about it.'

'I forgive you,' he said, walking over to kiss her. 'Do you want me to come with you?' He looked mollified after her apology, though still visibly wounded, and she always felt so terrible after she accused him of something. Maybe it really wasn't him. She left her door unlocked a lot, it could actually have been one of the other boarders, and looking at Steve's face, she was beginning to think so.

'I'll be okay. I'll call you if anything happens.' She ran down the stairs then, after kissing him again, and looking embarrassed, she asked Mrs.

Boslicki if she could borrow cab fare. And without hesitating, her landlady handed her ten dollars from her own purse. It was the first time Gabriella had ever asked her for anything, and she wasn't surprised, since everyone knew that she was supporting that deadbeat. They had all grown tired of him by then, with all his grand stories about Stanford and Yale, and his excuses about why he couldn't get a job. They couldn't see why, since everyone else did. Maybe he thought he was too good for the jobs he was being offered. He got enough phone calls, and they had to be for something. Mrs. Boslicki was sorry now that she had pushed Steve at Gabbie at Christmas. She thought she could do a lot better.

'Call and tell us how the professor is,' Mrs. Boslicki said as Gabriella flew out the door and ran down the street to hail a taxi.

And as soon as she saw him, she knew things were not going well. He looked restless and seemed to be in pain, and every time he looked at Gabbie, he got agitated and stared at her so intently, she was frightened. Eventually the nurses asked her to leave again, but she decided to stay anyway, and sleep on the couch in the ICU hallway, just in case something happened.

She went back and sat with him at dawn. The nurse on duty said he was awake, and he seemed a little more peaceful.

'Hi,' Gabbie whispered, as she sat down next to him. 'Everyone at the house said to say hello.' She had forgotten to tell him the night before, but she was sure he knew that anyway. 'And Mrs. Rosenstein said to tell you to take your medicine, and don't make a fuss about it.' She had actually

344

said that to her, dabbing at her eyes with a hankie. 'We all love you,' she said, and meant it more than she could ever tell him.

She had been thinking all night about taking some time off, and nursing him when he got home. She was sure Ian would understand, for a few weeks at least. She had some vacation time coming anyway, and there was nothing she wanted to do more now than be with him. She started telling him about a story she'd been working on the week before, and she told him that Steve really liked it. And as she said it, the professor frowned again and lifted his left hand and slowly wagged a finger at her. He was very weak and he could hardly raise even his good hand, and she smiled as she saw what Mrs. Rosenstein called his 'famous finger.' He was always pointing and waving a finger at someone to emphasize a point or warn them of something. She thought he was scolding her for not writing more often.

'I will,' she said, thinking she understood him, but she didn't. 'I've just been so busy, with work, and trying to help Steve, it's hard for him still being out of work,' she said gently, as the finger wagged again, and he looked like he was going to start crying. 'Don't try to talk,' she admonished him. 'They'll make me leave again if you get all worked up. When you come home, we'll go over some of the stories together.'

She hadn't sold a story since the first one, but she knew she wasn't working as much as she should have. The rest of her life seemed too distracting. And now this. She couldn't imagine writing a word while she was worried about him. All she wanted to do now was infuse him with life, and help him get

345

healthy. That was the only thing that mattered to her.

He closed his eyes again then, and slept for a while, but he stirred fitfully, and every time he opened his eyes and saw Gabbie sitting next to him, he stared at her intently, as though willing her to know what he was thinking. The nurse on duty that day was nice about letting her stay, the others all made her follow the rules of the ICU, and made her leave the room regularly. But this one just let her sit quietly in the corner, watching him sleep and praying for him. She hadn't prayed as hard or as long since her days in the convent. And she thought about the Sisters now, and Mother Gregoria, remembering the community they had been, their quiet strength and utter certainty that their God would always love and protect them. She wished for that now, to be able to draw on the faith that had brought her through everything, and she was willing Professor Thomas to feel it with her.

He was still dozing when she finally left him that afternoon, to go home and shower and change and report to the others. He seemed to have stabilized, and she thought he'd be all right for a while. She kissed his cheek gently before she left, but he didn't stir this time. He was in a deep sleep finally, and she turned to smile at him from the doorway. He was going to be okay, he was strong, and he was fighting to stay alive, she could feel it. And she tried to say as much to the others. Mrs. Rosenstein was going to visit him that afternoon, and Mrs. Boslicki was already talking about the food she was going to prepare for him when he got home. Steve was out when she got back, but he had left her a note. He'd gone to play ball in the park with a

346

friend, someone who knew about a job for him, and he promised to see her later.

Gabbie stood in the shower for a long time, letting the hot water run over her, and thinking of the man who was fighting for his life in the ICU, and all that he meant to her. He was so much more than just a friend to her, he was a part of her soul now, and she knew she could not lose him. She would do anything she had to, to keep him, she would pour her own life into him if she had to. God had given him to her, and she would not let him go now. She would not let Him take him from her. He had no right to. He had already taken far too many. And her own sense of justice told her she would not lose this one.

When she got back to see him at the hospital that afternoon, Mrs. Boslicki and Mrs. Rosenstein were just leaving. Both women were in tears, and they told her he had had some kind of a setback. The paralysis on his right side seemed to be worse, and he was having trouble breathing. They had finally done a tracheotomy on him, and attached him to a respirator, and when Gabbie saw him as she walked into the brightly lit room, he looked exhausted.

'I hear you've been misbehaving today,' she said as she sat down. 'They told me you've been pinching all the nurses.' His eyes smiled weakly at her, and he continued to look at her intensely. But the finger didn't wag, and he made no sound at her. He couldn't with the respirator. He seemed weaker to her, but his color was a little better. She chatted to him, knowing he could hear what she said, and telling him about the things they were going to do when he got home. She pretended to complain that he hadn't taken her to dinner in ages. 'Just because I have Steve in my life doesn't mean we can't go out. He's not jealous of you, you know, although he should be.' She kissed his cheek again and the eyes closed. He looked as though he were fighting a terrible battle. She told him Steve was playing ball that afternoon with someone who knew about a job, and his eyes flew open again and he stared at her, but the room was filled with silence. The sound of the machines keeping him alive and monitoring him were the only sound between them.

Gabbie stayed with him all that afternoon, and she was thinking about going home that night, but in the end she called the boardinghouse and talked to Steve, and told him she had decided to stay. He said he was having dinner with the guys he had played baseball with that afternoon. They'd had a great day, and his team had won. They were good guys and all worked at various firms on Wall Street. It was a terrific connection for him, and Gabbie was relieved that he was busy and didn't mind her staying. She had been feeling guilty for deserting him, and after she hung up, she wondered how he was going to pay for dinner. She was still pondering the question when she walked back into the ICU and took her familiar seat next to the professor.

He was quiet most of that night, the respirator seemed to be keeping him more peaceful. He didn't have to fight to breathe now. And halfway through the night, he reached for Gabbie's hand with his one good one, and he gently held it.

'I love you,' she whispered to him, and sometimes she wondered if he thought she was Charlotte. There was a gentle look in his eyes whenever he opened them. They were closed most of the time, but sometimes when she opened hers, she would see him looking at her. And she had an odd feeling late into the night that he was happy. Maybe he knew too that he was going to be all right, she thought. Maybe her strength had communicated itself to him, which was why she wanted to be there with him.

They both slept for a while, holding hands, as her head drooped and she thought of many things. She had odd dreams about Joe that night, and her father, and Steve, and the professor. She was thinking about him when she woke up. The sky was getting gray, and there were streaks of pink appearing on the horizon. It was the beginning of a new day, and the fight was still on. But she had no doubt now that he was going to make it, and when she turned to look at him, his eyes were closed, and his jaw was slack, he looked completely relaxed. The respirator was breathing for him rhythmically, and as she looked at it one of the monitors made a high-pitched whine and another one began beeping. She didn't have time to ask herself what it meant, as two of the nurses came running. A blue light went on, and two male nurses rushed in, and they pushed Gabbie aside as they began giving him CPR, pressing powerfully on his chest while silently counting compressions. The room filled with people suddenly and Gabbie watched, filled with dread, as she heard what they said and understood what had happened. The respirator was still breathing for him, but his heart had stopped. They worked frantically for a while, and then one of the men shook his head, and one of the nurses spoke gently to Gabbie.

'He's gone ... I'm very sorry...' She stood staring at them in disbelief, knowing they were lying to her. They had to be. He couldn't do that. He'd been right there next to her ... he had looked at her ... she had held his hand and willed him to live with every ounce of strength she had. He couldn't die now. He couldn't. She wouldn't let him. But he had. He had gently let go of life, and gone to be with his beloved Charlotte.

They turned the respirator off, and left the room, as Gabbie stood there silently, looking at him, refusing to believe what had just happened. She sat down next to him again and took his hand in her own, and spoke to him as though he could still hear her.

'You can't do this to me,' she whispered as tears ran down her face. 'I need you too much ... don't leave me alone here ... don't go away, please ... come back...' But she knew he wouldn't. He was peaceful now. He had had a full life. Eighty-one years. And he didn't belong to her. He never had. He had only been on loan to her for a short time, not long enough. He belonged to God, and to Charlotte. And just as everyone else had, he had left her. Without malice, without anger, without accusation, or recrimination. She had done nothing to hurt him or to send him away. He didn't blame her for anything. Only good things had passed between them. But he had still left anyway, on his own schedule, to another time, another place, where she couldn't be with him.

A nurse came and asked her if she needed anything, but she shook her head. She just wanted to be with him for as long as she could. And then they asked her about arrangements.

350

'I don't know. I'll have to check and see what he wanted.' She didn't even know who to ask. Mrs. Rosenstein maybe. He had no family, no children, no relatives, only the people at the boardinghouse where he'd lived for nearly twenty years, and Gabbie. It was a sad end to a full life, and a great loss to all of them. He had given her so much, so much love, so much wisdom, so much power about her writing. She couldn't imagine what she would do without him.

She stood up finally, and kissed him one last time, and she could sense that he was gone now. The spirit had flown, only the flesh remained, tired and broken and unimportant. The best part of him was no longer there. And as she set his hand down gently on the bed, she whispered, 'Say hi to Joe for me . . .' There was no doubt in her mind that they would be together.

She walked slowly out of the ICU, took the elevator downstairs, and walked out into the bright July sunshine. It was a beautiful day, and there were no clouds overhead. People were walking in and out of the hospital, and it seemed odd to hear them talking and laughing. It seemed so strange to her that life should go on, that the world hadn't stopped, even briefly, to acknowledge his passing. And the heavy weight on her heart reminded her of the day she had left the convent. She could almost hear a door closing behind her as she walked slowly uptown to the boardinghouse where they lived. She couldn't take a cab or the subway this time, and she didn't care. She had no money left in her purse, and she wanted the air, and time to think about him, all alone, and as she walked slowly home in the summer sunshine, she could almost feel him

351

near her. He hadn't deserted her after all. He had left her so many things, so many words, so many feelings, so many stories. And although he was gone, as the others were, she knew that this time was different.

CHAPTER TWENTY-TWO

Much to everyone's surprise, Professor Thomas had left all of his affairs in extremely good order. He had always seemed a little vague to all of them, and Gabbie had expected to find a mess, but instead he had left neat files, a sealed will, and careful instructions. He wanted a small memorial service, and not a funeral, preferably outdoors, and he wanted a passage read from Tennyson, and another small poem by Robert Browning, which had always reminded him of Charlotte. He had a safe-deposit box in a bank downtown, and a huge file cabinet filled with correspondence.

Mrs. Rosenstein was devastated, and behaved like a grieving widow. But Mrs. Boslicki and Steve were very helpful to everyone in making all of the arrangements. They went to a funeral parlor nearby and selected a somber casket. He was to be buried on Long Island, with Charlotte. And they did everything precisely as he had asked them.

A handful of them went to Long Island for the burial in a rented limousine, and Gabbie stood for a long moment alone at the grave site, and left a single red rose on his casket. And the only addition to the service he'd described was a poem Gabbie had written for him, and which she read herself, with a voice trembling with emotion. Steve stood next to her and held her hand, and she tried not to think of Joe as she read it. She was grateful for Steve's presence in her life, and the strength he gave her now. He had been wonderful to all of them, and had even redeemed himself with Mrs. Boslicki.

Professor Thomas had been buried in his one dark suit, and they gave the rest of his things away, to charity. A small obituary appeared in *The New York Times*, and it turned out his teaching career was filled with honors and awards that none of them had been aware of. There was a formal reading of the will, in the living room, conducted by one of the boarders, who was a retired attorney. He told them all exactly what to do, and the will was unsealed for the first time in the presence of all of them. It was written in the professor's neat, careful hand, and it was more a formality than a serious legal event, as they all knew he had very little.

But what the lawyer read astounded all of them, and as he read the bequests, his eyes widened, as everyone's did. The professor had been hoarding, and quietly investing, a great deal of money. And he had stayed at the boardinghouse not out of necessity, but only because he loved it.

To his good friends Martha Rosenstein and Emma Boslicki he had left, to each of them, the sum of fifty thousand dollars, with his love and gratitude for the kindness they had bestowed on him over many years of friendship. He left Mrs. Rosenstein his gold watch as well, which was his only piece of jewelry, and he knew it would mean a great deal to her. She cried as the lawyer read it. And as for the rest of his worldly goods, the only

353

thing that meant anything to him was his library, and he left all of it to his young friend, and protégée, Gabriella Harrison, as well as what remained of his bank accounts and investments, which, at the time of his death, amounted to slightly over six hundred thousand dollars. There was a sudden gasp in the room, as the attorney paused for breath and stared at Gabriella. His stock certificates were apparently all in his safety-deposit box in the bank, and everything was said to be in good order. But Gabriella could not believe what she had just heard the lawyer say. It was impossible, a joke. Why would he leave all that to her? But he had also explained that in his letter. He felt that she would use the money wisely and well, and it would help her to embark on a serious literary career without the burden of financial concern, which might otherwise hinder her progress. She was young enough, he felt, for the money to make a real difference to her, and to give her the kind of security she had not been fortunate enough to have in recent years, if ever. And he said as well that he had regarded her as the daughter he had never had, and what he gave, he gave with his love, and his heart, and his great admiration for her, as a writer and a person. He thanked them all then, and wished them well, and had signed the letter formally, Professor Theodore Rawson Thomas. The letter was properly dated and signed, and the lawyer assured them all that it was legally correct and in good order.

There was a stunned silence in the room when he was through, and then a sudden babble of voices, exclamations, and congratulations to Gabbie. They were sincerely pleased for her, and didn't begrudge her her good fortune. She felt like an heiress, and as she glanced at Steve, he was smiling at her. It was easy to see he was happy for her, and she was relieved to see that he didn't look angry or jealous. No one did. They all thought she deserved it.

'I suppose you'll be leaving us now,' Mrs. Boslicki said sadly. 'You can buy your own brownstone,' she said, smiling through tears, as Gabbie hugged her.

'Don't be silly, I'm not going anywhere.' She still couldn't believe it, and they were all amazed at the genteel fortune quietly amassed by the professor. No one had ever suspected that he had anything more than his social security checks, but it did explain his frequent generosity in taking Gabbie to dinner. The will explained a lot of things, mostly how he felt about her, and she was only sorry she couldn't thank him. The only thanks he had wanted from her was that she pursue her writing career, and she had every intention of doing that now, in his honor, as much as for her own pleasure.

'Well, princess, what now? A limousine or a vacation in Honolulu?' Steve was teasing her, as he put an arm around her. But even she had to admit it certainly took the edge off her problems. It changed a lot of things, and she was only sorry she couldn't share the news with Mother Gregoria, and the Sisters at St. Matthew's. Perhaps there was indeed a blessing in everything. Had they not closed the door on her, this would never have happened. It had been an extraordinary year for her, and it was hard to believe it had only been ten months since she left the convent. The professor had written his will in June, almost as though he had had a premonition that his time was coming. But with Mrs. Rosenstein getting ill that spring, and his own health growing more delicate, he had wanted to make his wishes known, which proved to be providential.

They all went out to dinner that night, and Gabriella treated them officially, although Mrs. Boslicki had to advance her the money. And when they got back, Gabbie went quietly to the professor's room, and looked over the library she had inherited. There were some beautiful books, including the ones she had given him the previous Christmas. She sat at the desk after that, and looked at his files, and then she opened one of the drawers to see if there were more papers in it, and she noticed a neat stack of letters marked 'Steve Porter.' She was surprised to see them there, and took them out. They were copies of all the correspondence he had shown Steve the week before. The letters to Stanford and Yale, and their responses, along with a series of letters from assorted departments of corrections, and as she looked at them, and read them carefully, one by one, her eyes widened in horror. She discovered in them a man she had never known, a number of them, a 'monster,' as the Professor had put it to him. She read the list of his various aliases, his crimes, his sentences, the time he had spent in various jails and prisons, mostly for forgery and extortion. He had bilked money from women in several states and was apparently known for the games he played, having affairs with them and then using them in every way he could until he exhausted their supply of money. He occasionally sold small quantities of drugs as well. He did whatever he had to do to extort money from everyone. And she noted in a letter based on a social worker's interview with him in jail that he had never finished high school. So much for Stanford and Yale. But the implications for her were far more terrifying than the lack of a diploma. She suddenly knew what had been happening to her for the past seven months, and what he'd been doing. He had used her, mercilessly, cruelly, he didn't give a damn about her, didn't care who she was. There had been no accident, no fiancée, his parents had died when he was a child, and he had grown up in foster homes and state institutions. There was no sick mother in Des Moines, his father had not died the previous year. Every single thing he'd told her to evoke her sympathy and get closer to her had been a lie. All of it. Even the name he used was not his true one. The Steve Porter she knew and thought she loved was entirely a fabrication.

It was worse than anything that had ever happened to her so far, worse even than losing Joe. That had been heartbreaking, but it was real and she knew he loved her. This man was a con artist and a criminal. He had lied to her, used her, stolen from her, and taken advantage of her in every way he could. She suddenly felt sick and dirty. It made her feel ill thinking of him now and the things he'd done to her, the intimacies they'd shared. She felt like a prostitute, except he was the prostitute. He was worse than that.

She sat for a long time with the letters in her hand, and then put them back in the drawer and locked it. She didn't know what to say to him, how to escape him. And then with a sense of terror, she suddenly wondered if the professor had confronted him, if Steve knew what the professor had discovered about him, and had somehow hurt him. The thought made her tremble. She felt sick as she thought of it, but she suddenly knew that something terrible had happened.

She left the room quietly and went back to her own room. She was sitting on the bed, trying to sort out her tangled thoughts about all of it as Steve came into the room and saw her.

'You okay?' She looked strange to him, but she'd had quite a day. It was a real bonus he had never expected. He had thought the old fool was dead broke, and all he had to go on was Gabriella's salary and meager savings. This was a real windfall, and he didn't doubt for a minute that he had her in his pocket.

'I have a terrible headache,' she said, sounding groggy. She was stunned by the realization of her discoveries in the professor's desk, and she turned to look at Steve now as though he were a stranger. He was, nothing of what she knew of him existed.

'Well, sweetheart,' he said glibly. He was in high spirits. 'You can buy a hell of a lot of aspirin with six hundred thousand dollars. What do you say we go out to dinner to celebrate tomorrow night? And then maybe go away somewhere . . . Paris . . . Rome . . . Atlantic City . . .' The possibilities were endless. He had some real work to do on her now, and Europe would be the perfect place to do it.

'I can't think about that now, Steve. Besides, I can't just leave Ian on the spur of the moment. And the professor wanted me to use the money so I can write. I can't just throw it around, that wouldn't be fair to him.' She didn't even know why she was wasting her breath on him, but she had to say something. She had to buy time until she could figure out what she was doing. But just looking at him now was painful, particularly if in some way he had been responsible for the professor's 'accident,' or his death, as she now suspected.

'Let me tell you something,' he said, looking amused by her pangs of conscience, 'the professor is never going to know what you do with it. It's yours now.' She nodded, unable to think of anything to say to him. Even now, his true colors were showing.

They slept in her room, as usual, that night. He used his as an office and a closet. And she told him again how ill she felt. She knew that if he tried to touch her, she would hit him. His was an abuse of a kind she had never known, but it was nonetheless clear to her now. It was no prettier than what her mother had done to her, it wasn't physical, but in its own way, it was just as ugly.

And in the morning, she pretended to go to work, just to get away from him, but she called Ian from a pay phone down the street, and told him she was ill. She went to the park then, and sat on a bench, trying to figure out what she was doing.

She knew that Steve was going out that day, to meet friends for lunch, and that morning he had talked to her again about going to Europe, but she had pretended to be too busy getting dressed to answer, and he had no reason to suspect anything.

Mrs. Boslicki was going out that day too, she said she had to buy a new bed, one of the mattresses had been burned by one of her last boarders. And Mrs. Rosenstein had an appointment with her doctor. And the others all

359

worked. She knew that if she waited till lunchtime, she could be alone in the house to go through the professor's room. She wanted to see if there were any more incriminating documents about Steve, and then she wanted to talk to the lawyer, to see what he thought she should do. But the one thing she knew was that she wanted Steve out of her life as soon as possible. She never wanted to spend another night with him, or have him touch her again. She wanted to ask Mrs. Boslicki to evict him. He hadn't paid his rent in months, and she knew that if she didn't pay it for him, he couldn't. But even that would take time, weeks at least. And she didn't know how to handle the situation ˙in the meantime. There was no one for her to talk to.

She went back to the house at noon, and knew she had waited long enough. The house was silent when she let herself in. Everyone was gone, as she hurried up the stairs to the professor's room, and left the door wide open. There was no one there to see what she was doing. She unlocked the desk, took out the stack of letters again, and they were even more horrifying this time when she read them. She pored over every detail, the aliases, the crimes, the list of women he had used all over the country. Considering his age, he had been very busy. And she was still engrossed in reading when she suddenly heard a sound behind her. She turned and saw Steve, smiling at her from the doorway.

'Counting your money so soon, Gabbie? Or hoping to find more? Now don't be greedy, baby.' There was a strange smile on his face, and she jumped when she saw him. Her face went instantly pale, and she didn't smile at him. She just couldn't.

'I just wanted to go through some of his things.

360

Ian gave me a long lunch break.' Steve said nothing as he sauntered slowly toward her. She wondered if he had canceled his lunch, or if that had been a lie too, or if this was all a trap, and he knew exactly what she'd been reading. Maybe he knew all along. She didn't know what to think now.

'Interesting reading, isn't it?' He pointed at the neat stack of letters, and she knew from the look in his eyes he'd seen them before. He didn't care what she knew now. He was in the money.

'I don't know what you mean,' she said, sounding vague, turning over one of the letters to conceal the others.

'Yes, you do. Did he manage to tell you before he died? Or did you just find them?' He had returned to the house to look for any copies of the letters that might still be around. The old bastard was just the kind of person who would protect himself.

'What is it you think I found?' She was playing cat and mouse with him, and they both knew it.

'My little history. The professor did some very thorough research. There's more, of course, but I think he managed to hit all the high spots.' He sounded proud of it, and he looked so sure of himself, it made her feel sick as she watched him. Who was this man? He was nothing to her. A total stranger. 'We had a conversation about it the day he . . . uh . . . fell.' He said it with careful emphasis and her eyes blazed as she stood up to face him.

'You did it, didn't you? You bastard.' She had never called anyone that before, but he deserved it. 'Did you hit him? Or just push him? What did you do to him, Steve?' She wanted to know now.

'Absolutely nothing. He made it easy for me. The

361

old fool got in such a state he did most of it to himself. I just helped a little. He was very worried about you. But I can see why now. I didn't realize you were his heiress. That was a lucky break, wasn't it? For both of us. Or did you know, and was all that surprise in front of the others just bullshit?'

'Of course I didn't know. How could I?'

'Maybe he told you.'

'I'm going to tell the others what you did,' she said boldly, convinced as she always was that justice could always prevail over evil. All you had to do was stand your ground and know the truth, and the devil would flee before you. But not this one. And not her mother before him either. 'And after I tell them, we're going to call the police. You'd better get the hell out of town, and fast, or you'll be very sorry.' She was shaking with rage as she faced him. One way or the other, even indirectly, she knew he had killed the professor.

'I don't think so, Gabbie.' He looked at her calmly. 'I don't think we're going to be telling anyone anything. Or at least you won't. I might. I could tell the police that you knew exactly what he was leaving you, that you talked to me about it many times and *wanted* me to kill him. I refused, of course, and talked you out of it. You even offered me money if I'd do it. Half the take. Three hundred thousand dollars. Pretty impressive. And all I did was talk to him, and he had a stroke. You can't go to jail for that, but you can for conspiring to have someone killed, someone you stood to inherit a great deal from. In fact, if I offer state's evidence, and turn you in, they'll offer me protection, and you about ten to fifteen in jail. How does that sound?' It sounded horrifying and

362

she couldn't believe what she was hearing. She was momentarily stunned into silence. 'In fact, I promise you that's what I'll do, unless you agree to give me five hundred thousand dollars right now. This is the Big Time, Gabbie. It's a small price to pay for your freedom. Think about it. Ten to fifteen. And jail is a pretty ugly place for a kid like you. I know. I've been there.'

'How can you do this to me?' she asked, her eyes suddenly swimming in tears. 'How could you?' He had told her that he loved her. He had pretended so many things, and now he was blackmailing her, threatening to destroy her life, for half a million dollars.

'This is easy, sweetheart. That's what this world is all about. Money. It's great stuff, when you got it. And I'm leaving you a hundred grand. You can't complain. You don't need much. You'd better make your mind up fast. If you drag this out, I'll take all of it. I think right now would be a fine time to call the bank and the lawyer.'

'How will you explain that I'm giving it all to you? Aren't you afraid of what it'll look like?'

'We'll work it out. Women do a lot of crazy things for love, Gabbie. I'm sure you know that.' After all, she had fallen in love with a priest and gotten pregnant by him. That was pretty crazy.

'I can't believe you'd do this.'

'Well, believe it, Gabbie. Five hundred thousand dollars, six if you don't hurry up, and I'm out of your life forever. The Big Bad Wolf will be gone, and you can cry about me and lie in a ball at the bottom of your bed for the rest of your life, and have nightmares, and whine about Joe and your mama.' He had used all her confidences against her.

'You bastard!' she said for the second time, and instinctively moved forward to slap him. He had killed the professor and now he was destroying her life, tearing it to shreds, and he had absolutely no conscience about it. He had killed a man, a man she loved and respected deeply, a good person who had been her only salvation for the past year, and now he was threatening to put her in jail and accuse her of trying to arrange his murder. The sheer horror of it overwhelmed her, and suddenly she knew she could not do this.

'Kill me if you want, tell the police anything, I'm not giving you a dime, Steve Porter, or whoever the hell you are. You took everything I had to give for the past seven months. You conned me into believing that you loved me, you used me, you lied to me ... you're not getting one thing more out of me. *Ever!*' And he could see in her eyes that she meant it, but he knew with total certainty that he was far more powerful than she was. And without saying a word to her, he walked over, grabbed a fistful of her hair, and yanked her head back.

'Don't ever talk to me like that again, Gabbie. Don't tell me what you will or won't do. You'll do *exactly* what I tell you, or I'll kill you.' Her eyes grew wide as she stared at him, and listening to him was like hearing an echo. 'I want the money. *Now.* Do you get that? Or are you even dumber than I thought? I'm not going to fuck around with this. Now call the lawyer.' He pointed to the phone and waited for her to come to her senses.

'I'm not calling anyone,' she said calmly, although her knees were shaking. 'The game is over.'

'No, it's not,' he said, releasing her again, wondering just how much roughing up it was going to take to make her understand that he meant it. Not much probably. She was scared of her own shadow. 'The game is just beginning. The romance is over. The bullshit. The pretense. I don't even have to tell you I love you now to get what I want. All I have to do is tell you what I'm going to do to you if I don't. Is that clear yet?' She didn't answer him, but stood facing him from a few feet away, wrestling with her own silent demons. 'Call the bank, Gabbie. Or I'm calling the police. The man is dead. You have his money. You had everything to gain from it. They'll believe me.' She wanted to kill him with her own hands, and the white rage he lit in her nearly overwhelmed her. She grabbed the phone off the desk and dialed the operator, and he saw it. 'What are you doing?' He looked instantly worried.

'I'm calling the police for you. Let's get it over with.' He yanked the phone out of her hands immediately and hung up, and then with a single gesture, he ripped it out of the wall, and handed it to her.

'Let's be sensible about this, or do we have to discuss it all afternoon? Why don't we just go to the bank and get it? That's nice and simple. Then I catch an airplane to Europe, and it's all over. For you. For me, it's just beginning.'

'How do I know you won't tell the police anyway that I paid you the money to kill him?' It was just the evidence he needed, and she could see now that he would stop at nothing.

'You don't know that, and actually it's not a bad idea. But you'll have to trust me. You have no choice now. If you don't give it to me, I might kill you. It might be worth it to me for all the aggravation you've caused me.' It was suddenly her fault again . . . she was the one . . . he had to do this because she'd been such a bad girl . . . it wasn't his fault . . . he didn't want to do it . . . she *made* him . . .

'Kill me,' she said bluntly. It didn't matter anymore. There was always someone, something, trying to hurt her, blaming her for everything. It was always her fault, and there was always going to be another one, hurting her, leaving her, lying to her, threatening to kill her in body and spirit. In their own way, they had already killed her, and she knew it.

'You're a fool,' he said, approaching her menacingly. He was not going to be beaten by this woman, this fool he had been living with, sharing the pittance she made, having to steal five-dollar bills from hidden envelopes she kept under her mattress. He had lived on crumbs for long enough. He wanted the whole pie now. 'Don't fuck with me, Gabbie.' But he could see in her eyes that he was getting nowhere with her, and he had no more time to waste. The others would be back soon, and he wanted his money. His money. It was his now. He had earned it.

Without saying a word, he put his hands around her neck and started to shake her, and she just stood there. She was letting him do it . . . just as she always had . . . she just stood there. She was the good little girl she always had been.

'I'm going to kill you, you fucking bitch,' he shouted at her. 'Don't you understand that?' But there was a force in her he couldn't contend with, a

366

bottomless place he could not reach and no one else had. He would have to kill her to do it, and he knew it. But he wanted the money from her more than he had ever wanted anything in his life, and he was not going to let her stop him.

'I hate you,' she said quietly, speaking not only to him, but to a chorus of others . . . 'I hate you, Steve Porter.' He slapped her hard across the face then, and the familiarity of it was terrifying. She knew the sound and the feel of it, the force of it as she reeled from the blow and struck her back against the corner of the desk just behind her. And seeing her begin to fall, he grabbed her arm and yanked her toward him, striking her again, with his fist this time. He landed a crashing blow on the side of her head, and she could hear a sound like sandbags hitting the pavement, but she had no eardrum for him to damage, there was nothing he could do to her that hadn't been done before. She had lived the same nightmare for the first ten years of her life and he couldn't touch her, as he sent her flying. He struck blow after blow, pummeling her face and her body. And then he beat her head into the floor and she could only hear him vaguely in the distance, saying something about the money. He had completely lost control by then, she was an animal that had to be destroyed, a beast who wanted to keep him from everything he deserved and had dreamed of.

He pulled her to her feet again then, and when he threw her against the wall, she knew her arm was broken. But she no longer cared, about any of it. He would get nothing from her, and the life he sought to take from her now meant nothing to her. There had been too many lies, too many

367

heartbreaks, too much pain, too many losses, and he was just one more. She saw a white light around her finally as she lay on the floor and he kicked her, screaming at her, to call the bank, to give him what he wanted, and telling her how hateful she was, how rotten, how he had never loved her. His words raged at her with as much venom as his fists did, and as she looked at him, she thought she saw Joe, and then the professor, and finally her mother, all saying something to her . . . Joe was telling her that he loved her and couldn't be with her . . . The professor was begging her not to let Steve do this to her, and her mother was telling her that it was all her fault, that she was as rotten as he said and she deserved it. But as she listened to all of them she knew the truth of what they were saying. That it was not her, but them . . . it was all their fault, not her own . . . it was Steve who was the villain . . . it was Steve who had killed the professor, and now her . . . and with a strength she never thought she could muster again, she staggered to her feet to face him. She was bleeding all over and her face was completely distorted. There was no way he could take her to the bank now, no way he could call the police, no way he could do anything but run, without the money. And with a final burst of rage, he lunged at her and tried to squeeze the last breath from her. He shook her until the room spun around her, and still she held on, still she clung to him, clawing his face and fighting back now. She would not let him do this to her, no one would ever do it to her again. She refused to let go of life as he tried to strangle her, and then finally he dropped her to the floor, kicked her one last time, and left her.

She didn't know if she'd won or lost as she lay there. And it didn't matter. They had all tried in their own way to kill her ... Joe ... her mother ... Steve ... her father ... they had tried and failed. They had reached down as far inside of her as they could get and tried to destroy her spirit, tried to extinguish it like a small flame but it was always out of reach, just beyond them, and for that they hated her more than ever. Gabbie rolled over on her back, and looked up at the ceiling with eyes filled with blood and pain, and she saw Joe standing there, looking down at her, telling her he was sorry. And this time, when he held a hand out to her, and beckoned her, she turned away, and walked slowly alone into the darkness.

CHAPTER TWENTY-THREE

Mrs. Rosenstein saw Gabriella lying there as she walked past the professor's room late that afternoon, on the way to her own room. There was blood everywhere, the furniture was overturned, and at first she didn't even see her. Gabriella looked like a limp rag doll. Her face was unrecognizable, her hair was matted with blood, there were bruises on her neck, and she lay so awkwardly, it seemed obvious to Mrs. Rosenstein that Gabriella was dead. She had to be, she appeared not to be breathing. And everyone in the house came when they heard Mrs. Rosenstein screaming.

One of the boarders called the operator immediately and saw that the phone had been torn out of the wall in the professor's room. He was one of the few guests with his own phone line.

Everyone in the house stood huddled and crying as they waited for the ambulance to come. One of the new boarders had searched for a pulse and said that she still had one, but barely. And it was impossible to know how much damage had been done, given the obvious blows to her head. It was entirely possible, one of the boarders whispered, that she'd be brain-damaged forever...so young... so beautiful ... So terrible ... they all whispered as Mrs. Boslicki sobbed, as they all asked each other who could have done this. For a moment Mrs. Boslicki wondered if Steve had done this and run away, but when someone looked in his room his things were all there. They were dreading telling him what had happened.

They were all standing around her like mourners at a wake as the ambulance attendants came running into the house. After one look at her, they moved her to the ambulance with lightning speed, and were gone in less than two minutes, with sirens screaming.

But Gabriella heard nothing this time as they drove. She saw no visions. Heard no voices. She had been in a coma since shortly after Steve had left her. She was in a faraway place free from all pain now.

The entire trauma unit team worked on her all afternoon, the arm was set, the wounds were sewn, the bruises were staggering, and this time nearly all her ribs were broken, but it was the head injuries that worried them. They did several EEGs, but the real test would be if her brain survived the swelling. Eventually a plastic surgeon came to work on her face. She had a long open wound on her chin, and another over her left eyebrow. But he was satisfied, when he was finished, with the repair work. He couldn't help noticing the bruises on her neck as well, and shook his head when he left her. He stopped to talk to the head of the trauma team, a young doctor he'd worked with before, he was the head of the department, Peter Mason.

'Nice job they did on her,' the plastic surgeon said, adding his notes to the chart. She'd already been in surgery twice that evening. Once with him, and the other time with the orthopedic man to put a pin in her elbow. 'She must have really pissed someone off.' It was nothing short of amazing that they hadn't killed her.

'Maybe it's her cooking,' Peter said without smiling. It was the kind of humor that kept them going. They saw too much of this, car accidents, people who jumped out of windows and survived despite their best efforts not to, and near-fatal beatings. What Peter hated most was seeing the children. The trauma unit was not a place that left you many illusions.

'Have the cops seen her yet?' the plastic surgeon asked casually, handing the chart back.

'They took a lot of pictures of her after we got the arm set. It wasn't pretty.' And it still wasn't. Neither of them had any way of gauging what she had once looked like.

'Think she'll make it?'

Peter Mason whistled before he answered. His whites were still covered with her blood, the list of her injuries seemed endless, and their X rays showed a fair amount of earlier damage, maybe a car accident, it was hard to say. But what had been done to her this time had been damn near fatal. Her liver and kidneys were in bad shape too from being kicked, it seems like there wasn't any part of her that wasn't damaged. 'I'd like to think she'll make it,' Peter Mason said optimistically, but he really didn't think she would. The head injuries just added one more complication. The rest would have been enough to kill her. Even one of her eyes had been affected.

'I hope they get the son of a bitch who did it,' the plastic surgeon said amiably, and went home to dinner.

'Probably her husband,' Peter muttered to himself. He had seen that before too. Husbands or boyfriends who were jealous or drunk or came unhinged for some minor reason that made sense to them and seemed to justify taking another life in order to soothe their egos. He'd seen too much of this in the past ten years. He was thirty-five years old, divorced, and afraid he was getting bitter. His wife had left him because she said she couldn't stand it anymore. He was never home, always on call, and even when he was with her, he wasn't. He was always thinking about his patients, or running out the door to save the victims of a car crash. She stuck it out for five years and left him for a plastic surgeon who only did face-lifts. And he wasn't sure he blamed her.

He checked on Gabbie himself several times that night, and everything seemed stable. She was in the trauma ICU along with a woman who had jumped out of a third-story window and landed on two children and killed them. There was a drug overdose in the bed next to hers who had fallen onto the tracks of the IRT subway, and wasn't

372

going to make it. But Gabbie was still a question. She could survive, if she fought hard enough, and wanted to, and if she came out of the coma.

The nurses said several people had called about her from the boardinghouse where she lived, but there was no next of kin, and no husband. Only a boyfriend apparently, and he hadn't been heard from. Peter wondered if he had done this to her, and figured it was more than likely. Intruders didn't put that much energy into it. This guy had pulled out all the stops and hit all the bases. The only thing he hadn't done was set fire to her.

'Any change?' he asked the nurse in the ICU, and she shook her head.

'She's just hanging in there.'

'Let's hope it stays that way,' he said. It was midnight by then, and he decided to take a nap while it was quiet. You never knew what was coming. They worked twenty-four-hour shifts in the trauma ICU, and his was just beginning. 'Call me if anything happens.' They exchanged a smile, and whenever she worked with him, she really enjoyed it. He was a nice guy and better-looking than she would ever have admitted to her husband. He had shaggy good looks, with rumpled brown hair and dark brown eyes the color of chocolate. But he was tough, too, not always easy to work for, but a hell of a good doctor.

He disappeared into the room he used when he needed some sleep. It was a supply room where they kept chemicals and a spare gurney, but it was useful.

And for the rest of the night, the nurses watched Gabriella. She never stirred, never moved, and she seemed to be barely breathing, but the monitors

373

showed her vital signs were constant. They did another EEG in the morning, and it seemed normal, but she still hadn't come out of the coma.

And at the boardinghouse, the mood was heavy. Mrs. Boslicki gave everyone bulletins as they left for work, and promised to call them if anything happened. It was the worst thing that had ever happened in her house other than the death of the professor. They were all aware of the fact that Steve hadn't come home that night, and he hadn't called her. Mrs. Boslicki reported his disappearance to the police that morning. The police had talked to everyone the night before, and asked a lot of questions about Steve. And it was interesting to realize how little they all knew about him. They knew he'd gone to Stanford and Yale, lived there for eight months, was unemployed, and was Gabriella's boyfriend. Beyond that, they knew nothing. But the police had taken a stack of messages from his phone calls, which Mrs. Boslicki was holding for him in her kitchen. But when she talked to the police that morning, even they knew nothing.

And by that afternoon, the reports from the hospital were depressing. There was no change in Gabriella's condition, and when Mrs. Rosenstein spoke to Dr. Mason, he didn't sound optimistic. He said the outlook for her was 'guarded,' whatever that meant. She was still listed in critical condition, and still in a coma. There was nothing more to say, but he promised to call if anything happened.

Peter was supposed to be off duty that afternoon, but the doctor supposed to be on this shift had called in, his wife had gone into labor, and he was upstairs in labor and delivery helping to

374

deliver his first baby. So Peter agreed to cover for him, which meant he was stuck here for another twenty-four hours. He was used to it and he had nothing else to do these days, but it was exactly the kind of thing that had cost him his marriage.

'Anything new?' Peter checked in at the desk when he came back from the cafeteria, and was told that two new cases had come in, a ten-year-old boy they'd transferred to the burn unit after a bad fire in Harlem, and an eighty-six-year-old woman who'd fallen down a marble staircase. In other words, nothing exciting.

And more out of routine than because anything was happening, he decided to check on Gabbie. He watched the monitors for a minute or two, and then examined her gently. But when he did, he saw an expression of pain flit across her face, and stopped to watch her. He touched her again, and saw the same thing happen, and it was hard to tell if she was coming out of it, or if it was just a reflex. He looked at the chart and read her name again, and moved a little closer to her.

'Gabriella?' . . . Gabriella . . . open your eyes if you can hear me.' There was nothing. He put a finger into her hand then, and curled her own fingers around it, and spoke to her. 'Squeeze my finger, Gabriella, if you can hear me.' He waited an instant and was about to take his finger away, when the smallest movement of her fingers touched him. She had heard him, and he couldn't help smiling at her. These were the victories he lived for, that he had given up a marriage and most of his life for. It wasn't much, but it was what made his life worth living. He tried it again, and this time her touch seemed stronger. 'Can you open your eyes for me?'

375

he asked softly. 'Or blink a little. Squeeze your eyes shut, or open them . . . I'd like to see you.' There was nothing for a long time, and then slowly the lashes fluttered, but her eyes never opened. But it meant that she heard him and her brain had stopped swelling. And it also meant their work was just beginning. He signaled to one of the nurses from where he was standing, and when she joined him, he told her what had happened.

'We're heading for first base. Why don't you talk to her for a while and see what happens. I'll come back and check her later.'

He then went to check on the woman who had fallen down the marble staircase, and found her in remarkably good condition. She was mad as hell to be there at all, had broken her pelvis and a hip, and she demanded to be sent home immediately. She said she had an appointment at the hair-dresser the next morning. And Peter was still smiling when he left her. She was outrageously crotchety and aristocratic, and he could just imagine her hitting him with a cane, if she'd had one at her disposal. He had promised to send her home as soon as she could manage with a walker. But she had to have surgery on the hip in the morning.

And after doing some paperwork, it was nearly midnight when he got back to Gabriella. 'What's new on Sleeping Beauty?' he asked the nurse easily, and she shrugged. There had been no further response from her all evening. Maybe it had been a reflex, or maybe she was just so beaten up, she wanted no part of the world anymore. She had withdrawn into a place where no one could touch her. Sometimes that happened.

He sat down in the chair next to her, and the

376

nurse left, and he put his finger in her hand again, but nothing happened. And she looked more than ever as though she were in a deep coma. He was just about to give up on her when he saw her move her arm in his direction, and stretch out two fingers toward him. Her eyes were closed, but he knew that she had heard him.

'Are you talking to me?' he asked gently. 'How about saying something to me?' They needed to know if she could speak, and eventually if she could reason. But right now a word, a look, a sound would have been enough for him. 'How about singing me a little song or something?' He had a funny, easy way with patients in the most devastating circumstances, which made both his patients and his nurses love him. And his remarkable skill in bringing people back from the dead, or damn close to it, had won him the respect of his colleagues.

'Come on, Gabriella, how about it? The "Star-Spangled Banner" maybe? Or what about "Twinkle, Twinkle"?' He sang it to her, softly, and very off-key, and a nurse wandering by grinned at him. He was a little crazy, but they loved him. 'What about "ABC"? It's the same tune, you know. I'll do "ABC," you do "Twinkle, Twinkle"?' And as he chattered on to her, suddenly there was a soft moan and a sound that was anything but human.

'Which one was that?' he asked, sensing victory beckoning him, and wanting to snatch it quickly. 'Was that "ABC" or "Twinkle, Twinkle"? I recognized the tune, but I didn't quite catch the lyrics.' She groaned again, louder this time, and he knew she was coming back to them. This was no reflex. And this time, her eyelids fluttered, and he could see that she was trying to open them, but her eyes were still very swollen. And very gently, he reached down and tried to help her. And just as he touched her, her eyes opened slowly. All she saw was a blur, but she could see the outline of someone standing there. She couldn't see the tears in his eyes as he watched her. He wanted to shout, 'Gotcha!' By sheer will, if nothing else, they had snatched her back from the dark recesses of death. And maybe, just maybe, she was going to make it.

'Hello, Gabriella. Welcome back, we missed you.' She groaned again. Her lips were still too swollen to speak clearly but he could see she was trying. There were a lot of questions they wanted to ask her, about what had happened and who had done this to her, but it was much too soon now. 'How do you feel, or is that a really stupid question?' This time she nodded, and then closed her eyes. Moving her head was excruciatingly painful. She moaned at him again, and opened her eyes a minute later. 'I bet you do.' He could give her something for the pain eventually, but having just come out of the coma, he didn't want to get her all doped up yet. She was going to have to live with it for a while longer. 'Do you think you can say anything to me yet? . . . I mean other than sing "Twinkle, Twinkle." ' He could see she was trying to smile at him, but the grimace she made instead was much too painful.

'Hurts,' was the one word she finally came up with. It was a cross between a groan and a whisper.

'I'll bet it does.' He couldn't begin to imagine where, there were so many possibilities to choose from. 'Your head?'

'Yes . . .' she whispered, and sounded a little less

378

croaky. 'Arm . . . face . . .' There weren't too many places on her body that hadn't been battered. But she was also coherent enough now that he knew there were other questions he had to ask her. The police were due back in the morning. They had been keeping close tabs on her. It was the worst assault they'd seen in years, and they wanted to catch the guy who did it.

'Do you know who did this to you?' he asked cautiously, and she didn't answer. She closed her eyes then, but he was persistent. 'If you know, I'd like you to tell me. You don't want him to do this to someone else, do you? I'd like you to think about it.' He sat very quietly and she opened her eyes and looked at him, she seemed to be thinking about it. She had always protected them, all of them, but even in the dark recesses of where she had been, she knew that this was different. 'Do you know who it was?' If it had been an intruder, she may not have known. But Peter suspected it wasn't. And she didn't answer his question. 'We can talk about it later.' She blinked agreement, and then tried to speak again.

'Name . . .'

'The name of the person who beat you up?' He was confused now, but she frowned and looked annoyed that he hadn't understood her. She pointed a finger at him then, barely lifting it off the covers. She wanted to know who he was. 'Peter . . . Peter Mason. I'm a doctor. And you're in the hospital. And we're going to get you all put back together and send you home, but we want you to be safe there. That's why we want to know who did it.' She only moaned again then, and closed her eyes, exhausted. She drifted off to sleep, and he watched

379

her for a minute and then left her. She was definitely thinking clearly. She had responded to everything he said, and she wanted to know who he was. It was a great beginning, and he was encouraged.

He slept for a short time that night, and came back to see her in the morning. She was looking brighter than she had the night before, and she was able to speak more clearly in a whisper, and she remembered that his name was Peter. The EEG looked good and so did all the other monitors. She was definitely up and running, by his standards at least, which didn't take much. And he was still with her when the police came to see her. They were pleased to hear she was no longer in a coma, and what they wanted now was information.

Peter warned them, as they approached her bed, to go easy. She had only been conscious since the previous evening. They asked her the same questions he had, although less gently. They told her they wanted to do everything they could to help and protect her, but they couldn't do it unless she told them who had attacked her, and she looked very pensive when they said it. She seemed to be weighing it all out, thinking about it, and she almost looked as though she were listening to something.

'You can't let this happen to you again,' Peter said quietly, standing next to her bed, and looking down at her with compassion. 'Next time you might not be as lucky. Whoever did this to you wanted to hurt you, Gabriella. He did everything he could to injure you and kill you.' He had kicked her, broken her, bruised her, tried to strangle her. This was not an accident, or even a crime of passion, in his mind.

380

It was a vicious attempt to destroy her, and he had very nearly been successful and she knew it.

'He wanted to do this to you. Now you have to help us catch him, so it doesn't happen again. You won't be safe until he's put away in jail where he belongs. Think about it.' She was, obviously, and she looked up at them, moving her eyes from one to the other. Her whole life had been spent protecting other people, hiding their crimes, making excuses for them, telling herself she deserved it, but suddenly she no longer believed that. She didn't deserve this. He did. She opened her mouth to speak, and then closed it again, unsure of herself. And the suspense was killing them. And then finally, when Peter was certain she wouldn't tell them, she looked directly at him, and nodded. Something he had said had gotten to her, and opened the door for her, and he knew it.

'Come on, Gabriella . . . tell us . . . you've got to. You don't deserve this.' She didn't, and she knew it. Just as she had known when he did it to her that he had no right to do it, no right to do what her mother had done, any more than she had. And it was exactly what she had said to Steve. It was over. She was never going to let this happen again. No one would ever again touch her, not like this, not to hurt her. She wouldn't let them.

'Steve,' she whispered almost inaudibly at first, 'Steve Porter.' But she knew she had to explain other things as well, and she barely had the strength to do it, but they were listening closely and one of the inspectors was scribbling. They knew Porter was her boyfriend and lived at the boarding-house, from what the other boarders had told him. 'Other names . . . letters in the professor's desk . . .

381

different names ... he's been in prison.' Both inspectors looked up simultaneously. This was going to be easy. Bingo.

'Do you remember what his aliases are, Miss Harrison?'

'Steve Johnson ... John Stevens ... Michael Houston.' She remembered them all with surprisingly little effort. And now she wanted to do this. She owed it to herself, after all these years, and she knew it. No one would ever hurt her again. Or break her. And Steve deserved everything that happened to him. 'He's been in prison in Kentucky ... Texas ... California ...'

'Do you know where he is now?' they asked her, and she told them she didn't. 'He hasn't been here, has he?' They looked up at the doctor and he shook his head. That crazy he wasn't. 'Do you know why he did this to you? Was he angry at you? Jealous? Were you trying to break off with him, or seeing another man?' Those were all the usual reasons.

'He wanted money from me ... I've been giving him money for months,' she whispered, and he'd been taking it, but she didn't have the strength to say that. She could tell them the rest later. 'And a friend just left me some money ... He wanted me to give him all of it, or most of it ... or he'd say I tried to have him kill the professor ... He left me the money. Steve wanted it all ... wanted to go to Europe ... said he'd kill me if I didn't give it to him.' And he had very nearly delivered on the promise. And then she added the final blow to what she had told them. 'I think he killed the professor ... tried to ... hurt him ... then he had a stroke ... he left me the money.' It was a little garbled, but they thought they could get the rest from the landlady and the other boarders at the boardinghouse, and there was plenty of time to ask Gabriella more questions later, when she felt better.

'Did he use any weapons on you?' they asked her then, and she was surprised by the question.

'Just hit me.'

'Nice guy.' They flipped their notebooks shut and thanked her and told her they'd come back when she felt better. They told her they hoped to have good news for her shortly, and she was surprised to realize as she lay back and closed her eyes that she wasn't sorry. She had done the right thing, and she knew it. It was time to stop the people who hurt her. Some of them couldn't help it, like Joe, and Mother Gregoria ... but her mother ... and maybe even her father ... they didn't have to do it ... and Steve ... all she could do now was stop him. It was too late for the others.

She opened her eyes again after they left and was surprised to see Peter still standing there, watching her. He was trying to guess what she was thinking, if she had really loved the guy, and was heartbroken over what had happened. She didn't look it. She looked happy, relieved in a way. And he could almost guess that underneath all the wounds and bruises and bandages, she might be pretty. He would have liked her anyway, he realized. There was something incredibly powerful about her. She had come through hell, and she was smiling at him.

'Good work,' he said.

'Bad person ... terrible ... he killed my friend.'

'He nearly killed you,' which was more

important to Peter. She was his patient. 'I hope they catch him.'

'Me too.'

Both their wishes were granted. The police came back at six o'clock that night just before Peter finally went off duty.

They had found Steve at four o'clock that afternoon, gambling in Atlantic City. The FBI had a file on him, and Texas and California had been very helpful. He had denied everything, of course, told them they were crazy, said Gabbie was psychotic and had threatened him. But with the condition she was in, he didn't have a prayer of anyone believing his story. It was all over for him. He had violated parole in three states, and even if he'd never laid a hand on her, he was going to be serving time all around the country. It was only miraculous that they hadn't caught him sooner. And if they had, maybe he wouldn't have hurt her. But after what he had done to her, he was going to be put away for a long time. They read him his rights and arrested him on the spot. They were charging him with attempted murder, and they were going to see if they could make manslaughter charges stick in the death of the professor. Steve had been right in the end. This was the Big Time. Gabbie listened to them in amazement.

'Will he go to jail?' she asked, still whispering. She didn't have the strength, and it still hurt too much to speak louder. Her ribs shrieked every time she moved or spoke, or even whispered.

'For a long time,' they reassured her, and she nodded. She was sorry all of it had happened. It was all so ugly, and so terrible, and she was still sick about the professor. She would much rather have had him than his money. Before the police left, they told her the boardinghouse was in an uproar that night, and everyone sent her their best wishes. But so far, no one had been allowed to visit. They would come as soon as the doctors let them.

'That's me. I'm the bad guy. You need to rest,' Peter said to her after the police left. 'How do you feel?' he asked her, looking concerned. She'd been through a lot of emotion since that morning. Deciding to turn the guy in couldn't have been easy for her, and now hearing the consequences of it. It was a hard thing knowing you had sent someone to prison, even if he deserved it. And for her, there had to be added conflict, since Peter assumed she had loved him. She had, in a way, but it had been more of an entanglement and an addiction. She hadn't known how to get out of it, how to stop giving money to him, particularly once he started pressing her for it. He had been a con man and he had manipulated her, and she had been easy prey for him. But she knew now that she had never really loved him.

'Are you okay?' Peter asked again, and she nodded.

'I think so.' She still wasn't sure what she felt, it was all so confusing.

'It must be difficult, thinking he was your friend.' He could only imagine that her sense of betrayal was beyond measure.

'I don't think I ever knew him. I don't know who he was,' she said quietly, and he saw something in her eyes that touched him. She looked up at him then with a question. 'How long will I be here?' She reminded him suddenly of the old lady who had fallen down the marble staircase the night before,

385

and wanted to get to the hairdresser in the morning.

'Do you have a hair appointment?' he asked, smiling at her.

'Not exactly.' Her hair was lost in the bandages somewhere. He could hardly guess what color it was, and hadn't really noticed. 'I just wondered.' She spoke very softly.

'A few weeks. Long enough to get you tap-dancing again, or whatever it is you do. What do you do?' He knew from her chart that she was twenty-three years old, single, had no apparent family, lived in a boardinghouse, and worked in a bookshop, and nothing much beyond that.

'I'm trying to be a writer,' she said shyly.

'Ever publish anything?' he asked with interest.

'Once. *The New Yorker* in March.' It was very prestigious and he was impressed to hear it.

'You must be pretty good.'

'Not yet,' she said modestly. 'I'm working on it.'

'Well, don't write about this one yet. Let's get you healthy first before you go back to work. Where did you meet this guy anyway? At a convention for ex-convicts?'

She smiled at him, she liked him. He'd been good to her, and she could see that he cared about what had happened to her. Everyone had been nice to her here, even the nurses. 'He lived in my boardinghouse.'

'Maybe you should think about getting an apartment. Speaking of which,' he said, glancing at his watch, 'I'm about to turn into a pumpkin. Try not to get into too much trouble. I'm off for two days.' And then he patted her leg gently under the covers. 'Take care, Gabriella.'

386

'Gabbie,' she corrected him. She had meant to do it earlier, but she kept forgetting. Gabriella sounded so formal after all they'd been through together. She was sorry to see him go, he was her only friend here. He waved as he left the room.

And when he came back two days later, she was the first patient he saw on his rounds, and he was impressed by her progress. She spoke almost in a normal voice, but it still hurt to laugh, and she didn't attempt it often. They had sat her up on the edge of her bed twice each day, and she could manage it now without fainting, which she had done the first time. And they were promising to get her out of bed by the end of the week, which seemed like an impossible goal to Gabbie. Mrs. Rosenstein and Mrs. Boslicki had come to see her by then, and all the others had sent cards and little gifts, and the two ladies had brought her roses.

Everyone was still upset about Steve, and there had been a big article in the paper about him, and the crimes he was accused of.

'Imagine, he was living with us!' Mrs. Rosenstein said with horror. And they were all upset about the possibility that he might have hurt the professor. It was hard to imagine.

Gabriella had heard nothing from Steve, and hoped she never would again. The thought that she had slept with him, lived with him, supported him, still turned her stomach. She would have to face him in court one day, and that would be difficult, and she was sure he would tell lies about her, but by then she would be stronger and better able to face him.

Ian Jones had called her from the bookstore and told her to take as long as she needed to to come back to work. She was going to keep her job, in spite of the money she had inherited. She loved working in the bookshop, and she still had plenty of time for her writing. And she had no plans to move out of Mrs. Boslicki's house. Now that Steve was gone, she felt safe there.

'So what have you been up to while I was gone?' Peter asked her after examining her. 'Dinner? Dancing? The usual?'

'Very usual. Someone came to wash my hair, and they still won't let me go to the bathroom.' She laughed, her victories were still very small here, but she was happy to see him.

'We might be able to change that.' He made a note on the chart, and looked at her arm, and how the plastic surgeon's work was repairing. She was doing nicely. And then he asked her something he had wondered about when he saw her X rays. 'Were you ever in a car accident, Gabbie? You look like you've had a few broken bones before. Your ribs look like they've been through the wars.' And he'd seen scars in her scalp when he was checking her head for swelling.

'More or less,' she answered vaguely, with an odd look in her eyes. He noticed her withdrawal immediately. She was a woman with a lot of secrets.

'That's an interesting answer. We'll have to talk about it sometime.' But he had other patients to see.

He came back later that night with a ginger ale for her and a cup of coffee.

'I thought I'd check on you. I just had dinner. They keep a stomach pump in the cafeteria in case they poison anyone. We use it at least four times

388

every evening.' He sat down in the chair and she laughed at him. She noticed that he looked tired tonight, and could see how hard he worked there.

He asked her about her writing, and where she went to school. He was from the Southwest, and in a way, she thought he had the look of a cowboy. He had a long, easy lope as he crossed the halls, and she'd noticed that he wore cowboy boots with his whites. He had noticed how blue her eyes were, and that as the swelling in her face went down, as he had suspected, she was very pretty. And very young. And very old at the same time. She was a woman of many contrasts. There was something very wise and sad about her eyes, which fascinated him, but then again, being beaten within an inch of her life by the man she'd lived with couldn't have been easy. He asked about him a little bit and she didn't seem anxious to talk about him. One of the nurses had shown him the article in the paper, but he didn't mention it to Gabbie.

'So where did you grow up?' he asked easily, curious about her, as he sipped his coffee. She was nice to talk to.

'Here. In New York.' But she didn't mention the convent. They discovered that they were both only children, and he had gone to Columbia Medical School, which was what had brought him to New York originally, and something they had in common. But in many ways, they seemed very different. He was very easy and open, and had seen a lot of cruelty in his life, but he had never lived it. There was something about her that suggested to him that she had seen more than most people her age, or many far older. There were doors that he knew were closed to him, but he didn't know how to find the key to unlock them. She seemed to do a lot of thinking.

And then, purely by coincidence, he mentioned that one of his friends from school had become a priest, and they had stayed close. He seemed very fond of him, and Gabriella smiled as she listened. He thought she was making fun of him, and he tried convincing her that even priests were people. She couldn't resist telling him then that she'd been a postulant, and grew up in a convent. But she didn't tell him about Joe or any of what had happened the year before.

He was fascinated by her history, and the fact that she'd almost been a nun, and eventually he asked her what had changed her mind about it.

'That's a long story,' she said with a sigh, ignoring the question.

He had to go back to work and promised to see her the next day. But he came back later that night, and was sure she'd be asleep by then, it was after midnight, and he was surprised to find she wasn't. She was lying in bed quietly, with her eyes open. There was something very quiet and peaceful about her.

'Can I come in?' He'd been thinking about her all evening, and felt drawn toward her room when he was passing it, when he finished with his patients.

'Sure.' She smiled and propped herself up on her good elbow. There was a small light on in the corner of the room, but it was mostly dark and cozy. She'd been lying there, reflecting about her parents. She had been doing that a lot lately, particularly her father.

'You looked pretty serious for a minute there.

Are you okay?'

She nodded. She was, actually, considering everything that had happened. Steve had disappeared from her life like a dream. It was almost as if he had never existed. In one way or another, all the people she had ever cared about had vanished, except lately she seemed to feel more peaceful about it.

'I was thinking about my parents,' she admitted, and he was sympathetic. Her chart said she had no next of kin, and he assumed they had died at some point, and he asked her when it happened. She hesitated before she answered. 'They didn't. I think my father is in Boston, and my mother lives in California. I haven't seen him in fourteen years, and my mother in thirteen.' He looked startled.

'Were you a bad girl? Did you run away to join the circus?' he asked, and she laughed at the image.

'No, I ran away to join the convent,' but he already knew that. 'It's a long story, but my father left when I was a kid, and then my mother dropped me off at the convent and never came back.' It sounded like a fairly simple story, but he suspected it wasn't.

'That's a little unusual. Why couldn't they keep you? Had you done anything to seriously annoy them?'

'They thought so. They weren't too keen on children.'

'They sound like lovely people,' he said, watching her, wishing he could move closer to her, but he was on duty, and she was his patient. He was already spending a lot of time with her, and he didn't want to cause any comment.

'They weren't,' Gabriella said softly, and then decided she had nothing to hide from him. She felt strangely safe talking to him. And it was their dark secret as much as her own. She had always felt so ashamed about it, but now she didn't. 'They were the car accident you asked me about. Or actually, she was. He was just the casual observer.'

'I'm not sure I understand.' He looked troubled as he said it. He didn't want to understand, couldn't conceive of what she was saying.

'The broken ribs. A Christmas present from my mother, several years in a row. It was her favorite gift, actually. She gave it to me often.' She tried to put a little levity into it, but it was a tough subject to lighten.

'She beat you?' He looked stunned. 'That's what I saw on the X rays?'

'Probably. I never broke anything any other way. She spent ten years beating me up constantly before she left me.' Her eyes were big and sad and he reached out and touched her. He held her hand in his own, as his heart went out to her. He couldn't imagine what she'd been through.

'Gabbie ... how awful ... didn't anybody help you, or stop her?' That was even more inconceivable to him, that she had been a child with no allies.

'No, my father used to watch, but he never said anything. He was afraid of her, I think. And finally, he just couldn't take it anymore, so he left her.'

'Why didn't he take you with him?' It was a question she had never dared ask herself, but she wondered now, and shrugged as she looked up at Peter.

'I don't know the answer to that. There are a lot

392

of answers I don't have about them. I've been thinking about it since all this happened. I know why Steve did it. It was right out front. I made him angry. He wanted money and I wouldn't give it to him. At least it was direct. But I never knew why they hated me, what made them hate me so much, I never understood it. They always said I was so bad ... so terrible ... that if I hadn't been so bad they wouldn't have had to do it. But how bad can a kid be?' It was a question that had begun to haunt her lately.

'Not bad enough to break bones about. I don't understand it either. Have you ever asked them?'

'I've never seen either of them again. I called my father once, a year ago, or tried to. But I couldn't find any listing for him in Boston.'

'What about your mother? She sounds like a good person to stay away from.'

'She was then,' Gabbie said honestly, the chords of memory still trembling deep within her. Steve's nearly killing her had awakened a lot of old feelings, and they were hard to still now. 'I keep wondering if she'd be different now, if she changed, if she could explain it to me, if she's sorry now that so many years have passed. It nearly ruined my life, it must have nearly ruined hers too.' Her eyes met his so squarely that it took his breath away, she was so open and so honest and so fearless. 'I keep wanting to know why she hated me so much. What was it about me that made her hate me?' It was important to her to know that.

'Some sickness in her own soul, I would guess,' he said thoughtfully. 'It couldn't have been you, Gabbie.' He had seen victims of child abuse in the trauma unit before, and they always broke his heart, those terrified eyes and broken little bodies, telling you it was no one's fault, no one had done it, and protecting their parents. They were so helpless and such victims of vicious, sick people. He had lost a child on the unit only two months ago, beaten until she was brain-dead, by her mother. It was not something he could ever accept, and all he wanted to do the night the child died was run out of the room and kill the mother. She was currently in jail, awaiting trial, and her lawyers were asking for probation.

'I don't know how you survived it,' he said gently. 'Did no one help you?'

'Never. Not till I got to the convent.'

'Were they good to you there?' He hoped so, he couldn't bear the thought of what her life must have been like before that. Although he scarcely knew her, it made him want to protect her. But all he could do now was listen.

'They were very good to me. I loved it, and I was very happy.'

'Then why did you leave?' There was so much to learn about her. And he wanted to know so much more about her.

'I had to leave. I did a terrible thing, and they couldn't let me stay.' In the past year, she had come to accept that, although she knew she would never be able to forgive herself completely.

'How terrible could it have been?' he said lightly. 'What did you do? Steal another nun's habit?'

'A man died because of me. I cost him his life. It's something I will have to live with. Always.'

He didn't know what to say to her for a moment. 'Was it an accident?' It must have been. She would never have killed anyone. As little as he knew her, he knew she couldn't. But she was looking long and hard at him, wondering just how much she could trust him. And for some odd reason, she knew she could trust him completely. She could feel it in him, and see it in his eyes as he watched her.

'He committed suicide because of me. He was a priest, and we were in love with each other. I was having his baby.' Peter looked at her in silent amazement. She had been to hell and back, and then some.

'How long ago was that?' Although he was not sure it really mattered.

'A year ago. Eleven months, actually. I don't know how it happened. I'd never looked at a man before. I don't think either of us understood what we were doing, until too late. It went on for three months. We were going to leave together. But he couldn't. He couldn't leave. It was the only life he'd ever known, and he had his own demons to live with. He couldn't bring himself to leave, and he couldn't leave me. So he killed himself, and left me a letter to explain it.'

'And the baby?' he asked, holding her hand tightly in his own, and desperately wanting to put his arms around her.

'I lost it.' It was all a blur now, a surrealistic impression of tragedy that always made her heart feel as though someone had just squeezed it. 'It was last September.'

'And now this. This hasn't been much of a year for you, Gabbie, has it?' It hadn't been much of a life for her before that either, parents who beat her, abandoned her in a convent, and a man who committed suicide rather than stand by her and her baby. It was a lot to live with. He was amazed that

395

she had survived it.

'This was different,' she said about Steve. 'In a funny way, it was more straightforward. I felt used by him, and betrayed, and it hurt terribly when I first found out, but I don't think I ever really loved him. I was just in a very awkward situation. Looking back, I realize he set me up right from the beginning.'

'You were easy prey for him,' Peter said sensibly, looking at her, appreciating who she was and what she had been through. 'I hope he gets a hell of a long sentence.' He was relieved to know that the police seemed to think that was more than likely. 'What are you going to do now?' he asked her, thinking about her.

'I don't know . . . write . . . work . . . start over . . . be smarter . . . I had a lot to learn when I came out of the convent. I had never been out in the world before, it's such an unreal life in there, so sheltered and protected. I think that's what frightened Joe. He didn't know how to survive without that.' But as far as Peter was concerned, suicide was not an option. Joe had left her alone to face the music herself, and be blamed for his death. It was only a solution for a weak, selfish man, and Peter didn't admire him for it, though he said nothing to Gabbie.

'You need time to heal,' he said quietly, 'not just from this. But from all of it. You've already been through ten lifetimes,' and none of them had been easy.

'Writing does that for me. It's been wonderful for me. The professor I told you about really helped me, he opened doors for me I never knew were there, into my heart and my mind, into the places I need to speak from, especially for my writing.'

'I'm not sure someone else can do that for you. I think it's within you, Gabbie, and probably always was. Maybe he just showed you where the key was.'

'Maybe,' she said, and a few minutes later one of the nurses came in. A four-year-old had been in a car accident without a seat belt.

'Oh God, I hate these,' he said, looking at her longingly. He would have liked to talk to her forever. He let her and told her he would see her in the morning.

And after he left, she lay in bed, thinking about him, surprised at the things she had told him. He knew it all now. And he had been so easy to talk to.

He came by later that night, and glanced into her room, and she was fast asleep. He stood looking at her for a long time, and then went back to the supply room to lie on the gurney. But the things she had told him kept him from sleeping. He wondered how any one human being could endure so much pain and disappointment, and why they would ever have to. It was a question she had often asked herself, and to which neither of them had an answer.

CHAPTER TWENTY-FOUR

The weeks of her recovery seemed long to both of them, but both Gabbie and Peter enjoyed the time they spent talking to each other. She needed therapy for her arm, and the ribs took a long time to heal, as did some of her head wounds, but at the end of four weeks, he could no longer find an excuse to keep her. She was almost healthy. And on her last morning in the hospital, Peter came to see her, and brought her flowers and told her how much he was going to miss her. In fact, there was something he had been meaning to ask her, but it had taken him a long time to get up his courage. He had never done anything like this before, and it was awkward for him while she was there, because she was one of his patients. But once she left, he was no longer under any restrictions about seeing her.

'I was wondering,' he said awkwardly, feeling very young suddenly and more than a little stupid, 'how would you feel about . . . if you . . . if we could have dinner sometime . . . or lunch . . . or coffee . . .' His own apartment was not very far from her in the East Eighties.

'I'd like that,' she said cautiously, but she had been thinking a great deal, and there was something she knew she needed to do first, for her own sake. And when she saw he was bothered by her hesitation, she tried to tell him about it. 'I'm going to try to find my parents.'

'Why?' After all she'd told him, he didn't want her seeing them, and he had an overwhelming urge to protect her from them. She was much more beautiful than he had imagined she would be at first, but also far more delicate, and in some ways very fragile. There was a strength about her that carried her on, but a vulnerability at the same time that had come to frighten him for her. 'Are you sure that's a good idea?' he asked, looking worried.

'Maybe not.' She smiled at him, braver than most, and much more so than he thought she

398

should be. But that was part of what he loved about her. She was willing to stand up and be counted, to stick her chin out for everything she stood for. But so far, it had cost her a lot of blows that had nearly killed her. And Peter knew better than anyone that she needed someone to protect her. He suspected he knew it even better than she did. He was twelve years older than she was, and wise in the ways of the world, and he understood now what she needed, and wanted to see if he could give it to her. He had made mistakes of his own in his life, and he had failed in his own marriage, but he had learned a lot from it, and he wanted to be someone better than he had been, to Gabbie. 'I just know I have to do this, Peter,' she explained to him, wanting to see her parents. 'If I don't, if I never get the answers from them, there will always be a piece of me missing.'

'Maybe it's already there, Gabbie. Maybe it's already a part of you. It could be that the answers are within you, and not from them.' He wasn't certain either, but he didn't want them hurting her, not again. All of that was behind her now, and she had so much to live for. But she knew that. He had come to mean a great deal to her too. And part of wanting him was wanting to be whole for him, and not a half person living in the past, and wondering why they had never loved her.

'I have to do it.' She had already decided to call Mother Gregoria and see what information she was willing to give her. But Gabbie knew even that would be painful. If the nun refused to speak to her it would remind her again of how much she had lost when she left the convent. They had never spoken since the day the door had closed behind her, and Gabriella knew she wasn't supposed to call her. But now she felt she had to, and she thought Mother Gregoria would understand that.

Peter was planning to be on duty for the next two days, and he was worried about her. He told her he'd call her that evening. And when he did, she was happy to hear from him. She admitted that she was tired, and getting up the stairs to her room had been difficult, and she realized when she saw it again, that the room itself seemed filled with memories of Steve, and she didn't want to be there. A few things had changed in the last month. The professor's room had been rented and the books he had left Gabbie were in boxes in the basement. Steve's room had also been rented.

She said that Mrs. Boslicki had been very good to her, and had brought her dinner. He hated thinking of her there, and now suddenly all he wanted was to be with her. After the ease of seeing her in the hospital every day, it seemed so odd now to be away from her. But she was still keeping a little distance between them. She wanted to pursue her past now, and she was not yet ready for her future.

She slept fitfully that night, thinking of the calls she had to make, and worrying about them. And as soon as she woke up, the next day, she called Mother Gregoria, and when she asked for her and gave her name, she was afraid they would tell her she couldn't speak to her. There was a long wait and the voice of the nun who answered the phone wasn't one Gabbie remembered. And then finally, she said she'd put the call through. There was a brief ring, and then suddenly Gabriella heard her. And it brought tears to her eyes the moment she

400

heard the voice she had loved and missed for so many months.

'Are you all right, Gabbie?' Mother Gregoria had read the article in the newspaper, and it had taken all her strength to follow her own vows of obedience and not call her. But she had called the hospital until she was reassured that Gabbie had come out of the coma.

'I'm fine, Mother. A little battered and bruised, but no worse than I'm used to,' she said softly, but they both knew it had been a lot worse. And then Gabriella explained why she was calling. She wanted to know the last addresses Mother Gregoria had had for her parents. The Mother Superior hesitated for a long time, she knew she was not supposed to give them to her, it had been her mother's request. But they hadn't heard from her mother in five years now, and in truth Mother Gregoria saw no real harm in it. If anything, it might be helpful to Gabbie to contact her. She understood perfectly why Gabbie wanted it. And she gave her her mother's last San Francisco address from five years before, and an address in the East Seventies for her father.

'In New York?' Gabbie sounded startled when she heard it. 'He's here? I never knew that.'

'He only stayed in Boston a few months, Gabbie. He's always been here.'

'Then why didn't he come to see me?'

'I don't know the answer to that question,' the old nun said softly, although she had her own suspicions.

'Did he ever call you?'

'Never. But your mother gave me his address in case I ever needed it, if something ever happened

401

to her. But we never needed to call him.'

'He must have never known where I was.' Now in retrospect that seemed so awful. He had only been a few blocks away from her, and she had always thought he was in Boston.

'You can tell him yourself now.' Mother Gregoria had given her both an office and a home address, and his phone numbers, though they were more than a dozen years old. But it was a start at least, and she was going to call him as soon as possible, and hopefully, someone at those numbers would know where he was now.

'Thank you, Mother,' Gabbie said softly, and then added cautiously, 'I've missed you so much.' So much had happened to her.

'We've prayed for you so often,' and then she smiled proudly. 'I read your story in *The New Yorker*. It was wonderful.' Gabbie told her about the professor then, and the money he had left her, how kind he had been to her, and the Mother Superior closed her eyes as she listened, reveling in the voice she had so loved, and the child she had cherished, grateful that at least one person had been kind to her since she left them. It was still forbidden to speak her name in the convent.

'May I write to you and tell you what happened with my parents?' Gabbie asked hesitantly, and there was a sad pause as she waited.

'No, my child. Neither of us can do that. God bless you, Gabbie.'

'I love you, Mother . . . I always will . . .' she said, choking on a sob.

'Take care of yourself,' Mother Gregoria whispered, unable to say more as tears streamed down her cheeks. She looked older than she had a year before. The loss had cost her dearly.

Gabbie had wanted to tell her about Peter, but she hadn't dared. There was so little to say yet. And perhaps he would forget her when she left the hospital, or think better of it, or maybe he only talked to her because she was there and it was easy. She had learned that she couldn't trust any man not to hurt her or leave her.

'God bless you, my child,' Mother Gregoria said again, and they were both crying when they hung up. Gabbie had no idea if she would ever speak to her again. It was nearly unbearable to think she wouldn't hear the Mother Superior's voice for the rest of her life, but she knew that, more than likely, she wouldn't.

She waited for a few minutes to catch her breath, and dialed the office number Mother Gregoria had given her. She didn't want to wait until he got home that night to call him. She knew that the number was old. It was from thirteen or fourteen years before, and he might no longer work there, but when she asked for John Harrison they seemed to know who she was asking about. They put her on hold and he came on the line very quickly.

'Gabriella?' he said in a single breath, sounding extremely surprised. But his voice was so precisely as she remembered it that all she could think of was the vision she still had of him as a child, when, to her, he looked like Prince Charming.

'Daddy?' She felt nine years old again, or much, much younger.

'Where are you?' He sounded worried.

'Here in New York. I just got your number for the first time in all these years. I thought you were in Boston.'

'I moved back thirteen years ago,' he said matter-of-factly, and she couldn't even begin to imagine what he was feeling. Probably the same things that she was. It was inconceivable to her that he wouldn't.

'Mommy left me in a convent,' she blurted out, still feeling like a child, and wanting to explain to him where she'd been, while he'd been missing.

'I know,' he said, sounding very quiet. 'She told me. She wrote me a letter from San Francisco.'

'When?' Gabriella was confused now. He'd known? Why hadn't he called or come to see her? What could possibly have kept him from calling?

'She wrote to me right after she got there. I never heard from her again. But she wanted to let me know where she'd left you. I believe she remarried,' he said calmly.

'You've known for thirteen years?' Gabriella sounded puzzled, and his response didn't give her the answer she wanted.

'Lives move on, Gabriella. Things change. People change. That was a hard time for me,' he said, as though expecting her to understand that. But it had been harder still for his daughter. Harder than he knew, or cared, or wanted to consider.

'When can I see you?' she asked bluntly.

'I . . .' He hadn't expected her to ask that, and wondered if she wanted money from him. His career hadn't been brilliant, but moderately successful, in investment banking. 'Are you sure that's a good idea?' He sounded uncertain.

'I'd like that very much,' she said, feeling very nervous. He hadn't sounded as excited to hear from her as she'd hoped he would. But fourteen years was a long time not to see someone, and she hadn't warned him she'd be calling. She wondered if she should have just walked into his office and surprised him. 'Could I come today?' She still had some of the exuberance of her childhood, and hearing him made her feel the same age she had been when she last saw him. It was hard to remember suddenly that she was a grown-up.

Again, he hesitated, and at his end, he was looking pained. He had no idea what to say to her. And then finally, she got what she wanted from him. 'Why don't you come and see me in the office this afternoon?' He wanted to get it over with. It was going to be painful for both of them. There was no point postponing it any longer. 'Three o'clock?'

'I'll be there.' She was beaming as she set the phone down.

She was a nervous wreck all afternoon, thinking about him, wondering how he would look, what he would say, how he would explain all that had happened. She needed to ask him. She knew it was her mother's fault, but she wanted to hear from him now why it had happened, and why he had let it.

She put on her best navy blue linen suit, which she wore to work sometimes, and treated herself to a taxi to go to Park Avenue and Fifty-third to his office. It was a distinguished-looking office building, and when she got upstairs, an impressive-looking office. He worked for a small firm, with an excellent reputation.

His secretary said he was expecting her, and at exactly 3:01, Gabriella was led down a long hall to a corner office, grinning broadly. She was so happy to see him she could hardly stand it, and as nervous as she was, she knew that her terrors would be dispelled the moment she saw him.

The door was opened very deliberately by the secretary, who then stood aside as Gabriella stepped into a room with a view, and standing there, behind the desk, she saw him. At first she thought he had hardly changed, he was as handsome as ever, and when she looked more carefully, she saw that there were a few lines in his face, and gray in his hair now. She could calculate easily that he had just turned fifty.

'Hello, Gabriella,' he said, watching her intently, surprised by how beautiful she was, and how graceful. She looked nothing like her mother though, but much more like him. She had his blond good looks, and his eyes were exactly the same color hers were. And as he looked at her, he made no move to come toward her. 'Sit down,' he said uneasily, pointing to a chair on the other side of his desk. She was desperate to come around the desk and hug him, and kiss him and touch him, but the surroundings seemed suddenly very daunting. She sat down in the chair then, and assumed he would come around to kiss her later, after they had caught up with each other and he knew her a little better.

She saw that there were photographs of several children on the desk, four of them, all in silver frames, two girls about her age, or perhaps a little older, and two boys who were much younger, and were obviously still children. The photographs looked recent. And there was a large photograph of a woman in a red dress, she looked a little stern, and not terribly happy. And Gabriella noticed immediately that there were no photographs of her from her childhood, but that was understandable, from what she could remember, there had been none.

'How have you been?' he asked formally, looking slightly pained, and she imagined that he must have felt guilty. He had left them, after all. It had to have been hard for him, or at least she imagined it was, and then she couldn't resist asking him a question.

'Are those your children, Daddy?' He nodded in answer.

'The two girls are Barbara's, the boys are our sons. Jeffrey and Winston. They're twelve and nine now.' And then he looked at her, anxious to get it over with, and get to the point of her visit. 'Why have you come to see me?'

'I wanted to find you. I never knew you were here in New York.' He had been so close by, with a family, leading his life entirely without her. Without further explanation, that was painful.

'Barbara didn't like Boston,' he said, as though that explained it. But in fact, for Gabbie, it explained nothing.

'If you knew I was there, why didn't you come to see me at the convent?' As she asked him the question, she saw a look that she remembered from her childhood, a helpless, cornered look that said he wasn't equal to the situation. He had worn the same look, watching her being beaten, from the doorway.

'What was the point of seeing you?' he asked painfully. 'We all had such terrible memories of my marriage to your mother. I'm sure that you do too.

407

I thought it was better if we all closed the door on it and tried to forget it.' But how could he forget his daughter? 'She was a very sick woman.' And then he added something that truly shocked her. 'I always thought she would kill you,' he said in a choked voice, and before she could stop herself, Gabbie asked him one of the questions that had waited her entire lifetime for an answer.

'Why didn't you stop her?' She held her breath as she listened. It was important for her to know that.

'I couldn't have stopped her. How could I?' Force, threats, removal, divorce, the police, there had been a lot of options. 'What could I do? If I criticized her for what she did to you, she was worse to both of us, to you particularly. All I could do was leave, and start a new life somewhere else. It was the only answer for me.' And what about me, she wanted to scream at him. What new life did I have? 'I thought you were better off with the Sisters. And your mother would never have let me take you.'

'Did you ever ask her, after she left me there?' She wanted to know it all. These were the answers she needed from him. They were the key to her life now.

'No, I didn't,' he said honestly. 'Barbara would have objected to it. You were part of another life, Gabriella. You didn't belong with us.' And then he delivered the final blow. 'You still don't. Our lives have gone separate ways for years, it's too late to recapture it now. And if Barbara knew I was seeing you today, she'd be furious with me. She'd feel it was a betrayal of our children.'

Gabriella was horrified at what he was saying.

408

He didn't want her, never had, and had simply walked away and left her to her own devices.

'But what about her daughters? Didn't they live with you?'

'Of course, but that was different.'

'What was different about it?'

'They're her children. All you were to me then was a bad memory, a relic of a nightmare I wanted to walk away from. I couldn't bring you with me. Just as I can't now. Gabriella, our lives have been separate for years. We no longer belong to each other.' But he had two sons and two stepchildren, and a wife. She had no one.

'How can you say something like that?' There were tears in her eyes, but she refused to allow them to overwhelm her.

'Because it's true. For both of us. Every time you saw me you'd remember the pain we inflicted on you, the times I was unable to help you. In time, you'd hate me for it.' She was already beginning to. He was none of the things she had dreamed about. He had been helpless then, and he still was. He didn't have the courage to be her father.

'How could you not call me for all these years?' she asked now, close to tears, but she no longer cared what he thought about her. He was indifferent and cruel and he had failed her completely. He had no love for her at all, and nothing to give anyone. He was selfish, and weak, and just as he had been ruled by her mother years before, he was now being ruled by a woman named Barbara.

'What was there to say to you, Gabriella?' He looked across his desk at her with exasperation. And it was clear to her that he didn't want her to be here. 'I didn't want to see you.' It was that simple. He had had nothing in his heart to give her, or possibly anyone, not even the pretty children in the pictures. She pitied all of them, and most of all him, for everything he wasn't. He wasn't even a person. He was a cardboard figure.

'Did you ever love me? Either of you?' she asked, choking on a sob now, and he found her demonstration of emotions distasteful. He looked agonized by it, and Gabriella knew he wished she would disappear. But she didn't care. This was for her, not for him. This was everything she needed to take with her to her future. He didn't answer her, and she looked at him with eyes that would not release him. 'I asked you a question.'

'I don't know what I felt then. Of course I must have loved you. You were a child.'

'But not enough to take me into the rest of your life. All I got was nine years. Why?'

'Because it was a failure. It was more than that, it was a disaster. And you were a symbol of that disaster.'

'I was a casualty of it.'

'That's unfortunate,' he said sadly, acknowledging it tacitly. 'We all were.'

'But you never wound up in the hospital. I did.' She was relentless now, in her pursuit of the truth, but painful as it was, she was glad she had come here.

'I knew you'd hate us for that. I told her so. She had no control over herself whatsoever.'

'Why did she hate me so much?' And why did you love me so little, was the question she didn't ask him. But she knew now that he wasn't capable of it, and probably never had been.

410

He sighed and sank back into his leather chair, looking exhausted. 'She was jealous of you. She always was. Right from the moment you were born. I don't think she had it in her to be a mother. I never realized that when I married her. I suppose I should have.' And he didn't have it in him to be a father, no matter how many pictures he had on his desk now. And then he looked at her, anxious to end the meeting. 'Is that it, Gabriella? Have I answered all your questions?'

'Most of them,' she said sadly, although she realized now that some of them would never be answered. He just didn't have what it took to be a father. He was less of a person than she had ever imagined. But maybe, in some secret part of her, she had always known that, and never wanted to face it. Maybe, as Peter said, the answers were within her.

Her father stood up then, and looked at her. He did not come around the desk as she had thought he would. He did not reach out and hug her, or try to touch her. He stayed as far away from her as possible, and even armed with what she knew now, it still hurt her.

'Thank you for your visit,' he said, indicating that the meeting was over. He pressed a button on his desk, and the secretary reappeared and stood holding the door open for Gabbie.

'Thank you,' Gabriella said. She did not call him 'Daddy' this time, or try to kiss him. There was no point. The man she remembered had been bad enough, this one was worse. And whatever he was, whoever he had been to her once, he was no longer her father. He had given up the job fourteen years before, and abdicated completely. That was

411

entirely clear now. The father she had known, such as he was, had died the day he left them.

She stood in the doorway for one last minute and looked at him, wanting to remember him, and then she turned around and walked away without saying another word to him. There was nothing left to say now. It was truly over.

And as soon as the secretary closed the door again, he came around his desk, looking pained. It was like looking through a window into the past for him, and remembering all that sorrow. She was a pretty girl, but he felt nothing for her. He had closed that door a long time before, and there was no opening it again. He had always known that. And trying not to think of her, and the look in her eyes that bore into him like hot coals, he opened a cabinet, mixed himself a stiff martini, and stood staring out the window as he drank it.

CHAPTER TWENTY FIVE

When Gabriella left her father that afternoon, she went straight to the ticket office on Fifth Avenue and bought a ticket to San Francisco. And as she purchased it, she was still thinking of the meeting with her father. Nothing about it had gone as she had expected. She felt sad in a way, and relieved too. She realized now that what had happened wasn't because of her, because in fact she had been so terrible, but because they were flawed. It was not because of who she was at the time, but who they weren't. And she had only just begun to understand that.

412

He was such an empty man, so cold, so frightened, so unable to cope with reality or honest emotions. It still stunned her that during the entire time in his office, he had never touched her, and would have shrunk from it if she tried to. He didn't want her in his life, and hadn't for years. In his mind, she was still too closely linked with her mother. But at least she understood something about him now. It was not that he had withheld something from her at the time, he had never had it to give her, or maybe even to give her mother. And he was right about one thing. It was too late now. As much as she had longed for him for all those years, and dreamed of him, and told herself that he would be there for her, if only he knew where she was, she now knew that he had known where she was all along, and didn't even care enough to see her. He didn't love or want her, there was no hiding from that fact now. It hurt to know that, but in its own way, it freed her. It was almost as though he had died fourteen years before, and she could lay the body to rest now. All these years, he had only been missing in action, and now she had a body to bury. She could still see him watching her as she left his office.

And when she got back to the boardinghouse, she found that Peter had called her from the hospital. She called and had him paged, and told him about the meeting.

'Do you feel better now?' he asked, sounding worried.

'Sort of,' she said honestly. It still hurt her that her father hadn't even wanted to hold her, or kiss her. But that was who he had always been. He had never held her then either, she now remembered.

413

Seeing him had brought back a lot of memories, none of which were pleasant. The only time she remembered him being tender with her, or even something close to it, was the night before he left them. And knowing what he was about to do, he probably felt guilty. 'You were right about one thing,' she told Peter, 'I think some of the answers are within me. I just didn't know it.' He was relieved to hear it. He was nervous about this odyssey of the past she had embarked on. He suspected that it was going to be very painful for her, and not the homecoming she wanted.

'What are you going to do now?' he asked. They had just paged him again, and he knew he couldn't talk much longer.

'I'm flying to San Francisco tomorrow.' He didn't know why, but he felt as though he should go with her. But he knew she'd never let him. She was determined to slay her dragons single-handed, no matter how dangerous, or how painful. And he admired her for it.

'Will you be all right out there all alone?'

'I think so,' she said honestly. It still frightened her to think of seeing her mother. But she knew she had to. She was the one with the real answers. And especially the one to the final question: Why didn't you ever love me? She felt like a child in a fairy tale, looking for answers under mushrooms. *Alice in Wonderland*, or Dorothy in *The Wizard of Oz*, and she said as much to Peter.

'If you wait a few days, I'll go out there with you. I've got some time off later this week, and it might be easier for you.'

'I need to do this,' she explained, and promised to call him from San Francisco.

'Take care of yourself, Gabbie.' And then unexpectedly, 'I miss you.'

'I miss you too,' she said softly. It was a prelude of better things to come between them, but not until she had resolved her past completely. She knew now, that without the answers, she had nothing to offer him, and he could never reach her. The pain of her childhood and knowing that she hadn't been loved would always stand between them. She would never believe him. And she would always believe that ultimately he would abandon her, just as they had. And the terror of waiting for it to happen would destroy them, or her, in the meantime.

'Call me when you get there,' he told her anxiously, and then he had to leave her to see patients.

She was very pensive as she walked upstairs to pack her suitcase, and as she had the night before, she found the room depressing. It was too full of Steve, and bad dreams, and ugly nightmares. She couldn't sleep all night thinking of the trip to San Francisco, but it was too far to go down four flights of stairs to call Peter, so she just lay there waiting for morning.

Everyone in the house was still asleep when she left, and she left a note for Mrs. Boslicki, telling her where she was going. 'I've gone to San Francisco to see my mother.' It would have had a nice ring to it, she thought, if it had been a different mother.

The flight to San Francisco passed uneventfully, and she took a bus into the city, with her small overnight bag. She was surprised by how cold it was, although it was August. There was a brisk wind, it was a foggy day, and it was decidedly chilly, which everyone said was typical of a San Francisco summer.

She stopped and had a bite to eat, and then called the telephone number she'd been given, and then realized instantly how foolish she'd been not to call first. What if they were away on vacation? But instead of that, there was a recording saying that the phone had been disconnected. She didn't know what to do then. She got a cab and drove by the address, but when she rang the bell they said that no one by that name lived there. She was almost in tears by then, and the cabdriver suggested they stop at a phone booth and call Information. All she knew was that the name of the man her mother had married years before was Frank Waterford. She remembered him vaguely as a nice-looking man who never talked to her. But surely he would now. And she followed the cabbie's suggestion, and it proved fruitful. Frank Waterford was listed on Twenty-eighth Avenue, in an area the driver said was called Seacliff.

She dialed the number she'd gotten from Information. A woman answered, but it did not sound like her mother. She asked for Mrs. Waterford and was told they were out, and would be back at four-thirty. She only had an hour to kill then, and debated between calling and showing up, and she finally decided to just go there. They drove up in front of the house at exactly four-thirty, and there was a silver Bentley parked in the driveway.

Gabriella held her suitcase in one hand, and rang the doorbell with the other. It was the same battered cardboard bag she'd been given when she left the convent. But although her wardrobe had improved in the last year, her luggage hadn't. This was the first trip she'd ever taken.

'Yes?' A woman in a yellow cashmere sweater opened the door. She was wearing a string of pearls, and had blond hair that had been 'assisted' in keeping its color, and she looked as though she was in her mid fifties. But she looked pleasantly at Gabriella. 'May I help you?' Gabriella looked like a runaway with her blond hair tousled by the wind, her big blue eyes, and her suitcase, and she looked younger than her twenty-three years. The woman who opened the door had no idea who she was, as Gabriella asked politely for 'Mrs. Waterford' and then looked stunned when the woman said she was. She had come to the wrong house after all, obviously a different Mr. and Mrs. Frank Waterford lived here. 'I'm sorry,' the woman said pleasantly, when Gabriella said she was looking for her mother, as a tall, well-built man with graying hair came up behind her. But he was the Frank Waterford she remembered, only thirteen years older than when she'd last seen him.

'Something wrong?' He looked concerned, and then saw the girl with the suitcase in the doorway. She looked lost but harmless.

'This young lady is looking for her mother,' his wife explained pleasantly, 'and she's come to the wrong address. I was trying to help her figure out what to do now.'

'Gabriella?' he asked, frowning at her in confusion. He had heard her say her name, and still remembered it, although he had hardly ever seen her, and she looked very different. She was all grown up now.

'Yes.' She nodded. 'Mr. Waterford?' He smiled

417

at her then, more than a little surprised to see her. 'I'm looking for my mother.' A glance was exchanged between the two Waterfords, who understood now. 'I take it she doesn't live here.'

'No, she doesn't,' he said carefully. 'Why don't you come in for a minute?' He looked much happier to see her than her father had, and seemed much kinder. They invited her to set down her bag, and come into the living room with them. He offered her a drink, and she said she'd be happy with a glass of water, and the woman with the blond hair went to get it for her.

'Are you and my mother divorced?' she asked, looking a little nervous, and he hesitated, but there was no way to keep the truth from her, and no reason to do it.

'No, Gabriella, we're not divorced. Your mother died four years ago. I'm very sorry.' For a moment, Gabriella was stunned into silence. She was gone, taking all her secrets with her. Gabriella knew instantly that she would never be free now.

'I felt sure your father would tell you.' He had a soft Southern drawl, which she remembered now, and thought she had heard her mother say he was originally from Texas. 'I sent him a copy of the obituary, just so he'd know, and I assumed he'd tell you.' The whole situation was puzzling to him until Gabriella explained it.

'I saw my father for the first time in fourteen years yesterday. He didn't say anything to me. But I didn't tell him I was going to come here.'

'But didn't you live with him?' Frank Waterford looked baffled. 'She told me she had given up full custody of you to him in order to marry me, and he never let her see you again. She never even put any

418

pictures of you anywhere, because she said it was too painful.' They were interesting people, her parents. What they had done to her was no accident, it had taken considerable effort.

She sighed as she answered him, amazed at the lies they had told their spouses, all in order to desert her. 'There were no pictures of me, Mr. Waterford, they never took any. And she left me at St. Matthew's convent in New York when she went to Reno. She never came back. I never heard from her again, she just sent a check every month to pay for my board there, and it stopped when I turned eighteen. And that was the end of it.'

'She died a year later,' he explained, putting the pieces of the story together finally. 'She always told me that was a charitable donation, that the nuns there had been good to her once. I never had any idea that you lived there.' He felt suddenly as though he should apologize to her, as though he had been part of the perfidy, but Gabriella knew he wasn't. It had all been her mother, and it was very like her.

'How did she die?'

'Of breast cancer,' he said, looking at Gabriella. There was something so sad in her eyes that he wanted to hug her. 'She wasn't a very happy woman,' he said diplomatically, not wanting to offend her daughter, or destroy her illusions about her. 'Maybe she missed you. I'm sure she must have.'

'That's why I came here,' Gabriella explained quietly, setting her glass down. 'There were some questions I wanted to ask her.'

'Maybe I can help you,' he offered, as his wife listened with compassion and interest.

419

'I don't think so. I wanted to ask her why she left me, and why,' she found herself struggling with tears in front of these people who were strangers to her, and it embarrassed her, but they were kind to her, and it was a difficult moment. 'I wanted to ask her why she did a lot of things before she left me.' He could see easily that her questions were painful, and he began to suspect that there was more to the story than he had ever dreamed of, and he decided to be honest with her. It was too late now to be otherwise. And he felt that Gabriella deserved at least that from him. It was all he had to give her.

'Gabriella, I'm going to level with you. You may not like it, but maybe it will help you. I was married to your mother for the worst nine years of my life. We were talking about getting a divorce when she got sick, but I didn't feel right about it under the circumstances. I thought I should stick by her, and I did. But she was a cold, difficult, angry, vicious, vengeful woman, and I don't think she had a kind bone in her body. I don't know what kind of a mother she was to you, but I'd venture to say that she was no nicer to you than she was to me, and maybe the nicest thing she ever did for you was leave you at St. Matthew's. She was a hateful woman.' He said it dispassionately, and his new wife patted his hand as he said it. 'I'm sorry she left you,' he went on, 'but I can't imagine you'd ever have been happy with her, even with me around. When I was going out with her in New York, she forbade me to speak to you, and I never understood it. You were the cutest little thing I'd ever seen, and I love kids. I have five of my own in Texas, but they wouldn't even come here to visit when I was married to her. She hated them, and

420

they hated her right up until the day she died, and I'm not sure I blame them. By the time she died, I wasn't too fond of her either. She was a woman without many redeeming features. Her obituary was the shortest one I've ever seen, because no one could think of anything nice to say about her.' And then, looking back into the past, he remembered something else he had forgotten. 'You know, back in New York, she tried to tell me that you had destroyed her marriage to your father. I never figured that one out, but I always got the feeling then that she was jealous of you, and that's why she gave up custody to your father. She didn't want you around, sweetheart. But I never figured for a minute she'd desert you. I wouldn't have married her if I knew that. Any woman who can do a thing like that . . . well, it tells you something about 'em . . . But knowing what she was, I believe it of her now. Amazing that for all those years, I never knew anything about it. I just figured it was painful for her talking about giving you up, so we never talked about you.'

It was indeed an amazing story. They had all forgotten her, buried her with the past, both her mother and her father. She truly had been abandoned by them.

And then she began telling the Waterfords what it had been like, what her mother had done to her, and how her father had let it happen, the beatings, the hospitals, the bruises, the hatred, the accusations. Her story went on for a long time and took a long time to tell, but when it was over, all three of them were crying, and Frank Waterford was holding her hand, and his wife, Jane, had an arm around her shoulders. They were the nicest

421

people she'd ever met, and she knew for a fact that her mother had never deserved him. She'd just been lucky, and he'd paid a high price for the pleasure of her company. He still looked grim when he talked about her, but so did Gabbie.

'I wanted to ask her,' Gabbie said tearfully, as she sat with them, 'why she never loved me.' It was the key to everything for her. The final answer. And now she would never know it. What was it about her that they couldn't love? Was it her or them? It was as though she had expected her mother to apologize, to beg her forgiveness, to tell her she had loved her but never knew how to show it. Anything would have been better than the raw hatred she had met at her hands and seen in her eyes for the ten years she had endured before her mother left her. But now she could not ask her.

'There's a very simple answer to that, Gabbie,' Frank said, wiping his eyes. 'She couldn't love anyone. She had nothing to give. I'm sorry to speak ill of the dead, but she was rotten to the core, mean as a snake. There was something wrong with her. No single human being can be that hateful. I always thought it was my fault. For the first five years of our marriage I thought it was me, that I had disappointed her somehow, or wasn't good enough, or had failed her. And then I realized it had nothing to do with me. It was her. It was a lot easier after that. I just felt sorry for her, but she still wasn't easy to live with.

'What she did to you is unforgivable, and you'll have to live with the scars of it for the rest of your life. You'll have to decide if you have it in your heart to forgive her, or if you just want to turn your back on her, as she did you, and forget her. But

422

whatever you decide, you have to know that it had nothing to do with you. Any other human being in the world, except those two you were related to, would have loved you. It was just bad luck. You wound up with rotten parents. Maybe that answer's too easy for you, but I think that's what it was. She was a terrible person. There was something very important missing in her, and always would be. If she were here today, she wouldn't be able to give you the answer either. She never had any love in her heart from the first day I met her. She was very beautiful, and a lot of fun sometimes in the beginning, but not for long. The meanness came out real quick, as soon as we were married. And that was it, until she died. It had nothing to do with you, Gabbie. You were in the wrong place, at the wrong time, and in the wrong line up in heaven, when they handed out the parents.'

That was it, then? she wondered. As simple as that? But as she listened to him, she knew it was true, it had nothing to do with her, and never had. She had her answer. It was all an accident of fate, a freak of nature, a collision of two planets that had never been meant to coexist side by side, and she had gotten caught in the resulting explosion. There was no answer to the question of why she had never loved her. Eloise Harrison Waterford had never loved anyone. She had no love to give, not even to her own daughter. And Gabbie felt oddly peaceful now as she listened. She knew that she had come to the end of the road finally, and she could go home now. It had been an odyssey that had taken her twenty-three years to accomplish. Other people's took longer. But she had been brave enough to face hers. She had wanted the answers. And she had the courage to go through the ordeals it had taken to get there. They had been right all along, all of them. She was strong. And she knew that now too. They couldn't hurt her with it now. She had survived them.

They asked her to stay for dinner that night, and she enjoyed being with them. The idea that Frank had been her stepfather for thirteen years and she'd never known him somehow touched her. And Jane was a lovely woman. She was a widow too, and they'd been married for three years and obviously loved each other. She said that Frank was a mess when she found him, and thanks to Eloise, was beginning to hate women, and she'd fixed that. And he laughed at her version of the story.

'Don't believe a word of that, Gabbie. She was a lonely widow and I rescued her, right from under the nose of some rich old fool from Palm Beach. I married her before he knew what hit him.' He smiled broadly as he said it.

They invited her to stay with them that night, but she didn't want to impose on them. She said she was going to get a hotel room at the airport and go home in the morning. But they wanted her to stay there, Frank said he owed her at least that after never having her around for all those years. And she couldn't help thinking about how different her life would have been if he had been. But her mother would have spoiled it for her anyway, and she had decided he was probably right. The best thing her mother had done for her was leave her. It had saved her ultimately, she couldn't have survived the beatings forever.

They gave her a lovely guest room with a view of the Bay and the Golden Gate Bridge, and in the morning a maid served her breakfast in bed. She felt like a princess. And she decided to call Peter before she left for the airport. He was off duty for a change, and thrilled to hear her.

She told him about the Waterfords, and he was happy it had gone so well, and he was also happy that her mother hadn't been there to see her. Like Frank Waterford, he was sure that nothing would have changed, and she would have found some way to hurt Gabbie. He wasn't surprised by anything Frank had said, and he was so relieved that her search was over. She sounded very peaceful. She said she was coming home that night, but as he listened to her, he had a better idea. He had four days off for once, and he said he loved San Francisco.

'Why don't you stay there?' he suggested. 'I'll meet you.' She hesitated for a long moment, not sure what to say to him. This was only the very beginning for them. But at least she felt as though she had finally left all the ghosts behind her. She had made peace with them at last. Joe, Steve, even her parents. She understood better now what had happened to her. Frank was right in a way. She hadn't been very lucky when they'd been handing out parents. It was like being struck by lightning. And for all those years, she had believed everything was her fault. The beatings, the cruelty, their abandoning her, even the fact that they hadn't loved her. She had been willing to accept the blame for everything. And she realized now that even what had happened to Joe hadn't been entirely her fault. Ultimately, he had made his own decision. 'What do you think?' Peter asked her about his coming out again, and slowly she smiled as she looked at the view from the Waterfords' guest room window.

'I'd like that,' she said, willing to let herself have it, able to let him in now. She didn't know what would happen between them, but if it was good, and right for them, it seemed possible now that she deserved it. She no longer felt as though she was eternally damned, or destined to be punished. That was why she had come here, to be relieved of the burdens they had doomed her to live with, and she had finally done it. Her life sentence had been lifted.

'I'll fly out this afternoon. I can meet you somewhere. I'll get a hotel room,' Peter said enthusiastically, but when she told the Waterfords he was coming out and she was moving to a hotel, they insisted she stay there with him. They were the kindest, most hospitable people she had ever met, and they seemed to genuinely want her to be there with them.

'I want to check out this new son-in-law of mine, before you make a mistake,' he teased Gabbie. She had told them how they had met, and what had happened with Steve Porter, or whatever his name was. They were horrified by the story, but anxious to meet Peter.

And after she left in a cab to go to the airport, Frank told his wife how sorry he felt about her, what hell her life must have been as a child. And he blamed himself for not seeing it, or Eloise for the monster she had been. It made him feel good now to do what he could to make it up to Gabbie. And he was pleased to see that she had a good head on her shoulders. He thought it remarkable that she had survived all she'd been through.

426

'She's a nice girl,' he said to Jane, and she agreed with him, and as they walked out in their garden to look at the view they enjoyed so much, Peter was landing at the airport.

CHAPTER TWENTY-SIX

His plane touched down easily on the runway as Gabriella watched it. She was excited to see him, but still a little nervous. They had talked so much in the hospital, but she hadn't seen him since, or out in the real world. It seemed hard to believe that she'd only been out of the hospital for three days. So much had happened, so many ghosts had been put to rest. And she was so glad she had come here. She and Peter had agreed to stay with the Waterfords for the weekend, and then he had to go back to the hospital, and she wanted to go back to the bookstore.

She was standing slightly to one side when he came off the plane, and he almost didn't see her. He was looking straight ahead, and he smiled broadly when she suddenly stepped forward and surprised him. And as he looked at her, with her blue eyes, and her shining blond hair, he had an overwhelming urge to kiss her. But instead, he put an arm around her shoulders and they began walking slowly through the airport. She was talking easily about the time she had spent here, and the discoveries she had made, and her eyes looked happier than he'd ever seen them. There was still the depth to them that he loved, and that had first drawn him to her, but she no longer looked so anguished. And then, as he listened to her, he stopped walking, and just looked down at her, smiling, and happy to see her.

'I've missed you. The trauma unit isn't the same without you.' Nothing had been. And he'd been worried sick about her ever since she came to California.

'I've missed you too, Peter.' She smiled up at him, with the eyes of a woman. They were wise eyes, strong eyes, brave eyes, eyes that were no longer afraid to see him. 'Thank you for coming out here.'

'Thank you for coming to the trauma unit,' for surviving it, for surviving her whole damn ugly life to get there. He had been waiting for her, for years, he just didn't know it. For all these years there had never been anyone he really cared about, no one who was right for him, no one who had the guts to stick by him, but somehow he knew she would. She wasn't afraid of anything, and if she was, he would be there for her, he would help her through it. Just as he knew she'd be there for him. They were both the kind of people who had the courage to do what they had to, to go after what they wanted, to be there for each other. They had both learned that the hard way. The road hadn't been easy for them, especially for Gabbie. She was the real hero in the piece, she had been to hell and back and survived, and now she was smiling up at him with all the courage she'd looked for all her life. The shadows were gone now.

He took her hand in his then, and held it firmly, and slowly they began walking toward the exit. He had his bag over his shoulder, and she had her freedom. They had nowhere special to go, and they were in no rush to get there. They had time, and a full life ahead of them, and there were no ghosts left to haunt them. All they needed now was each other, and the time to enjoy it. And she had no more answers to look for. She was free now.

And as they walked out into the August sunshine, hand in hand, he looked down at her, and she laughed up at him. It all seemed so easy. The road to get there had been tortuous and at times it had seemed endless. But now, looking down at the view from the mountaintop, the road didn't seem as rocky as it had been. It had been hard enough. And long enough. But wherever she was, she knew she was home now.

were in no rush to get there. They had time, and a
full life ahead of them, and there were no shops
left to haunt them. All they needed now was each
other, and the time to enjoy it. And she had the
more power to look for. She was free now.

And as she walked down the road, the sun on her
shoulder, hand in hand, he looked at down at her, and
she laughed up at him. Hand seemed so easy. The
paradise there had been hard won and, at times, it
had seemed endless. But it was looking up now at the
view from the mountaineer, the road didn't seem
sticky as it had been. It had been hard enough,
And long enough. But whatever it was, she knew
she was not alone...

The LARGE PRINT HOME LIBRARY

If you have enjoyed this Large Print book and would like to build up your own collection of Large Print books and have them delivered direct to your door, please contact The Large Print Home Library.

The Large Print Home Library offers you a full service:

☆ **Created to support your local library**

☆ **Delivery direct to your door**

☆ **Easy-to-read type & attractively bound**

☆ **The very best authors**

☆ **Special low prices**

For further details either call Customer Services on 01225 443400 or write to us at:

**The Large Print Home Library
FREEPOST (BA 1686/1)
Bath BA2 3SZ**